The Mini-Cycle

While scholars have been studying the short story cycle for some time now, this book discusses a form that has never before been identified and named, let alone analyzed: the mini-cycle. A mini-cycle is a short story cycle made up, in most cases, of only two or three stories. This study looks at mini-cycles spanning the period from Anton Chekhov's "little trilogy" (1898) to the "Alphinland" stories in Margaret Atwood's *Stone Mattress* (2014), including texts by such authors as Stephen Leacock, Alice Munro, Robert Olen Butler, and Clark Blaise. Consideration is also given to marginal examples, like Sherwood Anderson's "Godliness—A Tale in Four Parts" (1919), which can be seen as one story or four distinct texts unified under one title, and to what is called the "exploded" mini-cycle: one whose component stories are published with intervening stories between them rather than consecutively. For each mini-cycle, the analysis is based on close reading of both the linking elements—character, imagery, symbolism, and so forth—and the rhetorical and aesthetic effects of the mini-cycle being made up of distinct stories rather than constructed as one long narrative.

Allan Weiss received his Ph.D. in English from the University of Toronto (1985), with a specialization in Canadian literature. He has taught at York University since 1990 and is currently Associate Professor of English and Humanities. He has edited a number of collections of essays on Canadian fantastic literature, most recently *The Canadian Fantastic in Focus* (2014), a volume of proceedings of the Academic Conference on Canadian Science Fiction and Fantasy, of which he has been Chair since 1996. He has also published articles and given conference papers on Canadian fantastic literature both in Canada and internationally.

Routledge New Textual Studies in Literature
Series Editors: Jane Potter, Bonnie Latimer, and Kevin Killeen

For more information about this series, please visit: www.routledge.com/Routledge-New-Textual-Studies-in-Literature/book-series/NTSL

The Mini-Cycle

Allan Weiss

Routledge
Taylor & Francis Group

NEW YORK AND LONDON

First published 2021
by Routledge
52 Vanderbilt Avenue, New York, NY 10017

and by Routledge
2 Park Square, Milton Park, Abingdon, Oxon OX14 4RN

Routledge is an imprint of the Taylor & Francis Group, an informa business

© 2021 Taylor & Francis

Library of Congress Cataloging-in-Publication Data
Names: Weiss, Allan, 1956– author.
Title: The mini-cycle / Allan Weiss.
Description: New York, NY : Routledge, 2021. |
Series: Routledge new textual studies in literature |
Includes bibliographical references and index.
Identifiers: LCCN 2020053777 (print) | LCCN 2020053778 (ebook) |
ISBN 9780367691691 (hardback) | ISBN 9781003140672 (ebook)
Subjects: LCSH: Cycles (Literature) | Short story.
Classification: LCC PN3448.C94 W45 2021 (print) |
LCC PN3448.C94 (ebook) | DDC 808.3/1–dc23
LC record available at https://lccn.loc.gov/2020053777
LC ebook record available at https://lccn.loc.gov/2020053778

ISBN: 978-0-367-69169-1 (hbk)
ISBN: 978-0-367-69170-7 (pbk)
ISBN: 978-1-003-14067-2 (ebk)

Typeset in Sabon
by Newgen Publishing UK

With delight, I dedicate this study to J. R. (Tim) Struthers, a wonderful scholar and friend.

Contents

Preface

In 2004, I read two new short story collections that featured a remarkable coincidence. In Alice Munro's *Runaway*, three of the stories—"Chance," "Soon," and "Silence"—were linked to each other but had no connection to any of the other stories in the collection. Like most story cycles, the three stories are linked by character; the protagonist in all three is Juliet, and we trace, at decades-long intervals, the progress and decline of her relationship with her husband Eric and their daughter Penelope. Around the same time, I just happened to be reviewing Denise Roig's *Any Day Now*, a short story collection made up of what Roig called "trios": sets of three short stories that are linked by theme. I was struck by this foreshortened version of the story cycle, since cycles usually take up entire books and I had never seen any critical discussion of a set of linked stories that did not span an entire volume.

I began to notice, or was directed to, other mini-cycles written by authors in Canada, the United States, and elsewhere, and gave conference papers and wrote articles on them as constituting a distinct genre. I called the form the "mini-cycle," defining the mini-cycle as a two-, three-, or (rarely) four-story cycle that is not intended to form a book-length publication but be part of a larger collection. The most common number of stories in a mini-cycle is three, that magical number, and the mini-cycle is typically first published as a unit in a story collection made up of otherwise unrelated stories. It came as something of a surprise to realize that I was already familiar with one older mini-cycle, the three stories about Peter Pupkin and Zena Pepperleigh in Stephen Leacock's *Sunshine Sketches of a Little Town* (1912). Since nobody had ever analyzed the genre before, I could not recognize the stories as forming anything worth noting; all I knew about was the book-length story cycle, and so I saw the stories only in the context of their being part of the cycle as a whole.[1] That experience illustrates an important point about genres: the degree to which the definition of a genre plays a role in creating it as a literary phenomenon.

As it turned out, the mini-cycle proved to be an older and more pervasive form than I originally realized. For example, one of the scholars who helped me, J. R. (Tim) Struthers, pointed me in the direction of

Anton Chekhov's "Little Trilogy," likely the oldest example of the form. Struthers, in fact, was the one responsible for this book: knowing of my interest in the genre, he told me that I had to write a book about it, and to my dismay I recognized immediately that, as in most things, he was absolutely right. I was the logical person to prepare a book-length study of this non-book-length genre.

This book is a compilation of the studies that I have already done of the mini-cycle, in expanded and more coherent form, along with additional material. Unfortunately, since there is no bibliography of the mini-cycle, I have had to rely on sometimes accidental discoveries of examples. Given that I am a scholar of Canadian literature, I am aware of and have discussed a disproportionate number of Canadian texts, and I hope the imbalance is understandable and forgivable. I have also learned about American and Irish examples, sometimes from meeting their authors. I have no doubt that there are many other mini-cycles out there, but I hope that my comments on the ones discussed here can be extrapolated to these unknown texts and will illuminate them as well. The mini-cycle raises various broader questions about genre, literary form, and the economics of short story publishing, issues that I hope to address to some extent here. We cannot discuss the short story without confronting its social and economic history: all the paraliterary factors, such as the rise of the magazine, that contributed to the genre's evolution and indeed its very existence. The same is true of the story cycle and other forms of short story linking. The history and development of the mini-cycle is thus part of a much larger story, so to speak—a kind of mini-history of the short story itself.

Note

1 The only other recognition of the genre's existence that I am aware of is J. Gerald Kennedy's term "cluster," which he defines as "closely linked stories within a volume" (ix). Lundén uses the term somewhat differently to refer to loosely linked stories, offering as examples *Go Down, Moses* and *In Our Time* (38).

Acknowledgements

First and foremost, my thanks go to J. R. (Tim) Struthers for his advice and guidance, and for insisting that I write this book. To say it would not exist without him is no exaggeration.

I would also like to thank York University, which supplied me with the time to write the book during one of my sabbaticals among other forms of support—moral, administrative, and financial. The English Department has been wonderfully supportive of my explorations of genre; thanks especially to Chairs Maurice Elliott, Kim Michasiw, Julia Creet, Art Redding, Heather Campbell, and Lily Cho.

Also key to the book's development have been my fellow Board members of the Society for the Study of the Short Story, and the organizers of the International Conference on the Short Story in English, which I have attended regularly since it was inaugurated in 1988. Special thanks go to Claire Larriere, Mary Rohrberger, Maurice Lee, Susan Lohafer, Clark Blaise, Farhat Iftekharrudin, and all those who participated in my survey during the conference in Lisbon in 2018.

Thanks to the folks at Routledge, particularly Michelle Salyga and Bryony Reece, for all their contributions to the book's publication.

Of course, I must add my deepest gratitude to my family for their love and support.

Parts of this book have appeared previously and have been revised for publication here; thanks to those who have granted permission for their use:

Material in the Introduction and Chapter 7 was first published in the journal *Short Story*: "Cycles within Cycles: Mini-Cycles in Robert Olen Butler's Fiction" in *Short Story,* vol. 17, no. 1, 2009, pp. 65–80, and "Between Collection and Cycle: The Mini-Cycle" in *Short Story,* vol. 17, no. 2, 2009, pp. 78–90.

An earlier version of Chapter 8 was published as "The Mini-Cycle in Clark Blaise's *Resident Alien*" in *Clark Blaise: Essays on His Works,* edited by J.R. (Tim) Struthers, Guernica Editions, 2016, pp. 259–86. Reproduced with the kind permission of the publisher.

Introduction

This is a study of the genre I call the mini-cycle: a small set of linked short stories, generally two or three, that form a cycle. The mini-cycle is normally published in a story collection made up of otherwise unlinked stories; in only one instance, it seems—Biblioasis's 2012 publication of Anton Chekhov's "Little Trilogy" as a 110-page volume entitled *About Love: 3 Stories*—has a mini-cycle been published on its own. While the mini-cycle almost never appears by itself, it is possible for a volume to be composed entirely or almost entirely of mini-cycles, and examples of collections dominated by or containing nothing but mini-cycles are studied here. A mini-cycle may be part of a book-length story cycle; in such cases, the stories that form the mini-cycle are more strongly linked to each other than to the surrounding texts.

As the mini-cycle is a genre, one based on form, genre theory offers a fruitful way to analyze it. Obviously, there is no room here to go into great detail about genre theory, but a brief overview of this approach will clarify some of the points discussed below, such as the genre's relationship to other genres, especially the short story and the short story cycle.[1] The history of the mini-cycle is obviously bound up with the history of the short story and the various ways in which short stories have been linked. There have been numerous studies of the short story cycle, and some of the principles underlying scholarly analysis of that genre will inform the study of its smaller cousin.

Early genre theorists, from ancient Greek philosophers to Renaissance thinkers, believed that genre existed only at a high level of abstraction, indeed the highest they could think of, and limited their understanding of genre to a single feature. Plato, for example, saw genre as referring to very broad categories distinguished by mode of presentation—narration, imitation, or a combination of the two (see Book III of the *Republic*)— otherwise known as the ancient triad. Centuries later came the modern triad based on form: prose fiction, poetry, and drama. Futile efforts to fit all texts neatly into these three genres led theorists to come up with a proliferation of genres, as it soon became obvious that any attempt to construct a neat triad, particularly one based on form, was bound to fail.

Modern theorists have abandoned any effort to constrict genre to a triad or to define genre solely on the basis of one feature and have now established a few important principles that are the foundation for any study of a genre. Genres are socially defined; they are not Platonic ideals that pre-exist texts, nor are they rigid and prescriptive pigeonholes in which all texts must be stuffed, but rather they are social institutions—like literature itself. Human beings create and define genres, and modify them in accordance with social changes, although like other social institutions genres possess a remarkable degree of durability and consistency; genres persist because they become strongly embedded in a literature and, through other cultural institutions, produce offspring with a definite "genetic" resemblance to earlier texts in that genre. A variety of factors, both internal and external, affect how and the degree to which a genre evolves. Thus, the understanding of a genre must be based on recognition of both its synchronic and diachronic features. The synchronic features are the literary conventions that more or less define the genre. Some conventions are central to the genre's identity, such as the unhappy ending of a tragedy, while others are or become peripheral and disposable, such as the idea that a tragedy must be about a noble character. The diachronic features are those reflecting social changes, like the rise of the middle class that led to the parallel rise of the middle-class tragedy (Henrik Ibsen's *Hedda Gabler* [1891], Arthur Miller's *Death of a Salesman* [1949]), and those reflecting literary changes, like the exhaustion of conventions that devolve into clichés that in turn trigger ironic treatment of those conventions. Old genres like the epic die or are substantially recast, while new genres arise, generally through the combination of existing genres (e.g., the rise of the novel out of the autobiography, the history, the fable, and the *novelle*, among others). Old genres can beget new ones through the creation of anti-genres, like parody, the mock-epic, and the dystopia.

A genre can be based on any feature or combination of features, such as form (e.g., the sonnet), content or theme (e.g., science fiction, which can be in any form: short story, novel, poem, play, film, etc.), or function (e.g., horror, whose function is to frighten regardless of form or content). Also, genre exists at almost all levels of abstraction. Furthermore, genre is relational, meaning that a genre is in a sense defined by the existence of other genres at the same level of abstraction, and genre distinctions at a given level of abstraction can be made in various ways. Fiction, poetry, and drama are three broad genres of literature because if all literature were, say, poetry, the genre of "poetry" would not exist as it would be synonymous with literature and not a distinct type of it. At lower levels of abstraction, we have under "fiction" the form-based genres of the novel, the novella, and the short story, among others. On the other hand, we could distinguish fictional texts by content: science fiction novels, novellas, and short stories on the one hand, and mystery novels, novellas, and short stories on the other, because different content conventions exist at this level of abstraction, thus defining these as different genres.

In distinguishing genres, theorists have by and large accepted the idea that there are prototypical and more marginal examples. Prototypical examples serve to provide a focus for the features of a genre, while those texts that do not contain most or even a substantial number of these features are seen as less clearly members of that genre. In *Strategies of Fantasy*, Brian Attebery speaks of genres as "fuzzy sets" (12), a term he derives from the work of George Lakoff and Mark Johnson, although it is far more illuminating to see genres as classifications according to the work of Eleanor Rosch. In each of these approaches, there are boundaries to a genre where texts share little with other members of the genre on one hand, and share features with adjacent genres on the other. When it comes to the mini-cycle, there are a number of examples of the genre that adhere to a certain form or principle—for example, having the stories published together—while others, much fewer in number, depart from those core features and even suggest adjacent genres in their handling. Some of the key adjacent genres when it comes to the mini-cycle are the story collection, the story cycle, and the story series.

Also, throughout much of literary history there have been genre hierarchies, with certain genres treated as more prestigious or important than others: the epic in ancient and early modern times, the novel today. These hierarchies are never stable and are frequently overturned; the novel was not always considered the highest literary genre and was even considered quite low in its early days. Genre hierarchies require first that genres be recognized as such, and then these genres gain more or less prestige depending on a number of cultural factors. The fact that no one seems to have identified the mini-cycle before, let alone assigned it a place in the hierarchy of literary genres, signals that for one reason or another we have been culturally unable to see it. It may well be that the status of the short story has played a role in determining the degree to which we are aware of its myriad forms. Cultural blind spots are every bit as revealing as those areas considered worthy of attention.

The synchronic features of a genre that define and distinguish it are literary conventions and tropes. First, these need to be differentiated, as the term "trope" seldom receives proper attention in genre theory and analysis. In fact, the term seems to be used quite freely in public and academic discourse, without theoretical rigour, and standard dictionaries of literary terms tend to ignore it in its generic meaning. A convention is a structural feature or quality of language; *in medias res* is probably the best-known structural convention, while other conventions involve levels of style (e.g., the language of an epic *versus* the language of a farce) and plot elements. These conventions can apply to more than one genre, but their particular combination contributes to the definition of a genre. A trope is a more "concrete" element such as a character, object, or theme that is specific to a genre: in science fiction, an alien, a spaceship, or time travel; in detective fiction, a detective, a corpse, and pursuit. None of this is to imply that conventions and tropes of different genres cannot be mixed—the science fiction mysteries of Isaac Asimov come to mind here—nor that these are permanent features. Conventions and tropes come and go or become more or less important in a genre. For example, science fiction has always had neologisms, but these became more prominent in cyberpunk and post-cyberpunk fiction. As already noted, the convention that a tragic hero must be a royal or noble character, one that was once central to the genre, has disappeared.

Conventions and tropes constitute a type of contract between author and reader, signalling genre and therefore means of interpretation and evaluation. A number of scholars have examined social conventions and how they work, and literary conventions also act as a communicative shorthand. While some theorists argue for the primacy of the text in interpretation and evaluation, the fact is that the text is always made of far more than the words on the page. Conventions above all are unspoken yet no less powerful means of communication by which authors and readers contribute to the communicative act. Readers come to the act of reading armed with a set of competencies that facilitate understanding, competencies that are generated over time by experience with texts, cultural and other forms of education, and much else. The reader who comes to a text in an unfamiliar genre may have difficulty knowing what to make of it simply through ignorance of its conventions and tropes.[2] Authors, of course, often challenge the conventions of a genre in an effort to express a more personal vision, but they can never fully escape those conventions, if only as something to react against. As we look at some specific texts in detail, we will also be paying attention to some of the conventions of the mini-cycle as these have developed over time.

The most important genre adjacent to the mini-cycle is, obviously, the short story cycle, and so scholarship on the cycle can contribute to our understanding of its smaller cousin. What should be noted at the start, however, is that studies of short story linking tend to focus exclusively on the cycle, and other forms of linked stories are usually seen only as precursors of or inspirations for the cycle (see, for example, Nagel 3-5 and Dunn and Morris 21-29). A more precise approach is to recognize that there is a wide spectrum of types and degrees of linking. Not all sets of linked stories are collected in book form, and the line between the collection of unrelated stories and the clearly defined story cycle can be blurry when certain "weak" links are used. We need to review these various types of linking in order to provide context for, and perhaps even a better perspective on, the cycle and thus the mini-cycle.

Understanding the development of short story linking requires study of the diachronic element. The very emergence of a genre can represent such altered contexts, and the ways that, and the degree to which, conventions and tropes are modified over time are the product of both literary and extra-literary phenomena. Literary schools and even an individual author can change a genre for all time or be responsible for its birth or death. Economic forces, as scholars have come to recognize more and more, have shaped literary developments in profound ways, notably when it comes to genres like the short story that depend so heavily on modes of literary production and distribution. The sociology of literature is an especially relevant approach when it comes to the study of the short story and the ways in which stories have been linked, and therefore the origins of the cycle and the mini-cycle. The sociology of literature treats literature as a cultural phenomenon that is unavoidably embedded in a social and economic system, and some of its approaches see literature in a capitalist system as a commodity like any other. Thus, Robert Escarpit and others use the terms "production," "distribution," and "consumption" to refer to the writing, publishing, and reading of literature. When it comes to the short story, the role of modes of distribution has been especially important; in fact, it is almost a truism among critics that without the magazine, the short story as we understand it might never have evolved.

Thus, Chapter 1 reviews the role of periodicals in fostering the emergence and flourishing of the short story—in other words, how distribution contributed to the rise of the genre, one that is simultaneously very ancient and quite modern. Scholars have traced the short story to the tales published in the journals of the eighteenth century—like *The Tatler*, *The Spectator*, and *The Idler*—which were in most cases the products of individuals who wrote all or most of the contents, and the magazines of the nineteenth, which were money-making ventures offering the works of various authors who were paid for their works. We then turn to the sociology of short story linking, looking at the different types of linking, framing devices, short story series, and then the development of the short story cycle and the mini-cycle, and their relationship to the publishing of short stories. The approach to these linked genres is both formal and sociological, representing the synchronic and diachronic dimensions of the genres, respectively. The analysis in each case begins with a look at the aesthetic nature and function of each type of linking, focusing, for example, on how the genre relates to other genres, and then studies how the linked genre has been affected by means of distribution.

Later chapters look more closely at specific authors and texts, employing this dual approach to apply the theory to literary practice. The goal throughout this study is to examine how authors use the form to explore their themes and to create specific effects through writing short sets of linked stories. The most common, or prototypical, form of the mini-cycle is a set of three linked stories published together in a collection of otherwise unrelated texts, and so the first texts to be discussed are in this form. After that, variations on the form are analyzed: two- and four-story cycles, mini-cycles whose component stories are not published consecutively, and other forms that lie on the "fuzzy" boundaries. Authors have experimented with various ways of linking stories beyond the short story cycle, and the effects of their aesthetic choices are the main interest here.

Notes

1 The following discussion of genre is heavily indebted to the work of the following major theorists, among others: Brian Attebery, Mikhail Bakhtin, Thomas Beebee, John G. Cawelti, Ralph Cohen, Rosalie Colie, Heather Dubrow, David Duff, David Fishelov, Alistair Fowler, John Frow, Gerard Genette, Claudio Guillén, Paul Hernadi, Hans Robert Jauss, Thomas L. Kent, Carolyn R. Miller, Gary Saul Morson, Thomas Pavel, Janice A Radway, Eleanor Rosch, Marie-Laure Ryan, Jean-Marie Schaeffer, Viktor Shklovsky, Tzvetan Todorov, Karl Vietor, and Rene Wellek and Austin Warren.
2 I can testify to this fact after years of teaching science fiction to students—of whom there are always a few—who have never encountered it before; even those familiar with SF film occasionally have some difficulty reading fiction in the genre.

References

Attebery, Brian. *Strategies of Fantasy*. Indiana UP, 1992.

Chekhov, Anton. *About Love: 3 Stories*. Biblioasis, 2012.

Dunn, Maggie, and Ann Morris. *The Composite Novel: The Short Story Cycle in Transition*. Twayne, 1995.

Escarpit, Robert. *The Sociology of Literature*. Translated by Ernest Pick, introduction by Malcolm Bradbury and Bryan Wilson, Frank Cass, 1971.

Lakoff, George, and Mark Johnson. *Metaphors We Live By*. U of Chicago P, 1980.

Nagel, James. *The Contemporary American Short-Story Cycle: The Ethnic Resonance of Genre*. Louisiana State UP, 2001.

Rosch, Eleanor. "Principles of Categorization." *Cognition and Categorization*, edited by Rosch and Barbara B. Lloyd, Erlbaum, 1978, pp. 27–48.

1 The Sociology of the Short Story

Perhaps no genre has been as directly and obviously connected to extra-literary developments, i.e., material conditions, as the short story. That is, while scholars can trace literary sources for the modern short story—in fables, folk tales, fairy tales, and so on (see Edward W. R. Pitcher's introduction for a good survey)—its rise in the eighteenth and nineteenth centuries was inextricably linked to the emergence of a medium of distribution: the periodical press, and especially the magazine. The short story was the ideal form for this relatively new medium, as a genre that exactly suited the needs of both editors and readers, and the fortunes of the genre rose and fell in direct relation to those of the magazine.[1] Dean Baldwin is correct that "the rise and fall of the British short story is intimately connected to the economics of its writing and publishing" (1). In fact, according to Andrew Levy, Edgar Allan Poe's two important statements on the short story, his review of Hawthorne's *Twice-Told Tales* (1842) and "The Philosophy of Composition" (1846), had more to do with his ambition to found a literary magazine than the genre itself (Levy 14).

The number, nature, and variety of short stories published during the nineteenth century depended on when and how many magazines appeared and disappeared, and the "golden age" of the short story, from the 1880s to the early twentieth century, coincided with the period of the greatest number and variety of magazines, from high-brow publications like *The New Yorker* and *Yellow Book* to cheap pulp magazines featuring popular fiction in numerous genres and subgenres. Short stories had been appearing in British journals since the eighteenth century, including "oriental" tales, satires, moral tales, and short romances (see Boyce for a history and analysis), and in the nineteenth century in such professional periodicals as *New Monthly Magazine* and *Blackwood's Edinburgh Magazine*. Polsgrove's history of short fiction during the 1820s to the 1840s demonstrates the link between the genre and the medium in which they appeared, and the role of the professionalization of authorship in the rise of the short story (418–19; see also Baldwin 15–20, 36–48; and Killick, *British Short Fiction* 22–37). Wendell V. Harris and Harold Orel cover the Victorian period, showing how the short story flowered with the expansion of the periodical press. Levy quotes William

Dean Howells, editor of *Harper's New Monthly*, as saying in 1887 that the short story's "phenomenal success had been won simply because of the success of American magazines, which is nothing less than prodigious" (30). In 1885, there were about 3,300 magazines in the United States alone, to which were added another 7,500 by 1905 (Mott 11). According to Winnie Chan, "at the end of the nineteenth century, the growth of the periodical press made short stories a necessity to any periodical with aspirations to popularity" (x). She also comments that the profession of short story writer had been so well established that authors had become brand names (x). Magazine writing became more lucrative for authors than novel writing, as it could provide steady and immediate remuneration for fictional efforts (Baldwin 43, 51–65). The demise of the triple-decker novel opened the market for shorter fictional forms (see, e.g., Orel 11).

The very success of the commercial short story provoked a Modernist reaction, and the rise of such "high-brow" periodicals as *Yellow Book* (on the cultural status of the short story, see Ferguson, "The Short Story as Parvenu"; on the rise of the little magazines, see, among others, Harris 109–25 and Baldwin 67–82). Chan summarizes the ostensible conflict between money and art during the 1890s: " 'the short story' and short stories emerge as the product of both mass culture and the backlash against it. The aims of commercial success and literary value became incompatible precisely during the period of its definition" (xi). Nevertheless, as she points out, there was no very sharp divide between commerce and culture, between magazines like *The Strand* and *Yellow Book*; the latter "used its anti-commercialism as part of a commercial strategy" (xii). Scholars of the fin-de-siècle period have revealed the degree to which economic considerations played a role in the supposedly "pure" artistic motivations and choices of the Aesthetic and Decadent authors (Baldwin 155–60). During the 1890s, Baldwin states, "the market for short fiction became sufficiently broad, deep, varied, and flexible to accommodate all writers' talent and many of very limited abilities" (3). The issue of markets for short fiction will become important for our look at the mini-cycle in due course. Modernist authors did, however, engage in literary experimentation of the sort that led to the Joycean "epiphany" story, for example, and during the 1930s high-brow magazines sometimes published political fiction that popular magazines of the day might not have wanted to publish (see Martin).

The magazine imposed certain important formal as well as thematic restrictions on the short story that will prove relevant to our discussion. Stories had to be from about 2,000–10,000 words long; anything substantially longer had to be serialized. Baldwin goes into some detail about editorial requirements, noting that the six-part serial was considered best: "two or three part serials, however, fell between two stools. Some of the best stories of the period were published in this fashion, but editors preferred either whole, complete stories or full-length novels" (89).

Henry James felt too constrained to meet such limitations and benefited from the publication of "little" magazines that had looser length requirements. Those restrictions on form and others on content harmed the reputation of the short story, relegating it, for some critics, to the status of a standardized literary commodity: "The short story's continued involvement with journalism has damaged its standing while ensuring its popularity ... there is a suspicion that a storyteller's artistry may be far too closely tied up with external considerations like space limitations, restrictive house styles and editorial stipulations" (Shaw 7; see also Levy's discussion of the emergence of "how-to" manuals on short story writing and other factors on pp. 47–57).

Magazine publication led to book publication, as annuals and then story collections began to appear in an effort to capitalize on the popularity of the short story and the fame that authors had gained through magazine publication (see, e.g., Baldwin 6–7). According to Polsgrove, magazine appearances helped the writer establish a "readership that would buy book collections of his stories" (420). During the early period, she continues, book publication "was the goal of the writer who really wished to make money and who did not want his stories to vanish quickly in the ephemeral pages of the magazines and annuals ... the publication of their stories in book form suggests the strength of readers' new interest in short fiction" (421). From the very beginning of the publication of story collections, however, the market was weak; Baldwin comments, "while readers devoured short stories by the hundreds, even by the thousands in magazines, they shunned the form when it was published in a book" (99)—unless the stories were linked, and the volume could be passed off as a novel (102). Baldwin offers sales figures to prove the point that novels have always been much more popular than story collections, among readers and therefore among publishers—a phenomenon that persists to this day (109–14).

The Sociology of Short Story Linking

Studies of the cycle usually examine the genre in terms of its history and form; few scholars treat it from the perspective of the sociology of literature, except as part of a larger study of the short story. For example, the studies by Carol Polsgrove, Winnie Chan, Richard Ohmann, and Dean Baldwin discuss the short story in the context of the magazine publishing trade, dealing primarily with how short story writers during the nineteenth century earned a living, but spend little time on linked stories. What follows are some preliminary remarks about the relationship between magazine and book publishing on the one hand and short story linking on the other, applying the sociological approach to the various forms of linking.

Just as the short story itself is a creature of periodical publishing, the main forms of linking stories might not have come about, or taken the form that they did, without both periodical and book publishing and how these two trades related to each other. The short story was affected by changes in the periodical and book trades, and so, too, were the modes of short story linking. Much more study needs to be done to show the complex relationships between the forms of short story linking and the modes of publishing; studies of individual series and cycles, for example, can reveal the extent to which authors plan their cycles before periodical publication or turn series into cycles while preparing collections for book publication. For now, we can make a few general comments.

Among the earliest forms of short story linking is the collection of tales unified by a frame like the *Thousand and One Nights*, Giovanni Boccaccio's fourteenth century *Decameron*, and Geoffrey Chaucer's *The Canterbury Tales* (ca. 1400). The stories may have had their roots in the oral tradition, but as a collection they rely on their publication in a book for whatever link they have with each other. It might seem that the stories are entirely unrelated except for the community that produced them, but the frame assumes that the stories will be published together along with the frame, and therefore the book is really the only way in which the text can form a coherent whole. Furthermore, sometimes—as in Chaucer's collection—stories are responses to other stories, as the Reeve's tale is an answer to the Miller's. Such stories need to appear in the same collection to achieve their effect. Thus, even before the invention of moveable type, book publishing was a factor in short story linking. During the early nineteenth century, authors frequently added linking material like frames to lend cohesion to their volumes. As Killick writes,

> To collect tales together often (though not always) implies a connection between the individual stories. Many collections of the early nineteenth century employed devices such as framing narratives and thematic or character-based linkages which were derived in part from older epic or romance cycles such as the *Arabian Nights* and *Le Morte d'Arthur*. These strategies of organization gave writers of short fiction new ways of adding scope to their collections.
>
> (*British Short Fiction* 34–35)

Indeed, he continues, collecting "became a bolder artistic statement during the early nineteenth century, and moved from being an often indiscriminate amalgamation to a more considered and deliberate creative act" (35). Today, serious authors find ways to unify even the most ostensibly diverse collection of short stories.

Somewhat more strongly linked is the short story series, in which characters and/or settings recur, but there is no attempt to unify the stories to form a single narrative or to limit the number or types of stories for aesthetic purposes. Tracing the roots and branches of the short story series can provide insights into the relationship between linking and the economics of both the periodical and book trades. The origins of the story series lie in the myths and legends that represent our earliest form of storytelling: stories of the gods and goddesses and the adventures of figures like Hercules and King Arthur, while early fictional examples include the fabulous tales of Reynard the Fox. The modern story series' beginnings can be found in the sketch series. The sketch—the verbal "portrait" of an individual, a community, or a landscape—was written for the periodicals of the eighteenth and nineteenth centuries, at first by the editor-authors themselves, like Joseph Addison's and Richard Steele's anecdotes about running characters like Sir Roger de Coverly in *The Spectator*. These were not fully formed short stories, but rather short works designed to illustrate a philosophical, moral, or social point. At no point were these texts intended to constitute a greater unit, and only practical considerations—the lifespans of the periodicals and the authors—would prevent the series from going on forever.

In the early nineteenth century, the sketch was a popular and frequently published genre in the professional magazines. As the magazines became compendiums of a vast range of material, not just the opinions of their founders, and as authorship became professionalized, the sketches were written by others who were paid for their work. A notable example was Mary Russell Mitford, whose sketch collection *Our Village* (1824–1832) is often named in histories of the cycle but could just as well be treated as an important stage in the development of the series. Most of her sketches originally appeared in periodicals and are linked by theme and type of setting rather than character: each portrays a vivid figure or landscape in rural areas and villages in the English countryside (Dunn and Morris 23). Cross-references and motifs bind the sketches (Killick, *British Short Fiction* 93; see also his "Mary Russell Mitford" *passim*). Similar "local colour" work was being done by Washington Irving in the United States and Susanna Moodie in Canada. The narrator serves as another linking element; Mitford's and Moodie's narrators become the "running character" in their works, acting as the observing selves who judge, interpret, and respond emotionally to whomever and whatever they see.

Sketches like those by Mitford were sometimes collected in book form and frequently revised for book publication, while others were written expressly for the volumes. In "Foregrounding Nationalism," Kevin A. Morrison traces in detail the changes that Mitford made to her sketches in the move from periodical to book publication (280). Authors thereby gave the sketches a degree of coherence they were not designed to have in the periodicals.

Magazine editors during the first half of the nineteenth century quickly realized that having a known quantity—that is, the same author writing the same kind of text—would appeal to their readers and was therefore a good idea from a business point of view. What Susan Garland Mann says in her study of the cycle, that "Periodicals were ... frequently interested in stories by the same author dealing with a single character (or group of characters), setting, or topic" (8), was equally true of the sketch series. As

Barbara Onslow notes, "if a new series proved popular the writer would be encouraged to continue" (91). Collecting sketches in book form meant that publishers could capitalize on the author's fame while authors had an opportunity to earn money numerous times for the same piece.

It is worth noting that sketches and sketch series were written mainly by women, who could take a few moments during their housework to write brief, self-contained works for the periodical market. At the time, periodicals did not pay well, and authors relied on book publishing for the bulk of their income. Once women authors published enough sketches to make up a volume—and establish a devoted following—they sold the set to a book publisher, as we have seen. However, an emphasis on book publication draws attention away from the sketch series as a distinct genre on its own, one that offered steady income for women authors and a reliable form of periodical literature for editors and readers alike.

The short story series also had roots in series of tales unified by nationality. Allan Cunningham, James Hogg, and others published tales linked solely by being, or supposedly being, Scottish, Irish, or English folktales. Authors of such tales hoped for book publication at some point, but the immediate environment for the stories was the periodical, and the stories were shaped by the needs of the periodical press in terms of length, subject matter, and structure. Recent economic histories of the short story describe the ways in which nineteenth-century short fiction by these writers and others was affected by magazine publication, and time does not permit reviewing what Ohmann, Baldwin, and others have said. What we can say is that authors of both tales and sketches gained their fame through their periodical publications, and it is difficult to imagine that the books would have been published without the authors' having already become well known through their series.

The short story series emerged soon after the short story itself developed in the periodical press in the nineteenth century. Unlike a serialized novel, which is intended to have an endpoint, a climax in which there is some resolution, a short story series has no closure; the only climaxes or resolutions are in the individual stories. In the series, one or more running characters reappear in order to relieve the author from the need to create new characters for every story he or she writes and to meet public demand. Reader feedback played a strong role in ensuring that Auguste Dupin would return to solve more crimes, and in a famous example, readers prevented Sir Arthur Conan Doyle from killing off Sherlock Homes as he wished to do. The appeal of a popular character to authors, editors, and readers encouraged the writing of similar but unrelated stories that could go on indefinitely. Story series can be found in most of the popular genres, that is, those genres that lend themselves to the depiction of distinct adventures: detective and mystery, fantasy, science fiction, and Western. In popular fiction, plot tends to dominate while character development is secondary. Therefore, as long as the character does not change much, if at all, the author can continue to churn out separate adventures for that detective, adventurer, scientific genius, and so on.[2]

Normally, individual stories do not refer to others in the series or do so only in passing; it is part of their function to require no prior knowledge for their full enjoyment and understanding. That is because stories in a series are first—and often only—published in periodicals, and neither the author nor the editor can assume that readers have read earlier stories or remember details in them, particularly if the issues are published far apart. Thus, for a story series to work, each story must constitute an autonomous whole. Since the magazines are designed to be disposable, readers are unlikely to be able to refer to earlier stories in a series, and so a larger narrative arc is simply impractical. Of course, both authors and editors will hope that readers are already familiar with the series character—Sherlock Holmes, Conan the Barbarian, John Carter of Mars, G. K. Chesterton's Father Brown, any number of other detectives and cowboy heroes—and have become fans of the series, or will discover it and become fans, and seek out more stories about him or her.

Conan Doyle claimed credit for creating the first "true" short story series with his famous detective. What he says about Sherlock Holmes's origins and popularity is worth quoting in full, as it demonstrates that the economics of magazine publishing played at least an equal role in Conan Doyle's purposes as did aesthetic considerations. Hesketh Pearson introduces Conan Doyle's undated comments by saying, "The notion of writing a series of short stories round the character of Holmes came to Doyle when he read the monthly magazines that were then beginning to cater for the train-travelling public" (91). He then quotes Conan Doyle:

> Considering these various journals with their disconnected stories, it had struck me that a single character running through a series, if it only engaged the attention of the reader, would bind that reader to that particular magazine. On the other hand, it had long seemed to me that the ordinary serial might be an impediment rather than a help to a magazine, since, sooner or later, one missed one number and afterwards it had lost all interest. Clearly the ideal compromise was a character which carried through, and yet instalments which were each complete in themselves, so that the purchaser was always sure that he could relish the whole contents of the magazine. I believe that I was the first to realize this and *The Strand Magazine* the first to put it into practice.
>
> (91–92)

Pearson goes on to say that Conan Doyle's agent sent "A Scandal in Bohemia" to Greenhough Smith, editor of the *Strand*, "who liked it and encouraged Doyle to go ahead with the series" (Pearson 92).

Of course, Conan Doyle was by no means the first to write a series of stories featuring a linking character; Poe anticipated him by about half a century with his Auguste Dupin detective stories. It may well be true that no other series was so consistently and self-consciously maintained as Conan Doyle's—further research would be required to prove the point—and Mike Ashley is partly correct in saying of the *Strand* that "the magazine's greatest innovation was the *series short story*—a tight form, usually numbered and run in consecutive issues, essentially invented by Conan Doyle in July 1891 for his first Sherlock Holmes story-series" (11). Ashley, however, somewhat unfairly dismisses the Dupin stories as "an 'accidental' near-series, appearing in three different American magazines over a period of several years in the 1840s, rather than a series proper" (11). The fact that these short stories featured the same main character, even though they were published in different magazines, surely qualifies them as a series.

The success of the Sherlock Holmes series inspired numerous imitators in various genres, and one can even include P. G. Wodehouse's Jeeves and Wooster stories (Ashley 12). A particularly noteworthy example is William Gilbert Patten's long-running character, Frank Merriwell. The editors at *Street and Smith* magazine asked Patten to write a series of stories about a boy at a military academy in imitation of the highly popular British school stories like Thomas Hughes's novels about Tom Brown. Patten's creation, who first appeared in *Tip Top Weekly* in 1896, lasted twenty years in print and spawned radio, comic strip, and film series. Each of his "adventures" was self-contained, and the stories were never intended to become or be published as a unified set.

Like the sketch writers who preceded them, then, the authors of short story series relied on magazines, and editors in turn relied on them, in a mutually beneficial economic relationship. By the 1890s, the short story was enjoying its heyday—the period H. G. Wells called the genre's Golden Age—and the economics of periodical and book publishing had reversed. Between 1890 and the First World War, authors earned more from periodical sales than from their books. It would likely amaze authors today that writers wrote short stories to earn money in order to support their novel writing. Authors did not collect their texts in book form with the same degree of urgency as their predecessors, so story collections—whether of unlinked or series stories—represented welcome additional income but no more than that.

The rise of the periodical market for short stories thus fostered and encouraged the writing of short story series, as authors, editors, and readers became dependent upon quickly written, entirely self-contained, yet comfortingly familiar short stories featuring recognizable heroes and villains. Series later found their main homes not so much in the large-circulation, general-interest fiction magazines like *Blackwood's*, the *Saturday Evening Post*, and *Cornhill*, but rather in the pulp magazines that began appearing, particularly in the United States. For example, Robert E. Howard was simultaneously inspired by and sought to react against the Tarzan novels of Edgar Rice Burroughs, whose primitive

gentleman seemed highly unlikely. As a result, Howard created Conan
the Barbarian, for him a far more plausible example of humanity's fun-
damental barbarism when people lack or are deprived of the thin veneer
of civilization (Coffman 35–44). Howard published a number of Conan
"novelettes" (stories in the 10,000–20,000-word range) in *Weird Tales* and
Fantasy Fan Magazine from 1932 to 1934. Conan was not his first series
hero, but when these characters failed to catch on, Howard converted
one of his Kull of Atlantis stories into the first Conan tale. Conan became
immediately popular, and Howard's bread-and-butter. When *Weird Tales*
suffered financial problems due to the Great Depression, he stopped
writing Conan stories—not for any aesthetic reasons but only because he
was no longer being paid for them (Finn 174).[3] What Darrell Schweitzer
says of series clearly distinguishes the genre from the cycle:

> Many writers imagine a series character without consciously out-
> lining his future exploits, arranging the stories later when the char-
> acter grows popular ... an interesting story or character may develop
> into a series, forcing the writer to go back to the origins of his hero,
> and then forward again (although this is less commercially sound)
> to chronicle his eventual fate. Often, many important parts of the
> character's life don't occur to the author until the basic premise is set.
> (11)

The author, then, does not think of the stories as unified in any way, even
by consistency of character, until required to do so.

Story series provided additional pay for authors on those rare occasions
when the series were published in book form. When the stories in a series
are collected, they will not form a more cohesive sequence, and certainly
not the unity of a story cycle. The stories may be printed and read in any
order, depending on the wishes of the author, publisher, and reader. That
is not to say that an author cannot unify such a story collection after
the fact. In science fiction, a unique form developed that lies somewhere
between the series collection and the cycle: the "fix-up novel." In the
fix-up novel, short stories, novelettes, and novellas that were published
separately in the pulps are combined to form a book-length text that
is less coherent than a true novel but more unified than a conventional
story collection or cycle, as the author provides a frame and/or narrative
links to make the text novel-like. We cannot be certain whether an author
always intended the component texts to be brought together at some
point, although that was probably the case with Walter M. Miller, Jr.'s *A
Canticle for Leibowitz* (1960), which was originally published as three
novellas in *The Magazine of Fantasy and Science Fiction* (1955–57). In
some cases, it may be that the author found an opportunity to earn money
from a short text in many ways: initial periodical publication, anthology
reprints, and then novel publication. A. E. van Vogt, Henry Kuttner, and
Ray Bradbury were among many science-fiction authors from the 1940s

to the present who published fix-up novels.[4] Authors typically revise the original texts to unify them more strongly when preparing such novels for publication.

In a particularly interesting example of after-the-fact linking, Isaac Asimov published his robot stories in various science fiction magazines, and they were unified solely by the Three Laws of Robotics that governed the behaviour of all his positronic characters. When he collected a number of them in *I, Robot* (1950), he wrote linking passages foregrounding his running character, robopsychologist Susan Calvin, who reminisces about the "malfunctions" she dealt with. The implication is that all of the stories are set in the same universe, although there was never any hint of that when the stories were published in the magazines. The result is not a fix-up novel, but it is more than a story collection and yet not exactly a cycle.

Incidentally, as we know, serial publication of novels was common in the nineteenth century and remains a form of novel publication in some spheres of the literary world. Large-circulation magazines of the nineteenth and twentieth centuries frequently featured serialized novels among their offerings, and novels appeared in book form only after such serialization (for a discussion of the serialized novel, see Mayo). Returning to the world of science fiction, for much of the era of the pulp magazines (the Golden Age of Science Fiction, it is called), magazines published serialized novels along with short stories and other texts of intermediate length; indeed, until the paperback revolution of the 1940s and 1950s, the magazine was the primary venue for the publication of science fiction novels in the United States. Science fiction magazines continued to publish serialized novels long after other types of magazines dropped them, and *Analog* still does so. Today, the most important site of serialization of novels is the internet, where authors have rediscovered older forms of publication: not just serialization, but also subscription publication. Of course, the novel *per se* lies outside our purview, but we have to recall that the serialized novel exhibits many of the features of the story cycle, in that chapters or groups of chapters possess their own narrative and character arcs, forming units that are partially but unmistakably autonomous. Even the assigning of titles to chapters speaks volumes, as it were.[5]

Finally, we come to the short story cycle, also known as the "short story sequence" (Luscher, Kennedy), "composite novel" (Rabkin, Dunn and Morris), and "short story composite" (Lundén), among other terms. "Composite novel" is the least satisfactory term; Rabkin seems to have been somewhat confused by the genre, while Dunn and Morris offer no real rationale in their preface for calling the text a novel. The latter argue unconvincingly that the term "composite novel emphasizes the integrity of the whole, while short story cycle emphasizes the integrity of the parts ... it not only implies inferior status in the generic hierarchy, but also prescribes or at least suggests generic limitations" (5). This comment suggests that reference to the short story somehow implies lower generic status. It is true that some consider the short story a lesser form, but that is no reason to go along with that attitude. James Nagel points out the problems with the term "cycle" with its implication of circularity (12; see also Lundén 14, 17). On the other hand, he rejects "sequence" on the grounds that "in most such collections, 'sequentiality' is the least important aspect of the groupings of stories within a volume. The relationships among stories in a short-story cycle is [sic] far more complex than the simple following of one another in sequence" (12). However, authors carefully arrange the stories in any collection, on the (perhaps misguided) assumption that readers will read them in order (see below), and so sequentiality is not as insignificant as Nagel claims. In his introduction to *Modern American Short Story Sequences*, Kennedy justifies using the term instead of cycle "to emphasize its progressive unfolding and cumulative effects" (vii). He goes on to say that a sequence is a collection that the author has arranged him- or herself; the order of the stories is not the work of an editor (ix). The order is, therefore, aesthetically governed and not random.[6] Nagel defends the term "cycle" in part on the grounds that it is an established term for independent texts unified by some basic principle, dating back to ancient times and enduring through the Middle Ages in reference to plays (2). In this study, despite its evident problems, "cycle" will be used because it has become the most commonly accepted term for the genre, and contrary to the claims of its critics, it does not necessarily imply a circular structure.

James Nagel defines a cycle as "a collection of verse or narratives centering around some outstanding event or character" (1–2); for a collection of shorter pieces to be a cycle requires "that each contributing unit of the work be an independent narrative episode, and that there be some principle of unification that gives structure, movement, and thematic development to the whole" (2). Thus, "in the short story cycle each component work must stand alone (with a beginning, middle, and end) yet be enriched in the context of the interrelated stories" (15). Mann agrees, noting that "the stories are both self-sufficient and interrelated" (15). That balance or tension between the simultaneous autonomy and interconnectivity of the cycle is what most distinguishes it from other linked forms. For his part, Lundén broadens the range of binaries operating in dynamic balance within the cycle: "The tension between variety and unity, separateness and interconnectedness, fragmentation and continuity, openness and closure has been, if not ignored, at least given less attention than it deserves" (12). Later, he writes, "The short story composite ... is a form of narrative consisting of interlocking, autonomous stories, a narrative consciously constructed around the tension between simultaneous separateness and cohesion" (33). For Luscher, the cycle—or sequence, as he calls it—is "a volume of stories, collected and organized by their author, in which the reader successively realizes underlying patterns of coherence by continual modifications of his perceptions of pattern and theme" (148). Nagel argues that the short story cycle is the heir to an older narrative tradition than the novel: "The English 'novel,' as an extended narrative with a primary central character and a main plot that extends from beginning to end, is not as universal a form as a group of short stories linked to each other by consistent elements, whether ongoing characters, places, or situations" (5). He, Mann, Ian Reid (see p. 46), and others relate the cycle to other texts of linked shorter texts, notably framed tales and poetry sequences like Sir Philip Sidney's *Astrophil and Stella* (1591), James Thomson's *The Seasons* (1726–30), and Robert Browning's *The Ring and the Book* (1868–69).

The prototypical cycle is strongly linked, its constituent stories forming a narrative and/or thematic arc in which the artistic whole is greater than the sum of the short story parts. It is generally linked by character, setting, or—although whether such a set is a true cycle is not as clear—theme.[7] Cycles linked by character tend to portray a single protagonist's maturation in a chronological series of turning points in his or her life, as in Margaret Laurence's *A Bird in the House* (1970) and Alice Munro's *Who Do You Think You Are?* (1978). Those unified by setting portray the various inhabitants of a particular place and/or time: the physical setting can be anything from a city (e.g., James Joyce's *Dubliners* [1914]) to a town or village (Stephen Leacock's *Sunshine Sketches of a Little Town* [1912] and Eudora Welty's *The Golden Apples* [1949]) to a neighbourhood (Gloria Naylor's *The Women of Brewster Place* [1982]) to a single building (Rohinton Mistry's *Tales from Firozsha Baag* [1987]). Theme seldom constitutes the sole linking element in a cycle, so the theme-linked cycle is often unified by one of the other two elements as well. *Dubliners*, for example, is linked by setting as well as theme: Dublin as setting, paralysis as theme.

The strength of the linking of the stories depends on the linking element. The strongest linking is by character (a point with which Lundén agrees; see p. 165), the second-strongest is by setting, and the weakest is by theme. Thus, Alice Munro's *Who Do You Think You Are?* and *Lives of Girls and Women* (1971) portray Rose's and Del's growth, respectively, and are more tightly bonded, forming more cohesive aesthetic units over the course of the volumes, than setting-based cycles like Stephen Leacock's *Sunshine Sketches of a Little Town* and Sherwood Anderson's *Winesburg, Ohio* (1919). In setting-linked cycles, interaction among the characters in that setting provides stronger links; we see characters from their own and others' points of view, which adds a dimension of linking by character and greater unity to the cycle as a whole. The stories in Robert Olen Butler's *A Good Scent from a Strange Mountain* (1992) are all about the Vietnam War but provide more of a mosaic of characters' experiences of the conflict than a fully unified portrait.

One final point about generic identification: paratextual elements play a role in distinguishing story cycles from other kinds of text. Book titles can signal whether the focus of the work is on a theme, a symbol, or a place; for setting-linked stories, the name of the place usually provides the title. Seldom does the protagonist's name serve as the book's title the way it might for a novel.[8] As for generic subtitles, the term "A Story Cycle" is seldom if ever used, whereas tags like "Stories" and "A Novel" do appear; publishers prefer to use "A Novel in Stories" for cycles as a way to avoid scaring off potential customers, most of whom continue to prefer novels to story collections (more on that later). Back-cover blurbs and descriptions and a table of contents page are other ways a cycle can be identified as such. Novel chapters and parts can have titles, but those titles will not necessarily be listed in a table of contents, and where they are, they are often identified as chapters and parts. The issue of titles for the stories in a cycle will be taken up below; the matter can be complex and lead to some questions about how to deal with stories that have multiple and/or changing titles. Other considerations include the lengths of the constituent texts: one would not include a text made of brief anecdotes (too short and/or insufficiently "story-like") or a trilogy of novellas like *A Canticle for Leibowitz* (too long) (Lundén 47–49). Again, the author rather than an editor would have to be responsible for selecting and arranging the texts. Epigraphs, maps in setting-linked cycles, prefaces and epilogues, and other devices contribute to the volume's generic self-identification (Luscher 159).

As for the aesthetic nature of the cycle, scholars of the cycle generally agree that it is a liminal form, lying somewhere between the story collection—the volume of unrelated short stories—and the novel (e.g., Lundén 33, 36, 43–44; Lynch, *One and the Many* xi). Many theorists discuss the balance that the author seeks between what Lynch refers to as "the one and the many": the unity of the cycle and the diversity of its component stories (xvi; see also Struthers). Complicating the matter is that novels are normally constructed of discrete chapters, sometimes titled and each possessing a narrative arc or function of its own, and Lynch reviews the history of the English novel to show the degree to which its earliest manifestations, among them the works of Samuel Richardson, were "compilations" of shorter texts (*One and the Many* 15). Meanwhile, Lundén correctly points out that "a short story collection almost always possesses a measure of unity" (43), if only in style. In other words, linking involves less a set of strict divisions and more a spectrum that even takes in the adjacent genres: the novel at one end and the collection at the other.

While studies of the cycle commonly and properly relate it to the novel and the collection, however, scholars by and large neglect the role of the series in its history, form, and function. With its running characters, its common settings, and its thematic and other continuities, the cycle has obvious aesthetic links, so to speak, with the series. To the extent that the stories in a cycle function as stand-alone texts, and even lack direct references to each other, they are more like stories in a series than those in an unlinked collection. It would seem to be more just, then, to say that the cycle lies halfway between a *series* and a novel, with a book of unrelated stories possessing too few linkages to be related to the cycle the way critics often insist.

A related question is why an author would elect to write a set of linked short stories, particularly about the same protagonist, instead of a novel. That is, what does a set of discrete, self-contained stories convey that would not be communicated as well with the formal unity of a single narrative over the course of the entire volume? The form is often seen as particularly suitable in the modern and postmodern periods, which are characterized by a loss of faith in coherent narratives of the sort favoured by the novel. The short story cycle reflects the fragmentary and diverse nature of modern life, as both an illustration of and a way of depicting the complexity of life in the twentieth and twenty-first centuries (see, e.g., Lynch, *One and the Many* 17–18; Lundén argues that the composite or cycle "is more realistic, more closely rendering the indeterminacy of our lives, than both the short story and the novel" [89]). Analysts of the cycle assert that this fragmentation of experience and vision is better conveyed through a form that is more like a mosaic than a painting; in fact, Kennedy claims, "In its more experimental aspect ... the novel has for about seventy-five years been veering towards the story sequence as a decentred mode of narrative representation" (x). To a greater extent even than the modernist and postmodernist fragmentary novel, the story cycle communicates the modern and contemporary sensibility that rejects "grand narratives" or any such cohesive sense of the world. Story cycles express in form as much as content a view of experience as discontinuous, contingent, and incoherent. Lundén's position is that "In comparison with the traditional novel, the short story composite puts less emphasis on causality, temporality, plot, and character" (39).[9] He discusses at some length the genre's special handling of closure (52–77). Valerie Shaw also remarks on the way that the cycle resists conventionally linear narrative movement through its linking elements, including common characters, settings, and motifs: "all of these devices extend the scope of each individual piece without pretending to offer the type of progressive development associated with the novel" (159).

Scholars note how the form permits an author to accomplish certain artistic tasks, depending on the linking element. Forrest Ingram, the first critic to pay the genre due attention, endeavoured to distinguish types of cycles by authorial intention. He was rightly criticized for such an approach, one that begs many questions, yet artistic intention is an important factor in understanding an author's choice to employ this form. Modernism, for example, involved a growing interest in characters' psychological development rather than, say, plot, and in cycles linked by character, the author usually portrays distinct stages in the life of one character in the stories, perhaps to suggest that identity is shaped by discrete moments—incidents or epiphanies—rather than a coherent flow of experience: see Margaret Laurence's *A Bird in the House* and Alice Munro's *Who Do You Think You Are?*. Typically, the character-linked cycle takes the protagonist from childhood to adulthood, and often from farm or small town to city, and he or she undergoes a series of initiations—regarding death, sex, and so on—and revelations. The cycle lends itself to such key moments because "it allows the writer to focus on only those people and incidents that are essential to character development" (Mann 9). Those moments may involve different things for different groups of writers; for example, Mann says that female writers focus more on relationships than "the more introspective versions generally written by men" (9). The cycle may be better than the novel at portraying a character's isolation and alienation and the discontinuous nature of subjective time. *Kunstlerroman*-like cycles, such as *Winesburg, Ohio* and *A Bird in the House*, depict the stages in the growth of an artist, normally a writer, who is obliged both to separate him- or herself from family and community and to come to terms with the role these have played in shaping his or her mind and art. Often, the artist protagonist must learn that the very things he or she "escapes" are ultimately the material from which his/her art must be made. The stories often feature parallel structures so that they echo each other and thereby strengthen the unity of the text as a whole (Dunn and Morris 48). Dunn and Morris also identify "group" protagonists, such as the inhabitants of Dublin in Joyce's cycle and the family in Amy Tan's *The Joy Luck Club* (1989).

In stories linked by setting, the author can move from one character's point of view to another in order to provide a kaleidoscopic portrait of the setting, such as a small town or apartment building. Setting-linked cycles, like character-linked ones, illustrate the fragmentary nature of modern life by suggesting that no one perspective can give a full picture of a setting or a character. Rather, the diversity of spatial and social settings, such as richer and poorer areas of a city or town, and the points of view convey a sense that no place is one place. For example, Anderson's goal in *Winesburg, Ohio* was to portray the true lack of social cohesion and communication behind the façade of community in a small town (Reid 47–48; Kennedy, "From Anderson's Winesburg" 194–95). For Dunn and Morris, a "common setting, clearly defined, provides for the reader a necessary frame of reference" (30), one that guides the reader to the cycle's meaning and structure: again, they describe the characters in some setting-linked cycles as "collective" or "group" protagonists, citing the protagonists of Tama Janowitz's *Slaves of New York* (1986) as well as those of *Dubliners* as examples. Eleven of the stories in Janowitz's collection are linked by character, raising the question of whether these stories constitute a series or cycle of some kind.

Discussing contemporary cycles, Nagel writes that the "short-story cycle in modern American fiction is patently multicultural, deriving, perhaps, both from ethnic cross-fertilization within the literary community and from a shared legacy reaching back to ancient oral traditions in virtually every society throughout the world" (4–5); thus, "the story sequence offers not only a rich literary legacy but a vital technique for the exploration and depiction of the complex interactions of gender, ethnicity, and individual identity" (10). If the short story is suited to the expression of

Frank O'Connor's "lonely voice," the short story cycle, Nagel and others argue, is better than the novel for the marginalized voice.

Both character-linked and setting-linked story cycles, then, involve manipulation of point of view, a point that seems obvious in setting-linked story cycles, but even cycles linked by character, and depicting that common character's growth, portray the protagonist as subtly different in different stories. Instead of showing a character's coherent evolution, as would be the case in a novel, the character-linked story cycle captures separate and distinct moments in his or her development.

Furthermore, some scholars are more interested in the rhetorical effects of the form: that is, how the structure affects the reader. Luscher describes the cycle as "an open book, inviting the reader to construct a network of associations that binds the stories together and lends them cumulative thematic impact" and stresses the patterns and links that the reader perceives (149). The result is that cycles are "unique hybrids that combine two distinct reading pleasures: the patterned closure of individual stories and the discovery of larger unifying strategies that transcend the apparent gaps between stories" (150). While the short story conventionally seeks Poe's single effect, the cycle multiplies and complicates the effect, and requires the reader to do much of the work: "a certain amount of subjective activity must be left to the reader, who participates by supplying what the author leaves out" (152). Lundén describes the discontinuity and multiplicity created by the cycle, with gaps that the reader is required to fill or at the very least experience *as* gaps. He discusses "frontal" and "lateral" ellipses, meaning on one hand "a break in temporal continuity" and on the other "an omission of one or more components in a situation" (89). Information is missing between one story and the next, and the reader works to supply that information and interpret meaning. Much more is implicit than explicit (90). One way that many cycles affirm discontinuity, he notes, is by having the stories remain so discrete that they do not refer to events in other stories, despite the fact they may be about the same character, for example (90).

As with other collections of short stories, the individual texts are commonly first published in periodicals, and then, when collecting them, the author might add other stories to fill out the cycle and will arrange the stories in a way that assumes the reader will read the pieces in order. In fact, reader behaviour when it comes to story collections and anthologies is a little-studied field. However carefully the editor of an anthology or the author of a story collection might organize the volume, the reader may not read the stories in the order they are printed. Editors are known to arrange the stories in an anthology (or, indeed, the issues of a periodical) to create a rhythm of sorts, one that becomes lost on a reader who reads the stories at random or in an order based on personal interests and desires. More than an anthology or collection, a cycle requires orderly reading in order to convey the character and/or story arc intended. We will soon look at reading practices when it comes to short story collections and anthologies in some detail.

Periodical publication of the stories that compose a cycle raises a variety of formal questions. For example, were the stories always intended to be a cycle? Were they instead components in a short story series that were later shaped into a cycle through revision and organization, or were they more or less unrelated stories later revised to form a larger aesthetic unit? As Nagel says,

> Because the constituent stories of cycles often appear individually in magazines before being anthologized [sic; he means collected], they pose special interpretive problems for scholars … The most obvious of these kinds of changes would be the modification o[r] clarifications of family relationships, descriptions of locations and their distances from other places, and explanations of time parameters, matters essential in the appearance of individual stories published in separate places months or years apart from one another but redundant in a collected volume. For this and other reasons, the analysis of publication history is particularly important in the study of the genre.
>
> (14)

In the end, for the cycle to be read as a cycle, it must be published as a volume, that is, in book form; the cycle is therefore dependent upon the existence (and health) of the book trade. Like the novel, then, even though it may be published "serially" in periodicals, the story cycle is designed for ultimate publication as a volume. Anticipation of book publication will shape the way that the stories are written for the magazines, with linking characters and/or settings that may have to be elaborated upon each time; then, when the complete text is ready for book publication, redundant exposition might have to be excised and the author will make choices about story arrangement—choices the publisher might not agree with or even accept (deliberately or by error). Furthermore, as more than one author has experienced, book publishers may not be willing to publish collections of short stories even when the stories are closely linked, and if they do publish the work, they might insist that it be called a novel, or at least a "novel in stories." Munro's *Lives of Girls and Women* is referred to on the back cover of one of the paperback editions as a novel.

The cycle, then, is a creature of the modern book trade and its publishing of story collections, a practice that, as we have seen, dates back to the very earliest days of the short story but that has gone in cycles itself. During the short story's Golden Age, short story collections were easier to sell to both publishers and readers, but never easy; Ohmann demonstrates that story collections have always sold more poorly than novels (95–103). Even a popular writer like Robert E. Howard had trouble selling story collections. He tried to sell a collection of his Conan stories to Denis Archer Co., but one of its editors, Hugh G. Schonfield, replied, "The difficulty that arises about publication in book form, is the prejudice that is very strong over here just now against collections of short stories" (Schonfield to Howard 9 Jan. 1934, qtd. in Lord 142). Nevertheless, without the presence of a book trade and publishers willing to take a chance or even a loss on story collections, the short story cycle could not exist.

Now we come to the mini-cycle, which shares some formal and sociological features, challenges, and history with the cycle but which differs from its larger cousin in important ways as well. Again, we will begin with some formal questions and then move on to the sociological ones.

First, why would an author write a set of two, three, or four linked short stories instead of one text? That text would be fairly long for a single story—in fact, no longer qualifying as a short story by most definitions—but would not be long enough to qualify as a novel, either. At perhaps 20,000–40,000 words, that text would be a novella. The mini-cycle is thus similar to the cycle in that it is a text of similar length to an adjacent fictional form but involves a very different handling of the material by being composed of multiple texts rather than one longer narrative. Therefore, when it comes to identifying the mini-cycle generically, and thus relationally to other genres, the conclusion seems clear: *the mini-cycle is to the novella as the short story cycle is to the novel*. The mini-cycle constitutes a sort of liminal form between the short story collection or series and the novella, much as the story cycle exists on the border between the short story collection or series and the novel.

Just as understanding the novel contributes to our understanding of an author's choice to write a novel-length text as a set of linked stories, examining the novella helps us understand why an author would choose to write a novella-length text made up of discrete short stories. Again, to repeat a question posed earlier about the cycle, what can an author do in a mini-cycle that he or she could not accomplish by writing a novella?

We saw that one of the most significant distinguishing features of the cycle is how it permits greater diversification of point of view. In a cycle, the author can multiply the point of view either spatially—by "spreading out," so to speak, the point of view to encompass a number of characters—or temporally, by portraying the protagonist of a character-linked cycle at different stages of life. Does the same principle apply to the mini-cycle as it relates to the novella? To examine this question properly, we need to review the history and nature of the novella, particularly what theorists of the genre have said about point of view in it. Surprisingly little has been written about the novella as a genre, as Abby H. P. Werlock notes (485–86), and much of it is at least forty years old, but the analyses offer consistent insights into what distinguishes the novella from other forms, especially the short story and the novel. Studies by Ronald Paulson, Howard Nemerov, Judith Leibowitz, Bayard Quincy

Morgan, Mary Doyle Springer, and Charles E. May reveal that a tightly focused point of view is one of the distinguishing features of the novella and is apparently central to the genre to a greater degree than is the case with the novel.

The novella is a genre that has long suffered terminological confusion. The first significant texts called "novella" were the stories that Boccaccio collected and composed in the *Decameron* (see Good for a history of the early "*novelle*"). For many theorists, particularly those among the German Romantics, Boccaccio provided the model for what a "novelle" or "novella" should be: a short, realist story, often embedded in a framing narrative and featuring an "unheard-of" or novel event that produces a profound singular effect on the reader. The German theorists, like Johann Wolfgang von Goethe and Ludwig Tieck, were clearly influenced by Edgar Allan Poe's doctrine that a short story should offer unity of effect achieved through unusual situations and brevity that permitted the text to be read in a single sitting. For them, the *novelle* should have one dominant theme and/or mood, in order not to dilute the unity of effect, and be characterized by intensity through narrative concentration (Paine; May 3234–37). The German *novelle*, perhaps best represented by the works of Goethe, became the basis for later developments in the novella. Interestingly, Chekhov's "Little Trilogy" fits the nineteenth-century German definition of novella quite nicely: the three stories are frame narratives, as Burkin and Ivan Ivanovich are storytellers rather than protagonists, while Alyokhin acts as both. While the stories are linked by character, the main linking element in the mini-cycle is theme: all three stories illustrate the stultifying effects of materialism, narrowness of life and vision, and emotional and spiritual cowardice. In their function as *exempla*, the stories offer another link between the novella and the mini-cycle, as the exemplary novella—e.g., Cervantes's *Novelas ejemplares* (1613)—is seen as one of the early types of the genre (for modern examples, see Springer 56–76).

During the nineteenth century, fictional genres arose or gained new positions in the literary hierarchy, leading to generic redefinition and relabelling (for a history of the term "novella" see Gillespie). The rise of the short story, for example, necessitated changes in the term "novel," which came to refer to long works of prose fiction. In France, the terms *conte* and *nouvelle* were largely interchangeable, although some defined the first as referring to shorter, less mimetic texts while the latter was seen as applicable to longer and more realist works of fiction: the equivalents in French of "tale" and "short story." These terminological usages were not consistent, but for our purposes, the significance of this difference lies in how it affected the first major English-language theorist of the novella, Henry James. James used the term *nouvelle* to describe the longer realist stories he wrote for *Yellow Book*. As mentioned above, James chafed at the artistic confines of most magazines' word limits. In his preface to "The Lesson of the Master" (1888), his first story for *Yellow Book*,

James describes his pleasure at no longer being subject to these restrictive length requirements. The passage merits quotation in full, as it includes a number of relevant points:

> I was invited, and all urgently, to contribute to the first number, and was regaled with the golden truth that my composition might absolutely assume, might shamelessly parade in, its own organic form. It was disclosed to me, wonderfully, that—so golden the air pervading the enterprise—any projected contribution might conform, not only unchallenged but by this circumstance itself the more esteemed, to its true intelligible nature. For any idea I might wish to express I might have space, in other words, elegantly to express it—an offered licence that, on the spot, opened up the millennium to the "short story". One had so often known this product to struggle, in one's hands, under the rude prescription of brevity at any cost, with the opposition so offered to its really becoming a story, that my friend's emphasised indifference to the arbitrary limit of length struck me, I remember, as the fruit of the finest artistic intelligence. We had been at one—that we already knew—on the truth that the forms of wrought things, in this order, *were*, all exquisitely and effectively, the things; so that, for the delight of mankind, form might compete with form and might correspond to fitness; might, that is, in the given case, have an inevitability, a marked felicity. Among forms, moreover, we had had, on the dimensional ground—for length and breadth—our ideal, the beautiful and blest *nouvelle*; the generous, the enlightened hour for which appeared thus at last to shine. It was under the star of the *nouvelle* that, in other languages, a hundred interesting and charming results, such studies on the minor scale as the best of Turgenieff's, of Balzac's, of Maupassant's, of Bourget's, and just lately, in our own tongue, of Kipling's, had been, all economically, arrived at—thanks to their authors', as 'contributors', having been able to count, right and left, on a wise and liberal support. It had taken the blank misery of our Anglo-Saxon sense of such matters to organise, as might be said, the general indifference to this fine type of composition. In that dull view a "short story" was a "short story", and that was the end of it. Shades and differences, varieties and styles, the value above all of the idea happily *developed*, languished, to extinction, under the hard-and-fast rule of the "from six to eight thousand words"—when, for one's benefit, the rigour was a little relaxed. For myself, I delighted in the shapely *nouvelle*—as, for that matter, I had from time to time and here and there been almost encouraged to show.
>
> (219–20)

With the *nouvelle*, as Robert A. Lee says, "Length, focus, scale, are to be released from the constraints of the regulation short story, yet without the need to go to the other extreme of full-fledged novel-writing" (9).

Other authors, like Poe, Melville, Maupassant, and Chekhov, had worked in the genre of intermediate-length fiction, but only now did the modern novella begin to take its name and its place in the literary world. J. H. E. Paine goes into some detail about this development, tracing the rise of the modern novella from its Renaissance and nineteenth-century roots—particularly its realism, balance of the objective and subjective, and restrained scope.

James's comments reflect a practical concern that is pertinent to our genre: the difficulty of publishing novellas. His complaint refers to the fact that, with a few exceptions, both general-interest and literary magazines have always preferred to publish short stories, giving authors strict upper-word limits. Stories longer than 10,000 words—but not long enough to qualify as novels, which can be serialized or published separately—are difficult to place, and, as Greg Johnson points out, see print most often in short story collections:

> Beloved by writers, but often scorned by editors and readers, the novella has held a long but uncertain tenancy in the house of fiction. Traditionally considered too brief for individual publication in book form, but too lengthy for the format of most magazines and journals, the novella has broken into print most often as part of a short story collection or alongside several other novellas in a classroom anthology. A few contemporary writers have managed to publish single novellas (presumably because an established reputation makes such publication commercially feasible), and literary magazines will sometimes make room for an outstanding example of the form.
>
> (363; see also McGraw 808)

The resistance of periodical editors to publishing novellas has not been true for all genres; women's magazines frequently published "novelettes" (a term authors and critics have decried as demeaning), and science fiction magazines continue to publish novelettes and novellas as well as short stories and serialized novels. *The New Yorker* has demonstrated that it is prepared to publish very long "short stories" by authors like Alice Munro and Mavis Gallant, and a few literary journals like Toronto's now-defunct *Descant* have made room for novellas, but they have always been in a minority. It is noteworthy that novellas appear most frequently in the same venue as the mini-cycle: in a collection of otherwise unrelated stories. Authors will occasionally include a novella as the capstone or signature piece of a collection, like "The Dead" in *Dubliners*. Authors who incorporate mini-cycles in their collections are perhaps experimenting with the form of the collection of shorter pieces plus a longer work.

This is not the place to examine the features of the modern novella in great detail, but certain elements—some of which reflect the genre's roots in the *novelle*—are relevant to our study. Paulson, Nemerov, Springer, and Leibowitz agree that what distinguishes the novella from the novel is its goal of achieving unity of effect through limited scope: that is, its small number of characters, its narrow range of spatial and temporal setting, and its tight point of view (e.g., Nemerov 229–30). In his introduction to *The Novelette before 1900*, Paulson speaks of "the close structural unity around a single point" that leads to "the novella's tendency towards using first-person narrators to tell the story; the point of view is seldom omniscient" (v). Leibowitz describes the novella's "double effect of intensity and expansion" (16), with the expansion referring to a "theme-complex" rather than a single theme and the intensity deriving from repetition and other techniques that narrow the text's fictional scope. While the novel may involve multiple points of view, the novella maintains a sharper and more "intensive" perspective (see also Paine 56). Springer's somewhat rigid categorization and interpretation of novellas assigns techniques to what she calls the "apologue" (following Neo-Aristotelian critics like R. S. Crane and Sheldon Sacks) that can be found in the genre generally. Overall, she stresses the restricted spectrum of dominant themes, the low number of important characters, and in many cases the very tight focus on individual characters (see esp. 101–30). Charles E. May traces the modern novella's roots in forms like the parable and the Gothic, noting, "The novella alters these forms in significant ways, however, not the least of which is caused by the new importance that point of view or narrative voice assumes in the form" (3257). In his survey of the Canadian novella, Warren Cariou writes:

> The novella is generally not as formally experimental as the long story and the novel can be, and it usually lacks the subplots, the multiple points of view, and the generic adaptability that are common in the novel. It is most often concerned with personal and emotional development rather than with the larger social sphere. The novella generally retains something of the unity of impression that is a hallmark of the short story, but it also contains more highly developed characterization and more luxuriant description.
>
> (835; see also his comments on the status of
novella publishing in Canada)

The novella thus tends to favour strict limitations when it comes to point of view, as one might expect from a genre that seeks to create a strong effect through narrative focus. The novella strives for the compression of the short story while extending its themes beyond the confines of the short story's limits. In the process, the novella discourages multiple points of view or other formal experiments that would dilute its aesthetic effect. Within the confines of the same overall word-length, by contrast, the mini-cycle, like the story cycle *vis-à-vis* the novel, allows an author to multiply his or her points of view. By constructing a set of, say, three linked short stories rather than one unified narrative, the author can examine character relationships or themes from a variety of perspectives, highlighting the relative nature of those relationships or enriching the reader's awareness of the complexity of the emotions involved. Thus, the mini-cycle offers the author of a narrative totalling fifteen to fifty thousand words what the story cycle offers to the author of a novel-length text.

The mini-cycle not only allows for but actually encourages the examination of characters and themes from various perspectives. Like the story cycle, the mini-cycle provides a means to portray fragmentary experiences and reveal characters from various angles. The stories in a mini-cycle are closely linked through common characters, repetition and motif, and shared themes, but they remain discrete stories. As a result, the mini-cycle is both similar to and different from the novella, in much the same way that the story cycle is both similar to and very different from the novel. The component stories in a mini-cycle depict quite different perspectives by portraying different periods in a protagonist's life or having different protagonists or points of view. A study of the mini-cycle therefore offers an opportunity to see another way in which authors can expand the short story form to create larger narrative structures.

Turning now to the sociology or material conditions of the mini-cycle, we see that, like the novella, the most common form—the three-story mini-cycle, or story trilogy—does not fit well into the publishing requirements of professional or literary magazines, with their almost universal restrictions on word length. The stories would therefore have to be published separately, even in different periodicals, just like the components of a cycle. As far as I am aware, only once have the stories in a mini-cycle been published together in a periodical: Alice Munro's "Juliet Triptych" of "Chance," "Soon," and "Silence," which appeared as "Three Stories" in the 14 June 2004 issue of *The New Yorker* before their publication in *Runaway*. Clearly, the reason for the editors' exception is that she is Alice Munro; not many authors would be granted that indulgence. In a more usual example, the three short stories in the mini-cycle published in Clark Blaise's *Resident Alien* (1986) originally appeared on a radio programme ("South" on the CBC's "Anthology" series), an anthology ("Identity" in *81: Best Canadian Stories*), and a magazine ("North" in *Saturday Night*).

In addition, there has been a shift in the number and kinds of periodicals available to fiction authors. Instead of periodicals made up largely or even exclusively of fiction, weekly and monthly magazines since the middle of the twentieth century have become purveyors of mostly non-fictional content and many advertisements. Those general-interest magazines that still publish fiction normally publish one story per issue, so fiction has to compete for space to a far greater degree. That is of course not the case in online publishing, and there may well be online magazines that have published mini-cycles as units.

The mini-cycle is thus partly associated with periodical publishing, but its primary venue as a form is the collection, that is, the book. The individual stories may stand alone quite well, but they achieve their full effect when collected in book form, echoing and reinforcing each other and thereby influencing how we read them. With a couple of exceptions, then, the mini-cycle is only printed in a story collection, where author and editor have the freedom to incorporate stories of any length and to arrange them at will. Most of the time, authors choose to publish the stories in a mini-cycle consecutively, but occasionally the component stories are separated, in a form I call the "exploded" mini-cycle. Studying individual mini-cycles permits us to see both the most common methods of constructing them and such variations.

Short Story Volume Reading Practices

The construction of cycles and mini-cycles raises some intriguing questions about the reading of books of short stories: collections, cycles, and anthologies. Authors usually construct their cycles and mini-cycles carefully, arranging the component stories to create a certain effect. They may thus expect, assume, and hope that the reader will read the stories in the order in which they are printed. But is that always the case? What are the actual reading practices of readers of volumes of short stories?

Since the days of Hans Robert Jauss and Wolfgang Iser, scholars have been considering the role of readership in the construction of texts, but their work has been theoretical rather than empirical. It is one thing to discuss the ways in which the reader contributes to or even determines the final "meaning" of a text, but quite another to study how readers actually read a text like a book of short stories. Except in the case of experimental, "cut-up" examples, novels are meant to be read, and are always, or nearly always, read, from start to finish, but to my knowledge, no one has undertaken research on exactly how readers read volumes of short stories. Just because an author or editor designs a book of stories, or a mini-cycle, to be read in the same way as a novel—from the first page sequentially to the last—does not mean the reader will do what is desired or expected.

To fill in this gap, I conducted a survey of short story readers to establish their reading practices when it came to story collections, story cycles, and anthologies. I distributed a questionnaire at the Fifteenth International Conference on the Short Story in English, which was held from 27–30 June 2018, in Lisbon, Portugal. This seemed to me a logical venue for the survey, since the people in attendance were by virtue of their presence devoted short story readers and, in the case of a third of them, authors as well. It should be noted, however, that this was not a truly scientific survey, in that the respondents were by and large, and perhaps entirely, "professional" readers; that is, they were short story scholars, authors, and in many cases both. Results might well differ should the general reading public be sampled. Also, the response rate was low, with only 33 people submitting their survey forms. Nevertheless, the survey offers a valuable first look into short story reading practice, as the answers to my questions offer interesting insights into how people actually read books of short stories and illustrate in very real ways the potential for a substantial gap between what authors and anthology editors seek to accomplish and what actually happens when readers read their books.

For our purposes, the most important responses are those addressing the reading of story collections. That is because mini-cycles are normally published in collections of otherwise unrelated stories, and they are seldom identified as sets of linked stories. The components of a mini-cycle almost always have their own separate titles, titles that provide no clue that the stories belong to a linked set. A reader will not know, then, that the stories are designed to be read together or that they are linked at all until textual cues such as common characters and/or events signal the linking. Unlike the prototypical mini-cycle, a story cycle will have a single, overarching title, and that title might signal that the stories are linked—by naming the setting of a setting-linked cycle—or there may be other paratextual signals, such as a generic label like "story cycle" or the ambiguous "a novel in stories." A mini-cycle will generally not have any paratextual features identifying it as a mini-cycle; that is certainly the case with most of the mini-cycles discussed here. A reader will only know that the component stories of a mini-cycle are linked once he or she has read, or at least started to read, them. The linking will therefore come as more of a surprise than is the case with many story cycles. The surprise will be even greater in the case of exploded mini-cycles; the intervening stories will suggest to the reader that the characters are done with, the narrative arc completed, until he or she reaches the next story in the mini-cycle. We will see examples of this effect in the chapter on the form.

In the survey, I asked respondents to discuss how they read the three main types of short story volume: story collection, story cycle, and anthology. In each case, I asked readers whether they read the volumes in order—did they read the books from start to finish?—or, if not, what other principle(s) guided the order in which they read the stories.

Question 1 was: "How do you read a story collection? Do you read the stories in order from beginning to end, or in a different way?" Seven or 21% of respondents said that they always read story collections in order; ten or 30% replied that they usually read the stories in order, although one said that she would skip a story if it did not hold her interest; five or 15% said that they read the stories at random. When discussing other ways they decided to order their reading besides print order, seven or 21% cited story title; that is, they chose stories on the basis of whether the titles seemed interesting.

In their comments, respondents offered the following reasons for their choices in reading order:

- "I read first paragraphs and from my response keep reading, or put it aside."
- "I usually start reading the index and go strai[gh]t to the story that has the most interesting title."

- "Not always in the order from beginning to end. Sometimes just those which interest me most."
- "I mostly read in the order in which they are given. I assume that care has been put into their arrangement, even when the stories are not linked. I tend to 'read' collections with an expectation that they are probably cycles to some degree, or certainly with an eye on whether I could argue that they are cycles … However, I must confess I sometimes jump around the collection based on the length of stories; for example, if I don't have a lot of time, I might choose a shorter story to read, regardless of its position in the collection."
- "If I am very familiar with the author I select the stories I want to read first."
- "Usually from beginning to end, but if I have some special interest in some of the stories, I would read them first."
- "This depends on the author and my familiarity with the text, funnily enough. If I am encountering a new short story author whose works are new to me, I will read the book from start to finish in the order it is printed. If I am familiar with an author and I am buying a second/third/other collection of theirs, I may start with a story I know (such as if one had been published online/in journal prior to the publication of the collection) and then work outwards."
- "It depends on my goal concerning the reading, in terms of themes and subjects in the stories."
- "I read them out of order, seeing which titles appeal, or if an anthology, which authors. Once I have started that way, I scan the openings of the stories to see if I shall continue to read, which ideas grip me etc."
- "It depends on the collection. Sometimes I'm drawn to a particular title and will read that first. An e-book, I will work straight through. And more & more with hard copy, I do the same, respecting that there is a method to the order."
- "Sometimes I pick by intuition, or I have a brief look at the opening—the first sentences."
- "I usually read a story collection in the published order of the stories, but sometimes (if I don't intend to read cover to cover) I might cherry-pick stories at random—and pencil-tick the titles in the Contents list to remind me later."
- "If I haven't heard anything about the stories, I do tend to read them according to the appeal of the title. If I have heard or read something about any of the stories, then I still start by those who have already created some buzz."
- "I tend to browse story collections, checking out titles, and occasionally reading the start to see if the story is going to interest me."
- "I usually read a story collection by a favourite writer, or because of some critical comments on the writer or the collection which interest

me. I often read the stories in order from beginning to end, unless some stories are specifically commented [on]."

It is worth noting how large a role the reader's familiarity with the author and the title play in determining whether he or she will read the stories in order. As we will see, these considerations are even more important when it comes to anthologies.

Question 2 was: "Does your reading practice change if you know the book is a story cycle? Are you more likely to read it from beginning to end?" Here, the response was almost unanimous: all but one of the respondents said that they read story cycles sequentially. One, however, said, "I think I would. But you never know ... sometimes I just open a book and start reading."

As for anthologies, only three—fewer than 10%—of the respondents said that they read anthologies in order, while two more said they usually read the stories in order. Interestingly, those who read anthologies in order were among those who read story collections in order as well. One might speculate that novel-reading practice affected the way they read books of short stories. A few respondents said that what governed their reading choices depended on the kind of anthology it was, although they did not go into much detail about that. The most common reply was that readers first read stories by authors they knew (17 or 52%), and/or stories whose titles appealed to them: 8 or 24% said that they were drawn to the stories on the basis of their titles. One referred to "need" while another referred to "interest" without specifying what they meant by these terms, and one said she first read stories by authors she was researching. One said length was the determining factor. Five or 15% read the stories in an anthology at random.

The implications of the responses about story collection reading practice for the mini-cycle are clear. While authors may construct their mini-cycles intending readers to read the component texts together and in order, or in order but with gaps between them if they are exploded mini-cycles, readers will not necessarily read them that way. Only about 52% of readers always or usually read the stories in collections in order, meaning that what the author seeks to communicate through the placement and organization of mini-cycles is not necessarily what the reader receives. A reader might well read the consecutively printed stories in a mini-cycle separately from each other, and in a different or even reverse order. There is perhaps no better concrete illustration than this of the almost inevitable gap between authorial intention and reader experience.

Notes

1 My own research into the short story has dealt with the way the genre changed when the kind of magazine that published short stories changed in Canada

during the post-Second World War period, when the general-interest, large-circulation magazine was mostly replaced by the university-based literary magazine as the main publisher of short stories.

2 Some popular genres lend themselves less easily to story series, such as romance and sports fiction.

3 Howard wrote series in other genres as well, including Western, detective, and sports stories.

4 Disturbingly, the Wikipedia entry for "Fix-Up" includes a number of story cycles as examples.

5 Philip Stevick's *The Chapter in Fiction* (1970) is the classic study of division and closure in longer narrative forms.

6 Rolf Lundén, meanwhile, complains that the problem goes beyond the terminology, as scholars of the genre have tried too hard to impose cohesion on texts: "unity, coherence, and closure have been privileged at the expense of discontinuity, fragmentation, and openness" (8). That emphasis may be grounded in a desire to show how the cycle works as an aesthetic whole, while not losing sight of the cycle's inherently fragmented form.

7 If a set of stories with the same theme form a cycle, would a theme anthology qualify? We limit our definition of a cycle to a volume of works by the same author. Authors frequently deal with the same theme or themes in their stories, simply by virtue of their preoccupations. See the discussion below of degrees of linking.

8 In addition, while books of sketches would often be identified as such, either by having "sketch" itself or "patch-work" in the title (Dunn and Morris 22–23), few works of fiction will have "novel" or "stories" in their titles.

9 He may be making an unfair comparison here. After all, the same could be said of the modernist or postmodernist short story and its "traditional" predecessor.

References

Anderson, Sherwood. *Winesburg, Ohio*. Introduction by Malcolm Cowley, Penguin, 1976.

Ashley, Mike. *The Age of the Storytellers: British Popular Fiction Magazines 1880–1950*. British Library, 2006.

Asimov, Isaac. *I, Robot*. Gnome, 1950.

Baldwin, Dean. *Art and Commerce in the British Short Story, 1880–1950*. Pickering and Chatto, 2013.

Blaise, Clark. *Resident Alien*. Penguin, 1986.

Boyce, Benjamin. "English Short Fiction in the Eighteenth Century: A Preliminary View." *Studies in Short Fiction*, vol.5, no.2, Winter 1968, pp. 95–112.

Butler, Robert Olen. *A Good Scent from a Strange Mountain*. Holt, 1992.

Cariou, Warren. "Novella." *Encyclopedia of Literature in Canada*, edited by W. H. New, U of Toronto P, 2000, p. 835.

Chan, Winnie. *The Economy of the Short Story in British Periodicals of the 1890s*. Routledge, 2007.

Coffman, Frank. "Barbarian Ascendant: The Poetic and Epistolary Origins of the Character and His World." *Conan Meets the Academy: Multidisciplinary Essays on the Enduring Barbarian*, edited by Jonas Prida, McFarland, 2013, pp. 35–50.

Current-Garcia. Eugene. "Irving Sets the Pattern: Notes on Professionalism and the Art of the Short Story." *Studies in Short Fiction,* vol. 10, no. 4, Fall 1973, pp. 327–41.

Dunn, Maggie, and Ann Morris. *The Composite Novel: The Short Story Cycle in Transition.* Twayne, 1995.

Ferguson, Susan. "The Short Story as Parvenu in the Society of Genres." *Visions critiques,* no. 5, 1988, pp. 267–74.

Finn, Mark. *Blood & Thunder: The Life & Art of Robert E. Howard.* Monkey Brain, 2006.

Gillespie, Gerald. "Novella, Nouvelle, Novell[e], Short Novel?—A Review of Terms." *Neophilologus,* vol. 51, no. 2, Apr. 1967, pp. 117–27; vol. 51, no. 3, July 1967, pp. 225–30.

Good, Graham. "Notes on the Novella." *The New Short Story Theories,* edited by Charles May, Ohio UP, 1994, pp. 147–64.

Harris, Wendell V. *British Short Fiction in the Nineteenth Century: A Literary and Bibliographic Guide.* Wayne State UP, 1979.

Ingram, Forrest L. *Representative Short Story Cycles of the Twentieth Century: Studies in a Literary Genre.* Mouton, 1971.

Irving, Washington. *The Sketch Book.* Van Winkle, 1819–1820.

James, Henry. *The Art of the Novel: Critical Prefaces.* Edited by R. P. Blackmur, Scribner's Sons, 1934.

Janowitz, Tama. *Slaves of New York.* Crown Publishers, 1986.

Johnson, Greg. "Novellas for the Nineties." *Georgia Review,* vol. 45, no. 2, Summer 1991, pp. 363–71.

Joyce, James. *Dubliners.* G. Richards, 1914.

Kennedy, J. Gerald. "From Anderson's Winesburg to Carver's Cathedral: The Short Story Sequence and the Semblance of Community." Kennedy, pp. 194–215.

——. Introduction. Kennedy, pp. vii–xv.

——, editor. *Modern American Short Story Sequences: Composite Fictions and Fictive Communities.* Cambridge UP, 1995.

Killick, Tim. *British Short Fiction in the Early Nineteenth Century: The Rise of the Tale.* Ashgate, 2008.

——. "Mary Russell Mitford and the Topography of Short Fiction." *Journal of the Short Story in English,* no. 43, Autumn 2004, pp. 11–28.

Laurence, Margaret. *A Bird in the House.* McClelland and Stewart, 1974.

Leacock, Stephen. *Sunshine Sketches of a Little Town.* Edited by Gerald Lynch, Tecumseh, 1996.

Lee, Brian. *American Fiction 1865–1940.* Longman, 1987.

Lee, Robert A. Introduction. *The Modern American Novella,* edited by Lee, St. Martin's, 1989, pp. 7–12.

Leibowitz, Judith. *Narrative Purpose in the Novella.* Mouton, 1974.

Levy, Andrew. *The Culture and Commerce of the American Short Story.* Cambridge UP, 1993.

Lord, Glenn. "Robert E. Howard: Professional Writer." *The Dark Barbarian: The Writings of Robert E. Howard: A Critical Anthology.* Greenwood, 1984, pp. 135–47.

Lundén, Rolf. *The United Stories of America: Studies in the Short Story Composite.* Rodopi, 1999.

Luscher, Robert. "The Short Story Sequence: An Open Book." *Short Story Theory at a Crossroads*, edited by Susan Lohafer and Jo Ellen Clarey, Louisiana State UP, 1989, pp. 148–67.

Lynch, Gerald. *The One and the Many: English-Canadian Short Story Cycles*. U of Toronto P, 2001.

Mann, Susan Garland. *The Short Story Cycle: A Genre Companion and Reference Guide*. Greenwood, 1989.

Martin, Peter A. "The Short Story in England: 1930s Fiction Magazines." *Studies in Short Fiction*, vol. 14, no. 3, Summer 1977, pp. 233–40.

May, Charles E. "The Novella." *Critical Survey of Long Fiction: English Language Series*, edited by Frank N. McGill, vol. 8, Salem, 1983, pp. 3213–3339.

Mayo, Robert. *The English Novel in the Magazines 1740–1815*. Northwestern UP, 1962.

McGraw, Erin. "Nor Good Red Herring: Novellas and Stories." *Georgia Review*, vol. 50, no. 4, Winter 1996, pp. 808–18.

Miller, Jr., Walter M. *A Canticle for Leibowitz*. Lippincott, 1960.

Mistry, Rohinton. *Tales from Firozsha Baag*. Penguin, 1987.

Mitford, Mary Russell. *Our Village*. Macmillan, 1893.

Moodie, Susanna. *Roughing It in the Bush*. Norton, 2007.

Morgan, Bayard Quincy. "The Novelette as a Literary Form." *Symposium*, vol. 1, no. 1, 1 Nov. 1946, pp. 34–39.

Morrison, Kevin A. "Foregrounding Nationalism: Mary Russell Mitford's *Our Village* and the Effects of Publication Context." *European Romantic Review*, vol. 19, no. 3, July 2008, pp. 275–87.

Mott, Frank Luther. *A History of American Magazines*. Vol. 2: 1885–1905, Harvard UP, 1957.

Munro, Alice. *Lives of Girls and Women*. McGraw-Hill Ryerson, 1971.

——. *Runaway*. McClelland and Stewart, 2004.

——. *Who Do You Think You Are?* Macmillan, 1978.

Nagel, James. *The Contemporary American Short-Story Cycle: The Ethnic Resonance of Genre*. Louisiana State UP, 2001.

Naylor, Gloria. *The Women of Brewster Place*. Viking Press, 1982.

Nemerov, Howard. "Compositions and Fate in the Short Novel." *Poetry and Fiction: Essays*, Rutgers UP, 1963. 229–45.

Ohmann, Richard. *Selling Culture: Magazines, Markets, and Class at the Turn of the Century*. Verso, 1996.

Onslow, Barbara. *Women of the Press in Nineteenth-Century Britain*. Macmillan, 2000.

Orel, Harold. *The Victorian Short Story: Development and Triumph of a Literary Genre*. Cambridge UP, 1986.

Paine, J. H. E. *Theory and Criticism of the Novella*. Grundmann, 1979.

Paulson, Ronald. Introduction. *The Modern Novelette*, edited by Paulson, Prentice-Hall, 1965, pp. vi–x.

——. Introduction. *The Novelette before 1900*, edited by Paulson, Prentice-Hall, 1965, pp. v–viii.

Pearson, Hesketh. *Conan Doyle: His Life and Art*. Methuen, 1943.

Pitcher, Edward W. R., editor. *An Anthology of the Short Story in 18th and 19th Century America*. Vol. 1, Mellen, 2000.

Polsgrove, Carol. "They Made It Pay: British Short-Fiction Writers, 1820–1840." *Studies in Short Fiction*, vol. 11, no. 4. Fall 1974, pp. 417–21.

Rabkin, Eric S. "The Composite Novel in Science Fiction." *Foundation*, Spring 1996, pp. 93–100.

Reid, Ian. *The Short Story*. Methuen, 1977.

Schweitzer, Darrell. *Conan's World and Robert E. Howard*. Borgo Press, 1978.

Shaw, Valerie. *The Short Story: A Critical Introduction*. Longman, 1983.

Springer, Mary Doyle. *Forms of the Modern Novella*. U of Chicago P, 1975.

Stevick, Philip. *The Chapter in Fiction: Theories of Narrative Division*. Syracuse UP, 1970.

Struthers, J. R. (Tim). "Interesting Orbits: A Study of Selected Story Cycles by Hugh Hood, Jack Hodgins, Clark Blaise, and Alice Munro, in Their Literary Contexts." Diss. U of Western Ontario, 1981.

Tan, Amy. *The Joy Luck Club*. Putnam's, 1989.

Welty, Eudora. *The Golden Apples*. Harcourt, Brace, 1949.

Werlock, Abby H. P. "Novella." *The Facts on File Companion to the American Short Story*, Facts on File, 2000, pp. 317–21.

2   Anton Chekhov's "Little Trilogy"

The earliest mini-cycle I have so far identified is Chekhov's "little trilogy," made up of "Man in a Case," "Gooseberries," and "Concerning Love" (1898). It was in fact something of an "accidental" mini-cycle, as the stories were originally intended to form part of a larger cycle, one inspired by Ivan Turgenev's *A Sportsman's Sketches* (1852) (see Maxwell 53n.). Chekhov did not want the three tales published in the first *Collected Works* (published by A. F. Marks from 1899–1901) without the remainder of the cycle, indicating that he wished the whole cycle to be read as a unit.

Andrew R. Durkin outlines how the type of periodical affected the length, subject matter, and degree of complexity of the story that Chekhov published in it, and he was willing (if not necessarily happy) to meet the requirements of the three main kinds of periodical to which he submitted his fiction: humorous/satirical weeklies, newspapers, and "thick" literary—or high-brow—magazines. The greater aesthetic freedom permitted by the latter, including looser length requirements, encouraged Chekhov to experiment with form and genre, leading him to try his hand at a cycle. In terms reminiscent of Henry James's complaints about the restrictions of the popular journals and the benefits of the literary magazines, Chekhov wrote, "Collaboration in a thick journal can't be denied one advantage: a long piece is not fragmented and is published whole. When I write a long piece, I will send it to a thick journal, but short ones I will publish wherever the wind and my freedom take them" (qtd. in Durkin 237). The three stories in the "little trilogy" are around the same length as or perhaps a little longer than his satirical and newspaper works, and publishing in *Russian Thought* meant that Chekhov could write more allusively and explore philosophical themes. As Durkin says in reference to the "Little Trilogy," *Russian Thought* let Chekhov publish "stories of comparable length but with more complex relationships to the literary tradition" (241).

Chekhov published the three stories in two issues of *Russian Thought*: "The Man in a Case" in issue number 7 (July 1898) and the other two in number 8 (August 1898). One can guess that his reputation (like that of Alice Munro a century later) meant he could publish at least part of his mini-cycle together. Perhaps Chekhov intended to publish the remainder of the stories in his proposed cycle in the same journal, so that its regular readers would come to any later stories already familiar with the characters and setting and experience the cycle as a whole, even if month-long gaps separated individual stories.

Chekhov's mini-cycle is in the form of a framed collection in the manner of the *Canterbury Tales* and the *Decameron:* different characters who know each other and are together tell the stories to pass the time, make a moral point, or respond to the other stories they have heard. The narrator sets the scene in the frame; in his "Postscript" to *About Love*, David Helwig writes, "the outer narrative offers a vivid evocation of the Russian countryside, with a sense of history and geography complementing and containing the urgency of the tales" (107). The mini-cycle is linked primarily by theme; again, publication in a high-brow literary periodical like *Russian Thought* meant that Chekhov was freer to use a dominant idea, a philosophical problem, as his linking element. That theme is self-entrapment or self-enclosure due to misguided values—as Ronald Wilks puts it, "lack of will, moral cowardice, pettiness and bigotry generated by a complacent society" (21), or *"futliarnost,"* a term Irina Kirk translates as "an insular existence" (105). The protagonists of all three stories deny themselves freedom, emotional fulfilment, and true happiness out of fear or because they seek false, often artificial forms of satisfaction, particularly those promoted by modern society. Hingley comments that the characters "lack the kind of freedom which Chekhov considered necessary" (170). Joseph L. Conrad believes that another theme is just as important, arguing that in "The Man in a Case," the townspeople's pleasure at Belikov's death is "an admission that Burkin and his colleagues lacked a sense of responsibility, that they were, in fact, content to live without responsibility, as they had when they were children" (405). Chekhov's point is rather that society requires or encourages us to accept responsibilities that reduce or even destroy our freedom, and that is why, as we will see, childhood freedom becomes a motif with positive, not negative, connotations throughout the mini-cycle.

As Maxwell shows in some detail, the stories have parallel structures and portray similar emotional arcs on the parts of the protagonists, who begin with damaging dreams that they proceed to realize, at a heavy cost to their spiritual and emotional lives: "the character's dreams or fears have become a perverted reality" (38). Maxwell is correct to say that the case in the title of the first story is "a metaphor for the constricted life of the provincial town" (39); it could be said to symbolize all the cases in which the main characters of the stories live, like Nikolay's estate and Alyokhin's solitude. The constriction is also represented by the portrayal of characters' habits: Belikov's wearing of galoshes and carrying of an umbrella no matter what the weather; Nikolay's obsession with getting his own estate no matter what the consequences to others or himself; and Alyokhin's emotional cowardice. Furthermore, as Matthew Mangold shows in a recent article, freedom and entrapment are not stereotypically associated with the country and the city, respectively, but both settings can offer one or the other. In "Gooseberries," Ivan Illych's final speech expresses a view of city and country as a binary that appears throughout the mini-cycle (Mangold 85), yet neither city nor country guarantees freedom or its opposite (Mangold 94). The true source of freedom, for the most part, is nature, and the bathing scene is the only one in which the three storytellers seem truly free, yet the real chains are in the mind. Life in the country is stultifying in its isolation, cultural barrenness, and monotony; that sense of frustration, not yearning for Alyokhin, may be what Anna suffers from in "Concerning Love" (12; see Freedman 14).

While the stories are unified by theme, they are three distinct if linked narratives. As we have seen, one of the main functions of the mini-cycle form is to allow for a more complex handling of point of view, and Helwig notes that in these stories the "counterpoint of one voice with another, one mood with another, their contradiction, creates an ironic interplay" (109). The frame acts as a means to comment on or complicate the three stories: "Chekhov uses the frame for reflexive effect: at times the frame conversations elaborate on the stories, at times they nuance or critique the arguments of an interlocutor, and at times the silence of the characters creates a space for reflection" (Mangold 85). Composing separate stories permits Chekhov to manipulate point of view in two ways: first, by transferring the storytelling role to characters while still maintaining his own overall control in the frame; and second, by the relationship of each character to his subject. John Freedman discusses the handling of point of view in the mini-cycle in detail, writing that "each story contains its own point of view, its own inconsistencies, its own peculiarities, and the point of view of one teller does not necessarily belong to any other teller," including Chekhov himself (2).

Beginning with larger structural matters, the point of view moves progressively inward from story to story. First, the narrator portrays his three fictional storytellers coming together, exchanging tales, and reacting to each other's stories; Burkin narrates the life of a colleague, his fellow teacher Belikov; Ivan tells the story of his brother Nikolay; and Alyokhin's tale is about himself. In effect, then, if we count Chekhov among the storytellers, the tales get more personal and therefore the implications more private and emotional (Helwig 107). By constructing his text as a mini-cycle rather than a single narrative on the same theme, Chekhov can present four different points of view, and by ordering the stories the way he does, he can present these perspectives in a logical sequence from the most objective to the most subjective. Storytelling itself becomes the subject, lending a self-reflexive note to the text as a whole. Storytelling, "in addition to being a form of entertainment, is a way for people to share and participate in their lives" (Freedman 16), but the characters' efforts to reach out appear to be in vain as they remain alienated figures until the end. The movement from outer to inner, objective to subjective, begins with a description of the setting, that is, external to the characters to the point of not identifying them at first. Resting in Prokofy's barn triggers gossip about his wife, Mavra, who "had never been beyond her native village, had never seen a town nor a railway in her life, and had spent the last ten years sitting behind the stove, and only at night going out into the street" (350–51). Burkin tells Ivan Ivanych that she is not the only example of self-isolation, saying, "There are plenty of people in the world, solitary by temperament, who try to retreat into their shell like a hermit crab or a snail" (351). He then proceeds to tell the story of his fellow teacher, Belikov, as an example of such self-encasement. The bulk of the story is taken up with Burkin's monologue, with Ivan Ivanych interrupting only occasionally to make brief comments. At the end of the story, Burkin leaves the barn and enjoys a moment of repose in the silent night scene (361). Ivan Ivanych then provides the "moral" of the story, making again the point that being in a case is a universal condition:

> "Yes, that is just how it is," repeated Ivan Ivanovitch; "and isn't our living in town, airless and crowded, our writing useless papers, our playing *vint*—isn't that all a sort of case for us? And our spending our whole lives among trivial, fussy men and silly, idle women, our talking and our listening to all sorts of nonsense—isn't that a case for us, too?"
>
> (361)

He offers to tell his story, but Burkin says that it is time to sleep; they return to their shelter, re-encasing themselves in a way. At that point, Mavra walks by, her footsteps the only sound other than their own speech. In their repetitiveness, those footsteps—their "patter, patter again"—may be intended to echo the mechanical ticking of Belikov's watch. Ivan Ivanych continues with a diatribe against social hypocrisy:

> You endure insult and humiliation, and dare not openly say that you are on the side of the honest and the free, and you lie and smile yourself; and all that for the sake of a crust of bread, for the sake of a warm corner, for the sake of a wretched little worthless rank in the service. No, one can't go on living like this.
>
> (361)

Instead of agreeing, Burkin merely turns over to go to sleep, and Ivan Ivanych, too disturbed by the personal meaning of Burkin's story, goes back outside to smoke and think.

Ivan Ivanych's actions and above all his offer to tell Burkin "a very edifying story" (361) is an example of how, in a framed collection, one story can be a response to another; Johnson writes, "Burkin's story strikes a moral chord in Ivan that makes him want to relate his own tale" (R. Johnson 89). The offer foreshadows the following day's storytelling and creates anticipation in the reader. It should also be recalled that the story was published separately from the other two, so that readers of the text in the magazine would be encouraged by this "cliff-hanger" of sorts to buy the next issue of *Russian Thought* and "hear" Ivan Ivanych's tale.

The peaceful scene that ends "The Man in a Case" carries over into "Gooseberries": "The whole sky had been overcast with rain-clouds from early morning; it was a still day, not hot, but heavy, as it is in grey dull weather when the clouds have been hanging over the country for a long while, when one expects rain and it does not come" (362). Weather conditions reflect the characters' personalities and feelings throughout the mini-cycle, as Chekhov uses pathetic fallacy to create mood and/or foreshadow events (Wear 904). Here, the impression is of static, frustrated anticipation. We begin *in medias res*, as Burkin and Ivan Ivanych are "already tired from walking, and the fields seemed to them endless" (362). The narrator once again tells us the professions of these two characters—teacher and veterinarian—a relic of periodical publication. Chekhov might hope his readers had already read the first story, and remembered it, but could not count on that, and so needed to repeat the information. As in the first story, we are outside the village—that is, the setting is rural and the perspective is wide. Motifs connect the two stories: for example, in the first, we are told that Mavra has never seen railways, and here, one needs to climb the hillocks to see "the same vast plain, telegraph wires, and a train which in the distance looked like a crawling caterpillar" (362). The peaceful mood reminds Burkin of Ivan Ivanych's promise to tell his story, and the reader is reminded of the coming tale as well. Rain delays the narrative, however; with the downpour, Chekhov creates suspense, symbolically suggests that it will be a sad tale, and gives the characters a reason to take shelter in Alyokhin's house, thereby introducing the third storyteller.[1] As they make their way to Sofino, Alyokhin's home, they see the horses driving the windmill, living a mechanical existence not unlike their own. The communion with nature and with each other now ends for the two friends:

> It was damp, muddy, and desolate; the water looked cold and malignant. Ivan Ivanych and Burkin were already conscious of a feeling of wetness, messiness, and discomfort all over; their feet were heavy with mud, and when, crossing the dam, they went up to the barns, they were silent, as though they were angry with one another.
>
> (363)

Alyokhin, whom they find in one of the barns, is equally dirty and bedraggled-looking, and all will share the joy of a bath and a set of dry, clean clothes to follow (363).

As critics have long noted, the bathing scene is a rare experience of freedom for Ivan Ivanych, and some have tried to interpret it as an example of the liberating power of nature. It should be recalled, however, that he is bathing not in a purely natural body of water, but in the millpond. He has certainly felt free, briefly, but only within the confines of the farm and until his society summons him to return to it. Ivan Ivanych begins his story when all are suitably warm and comfortable, indulging in the benefits of civilization while being regarded by "the ladies, young and old, and the officers who looked down upon them sternly and calmly from their gold frames" (364). These portraits reinforce the sense that we are now back in society and subject to its long-standing rules of behaviour and constant supervision.

After telling his tale, Ivan Ivanych once again acts as the philosopher of the piece, advising the others not to be complacent but to seek freedom and happiness. Seeing his brother relishing the sour fruits of his ambition, Ivan Ivanych has an epiphany. He used to believe in mere contentment, but then:

> I went away from my brother's early in the morning, and ever since then it has been unbearable for me to be in town. I am oppressed by its peace and quiet; I am afraid to look at the windows, for there is no spectacle more painful to me now than the sight of a happy family sitting round the table drinking tea. I am old and am not fit for the struggle; I am not even capable of hatred; I can only grieve inwardly, feel irritated and vexed; but at night my head is hot from the rush of ideas, and I cannot sleep ... Ah, if I were young!
>
> (369)

Now we learn that the peacefulness of the village is a source of pain rather than comfort for him. The peace is that of inertness, complacent material satisfaction, and lack of freedom. The story ends with Ivan Ivanych urging Alyokhin to resist the temptation to accept such placid satisfaction:

> "Pavel Konstantinovitch," he said in an imploring voice, "don't be calm and contented, don't let yourself be put to sleep! While you are young, strong, confident, be not weary in well-doing! There is no happiness, and there ought not to be; but if there is a meaning and an object in life, that meaning and object is not our happiness, but something greater and more rational. Do good!"
>
> (370)

Burkin and Alyokhin react to Ivan Ivanych's call to action with discomfort, even hostility. They resist doing anything new or strange, preferring to remain encased in family tradition as represented by the family portraits, in old and established ways of doing things:

> When the generals and ladies gazed down from their gilt frames, looking in the dusk as though they were alive, it was dreary to listen to the story of the poor clerk who ate gooseberries ... their sitting

in the drawing-room where everything—the chandeliers in their covers, the arm-chairs, and the carpet under their feet—reminded them that those very people who were now looking down from their frames had once moved about, sat, drunk tea in this room, and the fact that lovely Pelageya was moving noiselessly about was better than any story.

(378)

Are they too mechanical and fearful to follow Ivan Ivanych's advice? Do they sense that their friend is being pompous and hypocritical? Either way, they prefer to go to bed rather than truly think about his words.

The transition between stories once again focuses on storytelling itself. Alyokhin stays awake well past the point of feeling "fearfully sleepy" (370) because he is "afraid his visitors might tell some interesting story after he had gone" and he would miss it—hardly the sentiments of someone willing to learn an important lesson from the story he has just heard (370). The line hints to the reader that there will be another story, and so we await the next tale. Burkin cannot sleep: Ivan Ivanych's pipe smells "strongly of stale tobacco, and Burkin … kept wondering where the oppressive smell came from" (370). Meanwhile, the now-oppressive rain continues to fall. Richard Wear, Mays, and Freedman interpret the bad smell coming from Ivan Ivanych's pipe as symbolic of his own corruption, hypocrisy, and self-encasement (Mays 67; Freedman 8). In fact, Burkin appears to be disturbed by the implications of Ivan Ivanych's story and message, seeking an explanation for his unpleasant feelings in the pipe, but it and the rain are only symbols of a deeper dissatisfaction.

Mays somewhat exaggerates the degree to which Ivan Ivanych is an unreliable narrator and therefore his philosophy is to be dismissed. The other characters react badly to his diatribe not because it is in bad taste or "a piece of flatulence" (Mays 65), but because it hits too close to home; Burkin tries to account for how he feels, but Chekhov is clear that the pipe-smoke—no matter how sour and symbolic of Ivan Ivanych's spiritual state it might be—is not the whole answer. Richard Wear is even more harsh about Ivan Ivanych, declaring him to be "the most reprehensible character in the trilogy, and thus the antithesis of what Chekhov stood for" (901). Wear condemns him for not living up to his own ideals, seeing his criticisms of his brother as "over-stated and, in light of Ivan's own life, grossly hypocritical" (904). But that does not mean his criticisms are invalid. Ivan Ivanych may not follow his own advice, but that does not invalidate the advice itself.[2]

The friends gather once more for a comfortable meal the following day, and the setting and atmosphere of one story flows into the next across the boundary of the mini-cycle, minus the overt distress created by the previous evening's story. "Concerning Love" features a radical shift in point of view: we move from third-person to first, as the pronouns change from "they" to "we," although the identity of the narrator is somewhat unclear. The tale that forms the core of the story comes not from the original narrator but from Alyokhin, who recounts his own experiences as a younger man. We therefore continue to hear things second-hand, from a distance even if that distance is decreased, and so Chekhov persists in reminding us that this is an individual's potentially biased account. The story begins with a description of the cook, Nikanor, who is the love interest of servant Pelageya. She wishes to live with him without benefit of marriage, but he refuses due to his supposed religious convictions—beliefs that do not stop him from indulging in drink and being violent toward her. Pelageya is a motif in the frame, representing love, and Alyokhin's remarks about the two characters inspire a conversation about love that leads to the host's autobiographical tale. He considers love a "great mystery" and objects to efforts by educated Russians to generalize and philosophize about it (371). On the other hand, he does much the same about his compatriots:

> Love is usually poeticized, decorated with roses, nightingales; we Russians decorate our loves with these momentous questions, and select the most uninteresting of them, too … when we are in love we are never tired of asking ourselves questions: whether it is honourable or dishonourable, sensible or stupid, what this love is leading up to, and so on. Whether it is a good thing or not I don't know, but that it is in the way, unsatisfactory, and irritating, I do know.
>
> (372)

Ivan Ivanych then detects that he seems to want to tell a story, thereby linking the previous and present stories by seeing in Alyokhin what Alyokhin thought might be the case in his friends. Ivan Ivanych interprets that desire as a symptom of Alyokhin's loneliness (372). The weather remains poor and therefore continues to offer good storytelling conditions (372). Once more, stories come when there is little opportunity for action, yet action is precisely what the stories preach. Chekhov establishes an unresolved tension between what the characters portray in their tales and what they actually do. After Alyokhin tells his story, the rain ends and the sun comes out, as if nature not only reflects the characters' mood but also now encourages them to leave their shelter and become active in the world. Alyokhin remains inside, while the other two go out on to the balcony,

> from which there was a beautiful view over the garden and the mill-pond, which was shining now in the sunshine like a mirror. They admired it, and at the same time they were sorry that this man with the kind, clever eyes, who had told them this story with such genuine feeling, should be rushing round and round this huge estate like a squirrel on a wheel instead of devoting himself to science or something else which would have made his life more pleasant.
>
> (378)

For all their sympathy with Alyokhin's feelings, they remain observers, admirers of other people's actions. They agree that Anna Alexyevna is beautiful, but neither has attempted to woo her; they feel that Nikanor does not deserve such a beautiful woman as Pelageya, but it is not just class difference that keeps them from pursuing her. These three characters lament their fears and inhibitions but do nothing to break out of the cases that contain them.

The frame, then, reflects the stories told in direct and ironic ways, and its structure highlights their (increasing) subjectivity. The distance between storyteller and story shrinks, so that we move inward from the Russian landscape to the self and progressively lose the spaciousness that Mangold writes about in his study of Chekhov's fiction. By choosing the cycle form, Chekhov has the freedom to move from one point of view to another—and he even shifts within the same story, it seems, in "Concerning Love"—as we progress from frame to core story, and then from one character to another. Reading the individual stories therefore requires that we always keep the context of each storyteller and of his protagonist in mind. Freedman notes that the tellers are always implicated in their tales, ironically revealing themselves even as they expose the flaws of their characters (even when the character is a past version of the self). The storytellers are no better than others whom they criticize for their fear and dependence on mechanical behaviour. Burkin, Ivan Ivanych, and Alyokhin condemn the fear- or folly-engendered self-encasement of their subjects, but the two who tell tales about others are no better than their protagonists, even while enjoying the benefits of a setting that ought to liberate them. Ivan Ivanych has been passive, waiting for something to happen; as Maxwell notes, "even a man cognizant of the limitlessness of his freedom and the nature of his responsibility to mankind hesitates to act" (44). "Gooseberries" is full of "unfulfilled expectations" (Maxwell 47), while in "Concerning Love," Alyokhin bemoans his lost love but does nothing more than talk about it, worrying so much about the consequences of his choices that he does not act. He loses his chance at love, and then "cut himself off from the future and completed yet another step in his progress toward complete emotional and physical isolation" (Maxwell 49). All three protagonists thus withdraw into shells out of fear of the disruption of their familiar ways of life or their materialistic dreams. Chekhov valued life over abstractions, complexity over hard and fast rules, the dynamic over the static, and so in all three stories the moral is that turning life experiences into philosophical statements hardly constitutes self-liberation (Mays 65; Hingley 169).

All three storytellers are trapped in "cases" of various kinds. In "The Man in a Case," Burkin tells us that Belikov keeps many of his possessions and even his body in cases: "the man displayed a constant and insurmountable impulse to wrap himself in a covering, to make himself, so to speak, a case which would isolate him and protect him from external influences" (351). He is full of fear, a man characterized by "constant apprehension"

(Kirk 105); according to Burkin, he always tries to protect himself from real experience, even through his specialization in the classical languages (351), and his bedroom, Burkin tells us, is "like a box" (353). Belikov is a creature of rules, in Hingley's words "a person smothered in self-imposed restrictions" (170), ready to condemn any who break them or in any way create disorder (352–53). Wilks calls Belikov "the very incarnation of petty tyranny" and states that "he has a deadening effect on his whole environment" (21); for Mangold, the story portrays "life in a Russian town that becomes increasingly claustrophobic" (86). However, Belikov is not entirely to blame for his behaviour or feelings: "Chekhov stresses the point that contemporary society as he saw it was the perfect breeding-ground for characters such as these" (Wilks 21; see also Mangold 86), one that particularly afflicts urban dwellers. The source of that disease is private property, Mangold continues, which divides individual from individual and creates a mechanical society symbolized by Belikov's watch (87–90). The story is thus in part a social satire, revealing the influence of Chekhov's earlier work in the satirical press and the stories of Gogol (Helwig 106). Belikov generates fear in the townspeople, yet it seems odd that someone with so little human connection, an introvert and a timid soul, could constitute such a threat to them, and so their fear says far more about them than about Belikov. Freedman rightly argues that "such exaggerated fear could not have been induced by the likes of a Belikov unless the townspeople themselves were Belikovs of a sort" (4). They engage in some match-making for him:

> All sorts of things are done in the provinces through boredom, all sorts of unnecessary and nonsensical things! And that is because what is necessary is not done at all ... The headmaster's wife, the inspector's wife, and all our high-school ladies, grew livelier and even better-looking, as though they had suddenly found a new object in life.
>
> (355)

Belikov hesitates, but eventually accedes to the town's wishes. Instead of joy, however, the approaching marriage to the vibrant Varenka becomes a source of suffering and worry (356). As he tells Burkin, "One may get married, and then, there is no knowing, one may find oneself in an unpleasant position" (356). Whether meant socially, morally, or sexually, his comment displays his paralyzing fear of human contact. To Belikov, propriety is everything, fear is his guide, and he knows nothing about the life of the heart, soul, or spirit. Due to social embarrassment, Belikov later gains his ultimate case, his coffin, and the response of the townspeople is appalling:

> One must confess that to bury people like Belikov is a great pleasure. As we were returning from the cemetery we wore discreet Lenten

faces; no one wanted to display this feeling of pleasure—a feeling like that we had experienced long, long ago as children when our elders had gone out and we ran about the garden for an hour or two, enjoying complete freedom. Ah, freedom, freedom! The merest hint, the faintest hope of its possibility gives wings to the soul, does it not? (360)

It becomes clear that Belikov is no eccentric in this town, but instead an embodiment of the people's own encased existence, to which they happily return.

Freedman points out that Burkin seems to know far more about Belikov's feelings and thoughts than he logically could, and so what we may be reading is the storyteller's, and the townspeople's, biased version of both Belikov and what occurs. In this way, Burkin becomes a creative writer rather than a reporter, and "Burkin's fictionalization of Belikov actually becomes a major element of the story" (6). If Freedman is correct, then Burkin's portrayal as an unreliable narrator foregrounds the role of point of view in the story, and by extension, its role in the mini-cycle as a whole. As the first story, it leads us to recognize that the tales are subjective responses to characters and events.

In "Gooseberries," Nikolay has convinced himself that the estate he desperately seeks will make him happy, thus exhibiting an obsession with trivial material objects reminiscent, Wilks notes, of the clerk in Gogol's "The Overcoat" (21). Like the townspeople, Ivan Ivanych and his brother were free during childhood: "we had spent our childhood running wild in the country" (364); adulthood means leaving that time behind while always hoping to return to that kind of life (364–65). Ivan Ivanych attributes Nikolay's ambition to the desire "to get into the country" and therefore to be free again. Ironically, the quest for that estate entraps rather than frees him. Ivan Ivanych says, "I never sympathized with this desire to shut himself up for the rest of his life in a little farm of his own" and then alludes to Leo Tolstoy's short story "How Much Land Does a Man Need?" (1886) by continuing, "It is the correct thing to say that a man needs no more than six feet of earth. But six feet is what a corpse needs, not a man" (365). Country life is no panacea; as we have seen, self-enclosure is as much a rural as an urban phenomenon. Mays and other critics have questioned his philosophy, but given Nikolay's fate, it is hard to disagree with his brother's assessment. Nikolay becomes obsessed with buying land, and above all planting gooseberries—the symbol for him of rural contentment and self-sufficiency (364–65). He ends up trapped by his own dream and gains not true happiness but purely material satisfaction; the estate itself, rather than what it was supposed to provide for him, has become his goal. That he has lost sight of his original goal and feels a false satisfaction in what he has gained is symbolized by his finding the "sour and unripe" gooseberries he eats delicious (368).

In "Concerning Love," Alyokhin "recalls an unsuccessful love affair of his own which might have turned out differently if he could have brought himself to act with imagination and enterprise" (Hingley 172). The story is also about rural life, but in this case the protagonist enters into it reluctantly—Alyokhin's goal is merely to pay off the estate's debts (372). It proves to be impossible to meld a farmer's and a cultural life, and he, like the others, feels trapped (372). His only escape comes when he is elected a justice of the peace and can once more mingle with educated men. Through a friend, Luganovich, he meets Anna Alexeyevna, Luganovich's wife, with whom he falls in love. Alyokhin struggles to explain the attraction, and his conclusion links him further with the other characters: "I felt her at once some one close and already familiar, as though that face, those cordial, intelligent eyes, I had seen somewhere in my childhood, in the album which lay on my mother's chest of drawers" (373). Once again, childhood—more than nature, more than conversation with fellow learned men—represents an ideal that a protagonist yearns for. He attaches himself to the couple, unable to stay away from Anna Alexeyevna, although there is no hint that she shares his romantic feelings (if that is indeed what they are). What is clear is that Alyokhin is quite lonely, and he needs at least the illusion of a close bond between them. Their relationship is full of silences, and it is difficult to know what feelings are really passing between them, particularly what Anna Alexeyevna's emotions are. Yet Alyokhin builds a fantasy out of their acquaintance:

> When I went to the town I saw every time from her eyes that she was expecting me, and she would confess to me herself that she had had a peculiar feeling all that day and had guessed that I should come. We talked a long time, and were silent, yet we did not confess our love to each other, but timidly and jealously concealed it. We were afraid of everything that might reveal our secret to ourselves. I loved her tenderly, deeply, but I reflected and kept asking myself what our love could lead to if we had not the strength to fight against it.
>
> (376)

What stops him from declaring his love is concern for the consequences:

> It seemed to be incredible that my gentle, sad love could all at once coarsely break up the even tenor of the life of her husband, her children, and all the household in which I was so loved and trusted. Would it be honourable? She would go away with me, but where? Where could I take her? ... And how long would our happiness last? What would happen to her in case I was ill, in case I died, or if we simply grew cold to one another?
>
> (376)

Alyokhin assumes that she shares his love and his reservations:

> She apparently reasoned in the same way. She thought of her hus-
> band, her children, and of her mother, who loved the husband like
> a son. If she abandoned herself to her feelings she would have to lie,
> or else to tell the truth, and in her position either would have been
> equally terrible and inconvenient. And she was tormented by the
> question whether her love would bring me happiness—would she not
> complicate my life, which, as it was, was hard enough and full of all
> sorts of trouble? She fancied she was not young enough for me, that
> she was not industrious nor energetic enough to begin a new life, and
> she often talked to her husband of the importance of my marrying a
> girl of intelligence and merit who would be a capable housewife and
> a help to me—and she would immediately add that it would be diffi-
> cult to find such a girl in the whole town.
>
> (376–77)

In fact, she never actually speaks any of these thoughts; these are all his
own beliefs about what she is thinking and feeling. At the end, he finally
kisses her as she is leaving on a train—a further instance of the railroad
motif we have seen in the frame:

> Kissing her face, her shoulders, her hands wet with tears—oh, how
> unhappy we were!—I confessed my love for her, and with a burning
> pain in my heart I realized how unnecessary, how petty, and how
> deceptive all that had hindered us from loving was. I understood
> that when you love you must either, in your reasonings about that
> love, start from what is highest, from what is more important than
> happiness or unhappiness, sin or virtue in their accepted meaning, or
> you must not reason at all.
>
> (378)

Maybe his belief that she shares his love is correct, but it is somewhat
past the time when he must act upon it. Alyokhin remains silent until
it is too late, and now regrets his hesitation. There is no guarantee that
she would have responded in kind, but even if her love is a figment of
his imagination, he has demonstrated an inexcusable cowardice. Like the
other characters, he has put worries about respectability and propriety
ahead of passion and has only himself to blame for missing out.

The story thus involves the sort of paradoxical relationship between
narrator and protagonist that confronts all first-person narratives.
Alyokhin is his own protagonist, and he tells the others what his younger
self did from an older and supposedly wiser position. He critiques his
own choices, but we cannot help wondering to what degree he is a reliable narrator and to what extent he has changed. Anna Alexeyevna may

indeed love him, but whether that love is romantic or maternal is open to question (Freedman 11).

Chekhov's "Little Trilogy," then, is carefully structured on recurring themes and images, motifs that connect the frame to the tales and the tales to each other. The form offers Chekhov the flexibility to manipulate point of view in order to provide a bigger, objective picture and then zoom into the lives and thoughts of his three storytellers. Thanks to the unresolved tension between first- and third-person perspectives, the stories remain open-ended and open to interpretation as well. The result is the foregrounding of storytelling itself, a self-reflexive mode that provokes the reader's awareness of the ultimate inaccessibility of that suspect abstract entity known as "Truth." Instead, we are made aware of life's variety and flux, of the impossibility of final and simple modes of understanding the complex, diverse, and dynamic human condition (see Gerhardie's discussion of Chekhov's philosophy of life and art on pp. 79– 85). The mini-cycle form is the ideal vehicle for such a vision, given its own tension between unity and multiplicity.

Notes

1 Perhaps Chekhov intended to introduce more characters had he succeeded in completing his cycle.
2 Conrad interprets the advice as referring mainly to educated people, who have the ability to improve society but who allow themselves to pursue less than noble goals and waste their talents—see pp. 406–08. He offers much textual evidence to prove the point. This is the responsibility that Conrad means, but freedom remains the primary value, since it is a responsibility to make society more free rather than passively allow it to direct people into ruts.

References

Chekhov, Anton. *About Love: 3 Stories by Anton Chekhov*. Translated and afterword by David Helwig, Biblioasis, 2012.
——. *Anton Chekhov's Selected Stories*. Edited by Cathy Popkin, Norton, 2014.
Conrad, Joseph L. "Cexov's *The Man in a Shell*: Freedom and Responsibility." *Slavic and East European Journal*, vol. 10, no. 4, Winter 1966, pp. 400–10.
Durkin, Andrew R. "Chekhov and the Journals of His Time." *Literary Journals in Imperial Russia*, edited by Deborah A. Martinsen, Cambridge UP, pp. 228–45.
Freedman, John. "Narrative Technique and the Art of Story-Telling in Anton Chekhov's 'Little Trilogy.'" *South Atlantic Review*, vol. 53 no. 1, Jan. 1988, pp. 1–18.
Gerhardie, William. *Anton Chehov: A Critical Study*. Macdonald, 1974.
Helwig, David. "Postscript." Chekhov, *About Love*, pp. 105–10.
Hingley, Ronald. *Anton Chekhov: A Biographical and Critical Study*. Barnes and Noble; George Allen and Unwin, 1966.
Johnson, Ronald L. *Anton Chekhov: A Study of the Short Fiction*. Twayne, 1993.
Kirk, Irina. *Anton Chekhov*. Twayne, 1987.

Mangold, Matthew. "Space and Storytelling in Late Imperial Russia: Tolstoy, Chekhov, and the Question of Property." *Russian Review*, vol. 76, no. 1, Jan. 2017, pp. 72–94.

Maxwell, David E. "The Unity of Chekhov's 'Little Trilogy.'" *Chekhov's Art of Writing: A Collection of Critical Essays*, edited by Paul Debreczeny and Thomas Eekman, Slavica, 1977, pp. 35–53.

Mays, Milton A. "Gooseberries and Chekhov's Concreteness." *Southern Humanities Review*, vol. 6, no. 1, Winter 1972, pp. 63–67.

Wear, Richard. "Chekhov's Trilogy: Another Look at Ivan Ivanych." *Revue belgique de philologie et d'histoire*, vol. 55, no. 3, 1977, pp. 897–906.

Wilks, Ronald. Introduction. *The Kiss and Other Stories*, by Anton Chekhov, Penguin, 1982, pp. 9–30.

3   The Mini-Cycle within a Cycle
Stephen Leacock's *Sunshine Sketches*

Stephen Leacock's mini-cycle in *Sunshine Sketches of a Little Town* (1912) is an unusual example of the genre, one that is part of a conventional story cycle. The cycle offers a kaleidoscopic portrait of Mariposa, while the three stories under review here stand apart as they portray the same set of characters and form a distinct, largely unified narrative separate from any other text in the cycle. Both sociological and structural considerations play a role in the mini-cycle's nature and effect.

The texts that make up *Sunshine Sketches of a Little Town* originally appeared serially in the *Montreal Daily Star* from 17 February to 22 June 1912, and the book was published a few weeks after the periodical appearances. As B. K. Sandwell tells us, Leacock's success with his first two books, *Literary Lapses* (1910) and *Nonsense Novels* (1911), led Edward Beck, managing editor of the *Star*, to ask Leacock for a series of short pieces for the Saturday issue (Sandwell 163; see Doyle for a detailed biography). Sandwell, Beck, and Leacock together "decided that the work would take the form of a serial rather than a series of unconnected pieces and that it would have a Canadian setting" (Moritz and Moritz 149).

Leacock's use of the term "sketch" for his stories is revealing; earlier, we saw that the sketch series was one of the source genres for the story cycle, and here Leacock is hearkening back to that form of linked texts. He saw his own cycle as a direct descendant of the genre employed by authors like Mary Russell Mitford: a series of character and setting portraits with little plot and much description and commentary. William H. Magee believes the term "shows that he was consciously avoiding the recognized genres of fiction" (33). Whatever his intention, his "sketches" feature too much narrative to fit that genre, and so the individual texts are regarded as short stories and the book as a whole as a cycle.[1]

Book publication supplemented the income Leacock received from the sale of the stories; like other authors, he sought to earn as much as he could from a work by publishing it in various formats (Lynch, "From Serial to Book" 98). Lynch's article provides details of Leacock's additions and revisions to the original stories to make a coherent book out of the original pieces. The revisions had no major significance for the stories in the mini-cycle; Leacock changed the names of some of the characters, but otherwise the texts are the same. The three stories, "The Extraordinary Entanglement of Mr. Pupkin," "The Fore-Ordained Attachment of Zena Pepperleigh and Peter Pupkin," and "The Mariposa Bank Mystery," appeared in the *Star* from 13 April to 4 May, meaning that regular readers of the newspaper would have seen them in order and with intervals of one week between the first two instalments and two weeks between the second and third. They recount Pupkin's progress in overcoming the challenges to gaining the hand of his true love, Zena.

The important formal question is why Leacock would write three separate stories instead of one unified narrative. First, practical considerations militated against attempting to make a longer text out of his material. He faced word-length constraints in selling the stories to the *Star*; the editor would likely not have accepted a single tale three times the length of each story—which were to be 4,000 words apiece (Moritz and Moritz 150)—i.e., one that would stretch to the dimensions of a novella. Furthermore, by publishing the texts serially, Leacock was able to sell three texts instead of one.

Perhaps more importantly, as some critics argue, Leacock was not suited to the writing of long narratives. According to Magee, he sought in vain for a fictional form that would permit him to incorporate his preferred kinds of humour, above all "quips" and parodies, into a fictional genre: "he needed larger patterns to give them durable form" (31; see also Bush 134). His favourite forms of humour, Magee writes, are the "exploded cliché"—turning a catch-phrase into sheer nonsense through exaggeration and distortion[2]—and the parody (32). The traditional English novel, Magee writes, "provided storytellers and humourists with both a principle of selection for individual scenes and a perspective for combining them into a unifying pattern of conflict and climax," but that sort of coherence over a long narrative did not accommodate Leacock's techniques (31; see also Lynch, *Stephen Leacock* for a study of his philosophy and techniques). For Magee, Leacock's characters were nearly all too static, and his parodies too direct and concise, to stretch over a long fictional work, despite the examples of his chief models, Mark Twain and Charles Dickens.

The problem may have been that the courtship plot was the only kind Leacock could imagine for a novel. That would explain his abortive plan to create a novel out of the periodical sketches based on his Pupkin/Pepperleigh stories; Ralph L. Curry informs us that Leacock originally intended the book to be a novel, and "the love story between Zena Pepperleigh and Peter Pupkin to be a central theme to unify the story" (97). His creative bent, however, worked against that effort, as he could not maintain the narrative beyond the mini-cycle, or even construct a single novella. Magee views this as an artistic limitation, but other critics see the choice of mini-cycle and story cycle as suitable on various grounds. Albert and Theresa Moritz interpret Leacock's choice of form as follows:

> Leacock was disappointed he had not developed *Sunshine Sketches*
> as a unified novel; he thought this failure stemmed from his inability
> to make the Pupkin-Pepperleigh romance a thread that ran through
> the entire book. In fact, the book seems to indicate that he could
> not create such a unity because he did not believe in it. The minor
> importance of the romance is in tune with his constant sense, both
> here and throughout his writings, that motives of self-interest, covet-
> ousness and status-seeking underlie romantic sentiments.
>
> (160)

While this may be somewhat harsh—as we will see, the stories do seem
to express a belief in love and its transformative powers, as Lynch argues
("Religion and Romance" 91)—it cannot be denied that Zena is quite
happy to discover that Peter is rich. Leacock wished to follow a romance-
and-marriage narrative beyond a single brief story, yet still accommodate
his creative strengths in humour, particularly in the joke or the brief scene
revealing a discrepancy between pretension and reality. His solution was
to make fun of the romantic plot; it was parody that made it possible for
Leacock to employ the plot in an extended narrative, but only up to a
point, meaning the writing of linked short texts (Magee 32).

As for the mini-cycle's role in the book, Gerald A. Lynch describes how
the stories in the cycle represent the political, economic, social, and religious aspects of Leacock's fictional society ("From Serial to Book" 105),
and the mini-cycle constitutes the "romance" section. Lynch believes that
Leacock arranged the stories to bracket the religious and romantic texts
with stories on economics and politics, and the romantic mini-cycle is
placed adjacent to the stories about the Church to convey a moral point:
"This contrived symmetrical centre of *Sunshine Sketches* opposes three
sketches on the failure of Mariposa's institutionalized Anglican religion
to meet simply the needs of its parishioners with three sketches on the
triumph of Mariposan romance, love, marriage, and family" (105). The
arrangement thereby highlights the contrast between institutionalized
and personal, very human relationships.

The three stories portray stages in the Peter–Zena love affair, beginning with an introduction to the main characters and Peter's romantic
interest in Zena in "The Extraordinary Entanglement of Mr. Pupkin."
Judge Pepperleigh is the one whom Mr. Smith foolishly shuts out of his
bar after hours, and who takes revenge by fining him for not permitting
the judge to partake of the illegally sold beverages (6). Pepperleigh's position as a force for strict law and order has thus already been undermined,
and so we cannot take him seriously as a blocker during the romance
plot. He also proves to be easily bribed, especially with a tasty game
pie (18), and enjoys social outings that are the real purpose behind the
Whirlwind Campaign (68). He has thus been established as a leading
figure in Mariposan society but only a parody of an authoritative figure
who might stand in Peter's way when it comes to wooing Zena.

The opening of the story purportedly depicts him as an "intimidating" personality, yet for every image like "you could see his spectacles flash like dynamite," we have one exhibiting his benign nature. Pepperleigh limits his fury to reports of Liberal electoral victories and flowers that do not bloom and birds that sing too much (84). His "judicial temper of mind" leads him to pass absurd judgments and impose ridiculous sentences on important foreign figures, including the Sultan of Turkey, the Emperor of Germany, and the Czar of Russia, all presented ironically as if his pronouncement could truly make "one's blood run cold" (84). While the Mariposan narrator may state, "So you can imagine that in some ways the judge's house was a pretty difficult house to go to," the reader has no fear for Peter when he makes the effort.

Peter is one of the would-be rescuers of the victims of the sinking of the Mariposa Belle ("The Marine Excursion of the Knights of Pythias") who need rescuing themselves. He springs into action largely because of the "danger" that Miss Lawson faces (51), thus demonstrating his romantic nature even before the mini-cycle. He is also mentioned among the bankers who contribute to the Whirlwind Campaign (69), and thus as a junior member of the social elite in Mariposa. As he arrives at Judge Pepperleigh's house, he comes across as a young man who, in Mariposan terms, is courageous and sophisticated, but who is in terms of the wider world feckless and true-hearted:

> I tell you it took some nerve to step up on that piazza and say, in a perfectly natural, off-hand way: "Oh, how do you do, judge? Is Miss Zena in? No, I won't stay, thanks; I think I ought to be going. I simply called." A man who can do that has got to have a pretty fair amount of savoir what do you call it, and he's got to be mighty well shaved and have his cameo pin put in his tie at a pretty undeniable angle before he can tackle it.
>
> (84)

He is a real, as opposed to idealized, romantic hero: "Still, that's what you call love, and if you've got it, and are well shaved, and your boots well blacked, you can do things that seem almost impossible. Yes, you can do anything, even if you do trip over the dog in getting off the piazza" (85). Subverting that image, however, is the reference to Miss Lawson—his feelings for her, strong enough to make him take to a boat to rescue her, are now thoroughly dismissed (88). No matter how poorly he fares in argument against pseudo-intellectual Mallory Tompkins (the "eggnostic" [89]), he shines by comparison in moral terms (89–90). He takes his job seriously, treating the minor financial secrets of the town as a sacred trust, except for occasional lapses that undercut his pretension to devout discretion (88).

The first story establishes the theme of romance versus reality, and the reality of true love, which dominates the mini-cycle (Lynch, "Religion and Romance" 90), mainly through our introduction to Zena. She, too, has appeared before: we learn in "The Ministrations of the Rev. Mr. Drone" that Peter first saw her while they sat together writing letters seeking donations to settle the church's debts (64). In "The Extraordinary Entanglement of Mr. Pupkin," Leacock shows us Zena's romantic nature through her voracious reading of novels with titles like *Errant Quest of the Palladin Pilgrim* and *Life of Sir Galahad* (85). On the other hand, love of all sorts, not just youthful romantic love, is the story's subject, as we see in the paragraphs about the judge's own marriage and the loss of his son (Lynch, "From Serial to Book" 106–07). When news comes of Neil's death, the judge's behaviour belies any suggestion that he is not affectionate with his wife, or any doubt how the parents feel about their son (87).

The narrator describes the lovers' first viewing of each other in a parody of the typical romance plot, in which the lovers are fated to meet. In typical Leacock style, this inevitable encounter of two people in a small town is presented in mock-heroic style as an act of the Fates:

> He first saw her—by one of the strangest coincidences in the world—on the Main Street of Mariposa. If he hadn't happened to be going up the street and she to be coming down it, the thing wouldn't have happened. Afterwards they both admitted that it was one of the most peculiar coincidences they ever heard of. Pupkin owned that he had had the strangest feeling that morning as if something were going to happen—a feeling not at all to be classed with the one of which he had once spoken to Miss Lawson, and which was, at the most, a mere anticipation of respect.
>
> (91)

The further reference to his earlier infatuation makes a mockery of his current one, but we do not feel that he is fickle, having developed too much sympathy for this foolish but sincere young man to think ill of him. The opening story therefore establishes not only the theme of the mini-cycle, but also the authenticity of the hero's feelings. Nothing actually happens in the story except the most important thing:

> For Pupkin, straight away the whole town was irradiated with sunshine, and there was such a singing of the birds, and such a dancing of the rippled waters of the lake, and such a kindliness in the faces of all the people, that only those who have lived in Mariposa, and been young there, can know at all what he felt.
>
> The simple fact is that just the moment he saw Zena Pepperleigh, Mr. Pupkin was clean, plumb, straight, flat, absolutely in love with her.
>
> Which fact is so important that it would be folly not to close the chapter and think about it.
>
> (92)

The final sentences highlight the unity of the collection, referring to the story as a "chapter" rather than a "short story" or "tale," and Leacock makes effective use of the break between stories for rhetorical purposes. The break obliges readers to consider what they have read before moving on to the story's sequel. The story thereby fulfils its role in the mini-cycle: giving us all the background we need for what happens in the other stories.

In "The Fore-Ordained Attachment of Zena Pepperleigh and Peter Pupkin," Leacock misleads us, for comic reasons, into thinking the lowly bank teller will have little chance of surmounting the social obstacles that stand between Peter and the judge's daughter. Leacock begins the story by portraying Zena's adolescent yearnings for a hero to sweep her off her feet, an image inspired by her reading (93): "She was always, as I say, being rescued and being borne away, and being parted, and reaching out her arms to France and to Spain and saying good-bye forever to Valladolid or the old grey towers of Hohenbranntwein" (93–94). Our first impression is that no real human being could live up to her image of an ideal mate. Only a Mariposan could claim that these dreams are at all plausible: "if you remember, too, that these are cultivated girls who have all been to the Mariposa high school and can do decimal fractions, you will understand that an Algerian corsair would sharpen his scimitar at the very sight of them" (94).

Leacock then blurs the line between romance and reality. He foreshadows the final paragraphs of the mini-cycle by suggesting that ordinary human love is little different from what is portrayed in these popular novels, in that it is every bit as capable of enchanting lovers as anything romantic fiction can devise (Lynch, "Religion and Romance" 90). Zena is like the other young girls in Mariposa, dreaming of grand heroes and gestures, and like them she will find her Prince Charming in the town:

> So it is that each one of them in due time marries an enchanted prince and goes to live in one of the little enchanted houses in the lower part of the town.
>
>   I don't know whether you know it, but you can rent an enchanted house in Mariposa for eight dollars a month, and some of the most completely enchanted are the cheapest. As for the enchanted princes, they find them in the strangest places, where you never expected to see them, working—under a spell, you understand,—in drug-stores and printing offices, and even selling things in shops. But to be able to find them you have first to read ever so many novels about Sir Galahad and the Errant Quest and that sort of thing.
>
> (94)

She has little regard for Peter at first, but it does not take long before she begins to see his rapid passing by her house on his bicycle as equivalent to "the last ride of Tancred the Inconsolable along the banks of the Danube" (95). Her head may have been turned by the books that shape her vision, but she is not so deluded as to miss the charms of a simple bank teller. Love, more than romance fiction, colours her view of him.

Peter, meanwhile, sees himself as a romantic hero pining for his idol, suggesting the illusions are not only Zena's. His error is that he takes what Zena says too literally:

> Every time that Pupkin watched Zena praying in church, he knew that she was too good for him. Every time that he came to call for her and found her reading Browning and Omar Khayyam he knew that she was too clever for him. And every time that he saw her at all he realized that she was too beautiful for him.
>
> You see, Pupkin knew that he wasn't a hero. When Zena would clasp her hands and talk rapturously about crusaders and soldiers and firemen and heroes generally, Pupkin knew just where he came in. Not in it, that was all. If a war could have broken out in Mariposa, or the judge's house been invaded by the Germans, he might have had a chance, but as it was—hopeless.
>
> (98)

He does not realize that he can certainly be her knight in shining armour simply by loving her. An additional problem for the couple is that he is earning "only" eight hundred dollars per year, and his bank has set the limit at a thousand (99). More importantly, Leacock refers to another potential barrier, Peter's parentage, implying that he has a socially disqualifying background: "Each time that he tried to talk to her about his home and his father and mother and found that something held him back, he realized more and more the kind of thing that stood between them ... Pupkin was ashamed of them, bitterly ashamed" (100). The reader naturally assumes that his family is poor or unrespectable, but it turns out that Leacock is playing with our own expectations generated by the same romantic fiction that has distorted Zena's view of the world, and Peter's as well: "What! You have mistaken my meaning? Ashamed of them because they were poor? Good heavens, no, but because they were rich!" (100). Leacock informs us that his father is one of the wealthiest men in the Maritime Provinces, and Peter's exile to Mariposa is merely a way of teaching him to fend for himself. Peter fears Pepperleigh's reaction to the news that he is rich because he has taken Judge Pepperleigh too literally as well, accepting the judge's complaints about rich people— that is, those who are richer than himself—as evidence of a hatred of wealth itself rather than simple envy (101). Zena has expressed similar sentiments against diamonds and yachts, but that is only because she does not have them (101–02). Peter always has great difficulty with literal meanings: for example, the narrator tells us that he has committed suicide three times out of shame over his parents (99), but the term is

Peter's and shows he does not know its meaning. The narrator tells us that he will explain what is meant later on (99), but the explanation does not come in this story; the reader is obliged to wait until the mini-cycle's next instalment.

The passage on Peter's parents, and indeed the story as a whole, reveals Peter's naiveté, erects parodic barriers to the fulfilment of their attachment, and generates suspense in the reader looking for the event that will bring them together. As a whole, the second story of the mini-cycle continues the process begun by the first: setting the scene, while undermining everything that the genre it is parodying might suggest. Again, Leacock is explicit about the function of the story and its nature as a "chapter" in a longer story—a chapter that ends with a cliff-hanger once Pupkin Senior's portfolio is fully described. Once again, Leacock uses the division between stories to foreshadow events to be narrated in the following story, and thereby create comic tension: "But surely after such reminiscences as these, the awful things that are impending over Mr. Pupkin must be kept for another chapter" (103).

Gerald Lynch somewhat harshly interprets the term "fore-ordained": "Those who help to 'fore-ordain' the attachment of Pupkin and Zena— Judge Pepperleigh and Pupkin Senior—are the representatives of law and order and the long-established business community" ("Religion and Romance" 90). The fact that they belong to the same class does facilitate their union, but what really "fore-ordain"s their "attachment" is that they love each other and that they are characters in a mock-romance. The genre and the author have fore-ordained the success of their relationship, although the genre also requires that they undergo trials before they can wed. The final lines foreshadow these trials, but the genre and tone prevent us from feeling too concerned about what will happen in the final story.

"The Mariposa Bank Mystery" brings together the themes and motifs of the other two stories. Peter, convinced that he will never win Zena's hand—particularly if he has to compete with poets, men from the city, and other powerful rivals—considers committing suicide four times in five weeks, but finds plenty of excuses for not following through (104–07). In his own mind, the thought of suicide is equivalent to the action and therefore enough to qualify him as a courtly lover and hero. Leacock here continues the theme that heroes are imaginative constructs, and that real people can in a sense become the figures in romantic poetry and bad novels if they see themselves or others see them that way.

Although certain he can never aspire to be the sort of hero Zena reads about, Peter nevertheless performs an act of heroism that is entirely real. He goes to the bank late at night to retrieve his revolver for another bound-to-be-abortive suicide attempt, and there becomes involved in a shoot-out with the bank's caretaker, Gillis (108–11). Both young men imagine they are in the process of thwarting an armed bank robbery, and both inflict similar wounds on each other, although of course they and the townspeople are incapable of figuring out this simple solution to the great "Mystery." Leacock's parody of the mystery story even extends to bringing in detectives from an unnamed "city" who are more interested in drinking and hunting than solving this (non-)crime (112–13). Now that he is the hero he believes Zena wants, he is emboldened to propose to her and she accepts.

The reality and romance of heroism is perhaps best expressed when Peter decides to confront the supposed bank robber. In a passage of rich irony, the narrator tells us what goes through Peter's mind:

> I think as Peter Pupkin stood, revolver in hand, in the office of the bank, he had forgotten all about the maudlin purpose of his first coming. He had forgotten for the moment all about heroes and love affairs, and his whole mind was focused, sharp and alert, with the intensity of the night-time, on the sounds that he heard in the vault and on the back-stairway of the bank.
>
> Straight away, Pupkin knew what it meant as plainly as if it were written in print. He had forgotten, I say, about being a hero and he only knew that there was sixty thousand dollars in the vault of the bank below, and that he was paid eight hundred dollars a year to look after it.
>
> (109–10)

He stops thinking about being an illusory "hero" and becomes a real one. While he may not really be prepared to give his life for his idealized love, he is willing to die to meet his responsibilities: "the robber who would take that sixty thousand dollars from the Mariposa bank must take it over the dead body of Peter Pupkin, teller" (110). Once he recovers from the minor wound he received in the exchange of gunfire, he will do the brave thing he has been afraid to do all along:

> He would do a thing seldom if ever done in Mariposa. He would propose to Zena Pepperleigh. In Mariposa this kind of step, I say, is seldom taken. The course of love runs on and on through all its stages of tennis playing and dancing and sleigh riding, till by sheer notoriety of circumstance an understanding is reached. To propose straight out would be thought priggish and affected and is supposed to belong only to people in books.
>
> But Pupkin felt that what ordinary people dare not do, heroes are allowed to attempt. He would propose to Zena, and more than that, he would tell her in a straight, manly way that he was rich and take the consequences.
>
> And he did it.
>
> (115–16)

The idea that proposing to Zena is "a thing seldom if ever done" is ludicrous, and the elevation of a proposal to a rare deed is absurd, but for him (and indeed for anyone) this is a momentous step.

Certain motifs reappear. As we have seen in the other stories, the idea of the non-coincidental "coincidence" is employed to parody the romance genre. Here, the supposed coincidence recurs in how the other family members treat Peter's proposal:

> By sheer good luck the judge had gone indoors to the library, and by a piece of rare good fortune Mrs. Pepperleigh had gone indoors to the sewing room, and by a happy trick of coincidence the servant was out and the dog was tied up—in fact, no such chain of circumstances was ever offered in favour of mortal man before.
>
> (116)

Also, Judge Pepperleigh has tried to convince his daughter to stop reading ridiculous novels about implausible heroes and events and stick to the real heroes of Canadian history (see pp. 85 and 92). At the beginning of "The Fore-Ordained Attachment of Zena Pepperleigh and Peter Pupkin," Zena hides her reading whenever she hears her father approach: she would "make a grab for the *Pioneers of Tecumseh Townships*, and start reading it like mad" (93). At the enquiry, Judge Pepperleigh congratulates Peter on his heroic act, saying that "his conduct was fit to rank among the annals of the pioneers of Tecumseh township" (115). For Gerald Lynch, Peter's behaviour in the bank is evidence that "Pupkin Senior has passed on to his son the real heroic virtues which make possible the resolution of the romantic complication [i.e.,] loyalty, duty, courage, and self-sacrifice": in other words, the qualities of a true United Empire Loyalist ("Religion and Romance" 92). Finally, the ending of the story, and therefore of the mini-cycle, reinforces the theme that real love turns real life into romance:

> So Pupkin and Zena in due course of time were married, and went to live in one of the enchanted houses on the hillside in the newer part of the town, where you may find them to this day.
>
> You may see Pupkin there at any time cutting enchanted grass on a little lawn in as gaudy a blazer as ever.
>
> But if you step up to speak to him or walk with him into the enchanted house, pray modulate your voice a little—musical though it is—for there is said to be an enchanted baby on the premises whose sleep must not lightly be disturbed.
>
> (117)

Daily life is full of heroism, wonder, and the glorious illusions, engendered by love, that turn men and women into handsome princes and beautiful princesses (Lynch, "Religion and Romance" 90).

The division of the narrative into three distinct but related stories, as opposed to one longer story incorporating the events of all three, thus provides Leacock with definite formal opportunities. He can lay the groundwork in the first story for what he can elaborate upon in the other two. Each story is unified on its own, while the transition from one to another permits the shifts in point of view as we move from the judge's perspective to Zena's to Peter's. Leacock can engage in ironic foreshadowing, implying relationships, character traits, and problems in one story that he can later undercut once the reader has completely fallen for Leacock's misdirections during the pauses between stories. The account of Peter's so-called "suicides" and later redemption as a true hero constitutes a unified narrative that lends itself to being written as a separate story.

Leacock's mini-cycle, like story cycles in general, thus operates in a liminal space between unity and diversity. Common threads like the characters, the tone, the imagery, the theme of love and marriage, and the genre of mock-romance tie the three stories together, but each separate tale fulfils its own separate function. The first story offers a sketch, in the true generic meaning of the word, of the principals in this narrative; the second depicts in ironic ways the supposed barriers to the couple's marriage, at all times simultaneously undercutting those barriers; the third narrates the central event that turns Peter into a true hero and brings him to ask Zena the question he has yearned to pose. Magee is therefore mistaken to say that Leacock was incapable of drawing characters who change, and that his true metier is the static figure and situation. It is Mariposa that must not change, and as he says later, "Peter Pupkin must be left mowing the lawn of his enchanted house forever" (37) so that Peter and his town can be an eternal source of nostalgic longing for the men at the Mausoleum Club. It is true that Leacock cannot seem to sustain a narrative for very long. The mini-cycle as a whole is over 10,000 words long, but it is made up of shorter and more focused texts, two of which lack plot, and so it seems that the form of the mini-cycle offered Leacock a way to extend his tale beyond the short story without pursuing a single, coherent narrative line, a way that best suits his talents and aesthetic goals.

Notes

1 I will refer to the texts as stories, defining them generically by their narrative structure instead of accepting Leacock's term. Conventions, not genre labels, define texts, even when the genre label is assigned by the author.
2 His best-known example is from "Gertrude the Governess" in *Nonsense Novels* (1911): "Lord Ronald said nothing; he flung himself from the room, flung himself upon his horse and rode off madly in all directions" (75).

References

Bush, Douglas. "Stephen Leacock." *The Canadian Imagination: Dimensions of a Literary Culture*, edited by David Staines, Harvard UP, 1977, pp. 123–51.

Curry, Ralph L. *Stephen Leacock: Humorist and Humanist.* 2nd ed., Leacock Museum, 2005.

Doyle, James. *Stephen Leacock: The Sage of Orillia.* ECW Press, 1992.

Leacock, Stephen. *Nonsense Novels.* J. Lane, 1911.

——. *Sunshine Sketches of a Little Town.* Edited by Gerald Lynch, Tecumseh, 1996.

Lynch, Gerald. "From Serial to Book: Leacock's Revisions to *Sunshine Sketches of a Little Town.*" *Studies in Canadian Literature,* vol. 36, no. 2, 2011, pp. 96–111.

——. "Religion and Romance in Mariposa." *Stephen Leacock: A Reappraisal,* edited by David Staines, U of Ottawa P, 1986, pp. 83–93.

——. *Stephen Leacock: Humour and Humanity.* McGill-Queen's UP, 1988.

Magee, William H. "Parody and Perspective: Form in Leacock's Sketches." *Thalia,* vol. 3, no. 2, Fall 1980, 31–37.

Moritz, Albert, and Theresa M. Moritz. *Stephen Leacock: His Remarkable Life.* Fitzhenry and Whiteside, 2002.

Sandwell, B. K. "How the 'Sketches' Started." *Sunshine Sketches of a Little Town: A Critical Edition,* edited by Gerald Lynch, Tecumseh Press, 1996, pp. 162–64.

4 The Prototypical Mini-Cycle I
Alice Munro's "Juliet Triptych"

Given the early examples by Chekhov and Leacock, and the more recent authors who have followed their lead—wittingly or not—the prototypical mini-cycle appears to be a set of three stories, and the mini-cycle is ultimately published, probably by design, sequentially in a collection. Chekhov wanted all of the stories in his cycle published together in his Collected Works, so we can assume that having the stories remain a unit was important to him, and Leacock published his three Pupkin/Pepperleigh stories in order in the *Star*, so one can similarly assume he always intended them to appear that way. As we turn to contemporary examples of the genre, then, it seems logical to begin with the three-story sequentially published mini-cycle. It also seems logical to begin with the collection that helped inspire this study.

Unlike *Sunshine Sketches of a Little Town*, Alice Munro's *Runaway* is not a story cycle, so the presence of three linked stories comes as somewhat more of a surprise than does the focus on Peter Pupkin in one-quarter of Leacock's cycle, where characters frequently recur. The publication history of Munro's mini-cycle, as already described above, is quite anomalous; I know of no other instance where an entire mini-cycle was published as a whole in one issue of a periodical (for an account of the collection's composition, publication, and reception, see Thacker, *Alice Munro* 498–524; on Munro's relationship with the magazine, see Beran). *The New Yorker* published the texts under the heading of "Three Stories"—that is, not a term that might signal that the stories form a unit—and so readers would not have known that the stories were linked till they reached the second in the set. We cannot know Munro's or the editors' purpose in these choices; how were readers supposed to react to the discovery that the stories were not unrelated texts but part of a larger unit? Is that surprise intended and part of the stories' designed effect?

Critics have dubbed the mini-cycle the "Juliet Triptych," as the stories depict various stages in Juliet's life and her relationships with her husband Eric and daughter Penelope. The stories are linked as much by common themes and motifs as by character: family, love, and the role of chance in our lives are the main themes here as in so much of Munro's fiction. Scholars who have analyzed the stories have agreed that like many of

Munro's characters, Juliet is subject to random events that govern the direction of her life, while at the same time she is the product of a family that shapes the kind of person she has become, and she herself determines, to a large degree, how her own children will evolve. As critics have noted for some time, Munro's fiction is characterized by paradox, and here we see again the clash of the seemingly contradictory forces of fate and randomness, of inescapable family heritage, and of the contingency of experience.

The formal question once again arises: why write three stories instead of a novella? What does Munro achieve by dividing her narrative this way? First, the tripartite structure allows her to portray three distinct and consequential periods in Juliet's life: the moment when she takes action to pursue her relationship with Eric despite the social pressures against such "forwardness"; her return home, where she reveals how much she is her parents' daughter; and a somewhat later period when the effects of her approach to family and romantic relationships exact a terrible price, assuming Penelope's actions are so easy to interpret. Each story has a fairly sharp focus in setting and plot: "Chance" is about two events six months apart and deals with the early days of the Juliet–Eric relationship; "Soon" is about an even shorter period of time and portrays the parent–daughter relationship in some depth; and "Silence" extends the parent–daughter theme to a later period when Juliet is the mother and Penelope is the self-distancing offspring. That is, the structure allows Munro to show one character experiencing both sides of one of her favourite subjects: the mother–daughter relationship. On the other hand, in her work Munro has never been averse to moving freely in a single text between widely separated periods in her protagonists' lives, from childhood to maturity and even to old age. What she does here by constructing three separate stories is to provide stronger divisions between periods and her protagonist's varied sensibilities, rather than anything radically different from what she does in other, particularly longer, stories.

Julie Rivkin interprets the tripartite structure in the light of classical models. She sees the mini-cycle as portraying the acting out of cosmic justice in circumstances involving guilt and multi-generational "pollution" or "contamination": "the trilogy form, which Munro adopts from the Greek dramatists, works well for the enactment of cosmic justice, guilty acts finding punishment over the course not only of generations but of subsequent plays or stories" (100). Her point, then, is that the guilt Juliet feels over her role in a stranger's suicide, symbolized by her blood on the tracks (Rivkin 102), continues to shape lives even into the next generation, i.e., Penelope's, thereby affecting relationships far beyond those of the people directly involved in the tragic incident.[1]

What Munro does with a mini-cycle parallels her technique and purpose in her story cycles, whose features are outlined by Balestra:

> Fragmentation, indeterminacy, discontinuity, ellipses and loose ends
> ... These features belong to each individual story and are expanded

in the short story cycle, where gaps are wider and a whole life is condensed, important parts of the biography are not incorporated in the narrative and yet inform the stories.

(Balestra 60)

In *Lives of Girls and Women* and *Who Do You Think You Are?*, the fragmentation and the continuities of character, setting, and motif work together to limn a picture that accommodates the incoherence of experience along with aesthetic unity. The same holds true for the mini-cycle.

"Chance" begins with and largely depicts Juliet's journey to Whale Bay, Eric's home, where Juliet hopes to rekindle the passion they felt during a train journey six months earlier. By the time we read the flashback showing how they met, we already know about her relationship with him, especially the accidents that brought them together, and we anticipate his arrival in her life. As Ailsa Cox writes, " 'Chance' is largely about causality and the unpredictable consequences of random events and irrational decisions" ("Almost Like a Ghost" 244). As the train passes through the Rockies, a man sits opposite Juliet and starts up a conversation with her. We quite naturally assume that this is Eric, until she makes it clear she is not interested in becoming his "chum" (56) and escapes to the observation car. There, the man who does turn out to be Eric sits with her, but he is somewhat less aggressive in his attempts to befriend her, and since they have little interaction, we wonder whether this might *not* be Eric. The original man commits suicide, and Juliet feels tremendous guilt at having spurned the approaches of a lonely man. Furthermore, she just happens to be having her period at the time, and the blood on the tracks is assumed to be his while she knows that it is her own—chance again plays a role in how she and other passengers act, react, and interpret events. The man's suicide, Rivkin writes, is one of "those moments where the journey encounters an obstacle, where it might go differently" (94). Had it not been for his approaches, she would have remained in her seat and in all likelihood would never have met Eric, nor been so open to him once she learned what her hesitation with the depressed man had led to. Had he not committed suicide, she would not have come to know Eric better during the train ride, nor felt so much guilt—a feeling that seems to have shaped many of her later choices—over her role in his death. In much of Munro's work, blind chance changes the directions of characters' lives, leading them into experiences and relationships that affect their lives but do not necessarily shape them forever. The story's title expresses this theme, one that links all the stories in *Runaway*. To that extent, then, while the mini-cycle exhibits a degree of unity that surpasses that of the collection as a whole because of the stories' common protagonist, the collection is not entirely without its own overall form of linking, however relatively "weak."

Juliet has decided to take "a little detour": to take a chance on the promise suggested by their meeting and seek out Eric's house instead of going home, that is, to her parents' house, after her contract teaching Classics ends (48). Rivkin points out that their meeting on the train was the initial "detour" in their lives, moving them in a very different direction from what Juliet and Eric may have originally planned (94; on the symbolic meaning of journeys in Munro's fiction, see York, "Distant Parts"). Juliet had been on one life "track" through her interest in Classics, and indeed she sees her world and herself through the lens of classical literature, such as the book by Dodd she is reading when the suicide occurs. In effect, she has assumed that life is governed by fate, but fate does not mean a single, clear path or direction: "What replaces personal fate is randomness; Juliet finds enchantment in having entered the landscape of chance" (Rivkin 96). She devotes much of her life to pursuing the intellectual and rational, and her contrast with Eric is evident throughout the story, as in her mythological rather than pragmatic way of looking at the constellations (Balestra 61). Now, she decides to indulge in the irrational, passionate, and Earth-bound. Much of the story's imagery concerns this move from the rational and orderly to the chaotic; for example, her bus ride involves going from the "lawns and gardens of Kerrisdale" and the "grounds of the school" that "were sheltered and civilized, enclosed by a stone wall" to "real forest" with "water and rocks, dark trees, hanging moss" and houses that are "damp and bettered-looking" with yards of random junk in them (50). That landscape is what triggers her memory of the Canadian wilderness the train passes through (52). This disorder is what she has sought: "What drew her in—enchanted her, actually—was the very indifference, the repetition, the carelessness and contempt for harmony, to be found on the scrambled surface of the Precambrian shield" (54). Balestra says that the "journey stands for open destiny, where chance and free will play their eternal game" (63). Juliet finds Eric's house the day after the funeral of his late wife, Ann, and is unsure what to do given that Eric is not home. Juliet refuses to leave and weathers the somewhat disdainful reactions of Ailo, the woman who had been nursing Ann. Juliet is somewhat intimidated by her, but insists on staying, revealing aspects of her personality we may respond to in different ways. For example, we perhaps wonder what makes her think she can resist the clearly expressed wish of someone very close to, and protective of, Ann that she leave. Her continued presence makes for an awkward situation, yet she will not succumb to the social pressure (even though exerted by only one person), and so we cannot help being puzzled by her sense of entitlement or possessiveness in the house of a man she has only recently met and briefly known.

The narrative shifts from present (the bus trip) to past (the train trip) to future, the latter reflected in frequent references to how events will one day be narrated by Juliet to a friend or family member at some point. She considers the lonely stranger unattractive, but "She would not have said, afterwards, that he was remarkably ugly" (55). This is how the reader learns about Christa, who will become a friend and who, we eventually discover, is Eric's current and future lover. The first reference makes no mention of Christa's relationship with Eric: the presence of Juliet's menstrual blood on the tracks is something she vows never to tell anyone about, but in fact "she did tell it, a few years later, to a woman named Christa, a woman whose name she did not yet know" (64). At the end of "Chance", Munro offers a foreshadowing of the two women's later relationship, as Christa "will become Juliet's great friend and mainstay during the years ahead—though she will never quite forgo a habit of sly teasing, the ironic flicker of a submerged rivalry" (86). The line has a complex function. It is a prolepsis and conveys to us that the narrator—presumably focalizing on an older Juliet recalling this period of her life—knows more than does the Juliet of the story's temporal setting. Isla Duncan analyzes the passage in narratological terms, writing that

> "Chance" is one of three linked stories, and in the third of these Christa will play an important role, as Juliet's friend and mentor; strictly speaking, then, the prediction does cover events within the narrative frame, and constitutes an internal prolepsis ... In the Juliet triptych ... the prolepses convey the panchronic authority of the narrator, moving freely along the axes of the characters' lives.
>
> (113)

Rivkin claims that "the fact that there are two stories ahead in the triptych suggests that we will arrive at the future alluded to here" (103). However, at this point there are no paratextual clues that the story is linked to the later ones; we have no reason to believe that Juliet's, Eric's, and Christa's story (or stories) will continue past the end of "Chance." Therefore, we do not know that we will actually see their fraught friendship dramatized. Prolepses, Duncan explains, "whet the reader's curiosity as to exactly how these [future circumstances] have been shaped" (113), and certainly Munro's reader wishes to hear more about her close but tense relationship with Christa—about whom we learn so little—struck by the idea that she met and became friends with another of Eric's lovers. Yet only once we have read all three stories do we see fully how the line works as more than just a signal of the temporal position of the narrator, but in fact a prediction of what will be dramatized later in the mini-cycle, and certain elements in "Chance" take on their full meaning. As Gianfranca Balestra argues, the story "undoubtedly acquires a different significance when studied as part of a composite" (59).

Furthermore, if Eric has had more than one lover, we must change our view of the relationship between Eric and Juliet; they no longer come across as figures in a conventional love story, thrown together by fate and enjoying a "happily ever after" fairy-tale romance. Eric is not the devoted, faithful husband of a sick woman, and Juliet is no longer the once-in-a-lifetime woman he falls madly in love with despite that devotion. Juliet is put in the position of having to decide whether she is willing to become another in a potentially long line of Eric's lovers (we might well wonder just how many there have been, especially after Ailo tells Juliet about another named Sandra [77]). She chooses to do so despite knowing about the others, setting herself up for betrayal later on. Eric reassures her during their conversation on the train that what seems important and overwhelming now—in this case, her guilt—will one day seem minor in the context of later experiences (68). His words will have inevitable implications for her compulsive feelings for him.

The story reveals much about her personality, information that will become very relevant in the other stories. From her parents she has learned to be a rebel, to care little for social conventions, particularly those governing women's roles and behaviour. As Isla Duncan argues, "noticeably in her later work, Munro writes stories in which women break loose from their conventional roles, shake off their customary or expected passivity" (113), and she cites Juliet's bus trip to Whale Bay to see Eric as an illustration of that. Juliet is willing to pursue him, even if it means being subjected to Ailo's possessive and disapproving scrutiny. She also resists the sexist discouragement of her professors (53). The problem lies not only with her instructors but also with her parents. They are supportive, but her mother wants her "to be popular" and her father "just wanted her to fit in" (53); "otherwise people will make your life hell" (54). She finds that attitude odd, as they "did not fit in so very well themselves" (54). What she will later learn is that being rebellious can indeed have consequences not only for herself but also for others. Juliet is certainly not trying to "fit in" in Eric's house; instead, she has barged in and stubbornly awaits Eric's arrival. She is far more like her parents than she or they might admit, and in a way she is both emulating and thumbing her nose at the extent to which they are "rebels."

Above all, we learn within the first two pages that Juliet has a somewhat qualified devotion to the truth. In the second paragraph, we are told that in speaking to a fellow teacher, Juliet has described Ann as "a total invalid, more or less brain-dead" (48), but then a letter from Eric arrives "as if conjured by such unworthy lies or half-lies" (49). From this point on, Juliet becomes an unreliable focalized character (she is not the narrator), and so we are put on guard against her judgments and declarations, particularly as Munro emphasizes her love of story-telling and embellishment of events, notably in her letters home (e.g., 64–65, where she entirely distorts what happened on the train). She plans to lie to Eric about why she is in Whale Bay, to claim that her friend and colleague Juanita has a cabin there and "is a fearless outdoor sort of woman (quite different from the real Juanita, who is seldom out of high heels)" (51). The story is about storytelling, such as what she will tell her parents and others about the blood on the tracks (64), and her account to Eric of the lonely man's efforts to befriend her; as for the latter, she omits "the expression *chum around*" because she is afraid she would cry again (or perhaps it would make her look worse) (67). She lies to the taxi driver bringing her to Eric's home about the purpose of her visit (74), and, during the flashback, to Eric about her virginity (80).[2] When Eric finally returns and she hears his truck door close, she thinks, "She wants to hide somewhere (she says later, *I could have crawled under the table*, but of course she does not think of doing anything so ridiculous)" (84). Such references to post-facto storytelling lend the story a degree of self-reflexivity. Because she is a student of the Classics, she tends to relate other people to historic and mythological parallels, thereby distancing herself from the people in her life—a depiction that foreshadows her later alienation from them.

A few motifs deserve mention, if only briefly. Ailo tells Juliet about Christa's talent with driftwood, which becomes a symbol of the contingent nature of the characters' lives. The titles of the other stories in the mini-cycle come up in passing. As Juliet is sitting in the observation car, she sees a wolf outside, for example, and wonders if the two women who are also sitting there have noticed it, too, but "neither broke the silence, and that was pleasing to her" (57). While waiting for Eric, she thinks of how she has put away her Greek vocabulary, like other forms of "bright treasure" in the mini-cycle (see Rivkin 107):

> And now and again you look in the closet for something else and you remember, and you think, soon. Then it becomes something that is just there, in the closet, and other things get crowded in front of it and on top of it and finally you don't think about it at all.
>
> The thing that was your bright treasure. You don't think about it. A loss you could not contemplate at one time, and now it becomes something you can barely remember.
>
> (83)

The story establishes some stylistic features that become prominent in "Soon" and "Silence." One paragraph describes the towns through which the bus passes in terms of what they are not: they "are not organized towns at all ... no paved streets, except the highway that goes through, no sidewalks. No big solid buildings to house Post Offices or Municipal offices, no ornamented blocks of stores, built to be noticed. No war monuments, drinking fountains, flowery little parks" (50–51). Such negative descriptions recur in the other stories.

Given what we learn about her, her parents, and her relationship with them, we are prepared in some ways for the visit home portrayed in the second story. Like "Chance," "Soon" is about a physical and emotional return, one that leads to flashbacks and provokes thoughts, feelings, and memories for Juliet. The consequences of the chance encounter on the train begin to reveal themselves in "Soon." Her relationship with Eric has become a source of contention between Juliet and her father. Juliet is living with Eric at a time when that sort of cohabitation is still socially unacceptable, and when the story begins, she is pregnant. Thus, she has obviously long been a defier of social conventions, someone who acts without much regard for the opinions or feelings of others. Christa makes an appearance, if only briefly, thus finally satisfying our desire at the end of "Chance" to see her "on stage," so to speak.

While making these connections between the two stories, however, Munro does not let us lose sight of the fact that "Soon" is a discrete story, such as through her handling of character relationships. The story opens with Juliet's purchase of a print of Marc Chagall's *I and the Village*, an ironic choice of gift for her parents considering the difficulties her father faces with the residents of his own, far less accepting town.[3] She is accompanied by Christa, who is described simply as "her friend who had come down with her from Whale Bay to do some shopping" (88); there is no mention of Christa's relationship to Eric, and all that we are told about her is that she likes to make jokes (88). It might seem odd that she is referred to as merely a "friend" despite the more complex and fraught relationship we already know that they have, but at this point Munro's purpose is to establish the story as both distinct from and linked to "Chance"; given that we are again in Juliet's perspective, this may well be how Juliet would describe Christa to others, in an attempt to hide uncomfortable truths about her participation in an extra-marital affair and a jealous rivalry over Eric. Dividing the stories permits Munro to portray the various meanings Christa has, had, and will have in Juliet's life—at this point, she is a friend only, while she is a rival for Eric's affections in the other stories. Christa also serves as a means by which we learn how Juliet views her parents, as Juliet tells her that "they lived in a curious but not unhappy isolation, though her father was a popular schoolteacher. Partly they were cut off by Sara's heart trouble, but also by their subscribing to magazines nobody around them read, listening to programs on the national radio network, which nobody around them listened to" (89). She projects her own intellectualism and rebelliousness on to them, believing they are far more independent and "modern" in their thinking than they later prove to be. To Juliet, Sam is intellectually superior and a free spirit, and a victim of the town's small-mindedness:

> He was a remarkable teacher, the one whose antics and energy everyone would remember, his Grade Six unlike any other year in his pupils' lives. Yet he had been passed over, time and again, and probably for that very reason. His methods could be seen to undercut authority. So you could imagine authority saying that he was not the sort of man to be in charge, he'd do less harm where he was.
>
> (93)

Yet she hesitates to tell her parents why Eric's medical career ended—while a medical student, he had performed an abortion on a friend (94)—because she is afraid "their broad-mindedness was possibly not so reliable as she had thought" (94–95).

During her visit, we learn much about the origins of Juliet's mental habits, the family traits of which she is clearly an heir. All these characters—Juliet, her father Sam, and her mother Sara—are similar in that each needs to tell stories about the others. The family is overburdened with secrets, lies, and incompatible images of each other. Juliet speaks separately with her father and mother and gains uncomfortable insights about each from the other. For example, when she speaks to Sara, she sees a heretofore unknown element of her parents' relationship as Sara tells her about Sam's need to defer to those who would presumably be beneath him socially: "'He has to suck up to them,' said Sara with a sudden change of tone, a wavering edge of viciousness, a weak chuckle" (101). Sam's behaviour toward service people is of course reminiscent of Juliet's toward Ailo in "Chance," and parallels her similar fearful feeling about Irene, Sara's care-giver. Munro makes it clear that all these instances of fear and deference are neither necessary nor justified. Also, Juliet is not the only one in the family who frequently lies. Her father tells her that the train no longer stops in town, but the truth is that he does not want the scandal of having to meet her at the station, in full view of his neighbours, given her "immoral" lifestyle of living with Eric. To protect both her and himself, he has her arrive at a nearby town instead. She is astonished when she realizes the truth (105). Here we see that he would like to "fit in" more than he is willing to admit, or she to believe. He has claimed that he quit his school teaching job voluntarily in order to become a fruit and vegetable seller, but the fact is that he was forced to quit his job over the scandal, and clearly harbours both resentment and pride over his defiance of the town's moral police (104). Considering the fact that he cannot just get up and leave the town the way Juliet did, and remains in that judgmental but inescapable social environment, we cannot help sympathizing with him and how difficult she has made life for him. When he challenges Juliet's lifestyle choices, she refuses to back down, and Sam counters by telling her about what her unconventionality means for him and Sara:

> "But you don't realize," said Juliet. "You don't *realize*. You don't realize just how *stupid* this is and what a disgusting place this is to live in, where people say that kind of thing, and how if I told people I know this they wouldn't believe it. It would seem like a joke."
> "Well. Unfortunately, your mother and I don't live where you live. Here is where we live. Does that fellow of yours think it's a joke too?"
>
> (105)

This community is—for better or worse—his home, and while she does not have to deal with the fallout from her cohabitation, he does. She does not realize that being a rebel affects not only her own life but others' as well. Sam tells Juliet about his own challenges to Authority: "there's times for sticking your neck out and times not to" (119). Sam obviously has feelings for Irene, perhaps because she has all the energy that Sara used to have and now lacks, but when Juliet confronts him about the matter, he is anything but forthright about it:

> "Does she want to get married? Irene?"
> This question startled Sam, coming as it did in that tone and after a considerable silence.
> "I don't know," he said.
> And after a moment, "I don't see how she could."
> "Ask her," Juliet said. "You must want to the way you feel about her."
> They drove for a mile or two before he spoke. It was clear she had given offense.
> "I don't know what you're talking about," he said.
>
> (114)

Juliet's own dishonesty and love of storytelling are elaborated and highlighted. While in the attic searching for a playpen, she recalls the times she spent up there "telling herself some story she had read, with certain additions or alterations" and "Dancing ... in front of an imaginary audience" (97). In a reversal of what happens in "Chance," where she tells others stories *about* Eric and Ann, Juliet sends a letter about her visit home *to* Eric in which she embellishes events to make them into a somewhat more colourful tale:

> The other day I rode around with him in the ancient vehicle delivering fresh raspberries and raspberry jam (made by a sort of junior Ilse Koch person who inhabits our kitchen) and newly dug first potatoes of the season. He is quite gung-ho. Sara stays in bed and dozes or looks at out-dated fashion magazines.
>
> (124)

We have already seen the conflict-filled reality behind this nearly bucolic picture, and it simply adds to our skepticism about her stories and honesty. That is, like so many of Munro's characters, Juliet is a performer, and we learn in "Silence" that she would later go on to become a television personality.

What becomes evident is that she appears to have learned much of her dramatizing storytelling and behaviour from her mother. Sara had also told dramatic stories as a child—in her case, about "the imaginary friends Rollo and Maxine who solved mysteries, even murders, like the characters in certain children's books" (100). Sara is a performer, too, someone who dresses in a flamboyant way to meet Juliet at the train station and reacts to Juliet's arrival in a manner that draws attention to herself (89–90). When Penelope, only a year old, recoils from Sara's attempt to embrace her, Sara makes a further scene:

Sara laughed. "Am I such a scarecrow?" Again her voice was ill controlled, rising to shrill peaks and falling away, drawing stares. This was new—though maybe not entirely. Juliet had an idea that people might always have looked her mother's way when she laughed or talked, but in the old days it would have been a spurt of merriment they noticed, something girlish and attractive (though not everybody would have liked that either, they would have said she was always trying to get attention).

(90)

One of the people who consider Sara to be an attention hound is Sam, as soon becomes evident: during the car ride home, explaining why he does not want to stop at a restaurant for ice cream, he comments, "Take her into anyplace for a treat, and she'll put on a show" (94).

Throughout the story, we see the family dynamic in detail, and the ways in which Juliet is very much her parents' daughter. Both Juliet and Sara notice the thick hair on Irene's arms and find it disgusting and frightening, even sharing a laugh about it (107), although it is clear that they fear her, too. More strikingly, Juliet is very young not only in years but also in her attitude and behaviour. Sara is similarly childlike in how she dresses, thinks, and behaves, as in her desire to go for ice cream. She suffers from heart problems, and while lying in bed she is "wearing woolly pink pajamas" and "with her white hair flying out in wisps, her bright eyes anxious under nearly nonexistent brows, she looked more like an oddly aged child" (98). A similar image comes to Juliet's mind when she bathes her daughter and mother together: "Sara, naked, did not look like an old woman as much as an old girl—a girl, say, who had suffered some exotic, wasting, desiccating disease" (115). Juliet recalls a children's theme park her parents used to take her to, and she and Sara try to remember the names of the Seven Dwarfs, which were used as the names of the caves children were allowed to explore (114–15). It is Sara who says, "We used to call it the Shrine of Strawberry Shortcake—oh, how I'd like to go again" (114–15). She informs Juliet that Sam only allowed her to come along for the ride to the train station to pick her up after she threw a fit (115), and refers to Sam as "Daddy," not because it is what Juliet called him but because she herself sees him as a father figure. Her inability to be a proper wife to Sam—as he tells it (111)—may explain his interest in the more competent, perhaps more mature, and certainly more vibrant Irene. When Juliet was a teenager, the two had been like close friends rather than mother and daughter, sharing hairdressing and "dressmaking sessions," suppers composed of "peanut-butter-and-tomato-and-mayonnaise sandwiches on the evenings Sam stayed late for a school meeting" (100). Later, Juliet outgrew their bizarre relationship:

Abruptly, Juliet hadn't wanted any more of it, she had wanted instead to talk to Sam late at night in the kitchen, to ask him about black holes, the Ice Age, God. She hated the way Sara undermined their talk with wide-eyed ingenuous questions, the way Sara always tried somehow to bring the subject back to herself. That was why the talks had to be late at night and there had to be the understanding neither she nor Sam ever spoke about. *Wait till we're rid of Sara.* Just for the time being, of course.

(100–01)

This passage suggests an equally disturbing relationship between Juliet and her father, implying a troubling degree of jealousy, secrecy, and resentment among the characters. It is not surprising that in such an environment Juliet's own attitudes toward romantic and parental relationships might become somewhat unhealthy.

Irene serves a number of functions in the story. As already noted, she echoes Ailo in "Chance" as the servant who knows and silently judges what is happening in the family she works for, or if she does not judge others believe that she does. Does Ailo really care about Eric's many lovers, and would Irene really quit if Sam put up Chagall's painting? The important thing is that other characters attribute these attitudes to them and adjust their behaviour accordingly. In reality, Irene is more like Sara—and by extension Juliet—than Sam or Juliet realize. She is around Juliet's age, and therefore much younger than Juliet had expected (91), and she is also childlike in her enjoyment of a Bullwinkle cartoon (95). Irene is another performer, at least in Sam's eyes; he recounts her family troubles, then says, "She may seem thick-skinned now but I guess she wasn't always. Maybe even now it's more of a masquerade" (110). For Sam, she is the female equivalent of Don, Sara's beloved minister, in that she offers—metaphorically speaking—a kind of spiritual relief: "She restored my faith in women" (113), he says, the way Don restored Sara's in God. She is also connected to the recurrence of the motif of a stored, hidden, and forgotten "bright treasure," which reappears in the form of the Chagall painting (Rivkin 110). Munro devotes three pages to portraying its careful purchase, only to show it later stashed away in the attic; Sam did not want to display it for fear of seeming to put on airs before the townspeople, especially Irene: as Sara explains, "I think it made Daddy uncomfortable. Or maybe looking at it with Irene looking at it—that made him uncomfortable. He might be afraid it would make her feel—oh, sort of contemptuous of us. You know—that we were weird. He wouldn't like for Irene to think we were that kind of people" (99). The parallels between Sam and Eric are obvious here: feeling deprived by having sick wives, both seek passion or attention elsewhere.

The story ends with an epiphany in which Juliet recognizes the effects of her choices and behaviour on the people around her. Once her mother has died, she realizes how little it would have taken for her to help Sara protect herself from a changing world through simple gestures, no matter how seemingly meaningless, like replying positively to her mother's desire to see her in spite of their religious and other differences:

> Some shift must have taken place, at that time, which she had not remembered. Some shift concerning where home was. Not at Whale Bay with Eric but back where it had been before, all her life before.
>
> Because it's what happens at home that you try to protect, as best you can, for as long as you can.
>
> But she had not protected Sara. When Sara had said, *soon I'll see Juliet*, Juliet had found no reply. Could it not have been managed? Why should it have been so difficult? Just to say *Yes*. To Sara it would have meant so much—to herself, surely, so little. But she had turned away, she had carried the tray to the kitchen, and there she washed and dried the cups and also the glass that had held grape soda. She had put everything away.
>
> (125)

She had indeed "put everything away": neatly organized her gestures and feelings to maintain a kind of intellectual integrity without accommodating the messy realities that characterize life. To her, devotion to political and philosophical principles is an obvious virtue, and being oblivious to public opinion is an obvious, easy choice. Eric Reeves argues that Sara "imposes at the end a finally selfish emotional burden on Juliet, switching from a discussion of religion and faith to 'faith' of a very different, finally deeply manipulative sort" (125). While it is true that Sara is juvenile and overly dependent on others, the fact remains that it would not have taken much for Juliet to satisfy Sara's needs.

What Juliet does not know, and what will only be revealed in the next story, is that this visit will have profound implications for her common-law marriage, since it is while she is visiting her parents that Eric renews his affair with Christa.

"Silence" is set nearly twenty years later. Penelope is now an adult and has joined a cult, thereby rebelling against her parents' atheism the way Juliet fought against her mother's spirituality represented by Don. The story recounts Juliet's efforts to find her daughter, a search she engages in frantically at first before coming to accept that Penelope does not want to be found. As critics have pointed out, between "Soon" and "Silence," Juliet has shifted position from daughter to mother, and the complex, not very happy relationships between mothers and daughters, so common in Munro's fiction (see Ferri, Heller, and Redekop), continue as the Sara/Juliet dynamic is replaced by the Juliet/Penelope one. Sara would have liked to see more of Juliet, and her hopes were invested in Juliet's possible visit—"*soon I'll see Juliet*"—and now Juliet is equally hopeful that soon she will see her own daughter. In the story, Duncan writes, "she is presented as a woman in her professional prime, a devoted mother excited at the prospect of being reunited with her beloved daughter"

(111). Like Sara, Juliet is fated to be disappointed and must ultimately accept that "she no longer knows her daughter, and her daughter does not wish to know about her, any more. She has become a wholly different person" (Duncan 111).

The Juliet–Penelope relationship comes to the fore with the departures of other major figures in Juliet's life. We have learned of Sara's death at the end of "Soon," and at the beginning of "Silence" Juliet recognizes her own appearance as that of "what her mother would have called a striking-looking woman" (126). In other words, despite her passing, Sara remains a strong presence in Juliet's mind and life. Later, we learn that Eric is dead, too. His fateful decision to perform an abortion destroyed his medical career and led to his becoming a prawn fisherman, a decision that in turn led to his death when he was caught out on the water during a storm. Choices and chance thus govern the characters' lives to the very end.

The "silence" of the title is Penelope's, but it is also the lack of real, sincere, and honest communication that has beset all the relationships to one degree or another. For instance, Juliet continues to exhibit her nature as a performer and storyteller, her preference for keeping secrets and telling tales to cover up the truth. She is now an interviewer on television—conversation as performance—and Eric's funeral is like a show in which she performs without really being engaged: "The storm, the recovery of the body, the burning on the beach—that was all like a pageant she had been compelled to watch and compelled to believe in, which still had nothing to do with Eric and herself" (146). Only later does the grief hit her, yet her first instinct is to hide it from Penelope (147–48). She takes a job in a library, then joins the Provincial Television channel, conducting interviews while "she cultivated a self-deprecating, faintly teasing manner that usually seemed to go over well. On camera, few things fazed her" (148).

She conceals the truth about where Penelope is through lies and stories, telling one woman, for example, that her daughter has simply gone on a "retreat" (127). We are told what "Juliet could have said" (128), not what she does say or is necessarily the truth. Even when it becomes clear that her daughter has cut herself off completely from Juliet, she continues to tell friends and acquaintances such stories (135). After she returns to her first love, Classics, she researches the Greek novelists of the first century and becomes particularly interested in Heliodorus's *Aethiopica* for obvious reasons: it is a mythological, fictional version of her own experiences with Penelope, a story that helps her distance herself from her daughter's disappearance and her feelings about it (151). She is surprised to discover from Penelope's friend Heather that instead of "being involved with transcendentalists" or "earning her living in a rough and risky way, fishing, perhaps with a husband, perhaps also with some husky little children, in the cold waters of the Inside Passage off the British Columbia coast" (155–56), she is living an ordinary middle-class life somewhere up north. Even this conventional version of Penelope's life is the subject of her fictionalizing, to the point of imagining their reunion. Her lying regarding Penelope does not stop; Juliet never tells her current boyfriend, Gary, about her (157). Once again, there is a long italicized passage presenting what she would have said had she been prepared to confide in him, to open herself to him, yet it, too, is filled with speculation and creative storytelling (157–58). Where she is most honest is in her admission that the real reason for Penelope's disappearance may be inaccessible: "*I think the reason may be something not so easily dug out. . . . Maybe she can't stand me. It's possible*" (158). The point is that there may be no rational explanation, that this is a mystery without a solution. On the other hand, perhaps Gianfranca Balestra is right that in Munro's work daughters often have to leave in order to create their own identities, and in Penelope's case the "daughter's need to detach herself from the maternal in order to forge an independent subjectivity is achieved in the most dramatic way" (67–68). That Juliet has herself used silence to cut herself off from Sara, denying her the reassurance her mother sought, highlights the persistence, and heightens the tragic nature, of this pattern.

When Juliet meets Heather by chance—again—she pretends to know all about Penelope's five children (154–55). It may well be that greater honesty would have led her to Penelope's whereabouts, but she eventually gives up her search and manages to build her life in her daughter's absence. The problem is that with all her falsehoods and performing, there is little left of her real self.[4] She seems to have no strong identity of her own, except as she has constructed it in order to impress, mislead, and above all protect herself from others. As the reviewer for *Kirkus Reviews* says, "a much older Juliet comes sorrowfully to terms with the emptiness in her that had forever alienated Penelope" (887). She has suffered in many ways for her insistence on dishonesty and role-playing—and the building of protective facades around herself—in her personal relationships and beyond. It becomes clear that the emotional distance and inability to communicate that Juliet has learned from her parents, and reinforced with her lovers, will be passed on to another generation.

Like her parents, Juliet wants her child to be more "normal"—more socially accepted and acceptable—than she herself is. At thirteen, Penelope goes away on a camping trip with a friend, something that pleases Juliet because that is "something that regular children did and that Juliet, as a child, had never had the chance to do ... she welcomed signs that Penelope was turning out to be a more normal sort of girl than she herself had been" (137). Juliet does not want her own child to experience the kind of alienation she and her father had endured for being misfits. Juliet created an image of her parents, especially her father, as courageous intellectuals in a town of Philistines; she does much the same image-mongering for her daughter, whom she sees as too intelligent to be "mixed up in anything like" what the Spiritual Balance Centre offers (131). This is how Juliet sees herself, as evidenced by her anthropological more than emotional response to the burning of Eric's drowned body (142–43). Once again, then, Juliet projects herself on to her loved ones, blinding herself to who they really are.

Juliet has another reason for wanting Penelope out of the way: she has just learned about Eric's affair and wants to thrash things out with him. Eric, on the other hand, prefers to put their problems away in the same manner that other things—"bright treasure's, Sara's dishes, and true feelings"—had been stored and forgotten:

> Eric, on the other hand, would have liked nothing better than to see their trouble smoothed over, hidden out of the way. To Eric's way of thinking, civility would restore good feeling, the semblance of love would be enough to get by on until love itself might be rediscovered.
> (138)

It is difficult to know what else Juliet could have expected from a man who had had more than one extra-marital affair before she came along. He revealed himself to be a superficial lover even before they moved in together, and she chose to get involved with him with her eyes wide open. She recalls: "She had known all about Christa then and she could not reasonably object to what had happened in the time before she and Eric were together. She did not. What she did object to—what she claimed had broken her heart—had happened after that. (But still a long time ago, said Eric.)" (138). She learns that the affair was not a one-time thing after all, but that they had slept together many times (139). What is interesting is the line about Juliet's having "claimed" that her heart was broken: Munro chose this skeptical word to convey the idea that Juliet had dramatized her own response in stories to others. Even her heartbreak is the subject of storytelling. After failing to see Penelope on Denman Island, she curiously finds in Christa a friend in whom she can confide. That she never truly hated Christa for the affair (139), and remains friends with her afterward, further calls the honesty of her "claim" of heartbreak into question.

Juliet's response to the affair reinforces our understanding of how much she is a product of her parents' way of thinking. It is Ailo who divulges Eric's affair, out of "a certain loyalty to Eric's dead wife and some reservations about Juliet" (138), and Juliet reacts to the revelation the way her father felt about the Chagall painting: "Her contentions were that he did not love her, had never loved her, had mocked her, with Christa, behind her back. He had made her a laughingstock in front of people like Ailo (who had always hated her)" (139). Appearances, including before the "help," matter to Juliet more than she will fully admit.

As she grows older, she becomes more like her parents: she turns to gardening, like her father, and as her hair changes colour she is "reminded of her mother, Sara. Sara's soft, fair, flyaway hair, going gray and then white" (150). She even withdraws from society, returning to her books as per her original tendencies, and as such recreates what her daughter did by withdrawing to the Centre (151). Penelope's disappearance may well reflect what she has learned from her mother about solitude. An earlier generation has shaped Juliet, and it is apparent that she has shaped the next one, at least for a time. That does not excuse Penelope's hard-hearted actions, however, and Reeves is correct when he says that in the story "there is an evident callousness, or perhaps self-protectiveness in Penelope as well" (128). As Lester E. Barber says, "Juliet was unfair to her mother, and Penelope is unfair to Juliet" ("Old Confusions" 149).

Motifs appearing in the other two stories continue to recur here. Like "Chance" and "Soon," the story is about a journey, one that explores a difficult relationship through voyages in space and time, in this case Juliet's trip to Denman Island to find her daughter. As a child, Penelope goes to the same private school in which Juliet had worked, Torrance House (137), and the train trip Juliet takes in "Chance" is to Vancouver to take up her position there. In "Silence," Christa's renewed affair with Eric triggers the break-up between him and Juliet, the aftermath of which is mentioned in "Chance." Thus, in the third story our understanding of the references in the previous two is enriched. Like Juliet, Christa is dishonest at times, as regards her affair with Eric; when Juliet suggests Penelope might have been in touch with Christa, the latter replies,

"She'd know I'd end up telling you."
Juliet was quiet for a moment, then she muttered sulkily, "There have been things you didn't tell me."
"Oh, for God's sake," said Christa, but without any animosity. "Not that again."

(134)

On the other hand, her motivations for dishonesty are more understandable than Juliet's. Christa lies to Penelope about Eric's death in order to speak to Heather's mother first (143), so that Juliet can break the news to her daughter herself, and when Juliet tells her that she no longer has as many meaningless affairs as she used to, Christa, to spare her feelings, refrains from saying "that this might be because of a lack of candidates" (149). Like Sara, Christa has a debilitating disease—in her case, multiple sclerosis (133). Penelope also parallels Sara; she looks somewhat like her grandmother (128) and is far more religious than Juliet. Sara has Don for spiritual guidance in "Soon," and in "Silence" Penelope runs off to join Mother Shipton's cult, although it becomes clear that the cult has disbanded given that Mother Shipton is now working in a Salvation Army Thrift Store (152). By no coincidence, one of the male denizens of the Spiritual Balance Centre is named Donny (129). Echoes of the other stories abound: for example, Ann's talent with driftwood is echoed in the reference to the driftwood used to burn Eric's body (141), and Juliet refers to her outrage at Eric for his affair with Christa as "fierce" (139), the same term Sara uses to describe Irene in "Soon" (107). The storage of treasures reappears with the bag of Penelope's possessions that Juliet refuses to throw out (136, 149).

The stories are thus distinct yet tightly connected. By choosing the form of the mini-cycle, Munro can portray distinct stages in her characters' lives, much as she does in story cycles like *Lives of Girls and Women* and *Who Do You Think You Are?*. In those works, each cycle features stories divided by both small and substantial gaps in time, permitting Munro to portray both the continuities and surprising changes in the lives of Del and Rose, respectively. Whether book-length or smaller, cycles permit Munro to return to her protagonists after major events like deaths in the family or divorces to see how such contingency in life shapes our sense of identity and our fates.

Also, as already noted, even in a mini-cycle in which there is a common point-of-view character, time renders the perspectives some-what different from each other from story to story. The three texts cover a substantial period of time, over the course of which Juliet exhibits both continuities and changes in her character. The form, in other words, gives Munro the opportunity to stretch the temporal setting to great lengths (Barber, "Old Confusions" 148), as she shows us how Juliet responds in various ways to her relationship with her husband Eric as she ages. In "Chance," she is twenty-one years old when she meets him and has no social or family responsibilities—none that she is willing to acknowledge, at least. In "Soon," she is a little older, but every bit as rebellious, and her confrontation with Don reveals her opinionated nature regarding religion, her unmarried status, and her thoughtlessness toward how her actions and beliefs may affect her parents' standing in their small town (119–21). From her viewpoint, she is being radical and independent, a champion of women's rights and a new morality, but as we look beyond her, we see the consequences of her choices for others to which she is blind. In "Silence," Eric is dead, and she has tried and failed to forge a bond with their daughter. For Barber, the mini-cycle form allows Munro greater breadth in which to portray Juliet more fully and from different angles:

> Munro is able to explore her character's motivations, reactions and self-assessment at greater leisure than is her norm, something more in the manner of a novelist. The reader appreciates the care with which Juliet is given a chance as an older woman to reflect back on key aspects of her life … The difference between the three Juliet stories and the others [in *Runaway*] is simply the amount of space Munro gives herself to explore the ironies, the self-assessments and understandings that come to her characters with age.
>
> ("Alice Munro" 150)

The mini-cycle provides a kaleidoscopic portrait of Juliet at quite different points in her life and above all in her family and other relationships, all unified by the theme of the failure of emotional and other forms of communication. Common thematic threads link stories separated by many years, by changes in Juliet's career and outlook, and by the sorts of relationships she has and how she understands, misunderstands, and resists full openness and vulnerability in them.

Notes

1 For more on the classical allusions in the mini-cycle and the role of shame and guilt, see Maja Čuk's and Gianfranca Balestra's articles.
2 For Rivkin, the latter lie "establishes a link between the concealment of blood and concealment of sexual relations" (104–05).
3 On the painting's symbolic significance, see Francesconi.
4 Munro dealt with the same idea in her earlier cycle, *Who Do You Think You Are?* (1974), in which Flo and Rose are both performers and the latter's identity is open to some question.

References

Balestra, Gianfranca. "Rituals of Life and Death in Alice Munro's 'Chance.'" Balestra et al., pp. 59–70.

Balestra, Gianfranca, Laura Ferri, and Caterina Ricciardi, editors. *Reading Alice Munro in Italy*. Frank Iacobucci Centre for Italian Studies, 2008.

Barber, Lester E. "Alice Munro: The Stories of *Runaway*." *ELOPE*, vol. 3, nos. 1–2, 2006, pp. 143–56.

——. "'Old Confusions or Obligations': Comic Vision in *Runaway*." Thacker, *Alice Munro*, pp. 136–58.

Beran, Carol L. "The Luxury of Excellence: Alice Munro in the *New Yorker*." Thacker, *Rest of the Story*, pp. 204–31.

Cox, Ailsa. "'Almost Like a Ghost': Spectral Figures in Alice Munro's Short Fiction." *Liminality and the Short Story: Boundary Crossings in American, Canadian, and British Writing*, edited by Jochen Achilles and Ina Bergmann, Routledge, 2015, pp. 238–50.

Čuk, Maya. "*Runaway*: Munro's Rewriting of Greek Mythology from a Feminist Perspective." *Alice Munro and the Anatomy of the Short Story*, edited by Oriana Palusci, Cambridge Scholars Press, 2017, pp. 83–94.

Duncan, Isla. *Alice Munro's Narrative Art*. Palgrave Macmillan, 2011.

Ferri, Laura. "Mothers and Other Secrets." *Open Letter*, series 11, no. 9 to series 12, no. 1, 2003–04, pp. 137–49.

Francesconi, Sabrina. "I and the Village: Locating Home and Self in Alice Munro's 'Soon.'" Balestra et al., pp. 71–81.

Heller, Deborah. *Daughters and Mothers in Alice Munro's Later Stories*. Workwomans Press, 2009.

Munro, Alice. *Lives of Girls and Women*. McGraw-Hill Ryerson, 1971.

——. *Runaway*. McClelland and Stewart, 2004.

——. *Who Do You Think You Are?* Macmillan, 1978.

Redekop, Magdalene. *Mothers and Other Clowns: The Stories of Alice Munro.* Routledge, 1992.

Reeves, Eric. "The Lives of Women and Men: Narrative Inflection in Alice Munro's *Runaway.*" Thacker, *Alice Munro*, pp. 114–36.

Review of *Runaway*, by Alice Munro. *Kirkus Reviews*, 15 Sept. 2005, p. 887.

Rivkin, Julie. "Sibyl at the Kitchen Table, or Translating the Classics in 'Hateship' and the Juliet Triptych." Thacker, *Alice Munro*, pp. 91–113.

Thacker, Robert, editor. *Alice Munro:* Hateship, Friendship, Courtship, Loveship, Marriage, Runaway, Dear Life. Bloomsbury, 2016.

York, Lorraine M. "'Distant Parts of Myself': The Topography of Alice Munro's Fiction." *American Review of Canadian Studies*, vol. 18, no. 1, Spring 1988, pp. 33–38.

5 The Prototypical Mini-Cycle II
Margaret Atwood's "Alphinland" Stories

The mini-cycle comprising the first three stories of Margaret Atwood's *Stone Mattress* (2014) is typical in that it is printed as a unit, and the point of view shifts from story to story. "Alphinland," "Revenant," and "Dark Lady" offer the very different perspectives of the characters involved in the stormy romantic relationships among Constance, Gavin, and Marjorie, as the stories reveal the myths, illusions, and emotional meanings that each character has created out of the others. The mini-cycle does this in a way that might not be possible, or at least as generically suitable, had it been written as a novella instead. We see the characters from within and without, and as one might expect, interpretations of their love affairs differ radically among them. Like Munro, Atwood links the stories in her mini-cycle not just by character but also by theme and motif, and the fantasy world of the first story's title tells us a great deal about the role of dream and illusion in all the characters' lives.

The protagonist of "Alphinland" is Constance, an aging author who achieved fame through her fantasy novels about the titular secondary world.[1] A recent widow, she is required to make do during a dangerous ice storm with the apparently ghostly advice of her late husband Ewan. She represents the imagination, while he represents practicality, perhaps her own practical side, as he aids her with advice on buying salt for the front steps and walk and on how to deal with a power failure. He remains, in her view, "so good at planning ahead" and recommends that she bring a flashlight when she goes out to buy the salt (7); when she discovers that there is no more salt to buy, he suggests that she substitute kitty litter (10). Their marriage persists even after Ewan's death, then.

As we learn, however, Constance's real love had been for the poet Gavin, and the story portrays her struggle to cope with her mixed feelings after she caught him cheating on her with Marjorie. Alphinland becomes the imaginary embodiment of her memory, the realm where she "stores" the men in her life, and Gavin will always have a place there: he is encased in a wine cask, but she has forgiven him his romantic trespasses so he is not suffering (19). She thinks,

One of the good things about Alphinland is that she can move the more disturbing items from her past through its stone gateway and store them in there on the memory palace model much in use in, when was it? The eighteenth century? You associate the things you want to remember with imaginary rooms, and when you want total recall you go into that room.

(18)

Thus, although it is a secondary world, Alphinland is strongly linked to the real world, and Gavin is hardly the only "real" person in it; for example, she gains revenge over an abusive boss by turning him into an evil sorcerer (8–9), and over Marjorie by immobilizing her and causing her to be stung daily by a hundred bees (25–26).

That Constance lives in the world of the imagination is made clear from the story's beginning. The ice storm has turned the outside world into a real version of her created one, at least on its surface, but she is now old enough to be aware of the romantic imagination's potential to delude and betray:

The freezing rain sifts down, handfuls of shining rice thrown by some unseen celebrant. Wherever it hits, it crystallizes into a granulated coating of ice. Under the streetlights, it looks so beautiful: like fairy silver, thinks Constance. But then, she would think that; she's far too prone to enchantment. The beauty is an illusion, and also a warning, there's a dark side to beauty, as with poisonous butterflies. She ought to be considering the dangers, the hazards, the grief this ice storm is going to bring to many.

(1)

Indeed, the news reports tell of car accidents, stranded airplanes, and fallen trees (2). There are hints here of her experience with Gavin: she learned the hard way what a mistake it was to romanticize and idealize him. The HD television on which she watches the news provides too clear a picture of reality: "there are some things that do not fare well in high definition. She resents the pores, the wrinkles, the nose hairs, the impossibly whitened teeth shoved right up in front of your eyes so you can't ignore them the way you would in real life" (1).

Still, Constance sees magic everywhere, even in the TV weather reports. The reporters gesture toward their maps like "magicians about to reveal the floating lady" (2). Outside, she sees "the world turn to diamonds—branches, rooftops, hydro lines, all glittering and sparkling" and then comments aloud, "Alphinland" (3). It is at this moment that Ewan speaks to her about the need to buy salt for the front steps. If he does represent the pragmatic world, he offers advice in a most unconventional way: from beyond the grave. When Constance created Alphinland, she became no longer able to drive because "she felt she was too distracted to drive.

Alphinland requires a lot of thought. It excludes peripheral details, such as stop signs" (6). Later, she sees the bushes in this dangerous landscape as looking "like fountains, their luminous foliage cascading gracefully to the ground" (12). She can never fully leave Alphinland, and her near-confinement to that secondary world is symbolized by her near-entrapment in her house by the ice storm. She scatters ashes around and behind her to provide traction on the slick steps and street, and the trail she leaves naturally reminds her of fairy tales: "Perhaps she'll be able to follow it home" (8). This is her world:

> It's the kind of thing that might occur in Alphinland—a trail of black ashes, mysterious, alluring, like glowing white stones in a forest, or bread crumbs—only there would be something extra about those ashes. Something you'd need to know about them, some verse or phrase to pronounce in order to keep their no doubt malevolent power at bay.
>
> (8)

She then brings up characters from her novels, such as Milzreth, an evil sorcerer. Light and dark, good and evil: Alphinland may be fantasy, but it is not idealized; rather, it is a place of archetypal forces, and one must navigate it carefully. If it represents her memory, then one can see why it is both beautiful and treacherous. Later in the story, she re-enters Alphinland as it exists on her computer, passing through the gateway Ewan had designed and moving once again through its irresistible landscape (16–17). She describes Gavin's attraction to her (as she sees it) in magical terms: "It was as if she radiated a ring of magic particles, as if she cast an irresistible spell, like Pheromonya of the Sapphire Tresses in Alphinland" (20). In an ironic passage, she recalls how her fans got upset about how she portrayed dragons and tried to "correct" her; she thinks, in a moment of self-blindness, "It's astonishing how folks can get so worked up over something that doesn't exist" (11).

She is at "constant" war with the realm of worldly concerns, embodied not just by Ewan but by her sons and their wives as well, who consider Alphinland a sign of insanity until it proves lucrative (4). They want her to move into a retirement home—the "practical" option—but she wishes to remain in her house as long as Ewan is there and has wisely not told them about hearing his voice (4–5). The clerk at the corner store informs her that the salt is sold out in a way that implies Constance should have been better prepared; she thinks, "How can you have a sense of wonder if you're prepared for everything? Prepared for the sunset. Prepared for the moonrise. Prepared for the ice storm. What a flat existence that would be" (9–10).

In fact, no character is either wholly imaginative or wholly pragmatic. Constance sardonically recalls her early life in Yorkville when she was broke: "she was young enough to find poverty glamorous. La Boheme, that was her" (21). We learn that she began writing the Alphinland stories not out of an outburst of imaginative excess but to earn money to support Gavin. She had little regard for her own literary creations: "she was not so stupid as to take this drivel seriously" (22). On the other hand, Alphinland becomes more and more meaningful to her over time for psychological, not aesthetic, reasons. In a lengthy flashback, Constance remembers her relationship with the egotistical, exploitative, sometimes abusive, hugely talented, and always exciting Gavin (17–26). She comes to realize that Gavin has not in fact been entranced by her but has begun addressing another "Dark Lady" in his poems (22), although the real identity of the Dark Lady is not revealed until the mini-cycle's second story. Here, Alphinland becomes

> her refuge, it was her stronghold; it was where she could go when things with Gavin weren't working out. She could walk in spirit through the invisible portal and wander through the darkling forests and over the shimmering fields, making alliances and defeating enemies, and no one else could come in unless she said they could because there was a five-dimensional spell guarding the entranceway.
> (22)

She finally discovers that he has become Marjorie's lover; he only wants Constance back when he learns how much money her Alphinland books are earning (25). In the present, for all her persistent romanticism, Constance exhibits a pragmatic streak of her own. She is somewhat proud of her ability to be practical when she buys candles and matches along with the kitty litter: "There. She's prepared" (11). Later, when the power goes out, she and Ewan both come up with measures to keep her warm and safe (29–30). She also shows the disillusioning effects of age; in the midst of a dramatic ice storm, the young reporters she watches are "excited; they say they've never seen anything like it. Of course they haven't, they're too young" (2). Meanwhile, the supposedly hard-headed characters do not lack a sense of the whimsical and imaginative. It was Ewan who constructed the gateway to Alphinland on her computer, and the very practical clerk sports a dragon tattoo. Thus, fantasy is everywhere, even among the defenders of reason and careful thought. Constance has pigeon-holed her lovers into extremes, but such easy categorizations of people simply cannot hold.

Constance is thus an unreliable narrator, but one who is occasionally aware of her unreliability—a fact that actually enhances her credibility without fully justifying her views. She does not know if she really remembers wartime bond-drive posters or only read about them (2), and "knows" that Ewan is not really speaking to her, that these are "aural hallucinations" (6)—but neither she nor the reader can be completely certain about that. She is (literally *and* figuratively?) haunted by the past in the guise of Ewan and Gavin, the emotional extremes of the men in her life. She does not light a fire because that (in her archetypal way of thinking) would be symbolic: "an act of renewal, of beginning, and she doesn't want to begin, she wants to continue. No: she wants to go back" (7). It is Ewan's past voice, the strong one he had before cancer struck, that she hears now (7). She does not remember turning on the porch light when she returns from her shopping excursion (12)—is she losing her memory or did Ewan do it? Her belief in his spectral reality is so strong that she refuses to refer to him as dead for fear of offending him (14). It might well be Ewan who tells her to shut off the computer just before the power goes out; there is no other explanation for such foresight (29). Nothing has changed between them despite his death: he remains as "mocking" and "teasing" as he was in life (4). Yet his feelings for her may have been stronger than she realizes, and the explanation for the harsh tone might be his awareness that her heart is elsewhere.

Constance assumes that the distance and coldness between them must have been the product of his having an affair, despite the absence of any evidence of infidelity (15). She confronts his ghost, and in her own mind—not any supposed outside voice—he responds to her accusatory question with the words he used so often whenever she became emotional: "*Ewan, are you seeing someone else? Pull yourself together. Use your common sense*" (16). She then asks him out loud if he was having an affair and he does not answer—probably because he does not need to (30). Deep down, she knows the real reason for her suspicion: guilt over the fact that she never felt for him the passion she never ceased to feel for Gavin. When she enters Alphinland in a dream sequence during the final pages of the story, she finds her own house there, but it is Gavin who comes to her, not Ewan, and they share a passionate kiss (30–31). Ewan asks her who "That man!" is; instead of telling him about Gavin, she once more asks him if he ever had an affair, and he fades away (32). The scene constitutes a final confrontation between dream and reality, myth and truth, and of course guilt and innocence. She concludes that Ewan has now entered Alphinland: "He's already lost. He's a stranger to Alphinland, he doesn't know its dangers. He's runeless, he's weaponless. He has no allies"—none, that is, "but her" (34). The story concludes when she decides to go in after him.

"Revenant" portrays the equally aged and far more frail Gavin, now living with his much younger wife Reynolds. He is an egomaniac and is verbally abusive towards Reynolds and indeed everyone else he speaks to, including the graduate student who comes to interview him. His egocentrism is evident from the story's first pages, when he recalls that he became attracted to Reynolds because "She herself had once been doing her thesis on his work ... It had been very seductive to him, then, to have an attractive young woman paying such concentrated attention to his every adjective" (40). He resented his children because "They and their pastel, urine-soaked paraphernalia had taken up so much space, they'd attracted so much attention that ought to have been his" (42).

He remains a glutton for attention; he is pleased to hear that Naveena, another graduate student, is coming to interview him, but learns to his horror that she has come to ask him about Constance's life and work, not his own:

> He's cornered. He can't pretend this matters to him—to be cast as a mere secondary source in the main action, the main action being Constance. Constance the fluffball, with her idiotic gnome stories. Constance the flake. Constance the bubblehead.
>
> (54)

In other words, it is clear that he has not changed at all from his youthful self, except perhaps to be aware of his physical failings. He is as arrogant as ever, but also recognizes that his body is betraying him. When Naveena shows him a video on YouTube of Constance at the World Fantasy Convention, he endures the same struggle between conflicting emotions as Constance had in the earlier story. The shock and his memories of their relationship lead him to suffer an attack of some kind, and he is confronted with the never-rivalled passion he once had for Constance. From her perspective, their relationship seemed entirely one-sided, but now we see that he had strong feelings for her after all. They seem to rejoin at the end, at his death, although whether their reunion is to be read as psychological, symbolic, or fantastically "real" is open to question.

The story's first line signals the link to "Alphinland" and the switch in point of view: "Reynolds bustles into the living room, carrying two pillows" (35). The reader may or may not remember that this is the name of Gavin's new and much younger wife, whose name Constance had derided as "dumb" (19), but then Gavin's own name appears just a few lines later. Gavin's comparison of the pillows to breasts displays his unaltered and somewhat adolescent perception of women in purely sexual terms, and his preoccupation with women's appearance, especially their behinds, pervades the story (44, 46, 63, etc.). He is also dishonest, as Reynolds warns Naveena and the reader (61): after he claims not to have read Constance's work, he thinks, "False: he has read it" (62). That fact makes him a more unreliable focalized character than Constance, meaning we have to treat his internal and external statements with great skepticism. We know that he has been contemptuous of Constance's writing and that feeling is on full display here: "Not only was Constance a bad poet, back when she was trying to be one, but she's a terrible prose writer as well. *Alphinland*: the title says it all. *Aphidland* would be even more accurate" (62). A particularly striking and revealing example of how the switch in point of view works concerns how Constance and Gavin view Marjorie. For Constance, the discovery of Gavin's affair with Marjorie is a major turning point in her life, as she ceases to be merely his plaything and supporter and becomes her own person—and an author in her own right. By contrast,

Gavin cannot even remember Marjorie's name without some effort: "He's forgotten why they broke up. It was a trivial thing; nothing that should have mattered to her. Some other woman he'd gone to bed with. Melanie, Megan, Marjorie" (52). There can be no clearer example of how two characters perceive the same incident in very different ways, and of how changing the point of view from one story in a cycle or mini-cycle to another can display that difference.

"Revenant" echoes many of the specific scenes and broader motifs in "Alphinland." Just as Ewan recommends to Constance in "Alphinland" that she take a flashlight when she leaves the house (7), Reynolds does the same to Gavin at the park when he goes into the woods to urinate (65). Constance tortures her enemies in Alphinland, and Reynolds inflicts verbal tortures on Gavin. She might well have known what Naveena is really working on and bringing her in to spring this surprise on Gavin may have been designed to give Reynolds a great deal of sadistic satisfaction (54). Evidence that Reynolds knew exactly what she was doing comes when she asks, "Did Naveena show you the video clips yet? They're fascinating! She sent them to me in a Dropbox" (55). As the video runs, Reynolds is catty about Constance and at the same time sympathetic when it comes to what Constance had to put up with during her youthful relationship with Gavin: " 'She must be tired,' says Reynolds, with satisfaction. 'Check out those bags under her eyes. Big dark circles. She must be really whipped' " (56). Gavin's response is revealing:

> "Tired?" says Gavin. He never thought of Constance as being tired.
>
> "Well, I guess she would be tired," says Naveena. "Think of all she was writing then! It was epic! She practically created the whole Alphinland ground plan, in such a short time! Plus she had that job, with the fried-chicken place."
>
> "She never said she was tired," says Gavin, because the two of them are staring at him with what might possibly be reproach. "She had a lot of stamina."
>
> "She wrote to you about it," says Naveena. "About being tired. Though she said she was never too tired for you! ..."
>
> (56)

The passage reveals much. First, Reynold's resentment, that is, jealousy, towards Constance is evident in her satisfaction at the latter's signs of exhaustion. Second, Gavin's insensitivity about what Constance was enduring is clear; we can interpret his ignorance of her being tired as pure self-absorption, or perhaps he idealized her to the point of being blind to her suffering. He seems completely stunned by the thought that she could be tired. Third, we now see Constance from the outside and how her life is interpreted by those who never met her as well as by Gavin. Constance considered her work at the restaurant to be what devoted mates of great poets ought to do, yet she harboured her own degree of resentment as his exploitation of her, too. Now, we see the outward signs of what that job was doing to her.

"Alphinland" satirizes the pretentious and hypocritical world of 1960s Yorkville culture, more specifically the poets whose devotion to art sometimes came second to their efforts to seduce women. "Revenant" also treats art satirically, skewering self-consciously "artsy" endeavours such as the grotesque production of Richard III in the park (38–39). The impression we get of the young Gavin and the people around him in "Alphinland" is confirmed in "Revenant." He had played the role of the Great Artist, but much of his approach to art was quite cynical. He had written poetry designed to break generic rules, like a revolutionary poet, but has little respect for what he had been doing:

> Those sonnets were noteworthy, first of all because they were sonnets in name only—how daring of him!—and secondly because they broke new ground and pushed the boundaries of language. Or so it said on the back of the book. In any case, that book snagged his first-ever prize. He'd pretended to view it with indifference, even disdain—what were prizes but one more level of control imposed on Art by the establishment?—but he'd cashed the cheque.
>
> (53)

Now, he writhes under the burden of who he is: Reynolds has made "shrines" out of his studies, carefully preparing his writing implements and ensuring he will not be interrupted: "Then she tiptoes around outside as if he's on life support, and then he can't write a word. He can't spin straw into gold, not in that mausoleum of a study" (47).

More importantly, the story also explores the theme of the relationship between art or the realm of imagination on the one hand and reality on the other. The production of Richard III includes oversized props that are, according to the director's notes, "symbols of Richard's unconscious, which accounted for their enlargement" (38). As outward signs of inward traits and emotions, the props and set parallel Alphinland's meaning for Constance. Alphinland is where Ewan gets lost, Constance believes, and Gavin gets lost in the park when he looks for somewhere to urinate (65). Art is thus associated in both stories with physical and emotional confusion and disorientation. Gavin's and Reynold's sexual role-playing reminds us of Alphinland's function for Constance: a world of invented but meaningful fantasy (41), one that highlights the inadequacies of real life (41). Gavin believes that Reynolds had invented a future for the two of them that soon collided with mundane life:

> This isn't what she signed up for when she married him. She most likely envisioned a fascinating life, filled with glamorous, creative people and stimulating intellectual chit-chat. And that did happen some, when they were first married; that, and the flare-up of his still

active hormones. The last kaboom of the firecracker before it fizzled; but now she's stuck with the burnt-out aftermath.

(41–42)

Meanwhile, Constance takes her own art more seriously than Gavin is willing to credit, the seriousness coming from Alphinland's status as more than pure escapist trash. Milzreth of the Red Hand, the evil wizard, returns as a character based on a real person (60). Watching Constance being interviewed at the World Fantasy Convention, Gavin sneers at what he considers her pretensions at seriousness: "That seriousness, too, he had found charming; now he finds it bogus. What right has she to be serious?" (59). We have learned from "Alphinland" that Constance took her work more and more seriously as it took on a more personal meaning for her, and now we see how that process looks from the point of view of another character, one who has personal reasons for refusing to believe it. In addition, it is surely no coincidence that the journal Gavin and Constance once used to send notes to each other is, Naveena tells Gavin, "the same sort of journal she used for the Alphinland lists and maps" (57). The notebooks symbolize the inextricable link between reality and fantasy in her life. Atwood thus establishes a point in the first story that then becomes a source of discomfort and self-serving skepticism for a different character in the second. The form of the mini-cycle allows for this kaleidoscopic perspective.

Another link is provided by the interviews in the stories: one involves a "smart-alecky young interviewer" in "Alphinland" who interprets the land's name as an attack on "alpha males" (28); the other is Naveena's interview with Gavin. Constance wants nothing to do with interviewers or fans and can no longer bear to go to conventions and see her characters demeaned by her fans' costumes and behaviour (28). Gavin, by contrast, is an attention hound, and it is a truly delightful ironic turn that Naveena's interview is not about him but about the very person who least wants that attention.

Constance represents all that Gavin has lost over time, the supposed "real love" he has thrown away or covered up under a façade of cynicism and irony. His declaration to Reynolds, "I should have married Constance" (44), may well be not just a powerless weapon to be thrown at his wife but also a truer statement than he knows. She was "His first live-in, Eve to his Adam. Nothing could ever replace that" (50). On the other hand, what appealed to him was how "pliable" she was (50), so she herself seems to have been less important to him than how she submitted to him. During the ice storm, he "imagines her holding out her arms to him, clothed in nothing but snow, with an unearthly radiance streaming out from around her. His lady of the moonglow" (52). These are, however, the lines that immediately precede his futile efforts to recall why they broke up—his betrayal seems to have meant little to *him*, suggesting his yearning for her is more about himself than her. The early film shows them as innocent young people, exhibiting all the appealing worship with which Constance treated him:

> He isn't looking at her, he's looking at the stage. She's looking at him, though. She was always looking at him. They're so sweet, the two of them, so unscarred, so filled with energy then, and hope, like children. So unaware of the winds of fate that were soon to sweep them apart. He wants to cry.
>
> (56)

It was not "fate" that separated them, of course, no matter how much he tries to attribute their break-up to great powers beyond their control, but his infidelity. He cannot help preferring Constance's past worship to Reynolds' present-day contempt.

The two stories are thus simultaneously different in how they portray the Constance and Gavin relationship and linked by common characters and motifs. Unalike as they are, Constance and Gavin share artistic temperaments and ambitions (although Gavin would bristle at such a suggestion), and they are equally good at creating imaginary worlds that represent internal states. They are profoundly drawn and connected to each other, although, at the end of the stories, while Gavin goes in search of Constance, she in turn searches for Ewan. Love, or whatever Gavin substitutes for love, ultimately leads them to seek the ones who can fulfil their deepest needs.

The third story concerns Marjorie, whose hobby at her advanced age is attending the funerals of people she did not like, in order to celebrate their deaths: "She wants to tap dance on the graves, figuratively speaking" (70). Like the other protagonists, she is aging and frail, and neither she nor her brother "is up to the actual dancing any more" (70). She learns that Gavin has died and attends his funeral in part to pay her disrespects and in part to try to meet Constance. She succeeds on both counts and, along with the reader, gains a new perspective on her former rival for Gavin's less-than-devoted affections. Like the other stories in the mini-cycle, "Dark Lady" is in third-person limited point of view; throughout the mini-cycle, then, we see the love triangle through the perceptions of all three participants, but at an ironic distance. In fact, "Dark Lady" is primarily in the point of view not of Marjorie but of Tin, her brother, through whom the reader gains yet another perspective on the triangle. The twins' points of view let us see the other characters in yet another way, and comments about Constance's and Reynolds's appearance and personality traits offer new angles on them as individuals.

The title signals that the story is linked to the others, and initially that is the only clue. Marjorie is identified by her nickname Jorrie here, and since we have never seen the nickname before, we do not immediately make the connection to the third person in the love triangle. In this story, the key relationship is not between Gavin and one of his lovers but between Marjorie and Martin, who is known by his nickname. The two put on façades in their dealings with others, including Tin's pretence that he is straight—the way that Constance uses a gender-neutral pseudonym, for example—but Tin claims they are entirely open and honest with each other: "Because they're twins they can be who they really are with each other, a thing they haven't managed very well with anyone else" (72). In truth, they are not at all "transparent" with each other, and Tin admits (internally) that he frequently lies to Jorrie to spare her feelings or avoid setting off her volatile temper (e.g., 76, 88, and 102). No one in the mini-cycle, then, is a fully reliable focalizer, and the misunderstandings multiply until the three key women in Gavin's life—Constance, Jorrie, and Reynolds—meet at his funeral.

It is during that encounter that the effects of Atwood's manipulation of point of view becomes most striking. We have seen both Constance and Gavin from the inside in the previous stories, along with a little from other characters' perspectives. In "Dark Lady," we see them mainly from the point of view of someone who barely knew Constance long ago, as well as from that of the woman responsible for the end of their relationship. Constance and Gavin are at times unrecognizable as seen through the eyes of Tin and, at one remove, Jorrie. To Jorrie or perhaps Tin—the third-person narration makes it unclear—Constance is "the embodiment of that very same wispiness and sentimentality so despised by the Poetaster" (88), and Jorrie considers her unwillingness to fight for Gavin evidence of weakness and lack of passion: "Jorrie herself would have done some hair-pulling and slapping at the very least, she claimed" (88). What we know from "Alphinland" is that Constance already suspected Gavin of being unfaithful and resented his parasitical attitude toward her, and she was more prepared to walk out on him than fight for him. Tin does not want to attend Gavin's funeral if it "is going to be all about Constance W. Starr" because Constance holds the moral high ground and Jorrie will inevitably lose the encounter (93). He sees a strength in Constance that is not evident in the story about her. Jorrie counters, "How could it be about her when I can't even remember her *name*? Anyway, she was so wispy! She was such a *pipsqueak*! I could have blown her over with a *sneeze*!" While Constance may not be a powerful individual, she is also not as delicate or "wispy" as Jorrie imagines: she had the strength to support herself and Gavin, to leave when she had to, and to write commercial fiction when she needed to make money. She was hardly a Romantic figure without grounding in the real world. Now, when they see Constance, her appearance is that of an ordinary older woman: "A short, white-haired old lady in a frumpy quilted coat. No glitter powder on her; in fact, no hint of makeup at all" (103). She is thus the opposite of Jorrie, eschewing any of the consideration of clothes and makeup that preoccupy Jorrie, and therefore someone more comfortable in her own skin. If anyone is being pretentious, it is Jorrie herself.

Gavin is subject to fairly unsympathetic comments from both twins. Jorrie refers to him as "Big Dick Metaphor" (82), and when he began pining for Constance, she called him "*pussy-whipped*" and "*limp prick*" (89). She and Tin make it clear Jorrie's interest in him had been purely sexual:

> "Just don't claim you were in love with him," says Tin. "It was low, sordid lust. You were out of your mind on hormones." ...
> Jorrie sighs. "He had a great body," she says. "While it lasted."
>
> (91)

Yet she did have some real feelings for him, as she cries at his funeral (101–02). Tin, meanwhile, refers to him as a "self-styled poet" (83), "the Poetaster" (88), and "the Poet of the Sprightly Prick" (90), among other epithets. Most importantly, Tin remembers Gavin in a very different way from Constance and Gavin himself: "He was so derivative, him and his poetry both. Sentimental trash. Quite gruesomely putrid" (83). Whether this is spoken out of sincere critical disapproval or resentment over how Gavin treated his sister is unclear, but that Gavin was hardly the original genius he and his reviewers claimed he was becomes clear later.

The character who fares the worst in the meeting of Gavin's lovers is Reynolds. She has been portrayed in "Revenant" as controlling, but in "Dark Lady" we also see her as possessive when it comes to her husband. She believed that she knew everything about him, and is shocked when Naveena tells her that Gavin is in Alphinland despite his denials:

> "He said there were a lot of things he never told you," says Naveena. "To spare your feelings. He didn't want you to feel left out because you weren't in Alphinland yourself."
> "You're lying!" says Reynolds. "He always told me everything! He thought Alphinland was drivel!"
> "Actually," says Constance, "I did put Gavin into Alphinland ... To keep him safe."
>
> (104–05)

This we have not been told before. In "Alphinland," all Constance would divulge is that she put him there to entrap him without making him suffer, but now we learn—if Constance is indeed being truthful—that she wanted to protect him, as she tells Jorrie, from the latter's "ill will ... Coupled with your anger. It's a very potent spell, you know. As long as his spirit still had a flesh container on this side, he was at risk" (105). Reynolds continues to refuse to believe that Gavin is anywhere in Alphinland, that is, that he is a continuing presence in Constance's world: " 'Gavin is not in that fucking *book*! Gavin is *dead*,' says Reynolds. She's beginning to cry" (105). With his death, he is free from her hostile "spell." Jorrie tells Constance that Gavin had broken off their relationship, but Constance "thought it was the other way around. I thought you'd wounded him" (106). As Constance and Jorrie reconcile, Reynolds is left on the outside looking in, newly aware that Gavin's life and memory belong to others perhaps more than to herself. The scene is presented from Tin's point of view, so that he and the reader witness the confrontation and resolution from a slightly distanced position.

The characters in "Dark Lady" echo those in the preceding story in much the same way that those in "Revenant" recall the ones in "Alphinland." For example, Tin controls Jorrie the way that Reynolds controls Gavin. He is a cautious manipulator: "It's best not to overreact to her. Push, and she pushes back ... So he avoids confrontation. Languor is a more efficient method of control" (75). Like Gavin, Jorrie enjoys being the centre of attention and dresses and makes herself up accordingly: Tin notes, "Jorrie wants to draw undue attention: that's the whole idea! If any of Gavin's wives are there, and especially if What's-her-name shows up, she longs to have them notice her the moment she walks in" (95). Also, Tin, like Naveena, was once a graduate student writing about an author (84).

While some motifs link pairs of the stories, other themes, symbols, and images run through all three. In effect, then, the stories mirror each other. For example, Constance watches the television news and weather; Gavin watches Richard III's corpse being excavated from a London parking lot (37), and then a report on what must be the same storm that Constance endures: "He's seen the pictures of the blizzards, the ice storms, the overturned cars and broken trees. That's where Constance must be right now: in the eye of the storm" (52). The icy conditions with which Constance copes are echoed when Naveena says about her high-heel boots, "they're comfortable, though maybe I shouldn't wear them when there's ice on the sidewalks" (51). Gavin later goes out to the patio to write: "The patio is tiled too, and can be slippery around the pool" (64). Since Gavin's funeral takes place during the same harsh winter as the other two stories are set in, the conditions in "Dark Lady" naturally remain treacherous for senior citizens, whether walking or driving (96). Characters in Constance's stories are mentioned in all three stories, particularly Milzreth of the Red Hand (pp. 28, 60, and 92).

Food is an important linking motif in the mini-cycle—just as it plays a key role throughout Atwood's fiction—as the amount the characters eat and do not eat signals their physical well-being and perhaps their diminishing interest in the world of the living. In "Alphinland," Constance has largely stopped eating, apart from cheese, crackers, and peanut butter (5), provoking concern in her family. In his final days, Ewan also stopped eating and had strong beliefs about food that was healthy and unhealthy, although he would be known to violate his own strict principles (10). Having accomplished her mission to buy something to keep her walk and steps safe, Constance suddenly feels hungry and begins to eat the chicken she bought on a whim: she has rejoined the world of the living in a more full way than has Ewan (13). Even in this act, she cannot resist associating her actions to Alphinland: "This is what people do in Alphinland when they've been rescued from something—dungeons, moors, iron cages, drifting boats: they eat with their hands" (13). Nothing in her life, it seems, is random; everything is meaningful, connected in some way with the metaphysical world she has created, even the everyday act of eating. When they were young and (she is convinced) madly in love with each other, Constance supported Gavin by working in a hillbilly-themed restaurant, sneaking out food for him (21). In "Revenant," Reynolds controls Gavin in part by promising him cookies (45, 55), and Gavin cannot control his mouth when he imagines saying to Naveena, " 'I could eat you all up' ... Mmm, mmm. Rrrr, rrrr. Oh yes!" (51), and then actually says it or makes those appalling noises. Gavin's funeral features "traditional" treats, both real and metaphorical: there are "crustless sandwiches" and lemon squares—Tin thinks, "what is a funerary occasion without a lemon square" (102)—and during the service, the "next funeral baked meat treat is not long in coming. One of the less successful Riverboat-era folksingers, much bewrinkled and with a straggling goatee that looks like the underside of a centipede, arises to favour them with a song from the period: 'Mister Tambourine Man' " (100).

Given the age of the protagonists and what happens to Gavin, it is not surprising that the passage of time, aging, and death constitute an important theme or set of themes in the mini-cycle. The past is an ongoing presence in the characters' lives, and they have different ways of preserving, or at least seeking to preserve, the past. For Constance, as we have seen, Alphinland is a kind of house of memory, where people from her past can be maintained and protected or tortured (or, in the case of Gavin, both). In "Revenant," Gavin to some extent lives in the past and looks to Constance for a means by which to return to his happier and more vigorous days. Constance's memories of her fight to maintain her independence and not be moved into a retirement home are echoed by Gavin's experiences in being cared for by Reynolds, who is as much a nurse as a wife (48). Viewing the film showing them back in 1965 is "like being drawn into a time tunnel" (55), and as Gavin dies, he is indeed transported back to their youth: "there is his Constance, young again and welcoming, the way she used to be" (68). Tin and Jorrie look at a photo of themselves in matching sailor suits:

> Gazing at their past selves, Jorrie and Tin feel a tenderness they seldom display to anyone in the present. They'd like to hug those scrumptious little scamps, those yellowing, fading echoes. They'd like to assure the pint-sized seafarers that, though their voyage through time is about to take a turn for the worse and will remain worse for a while, it will all work out in the end. Or near the end; which is, let's face it, where they are now.

> Because, voila, here they are together again. Full circle. A few inner wounds, a few scars, a few abrasions, but still standing.
>
> (76)

All three stories portray the effects of time and aging on the characters' bodies, minds, and emotions, and the protagonists are conscious of and self-conscious about their aging bodies. "Revenant" repeatedly portrays how weak Gavin has become—he is older than Constance, and much less capable of being self-sufficient. Gavin thinks of a "girl Pilates instructor" who would "contort his stringy, knobbled limbs while comparing the dashing protagonist of his earlier poems, replete with sexual alacrity and sardonic wit, to the atrophied bundle of twine and sticks he has become" (37). Because Reynolds is essentially Gavin's nurse, he is entirely at her mercy, and she certainly appears to take advantage of their new roles. More humiliatingly, she treats him like a child, giving him names for his various moods ("Mr. Grumpy, Mr. Sleepy, Dr. Ironic, Sir Sardonic, and sometimes, when she's being sarcastic or possibly nostalgic, Mr. Romantic"), and has named his penis "Mr. Wiggly" (40). Like Constance, he wants to return to the past, a time of romance and idealism, and just as (if not more) importantly creative vigour, and that explains his sudden desire to be with her again:

> In the '60s, when he was living with Constance in that cramped, sultry steam bath of a room where they stewed like prunes, back when they had no money and he certainly had no la-de-dah *study*, he could write anywhere—in bars, in fast-food joints, in coffee shops— and the words would flow out of him and through the pencil or the ballpoint onto anything flat and handy. Envelopes, paper napkins; a cliché, granted, but it was true all the same.
>
> How to get back there? How to get that back?
>
> (48)

He and Constance are trapped in time in much the same way his avatar is trapped inside the wine cask:

> Why couldn't the two of them have gone on and on forever? Himself and Constance, sun and moon, each one of them shining, though in different ways. Instead of which he's here, forsaken by her, abandoned. In time, which fails to sustain him. In space, which fails to cradle him.
>
> (52)

Tin thinks of his "wizened crotch" (73), and while he and Jorrie seem to be like the wise-cracking teams in movies of the 1930s, they can no longer maintain the "chain-drinking of martinis" the way they used to (78). Tin is Jorrie's fashion consultant and recommends she wears a scarf; when she says, "To cover up my scraggy neck?" he replies, "You said it, not me" (95). He also notices that the attendees at Gavin's funeral are mostly "the geezer generation, like Tin and Jorrie" (97). That death is one of the main themes of the mini-cycle requires little proof. Ewan has just died, although he seems unable or unwilling to disappear; Gavin dies at the end of "Revenant"; and there are numerous references to death and killing in "Dark Lady."

Identity, and in particular fluid identities, is also a central theme. In "Alphinland," Constance allows Gavin to absorb her and turn her into nothing more than his consort, until she breaks free and begins writing her Alphinland stories. Gavin engages in sexual role-playing with Reynolds, both acknowledged and unacknowledged, and with his fellow poets and other *artistes* self-consciously cultivates the image of the dis-affected Poet while also being every bit as egotistical as the persona he adopts. He wants both the acclaim and attention *and* the cheques that go with his position. Disguises abound, particularly in "Dark Lady," where Jorrie uses make-up to become different, mainly younger selves (74). Like both Constance and Gavin, then, she yearns to return to a lost youth; for his part, Tin pretends to be straight for many years, in his own form of role-playing. Changing names also recur. We do not learn until "Revenant" that Constance wrote her Alphinland stories under a pseudonym, C. W. Starr (54); that is, she has had to surrender her real identity in order to gain her own life beyond Gavin, as well as to sat-isfy a market (science fiction and fantasy fandom) that for many years discouraged women writers from writing under their full real names, leading them to hide their gender under pseudonyms and initials (e.g., James Tiptree, Jr. and C. L. Moore). Marjorie and Martin adopt their own pseudonyms, dropping the "Mar" part of their names; similarly, Jorrie refers to Gavin as "Gav" (88). In another parallel pertaining to characters' names, Constance sneers at Reynolds's name, and Jorrie does the same at Constance's: "How prissy!" (88); she then refuses to say the name, calling her "What's-her-name" through most of the story.

The possible fantastic elements in the stories, especially "Alphinland," contribute to the parallels. Characters frequently have premonitions or an ability to anticipate crises: Ewan warns and advises Constance about the ice storm, while Jorrie's and Tin's mother believes that her poorly centred photograph of her husband, one that visually cut off the top of his head, somehow contributed to his death (76). There are metaphor-ical and possible literal ghosts in all three stories. Is Ewan really a ghost, or is he Constance's conscience or practical side? The advice that Ewan gives her as the ice storm hits is uncannily prescient, suggesting that he is not just a personified part of herself but a real ghost. If he is not, and this is indeed Constance's "Ewan"-like side, then Constance and Ewan are far more alike than she realizes or perhaps wishes to believe. The title of "Revenant" refers to various characters: Ewan, Constance as she is reborn at the end of "Alphinland," and particularly Gavin, who rises up in fury when it becomes clear that Naveena is there to research Constance and Alphinland. His past is brought back to life, and at first he wallows in the ego-stroking that the interview seems to provide, but then finds himself a bit player in the story of the Alphinland's origins. Gavin echoes Ewan in his behaviour and language. He is a cynical and insulting ego-maniac, launching barbs at Constance and Reynolds—much like Ewan's put-downs of Constance—and everyone else. At one point, as Gavin starts making nasty comments about the play in the park, Reynolds warns him to be careful: " 'Your voice is louder than you think,' she whispered" (38). Thus, both Gavin and Ewan speak when they should not—Gavin because he is being rude, Ewan because he is dead. Later, when he muses about his funeral, Gavin thinks, "If only he could hover around in mid-air to watch!" (43). That is, he also becomes a ghost, if only in his imagination. The leaves that Maria skims are "already dead" yet in his poem about her Gavin revives them by referring to them as "dying" (46). The poem depicts her as the Angel of Death who has come to get him along with the leaves, so Maria is the ultimate "Dark Lady": "Is she the Angel of Death, with her dark hair,/ with her darkness, come to gather me in?" (64). At Gavin's funeral, Tin recognizes that we all become "revenants" through memory, and wonders what Gavin's ghost would be like: "All you have to do is kick the bucket and you're right back in the memory spotlight, thinks Tin. He hopes the lingering shade of Gavin Putnam will prove a friendly one, supposing it is indeed lingering" (90).

Other seemingly psychic references abound. Reynolds, Gavin believes, "casts herself as his interpreter; as if he's an oracle, spouting gnomic sayings that only the high priestess can decipher" (49). As Naveena tries to decipher which Alphinland character is based on which real person, she speaks of Gavin as possibly the source for Thomas the Rhymer "because he's the only poet in the series. Though maybe he's more of a prophet—he has the second sight as his special power" (61). When Gavin is lost in the park, who saves him? (66). Is it really Reynolds who leads him out, or has Constance magically done so? In "Dark Lady," Jorrie does hover at various funerals to which she has not been invited, if only to gloat, and Tin has barely prevented her from dyeing her hair black because it would be "way too Undead with her present-day skin tone" (73). During their conversation, Tin recites to himself, "Like the vampire, I have been dead many times" (73), thereby calling himself a revenant and unwittingly associating himself with Gavin. Psychic and magical abilities appear throughout the mini-cycle, not just in "Alphinland"; again, Jorrie and Tin are practically of one mind—"to each other they're transparent as guppies, they can see each other's innards"—but only up to a point (72). Furthermore, at Gavin's funeral, Jorrie and Constance meet and realize they are sisters under the skin. Myths, legends, and fairy tales are alluded to throughout: Tin wonders how many of his childhood memories are myths, relating them generically to the stories of Oedipus and Jason (79). Atwood's characters frequently refer to fairy-tale creatures, notably trolls:

in describing his inability to write when Reynolds treats him as a literary icon, Gavin thinks, "Rumpelstiltskin, the malicious dwarf who's the most likely shape of his Muse these days—tardy Rumpelstiltskin never shows up" (47). A few pages later, he "leers like a troll" at Naveena (49), and in "Dark Lady" Jorrie says that when she was young she "was ravished by a troll!" (82). In the latter story, Jorrie's make-up looks to Tin like "dragon scales" (103).

Perhaps the most striking motif running through and thereby connecting the three stories is the mirror: mirrors and mirroring play a role at both the symbolic and structural levels.[2] Alphinland is of course a mirror of Constance's mind, although rather than offering a faithful image, it is more like a funhouse mirror, exaggerating and rendering grotesque what it reflects. There are recurrent references to mirrors in scenes in which characters confront their deeper selves or less pleasant attributes. The stories mirror each other in various ways, most notably in how the characters relate to one another and in the theme of art and the role of the imagination. The characters frequently repeat each other's words and actions, sharing each other's thoughts, emotions, preoccupations, and motivations. Constance, Gavin, and Ewan seem at times less like individuals and more like reflections of each other. During Constance's apparent conversations with Ewan, Atwood is deliberately ambiguous about where Constance's voice ends and Ewan's begins (16), and at one point she admonishes herself—"*Constance … You're out of control*"— in a voice indistinguishable from Ewan's (32). They mirror each other's suspicions and accusations. Meanwhile, Gavin is living with his third wife, Reynolds, and we learn in "Revenant" that he is every bit as suspicious of her as Constance is of Ewan: "She must be finding consolation elsewhere. He would if he was her" (42). As for Constance and Gavin, both were romantics and poets, but her identity soon becomes subsumed into his, and she takes for granted—as does Marjorie—that she is the Dark Lady of his poems (17–18): that is, less a person than a source of inspiration. They eventually grow apart, as she finds a way to make money from her writing with her Alphinland stories and resentment at his financial dependence on her, and the final break occurs when she catches him with Marjorie. Nevertheless, they remain closely linked through their shared passion, and the stories in the mini-cycle make that link clear through some key symbols. The gateway to Alphinland is her literal and metaphorical portal to her inner life. In "Revenant," we find Gavin also looking through portals into other worlds: he stares out at a world he has little or no part of, one that also features a gate: "The window gives onto a fenced enclosure in which there's a palm tree … There's a swimming pool that he never uses, although it's heated … A girl comes by three times a week and skims them out with a net on a long handle … She lets herself in through the garden gate with a key" (45). Later, he regrets letting himself become so dependent on Reynolds: "handing over control of his correspondence to Reynolds has been a mistake, because it's given her the keys to the kingdom: she's now the gatekeeper to the Kingdom of Gavin" (46). Another poet in the mini-cycle who is dealing with life and death is Tin; he is a creative translator of Martial, and someone who has little regard for Gavin's work, yet as such is Gavin's mirror-image in his sardonic, critical stance toward others (98–99). Through Tin, we learn that Gavin was a derivative poet: Atwood therefore has made Tin a classicist solely to undercut Gavin's pretensions of revolutionary genius. Jorrie and Constance both claim to be the Dark Lady, but Maria as the Angel of Death is the real one.

Alphinland embodies the way a fantasy world can show us the real one. As already discussed, it is a reflection of Constance's mind, at once beyond reality—one that, again, "excludes peripheral details, such as stop signs" (6)—and part of it. The porous boundaries between fantasy and reality are starkly portrayed as Constance makes her ash trail (11), and her fans cannot seem to distinguish between fantasy and reality, certain as they are about what dragons are "really" like. Is she any better at seeing the distinction? At the end of the story, she believes that Ewan has disappeared into Alphinland, despite his having hated it all through their relationship:

> Secretly he hated its fame, he thought it was silly, he was humiliated by its intellectual shallowness. He resented her deep immersion in it, even while indulging her about it. And he's excluded from it, from her private world: invisible bars keep him out. They've always kept him out, ever since they met. He can't go in there.
>
> Or can he? Maybe he can. Maybe the rules of Alphinland no longer hold.
>
> (34)

In death, Ewan has invaded, that is, become part of, her past, but without the romantic imagination or passion to find his way around, or so she believes. She therefore goes after him, to save him from his alienation from her and her dreams.

The realm of art, then, is a mirror world of our own, exaggerating, distorting, and yet reflecting reality. In the stories, however, the mirrors are not just metaphorical; there are literal mirrors as well. For example, in "Alphinland," Constance compares watching high-definition television to looking into a magnifying mirror, one that reveals much but ironically presents a grotesquely distorted rather than more accurate picture of life: "It's like being forced to act as someone else's bathroom mirror, the magnifying kind: seldom a happy experience, those mirrors" (1–2). During her time with Gavin, Constance tries to see if she really is the Dark Lady of his poetry by comparing her own body to the one in the poems:

> With the aid of a hand-held mirror, Constance examined her back view. No way to rationalize it: there was no comparison. Could it

> be that when Constance was working her formerly poeticized ass off waiting tables at Snuffy's … Gavin was rolling around on their lumpy mattress with a fresh and sprightly new truelove? One with a gripping ass?
>
> (23)

In this case, the mirror provides her with a better view of reality and helps her gain a more solid footing in the world, albeit at the cost of losing her youthful passion in favour of pragmatism.

One further point on the question of art and imagination in the stories needs to be addressed: their self-reflexive elements. The first two are about writers, a feature that in itself foregrounds writing and thus, by implication, the composition of the texts themselves, while the third is about a reader, scholar, and, as translator, a creator in his own right, and it should be noted that Jorrie also had a brief career as a freelance writer (94). "Alphinland" is not just about a fantasy world but is also possibly a fantasy story, depending on whether we believe that Ewan is actually a ghost. Like Alphinland, the story is a site of memory storage and of the confluence of past and present. In "Revenant," Gavin assumes that Reynolds is preparing to play a role—to be a character in Gavin's life story, one that she wishes to control the way an author controls her own characters:

> She's polishing up her widow act; she wouldn't want it to go to waste. She's so competitive that she'll hang in there to make sure neither of the two previous wives can lay claim to any part of him, literary or otherwise. She'll want to control his narrative, she'll want to help write the biography, if any.
>
> (42)

Later, as he tries to maintain his focus on the upcoming interview with Naveena, he thinks—using literary terminology—"He must show her that he isn't drifting away, losing the plot" (52). Tin keeps a journal (80), a fact that in itself makes him a writer, too, and one that may remind us of Gavin's journals. Also, Naveena may be a scholarly rather than a creative writer, but her metafictional role is also significant. At the end of "Dark Lady," she becomes an embodiment of Alphinland, its author, and Constance's lovers simply by virtue of writing about them, as she becomes another in a series of characters who preserve memories through the act of composition:

> Young Naveena can scarcely believe her luck. Her mouth's half open, she's biting the tips of her fingers, she's holding her breath. She's embedding us in amber, thinks Tin. Like ancient insects. Preserving us forever. In amber beads, in amber words. Right before our eyes.
>
> (107)

Like any cycle, the Alphinland mini-cycle achieves its effect by balancing the autonomy of the individual stories and their links. The stories portray the same characters, but show them to us from different angles, inside and out, while always exhibiting their unity through common images and symbols as well. By composing the Constance–Gavin–Marjorie narrative as three separate yet tightly linked stories, Atwood succeeds in both shifting point-of-view from story to story and creating a single narrative arc out of the component texts.

Notes

1 Atwood has long been interested in popular fiction, including such genres as gothic literature, science fiction, and fantasy, as can be seen in her non-fiction text *In Other Worlds: SF and the Human Imagination* (2011) as well as novels like *Lady Oracle* (1976), *The Handmaid's Tale* (1985), *The Blind Assassin* (2000), and the MaddAddam Trilogy: *Oryx and Crake* (2003), *The Year of the Flood* (2009), and *MaddAddam* (2013). Commentary on her fantastic works in both long and short forms is extensive.

2 On mirroring and dualities in Atwood's fiction, see the studies by Sherrill Grace, Russell M. Brown (esp. p. 34), Frank Davey, J. Brooks Bouson, Nora Foster Stovel, Coral Ann Howells, Gloria Onley, Eleonora Rao, Jerome H. Rosenberg, Sharon Rose Wilson, and Lorraine M. York, among many others.

References

Atwood, Margaret. *The Blind Assassin*. McClelland and Stewart, 2000.

——. *The Handmaid's Tale*. McClelland and Stewart, 1985.

——. *In Other Worlds: SF and the Human Imagination*. Signal, 2011.

——. *Lady Oracle*. McClelland and Stewart, 1976.

——. *MaddAddam*. McClelland and Stewart, 2013.

——. *Oryx and Crake*. McClelland and Stewart, 2003.

——. *Stone Mattress: Nine Tales*. Toronto: McClelland and Stewart, 2014.

——. *The Year of the Flood*. McClelland and Stewart, 2009.

Bouson, J. Brooks. *Brutal Choreographies: Oppositional Strategies and Narrative Design in the Novels of Margaret Atwood*. U of Massachusetts P, 1993.

Brown, Russell M. "Atwood's Sacred Wells." *Essays on Canadian Writing*, no. 17, Spring 1980, pp. 5–43.

Davey, Frank. "Alternate Stories: The Short Fiction of Audrey Thomas and Margaret Atwood." *Canadian Literature*, no. 109, Summer 1986, pp. 5–14.

Grace, Sherrill. *Violent Duality: A Study of Margaret Atwood*. Véhicule Press, 1980.

Howells, Coral Ann. *Margaret Atwood*. St. Martin's Press, 1995.

Onley, Gloria. "Power Politics in Bluebeard's Castle." *Canadian Literature*, no. 60, Spring 1974, pp. 21–42.

Rao, Eleonora. *Strategies for Identity: The Fiction of Margaret Atwood*. Peter Lang, 1993.

Rosenberg, Jerome H. *Margaret Atwood*. Twayne, 1984.

Stovel, Nora Foster. "Reflections on Mirror Images: Double and Identity in the Novels of Margaret Atwood." *Essays on Canadian Writing*, no. 33, Fall 1986, pp. 50–67.

Wilson, Sharon Rose. *Margaret Atwood's Fairy-Tale Sexual Politics*. U of Mississippi P, 1983.

York, Lorraine M, editor. *Various Atwoods: Essays on the Later Poems, Short Fiction, and Novels*. House of Anansi Press, 1995.

6 The Collection of Mini-Cycles

An especially noteworthy, and one can even say radical, example of the three-story mini-cycle can be seen in Denise Roig's *Any Day Now* (2004; see my review). The collection is made up entirely of story trilogies, or what she calls "trios," and they are quite different from the ones we have analyzed thus far. The stories in each mini-cycle are largely linked by setting, and the first and third stories deal with the same characters, albeit at different periods in their lives. Roig explains in her preface that the collection's formal roots lie not in literature but in music and dance:

> In the 1920s, Martha Graham and Louis Horst developed a method of making modern dance based on the sonata, or A-B-A, form: exposition, development, recapitulation. I learned to choreograph this way as a dance student at the Juilliard School of Music. It was, I soon saw, a way to order space; make connections; tell a story. Beginning, middle, and end. Forty years later, I have returned to this structure with these trios of short stories.
>
> (11)

As I noted in my review of the work, "Roig is interested in exploring the wider artistic opportunities afforded by such a flexible form" (17). We do not have space to look at all the mini-cycles, of course, but a close reading of a representative example will convey a sense of Roig's technique.

The second mini-cycle is entitled, "After Quebec," and is made up of "Good Men," "Un, Deux, Trois ... Soleil!" and "Top of the World." All three are about French-Canadian families who have moved down to Massachusetts to work in the textile mills there. The protagonists face the divided cultural identity that such economic exile almost inevitably produces. In "Good Men," the protagonist is Alexandrine Lachance, a grandmother who complains bitterly—but comically—about her husband's compulsive acts of charity and her grown children's constant reliance and even dependence on her babysitting services. Both involve sacrifices on her part; Benoit's food and financial donations mean she must do with less, although not substantially so (41–42), and the babysitting is a drain on her time and energy. Benoit certainly seems obsessed with shopping for the poor, although we later discover that he has long found in the supermarket a place where he can escape the chaos of their big family (49). As for the other problem, her daughter Chantal does indeed phone during the narrative to ask her to baby-sit so that she can go to a concert with a friend (49). Alexandrine, taking a stand at last, refuses, but not long afterward Jacinthe calls begging her to babysit her son Joey so that Jacinthe can go out and search for her current boy-friend, with whom she is, as she is with every man, "crazy in love" (50). Alexandrine relents after Jacinthe's second desperate phone call.

We are also told that Benoit has never sexually satisfied her, except for one time when she had felt "flutters down there" (42), and now he has no interest in sex at all. She thinks, "She didn't miss it—how can you miss what you don't like?—but it left a space in the nights somehow" (42). She hopes that Jacinthe is not sleeping with her boyfriend, Jess, but thinks that is unlikely: "she had to assume that the crazy in love might have something to do with that" (50). Alexandrine may be jealous of her daughter's more active, and presumably more satisfying, sex life. Sexual frustration, we will see, is one of the motifs linking "Good Men" and "Top of the World."

In the opening scene, Benoit is late for church because of one of his charitable shopping expeditions, and when he finally arrives, Father Bruce praises him for exhibiting the true spirit of the Christmas season. Both the priest and Benoit are clearly "good men," but for Alexandrine, Benoit is too concerned about others and not enough about her. Alexandrine believes strongly in maintaining the community's roots in Québec. Father Bruce also comes from a Québécois family, but his parents had fully assimilated—thus his very English name—and never taught him proper French. For Alexandrine, this is a horrible betrayal:

> Why hadn't his parents spoken French to him at home? Alexandrine wondered, not for the first time. Unlike *her* parents who, bless their dear, departed, French-Canadian souls, never did quite get the hang of English, Father Bruce's parents had been way too eager to get American.
>
> (44)

On the other hand, she is angry at Benoit's friend Pierre Lafleur for intro-ducing him to the Québécois custom of *la Guignolée*, which here and now involves "singing off-key, ringing doorbells, dressed in Santa suits, asking neighbours for handouts so they could give it to some poor Puerto Rican" (46). The issue of French-Canadian versus American identity becomes a central theme throughout the mini-cycle.

As far as Alexandrine is concerned, Benoit has gone too far in his charitable work, to the point of insanity (e.g., 42, 46). She does not know what to do with or about him and wishes that she could ask her late mother for advice. Unfortunately, Maman is dead and has taken her ancient wisdom with her. The idea that the dead have advice for the living will recur in the final story. The older generation represents not just wisdom but narrow-mindedness and stubbornness as well. Maman had not approved of Benoit as a husband for Alexandrine because of his looks, and Alexandrine had defended him on the grounds that he was "a good, decent, French-Canadian Catholic" (47): in other words, she had used her mother's prejudice against her. She in fact shares that prejudice and has taught her own children that "Too many spices spoil the soup. A little salt, hold the pepper, you're just fine, she said. *Marry your own*" (48). She watches only the cable Catholic station on the TV and regularly says her rosary (48–49). While she has adopted her mother's strict beliefs, other children and grandchildren have rebelled against these edicts, or tried to, with mixed results (48). These conflicts between the generations will be echoed in the other stories in the mini-cycle.

Benoit is away yet again helping others when Jacinthe drops off her son, so Alexandrine has to deal with him alone. What Jacinthe has not told her is that Joey is sick, and now Alexandrine has to cope with a feverish, vomiting four-year-old. To make matters worse, two men break into the house while she is in the bathroom tending to Joey (55). She hides from them in the bathtub and never sees them; she only realizes that they are strangers when she hears them swear in English. Through much of the story she has revealed not only her strong belief in the merits of French but also her hatred of swearing (e.g., 42, 54), although she exhibits her somewhat flexible moral principles by often using phrases that include "shit." Joey whimpers in her arms, but the thieves seem not to have heard him and leave the house without looking in the bathroom.

After a scene break, it is some hours later, when Alexandrine is telling her story to two policemen—one of whom, it turns out, is also of French-Canadian origins (as revealed in his reference to his "Mémé") (56). Benoit has finally returned home, and Jacinthe eventually arrives to comfort her mother and child. It does not take long after the officers have departed for Alexandrine to be obliged to revert to her maternal role, however. Jacinthe tells her that Jess does not want her any more, and Alexandrine comforts her the way she had had to comfort Joey through his brief illness (58).

That night, Alexandrine blames Benoit's poor people for the break-in and believes that she is fortunate she and Joey were not found and murdered by the thieves. But then she recalls that the "boots had stopped at the door just before Joey had whimpered" and that she and Joey had made other sounds as well (59). She realizes, "*They knew we were there*" (59). Out of gratitude and respect for Benoit, they chose to leave her unharmed. She gains a new appreciation for her husband's status as a "good man"; she is also relieved that old-fashioned values still count for something even in this new American home, and is ashamed of her lack of faith:

Benoit wasn't going to change and those men had spared them, her and little Joey, and suddenly she was weeping. Maybe it was true. Everything she'd been taught by the nuns, the priests, all those sermons dished up and delivered, all those words from the apostles. Maybe God did protect them. And loved them! Loved them to distraction, without limit. She wept at the thought of all that love, wept for all the years before she'd known this.

(60)

The physical love she had been missing in her marriage is compensated for by the divine love she sees in her and Joey's being spared any harm.

In keeping with the A-B-A structure of the mini-cycles, "Un, Deux, Trois … Soleil!" is about an entirely different set of characters, yet the story is linked at the thematic level, and through common motifs, with the first and third stories. The focus again is on a family of Franco-Americans in Massachusetts. Teenager J-P (Jean-Pierre) is reluctantly attending the funeral of his aunt Jocelyne in Québec; he chooses to go "because *ma tante* Jocelyne had been pretty cool and because Isabelle and all the other cousins would be there" (61). Jocelyne, J-P recalls, was "the funniest of the Quebec gang, the one who swore and chain-smoked, the only one who'd never married" (62). The reference to swearing is just one of many motifs connecting this text to the two "A" stories. In another link, the story begins with Jocelyne's funeral, and the church setting recalls the early scene in the church in "Good Men." Benoit had been quite disruptive in his late entrance into the church after picking up supplies for the poor, and J-P and other family members are distracted by what is happening at the back of the church as well, all staring as his uncles Sylvain and Antoine struggle with the coffin (61). Sexuality is another linking theme; hints of J-P's attraction to Isabelle come when he singles her out among the cousins he hopes to see at the funeral (61), and at the church he thinks, "Isabelle was busting out—J-P felt a little flush building—of a short, black, clingy dress" (63). He and Isabelle walk together to the cemetery, and Isabelle takes his arm (64).

Other themes form much more important links among the stories. That of linguistic, cultural, and physical borders, so prominent in "Good Men," appears early on. The family is now in an entirely English environment, but J-P thinks of his aunt by her French title (*"tante"*) and, when they cross the border into Canada, Norm reverts to his real name, Normand. Throughout the story, J-P is in the wider family circle that his Americanized immediate family had to leave behind in order to assimilate. Jocelyne, in her association with humour, smoking, and swearing, represents the vitality that has been sacrificed in the family's move south. J-P has lost his French skills, and his high-school lessons have done little to help him follow the funeral service: *"Je comprends, je comprends!* He was used to waving everyone off with this, grinning, throwing in a couple of not too objectionable Québécois swear words so none of the cousins would come to his rescue" (62). Again, swearing plays a role, if minor, in the story's language theme. At the post-funeral reception, his family members pronounce his initials in the French way: "Jee-Pay!" (66), and while surprised at first he grows used to it, as he always does at such gatherings—a point to which we will return.

After the funeral, as the family prepares to leave for the reception, J-P recalls the stories he had heard about why his family moved south and the harsh feelings that the move created:

> There'd been rough times up here on the farms back in the fifties, not enough work and too many kids, and so lots of families had had to send some of the older children south, mostly to places like western Massachusetts where they could find work in the mills that made paper or shoes or textiles ... According to Ma, Sylvain and Antoine resented Pa's being able to escape the family dramas, to go to the great U.S. of A., learn English, attend trade school and become a mechanic with his own garage. Meanwhile, Pa resented being sent away. He'd missed out big, he said, on the important stuff, like family, like feeling he belonged somewhere.
>
> (65)

His family ties were strained both physically and emotionally by the move. For such a close family, they seem to communicate little: presumably knowing how Normand felt would have relieved Sylvain and Antoine of their resentment. Ironically, Normand's family exists precisely because he moved to the United States and met his future wife there.

Instead of constant bickering and resentment between mother and daughter, as in the first story, here the main family conflict is between father and son. Parental authority and child rebellion here parallel what occurs in the other stories. At first, J-P does not want to go to the funeral, but Pa would not accept the embarrassment if other family members brought children and he did not (61). Still, it remains J-P's decision, and he chooses to go as long as it is finally up to him. J-P resents Norm's authoritarian approach to parenting, like his "usual on-his-ass alerts" about how to behave (61). At the funeral, J-P watches his father carrying the coffin: "now as Pa came up the aisle, he looked his normal stick-up-the-ass self" (62). Normand is thus a constant voice in J-P's head, judging and condemning, and J-P does not need his father to speak to know what he will say, such as how he would react to cousin Isabelle's dress (63). Yet J-P is very much his father's son and sits as motionlessly as possible during the funeral to avoid giving his family members reason to accuse him of not paying attention (63). Like his father, J-P is concerned about appearances and does not want to face criticism from relatives. Perhaps the voice he hears in his head is not entirely his father's now.

The theme of family is illustrated in another and more significant way: the fact that none of these characters is a separate individual, but all are products of and embedded in the family. J-P is struck with this truth when he sees the backs of his father's and uncles' heads, "seeing for the first time that Pa and the uncles all parted their hair the same way—long strands brushed up and over to the right. They sat there like balding triplets, probably thinking they were fooling everyone with their comb-overs" (63). The similar way they wear their hair symbolizes the brothers' family connection; it is unclear whether J-P understands it, but what he is being shown is proof that Pa—in all his traits, good and bad—is not just himself but also a single element in a larger whole. Even more startling is that he sees Jocelyne herself sitting on one of the pews, attending her own funeral:

> Yeah, it was her. She was wearing her usual outfit: tight jeans with a long T-shirt; but she looked as if she'd just come from the hairdresser's … *Tante* Jocelyne turned around and smiled. Was she smiling at him? They'd always had a special something, even if he'd barely under-stood her. Then she wasn't there anymore and J-P was glad and sad, disappointed and relieved. Some tears finally came.
>
> (64)

Throughout the story, J-P moves back and forth between past and pre-sent, Massachusetts and Québec, beginning with his memories of the church and comparisons with the one he now attends in Granby (63). He recalls receptions at other similar family events: "This was the best part of any visit, but the worst, too, because it was when he had to talk" (66). *Tante* Jocelyne's appearances are one way in which the past refuses to be left behind. J-P, like the other members of the family, is haunted and made who he is by the family that produced him. The story is ultimately about his acceptance of his family as the shaper of his identity. Earlier, we saw that he grows accustomed at every family gathering to the French pronunciation of his initials, and his response is revealing:

> By the end of any visit it felt as if this was the only way to say his name. Truth was, by the end of most visits he didn't feel much like going home … Granby, Massachusetts, was OK as places go, and he had some good, old friends like Josh whom he'd known since kinder-garten. But life wasn't thick with people like it was here.
>
> (66)

His father could not have expressed it any better.

It is at this point that J-P hears the younger cousins playing the same game that he used to play with the cousins of his own age—the name of which lends the story its title—and that Jocelyne had insisted he play. The cousins were always better at the game than he, something that used to frustrate him as he tried to fit in. Now, as he is reminded of this family legacy by its continuation among the current generation of young children, Jocelyne reappears. She speaks to him in French, and he asks her to switch to English, but she refuses, assuring him, "*Mais tu comprendras toute, je te promets* [But you will understand everything, I promise]" (67). She tells him what life was like for her, Normand, and their brothers under the authoritarian rule of their father: "In our family, we've had lots of papas like this ... Full of corrections when they should have been full of love" (68). She then describes Jean-François's grief when Normand moved to the United States, as he revealed the depth of his love too late for Normand to see it (68). At the end, on his way home, J-P thinks about her final words to him: "Love him for me?" (69). Thanks to his encounter with his family's past, in the form of Jocelyne's ghost, he learns he must overcome his own resentments toward his father, to see the love behind the harsh façade, and thereby come to terms with the past and its role in shaping his father and himself as he strives for the future.

In "Top of the World," Jacinthe returns as Jackie; it is now five years later, and she is more fully Americanized, as reflected in her name change— one that parallels Normand's—while Joey has grown into a troubled youth. The story is narrated from the perspective of a man named Ben, and so we see Jackie through the eyes of a man who is only interested in picking up a woman for a brief sexual encounter. The story begins as the characters sit in a bar, and Ben overhears Jackie and her friend speaking about Joey, whom Jackie refers to as "psycho. Five hundred percent" (70), an echo of Alexandrine's silent declarations about her husband's insanity. Ben focuses far more on her physical appearance: "Slender legs, and—he leaned a little into his curved end of the bar to get the fuller picture—yes, large breasts" (70). After a brief conversation, they go back to her apartment for sex, and after their shower she is as conscious of the quality of her physique as he is: "Her breasts (firm! spectacular!) were part of the conditioned package. Could an amazing body be the basis of a relationship? Yes, by God, yes" (72). He, by contrast, is ashamed of "his desk-job paunch" (72). His shallowness is further illustrated when he wonders if "at one point he could get up, walk across the room, open, then close, the door and have it be OK that they'd never see each other again," but changes his mind when he sees her body inside her T-shirt (72). We soon discover that he is divorced due to an equally superficial sexual act with his secretary (74).

Jackie asks him his last name, and that is when she learns that Ben's family is also originally from Québec and even from the same part of it. In fact, he divulges later in the story that he is another Benoit, and like so many other characters in the mini-cycle is now going by an anglicized version of his name. Jackie responds, "That's my Dad's name ... Don't make me cry" (77). This touch of home and a somewhat happier past raises her hopes for their relationship, which are soon to be dashed. He is a corrupt version of her father, a man without faith, love, or charity. After their initial encounter, Ben does not call her for some time, and in the interlude we learn about his infidelity to his ex-wife: he "even confessed to Dayna. But it figured in both their (complicated, modern) Catholic codes as betrayal" (74). He is a Catholic when it comes to guilt and is prepared to accept the consequences of that betrayal, but certainly does not act in accordance with Catholic principles. He has also lost much of his French, like the more Americanized characters in the other stories, and can only manage "*C'est vrai* [That's true]" during one of his conversations with Jackie (77).

He finally phones Jackie on his return from a business trip, invites her to his condominium, and again he seems mostly interested in her appearance: "She looked small but built" (74). She tells him about her day dealing with a difficult mother at the day-care where she works, and as is her habit, perhaps one she inherited from her mother, she calls the mother "crazy," too (75). In fact, this is a term she will also apply to her own mother when she and Ben compare notes on their mothers: "Mine drives me crazy" (77). The narrator, using Ben's words, describes what they have together in familiar terms: "It was crazy, but lust was crazy. In the days after, he couldn't stop thinking about the way they were together, the things they made each other feel. Dayna could really get into sex, but on her terms and timing, and some of the women since had been pretty hot. But not like this" (76). It is "crazy" because it is mindless and emotionless, and he has also become somewhat addicted to Jackie. Perhaps he sees in her a suggestion of something more, however: she might represent a different, more settled life.

That may be why Ben is so curious about Joey. During their first sexual encounter, he asks her to explain why she said that her son was insane, expressing doubt that she meant it, but she reassures him that she did (71–72). The way she talks about Joey becomes a source of concern for Ben, for reasons that are never clear to him, and when she asks him if he has children, he replies, " 'Nope' … because why get into it?" (73). He may be so interested in Joey because he and Dayna never had children. Jackie divulges that Joey has epilepsy and behavioural problems, and that his father was a deadbeat dad (73). Parent–child relationships are quite fraught in the story, then, and as we learn about Joey in some detail, we are left to imagine how Ben—still affected by his Catholic upbringing—feels about never becoming a father. That there is a secret yearning in him for a family only becomes clear toward the end of the story. The theme of family is thus stronger here than one might expect in a story about casual sex. The comparison that Jackie and Ben make between their mothers shows that like Alexandrine, Ben's mother judges others by how Catholic they are—more specifically, by whether they attend Mass: "Like it's the only thing that makes a person a good person, you know?" he says. The term "good" is likely an allusion to the first story.

The title of the story refers to the Carpenters song, a happy love song sung by a troubled woman. It is playing in the bar when Jackie and Ben meet and it spurs their first conversation; Jackie sings it toward the end of their "date"—if it can be called that—to Ben's insincere compliments on her musical skills (73). They have a date at the same bar where they met, and he puts "Top of the World" on the jukebox as if it is "their" song—their relationship is a parody or vulgar version of a romantic one. He sings it to her after they have revealed their true, French names to each other: it is as if they have experienced a communion of sorts, a real connection that both pleases and frightens them (77).

In the last part of the story, Ben, like the elder Benoit, makes an effort to be a "good man." The babysitting issue returns: Jackie and Ben plan a date, and when her efforts at making babysitting arrangements for their date (including asking her mother, of course) fail, he invites her to bring Joey along. He seems to be moving toward a more serious involvement with Jackie:

> He couldn't avoid the boy forever and it did look as if they were going to be a thing for a while. and maybe it would even do Joey some good having a man around, and be good for Jackie, too, just a bit of relief, another adult, someone to count on, and it was time to take some responsibility.
>
> (78)

Remarkably, then, he is thinking about someone else's needs for a change. They plan to meet at an A&W, whose décor reminds Ben of his youth—as with J-P, the past is present in profound ways for Ben.

Unlike Jackie's father, however, this Benoit is only half-heartedly attempting to be a "good man"; Joey acts up at the restaurant, calling Ben and his mother "dumbhead" and compulsively drumming on the table. Jackie takes the boy into the bathroom, since Joey has a history of making messes if left on his own; the reader cannot help recalling Joey's illness and the bathroom scene in "Good Men." Ben goes up to the counter to order for them and sees the fast-food image of family portrayed on the menu, a romanticized version of family in the same way that Karen Carpenter's song is the idealized version of love. He leaves the restaurant and drives off. At the end, he remembers his ex's philosophy, one reminiscent of the older Benoit's determination to do the right thing:

> "Feel equal to high and splendid braveries." The quote Dayna had taped to her computer came back like an old catechism. It had still been there on the stick-it note when he'd packed it up for her. Well, now he knew: He wasn't equal to such things. His hands shook on the wheel, but he didn't turn back.
>
> (80)

Ben is a corrupted version of Benoit in more than name.

A few further points can be made about the way Roig has constructed the mini-cycle. The theme of border-crossing is reflected in the fact that the first story is set in the United States, the second involves crossing into Québec, and the third crosses back, in a sense, into the US. The setting thus recapitulates the movements of the families. Also, the stories reflect the changes in point of view that characterize the genre, particularly between the first and third stories. Babysitting and whether children can be left on their own is a common theme in the "A" stories and in "Un, Deux, Trois ... Soleil!" where J-P is old enough to stay home but elects not to. The first story prepares us for Jacinthe's babysitting difficulties not only in "Good Men" but also in the final story, and we see the issue from both the long-suffering mother's and the house-bound daughter's perspectives. Alexandrine does not want to revert to motherhood, feeling that she has done her share of child-raising; meanwhile, Jacinthe wants to move forward, to establish a new relationship or simply have sexual experiences. In the first story, Alexandrine suffers a disastrous evening because she has Joey; in the third, Jacinthe suffers a disastrous date for the same reason. Jacinthe is socially and sexually frustrated, and has good practical reasons for wanting to date, marry, and gain the benefits of having another breadwinner around. We have already learned, however, that she has gone to this particular child-care well too often and suffers the consequences of that history.

The "B" story also deals with generational relationships, this time portraying an older child and a posthumously child-rearing aunt. That is, Jocelyne is the counterpart to Alexandrine: each becomes directly involved in the raising of a family child that is not her own. J-P, however, is old enough to be the point of view character and to learn a lesson about family bonds. As an adolescent, he naturally resents being forced to attend family functions, but the occasion proves educational for him, particularly in seeing his father and himself as inextricably bound in their family. The A-B-A structure provides both unity and distinctness among the stories, reinforcing the balance between "the one and the many" Lynch and others describe as a hallmark of short story cycles.

It should be noted that *Any Day Now* is not the only story collection to contain more than one mini-cycle. Deena Goldstone's *Tell Me One Thing* (2014), for example, is made up of eight stories, six of which belong to a pair of unrelated three-story mini-cycles: the first comprises "Get Your Dead Man's Clothes," "Irish Twins," and "Aftermath," while the second is made up of "What We Give," "The Neighbor," and "Wishing." Each is primarily linked by character, and the first features shifts in point of view to portray the same family from different perspectives. Space does not permit further analysis of these mini-cycles, but Goldstone's collection shows that Roig's multi-mini-cycle collection is not unique; further research will be needed to identify more.

References

Goldstone, Deena. *Tell Me One Thing*. Doubleday, 2014.

Roig, Denise. *Any Day Now*. Signature, 2004.

Weiss, Allan. "A Sextet of Trios." Review of *Any Day Now*, by Denise Roig, *Literary Review of Canada,* July-Aug. 2005, p. 17.

7   The Two-Story Mini-Cycle

Most mini-cycles appear to be composed of three stories, but a number of them are made up of only two. These pairs of stories appear in both book-length cycles and in story collections. The cycles in which two-story mini-cycles appear are generally linked by theme, while the mini-cycles are linked by character. When the mini-cycle is published in a collection of otherwise unrelated stories, the two stories tend to be printed together at the beginning of the book. Of course, there are no universal conventions about how two-story mini-cycles are published, but it is remarkable how often authors follow these principles. Furthermore, while the three-story mini-cycle features shifts either in point of view or in temporal setting, the two-story mini-cycle favours less radical manipulation of point of view or time, and the stories, as one might expect, act as mirrors of each other. A few examples of the form will illustrate the ways in which authors use it, above all to show two sides of an incident, relationship, or theme.

The component stories of the mini-cycle in Sandra Birdsell's *The Two-Headed Calf* (1997) concern a divorced writer, Lorraine, and her daughter Christina. "I Used to Play Bass in a Band" is narrated in the first person by Lorraine, while "The Midnight Hour" is in third-person limited with Christina as the focalized character. We see each of the two protagonists from the other's perspective and learn about the complex nature of their relationship in the light of generational differences and the fact that Lorraine is an artist, a mother, and, whether she realizes it or not, a somewhat lonely person. The stories are in reverse chronological order, with the second set a few years before the first. They mirror each other in a variety of ways, sharing common themes, images, and symbols while treating these elements in ways shaped by the generational and other differences between the protagonists. Both stories are dominated by motifs involving music and housing, include characters who are misfits and, in some cases, suicidally depressed, and offer portraits of the rebellious or confused younger generation, first through Christina and the brothers she introduces her mother to in "I Used to Play Bass in a Band," and then through Christina herself, her group of friends, and the potentially dangerous young man they meet in "The Midnight Hour."

In "I Used to Play Bass in a Band," Lorraine has just returned home to Winnipeg from house-sitting on the West Coast. Christina has recently moved out, and Lorraine accepted the invitation to go west because she found the house too quiet and empty without her daughter: "Months after Christina had left I ran away from the silence" (9). She found Vancouver a vibrant, exotic place, but what Lorraine most wants now is to repossess her home, which she had rented out to a musician/music teacher, and make it her own once more. Roland, a friend and "historian and custodian" of the community (1)—that is, the local gossip—visits to bring her up to speed on what has been happening in the neighbourhood. At first, she is unaccustomed to the city and her space: "Winnipeg, my street, and Roland seemed blunt and excessively ordinary" (1). Yet the very ordinariness of her house, neighbourhood, and neighbours is what she hungers for, because they are sources of comforting certainty and familiarity. Lorraine seeks to preserve the past, if only on her own terms. The story opens with her "salvaging the clematis vines that had become intertwined with fleabane, amazed as always at how the wilderness of the prairie is only as far as the back gate and marches in at the slightest whiff of carelessness" (1). That is, she is trying to keep the outside world out. A stranger named Terry arrives and mistakes her for her tenant; he proves to be another Roland, someone whose knowledge of the neighbourhood extends well beyond Roland's, even to its prehistory (7). Lorraine describes the neighbourhood as a holdover from the 1960s—"what was once Winnipeg's granola belt" (6)—complete with trees that are survivors of Dutch elm disease (6). She wants her house to be a solitary refuge, and toward her goal of "reclaiming" (2) her house, she considers redecorating and even repainting it to eliminate all traces of the musician (2–3). She interrupts her plans when a bag of photographs strangely falls from its shelf, and she organizes the photos into albums as if determined to impose order on her home: "Eleven identical albums, their spines dated and subjects listed, now line a shelf in the living room for my children to invent histories to puzzle over" (5).

Lorraine's desire to erase the tenant's lingering presence in the house has led her to make no mention of her name; when Terry calls her "Marion," she says, "I forgot to say that my tenant's name was Marion Turnbell" (5). It is an odd admission for a narrator to make to her reader; narrators conventionally do not "forget" things and simply divulge information when it is the appropriate time to do so. What the line signals to the reader is that Lorraine feels she *should* give all the information she can, but for some reason she "forgot" a key detail about a character. She is thus a self-conscious narrator aware of her responsibility to tell everything she knows, yet also asserting and exercising full control over her material as well as her house. Had Terry not called out Marion's name, Lorraine presumably would have continued to "forget" to say it.

Lorraine plays the role of a good host and brings Terry refreshments. Terry takes an offered glass of iced tea "as though it had his name on it" (5), a comment that both suggests her compulsive possessiveness and foreshadows a revelation she will shortly have about him. When he unhesitatingly grabs a handful of nuts from a bowl and refers to all the books and the print of van Gogh's *Starry Night* that she has, he reveals a disturbing familiarity with her house (8). It turns out that he and Marion had been lovers. Toward the end of the story, Terry returns the *Rocks and Minerals Guide* that Marion had lent him, even though it is Lorraine's (21). None of her property rights had been respected, much to Roland's amusement.

Despite all her efforts at preserving her privacy and protecting her space, people and other creatures keep coming to or returning to her house. When she bought it, she discovered that it came with a cat that somehow manages to return to it no matter how hard she tries to send it away (3–4). In fact, much of the story is about the "home invaders" with which she must cope: not only her tenant, but also the band that Christina brought home—without consulting Lorraine first—allowing them to use the garage to practice and to store their possessions in after becoming homeless (9). At age four, Christina had threatened to run away from home, and Lorraine says, "The trick to keeping her put, I eventually realized, would be to let her bring the world home. Thus the cats, the dogs, the band" (10). Birdsell creates a link between the various human violators of Lorraine's personal space by making them all musicians: the band, the tenant who played "double-bass" in the Winnipeg Symphony, and eventually Terry, who will soon become the latest rescued being.

What Lorraine may not see is that if Christina insists on taking in strays, it is only because she has learned to do so from her mother, who is a compulsive care-giver and rescuer. We learn early that Lorraine has a strong nurturing instinct. As we have seen, the story begins with her tending to her plants, trying to save them from "foreign" invaders. Like Christina, she cannot resist trying to rescue anyone or anything needing to be saved. When Terry comes by seeking Marion, Lorraine immediately thinks of him as someone she must help: "His breathless run-on way of talking, his young voice scooping up at the end of each sentence in a question, had a disarming quality; I recognized the wooing call of the vulnerable in it. Against my new spirit of non-involvement, I was intrigued by his appearance" (6). Later, as he is leaving, she thinks, "In the glare of the streetlight, he looked undernourished and too pale" (21).

She becomes strongly involved in the lives of Glenn, Jason, and Michael, the members of the band, now that their mother has died and left them homeless (11–12). She had already exhibited continuing and compulsive concern for one of Christina's boyfriends, an asthmatic, even after they broke up (13), sympathy for lost and abandoned children all over the world, and strays in general (13–14). When she agrees to take the band members in, she thinks about them in the same terms as the prairie plants: "I saw spores, and tufts of white wind-blown seeds, seeds parachuting into my flower beds about to take root" (15)—but that does not stop her from caring for and about them. The three brothers even take to calling her "Mom" (19, 22), and she has planned to teach Jason, who is illiterate, to read. The brothers eventually find an apartment of their own, and Christina, having become lovers with Glenn, moves in with them. Lorraine's self-isolation is half-hearted at most; she provides them all with food and recipes, and misses her daughter, imagining that Christina is still upstairs when she hears the ceiling creak (15). They invite Lorraine over for dinner, and seeing them, and how they live, incites all her maternal instincts: "I wished for earth mothers, for women with large breasts to come to their rescue; women other than myself or my daughter" (18). Christina shows Lorraine a box of their family photographs, like the ones Lorraine herself had put in albums, and Glenn gives Christina some of his mother's costume jewellery, a pathetic and endearing gesture (18).

However, Christina gets an offer to teach in Japan, a position that will require her to finish her education, and the relationship with Glenn is doomed (19). Christina even leaves the box of jewellery on her bed, asking that Lorraine return it to Glenn. But Lorraine is unable to cut the brothers off; her refusal to let the asthmatic boyfriend go foreshadows her unwillingness to abandon these lost children. Roland expresses bemused exasperation with her: "Lorraine, Lorraine, Roland had said to me, those boys don't need you. They don't even want rescuing. They're too far gone into their lifestyle to ever be rescued" (20).

She sees them once on the street; they have become "boggans"— Roland's term for people who use grocery carts on moving day—and she cannot help approaching them to see how they are doing. They have likely left behind all traces of their mother, the way Lorraine had wanted to delete everything associated with her tenant, even the jewellery box: "they must have had to shed their mother's life, piece by piece. It had become too much for them to carry, too much for what had become lives without any rooms. I came to think of the box sitting on Christina's bedside table as an urn, holding the remains of a vanished family" (19–20). What this tells us is that Lorraine did not try to return the box to Glenn, as if their mother's life belonged to her now; that is, since their family's story has become Lorraine's story, she feels entitled to keep it. When Jason commits suicide after a fight with Glenn, Lorraine feels as if she has lost one of her own children (22–24). For reasons that only become clear in the second story, she does not tell her daughter that Jason's death was a suicide, preferring to make it sound like an accident.

During Lorraine's conversation with him, Terry refers to "Trilobites in the sky" (8), a bizarre image that reminds her of something a strange woman had said to her about cats "flying in the sky" (8). She wonders "if something had slipped past me. A mood, or a suspension of laws" (8). In fact, images of supernatural events and beings are a motif that runs through the story: the bag of photographs falls "as if an imp had been waiting in the rafters for me to return and on a cue had opened a trapdoor" (3); when the cat that came with the house finds its way back from her sister's farm, Lorraine says, "I thought it was a phantom come to haunt me"; as Terry approaches Lorraine, having mistaken her for the tenant, she describes him as looking like "a grey spectre" (5). These images represent the ghosts and uncontrollable powers that challenge her efforts at ordering her environment. She is being haunted by beings of the past and, it turns out, the future, who refuse to let her withdraw into comfortable isolation.

Later in the conversation comes another metafictional moment, like those cited above, when Terry says, "I used to play bass in a band" and the narrator thinks, "Good title for a story" (9). These instances of self-reflexivity suggest another interpretation for Lorraine's simultaneous living in the world of the ordinary and openness—no matter what she pretends—to intrusion, and even possession, by the extraordinary. Perhaps the house symbolizes the writer's everyday life now invaded by characters who insist on being accommodated, that is, written about. The magical creatures inhabiting the story are not just images of the past but also symbols of the otherworldly fictional beings disrupting daily life and enriching it. Among the creatures Lorraine refers to are angels, which appear frequently in different contexts. For example, Lorraine says that there is "a kind of holiness about children who have lost their parents"— orphans "spooning food into their mouths, chewing and swallowing as though they are normal, everyday children, and not part angel" (14). When she agrees to take in the band, she describes their admittance by bringing together the story's weird images and beings: "Cats are flying in the sky. Trilobites have left the water and, upstairs, angels float in my bathtub" (15). For all her hesitation, she has let in all the strange entities that are the stuff of art. Towards the end of his conversation with Lorraine, Terry suggests that van Gogh's art might not have been inspired solely by madness or alcohol: "Van Gogh had an alternate sense of reality. Probably all artists do" (21). The implications for Lorraine, the literary artist, are obvious.

The metafictional element explains the parallels that Birdsell establishes between Lorraine and other characters, thus reinforcing connections that the narrator may deny. She, Marion, and the band members are all "autistic," to use Roland's word for artistic types (2). Lorraine stops wanting to redecorate when she finds things her tenant had left behind that convince her the two were sufficiently alike to get along. Like Lorraine, the band had made a trip to the West Coast, using the money from their mother's insurance policy, and had felt out of place (13). Even Roland and Terry are fellow storytellers—artists in their own right—and Christina has, from an early age, found ways to manipulate her mother through dramatic performances Lorraine cannot resist (16–17).

At the end, going through one of her photo albums, Lorraine hears a sound outside and sees Terry scrounging through the remains of a neighbour's garage sale. She will try to save him, too: "And then I thought, what harm? What could go wrong in just lending him books? Lorraine,

Lorraine, this one's not even a christly boggan. At least this one can read, I thought. And anyway, every band needs a bass player, I thought. A heart, throbbing" (25). Like Christina, she cannot help inviting lost souls, or strays, to enter her home and her life. More importantly, like any good author, she will open her world to any creature from an alternate reality and make him or her a part of herself and her art.

The second story, "The Midnight Hour," is set some years earlier, while Christina is still living at home. We know by now that Lorraine is divorced and that Christina can easily elude her mother's oversight through emotional blackmail. Christina, like her mother, is a collector of misfits and strays, and is sexually active and not particularly interested in serious relationships (33). As we know from "I Used to Play Bass in a Band," Christina tends to choose friends who are unlikely to make her mother comfortable; in this story, Lorraine dislikes Pam and Lisa for their lack of candour—they will not make eye contact with her (26)—and, as the story unfolds, their willingness to take unnecessary chances with their safety. Christina smokes, more to be rebellious than anything else, and steals her mother's cigarettes to do so (31). Assuming the reader comes to this story after having read "I Used to Play Bass in a Band," then, she or he will enter it already familiar with the main outlines of Christina's traits and may well anticipate that she will find someone to rescue.

Christina's reported ability to manipulate her mother is depicted in the first paragraph, when we are told that she "would like to go into her mother's room, drop a book on the floor to wake her and say, For your information: I'm going suntanning in Assiniboine Park with Pam and Lisa. Not ask, just tell" (26). She realizes, however, that her mother would object, and a face-to-face confrontation might lead to complications, or refusal, so she leaves a note. As we saw in the previous story, mother and daughter are very much alike, so it is not surprising that Christina can hear her mother's voice in her head, leading her to add "and to hang around" in anticipation of what Lorraine would say (26). She later anticipates Lorraine saying, "Chris? You're not going to the park and that's that" (31) and proves to be right (34). She also plays her parents off against each other. It is the day after her birthday, and she asked her father during their conversation the previous evening, "Will you please reason with the other half of my parental unit?" (27), referring to her parents with a term she would continue to use in later years, as we see in "I Used to Play Bass in a Band" (15). When he asks her what she wants for her birthday, she asks for or hints at far more than she could reasonably get (27–28). As an aside, she mentions the suicide of her classmate Calvin—an event that now explains Lorraine's reluctance to tell her about Jason's suicide in the other story, as doing so would call up painful memories. All Christina gets from her father, however, is a box of toffee deposited on the bottom step of her building (37).

Lorraine's house is a key symbol in "I Used to Play Bass in a Band," and housing is also significant in "The Midnight Hour," as the divorce has obliged Lorraine and her ex-husband to sell their house in order to pay off debts. Now, Lorraine and Christina are living in an apartment, and Christina is unaccustomed to having to share a building with others whom she can hear above and around her (30). She has detested the apartment from the beginning, because it represents both their decline in wealth and class and Christina's loss of her "real" home and pre-divorce life: Lorraine promises her another house, but "Christina doesn't want another house. She wants the old one back" (31). She even pays periodic nostalgic visits to her old house (35). Like Lorraine in "I Used to Play Bass in a Band," Christina has declared possession of her house but, unfortunately, she is unable to maintain it. In fact, Christina often thinks back to life before the divorce and even dreams of herself as a baby (35). She wishes to go back in time and cancel all the traumas she has faced recently. The box of toffee she gets from her father triggers memories of how he used to feed frozen toffee to her when she was small (37). In the park, the miniature train reminds her of her own rides on it with him (40–41). A typical adolescent, Christina wants both to rebel and to be a child again.

The four-plex, like the house Lorraine will later live in, is full of reminders of previous tenants; Christina finds their graffiti on the water pipes. There are even ghosts of a sort: the former residents of the building when it was "a home for girls," and on "nights when she can't fall asleep it's because she feels she's being watched" (35). Lorraine is no happier here and is also unable to sleep when the sounds of the upstairs neighbours having sex come through the ceiling. She is worried about money, and instead of creative ideas, her imagination is devoted to embellishing the dangers that Christina will face in the park. Her writing career is not going well, and she is struggling with her current project (28).

As in the first story, music plays a major role. Lorraine's birthday present for her is a Billy Idol cassette, while Christina dons a Walkman for her journey to the park and listens to a cassette of Yo-Yo Ma (26), whose music reminds her of Calvin's suicide note. Later, she thinks, "She doesn't know why she likes the music, because sometimes it's confusing. The cello has so many sounds, it seems to work around the melody, to hide its message. And then suddenly, the melody pushes through the confusion, clear, easy to follow. She was with Pam and Lisa in Eaton's when she stole the tapes" (38). Lorraine has clearly been right to worry about Pam's and Lisa's influence on her daughter, and the music embodies the moral corruption they represent as well as the beauty of art. Considering everything that has happened—Calvin's suicide, her parents' divorce—Christina's definition of tragedy is nevertheless a teenager's: "She chose for her Social Studies newspaper project the topic of rock stars involved in car accidents ... A one-armed drummer is tragic, too, she thinks" (30). Darren, a young man whom Christina, Pam, and Lisa meet in the park, is also a musician of sorts, or at least someone who pretends to be. She and the other girls first see him playing Frisbee with himself—a red flag in Christina's view (40). While she sleeps, Pam and Lisa get to know him, and Christina learns that he has invited them to see his room. In appearance and unconventional demeanour, Darren is much like the other young men in the mini-cycle. For example, like Terry Darren speaks in riddles, asking the girls if they like "monkey's lunch," which he never explains to them (42). Also, Darren's hair reminds us not only of Terry, who is said to have "long coppery hair" (5), but also Glenn, who has long blond hair, and Michael, who is described as having "dark red hair that lay in tight curls like a cap" (11). As they walk toward his house, "He punches the air as he walks, lips moving constantly, as though he's plugged into music" (43). At his apartment, he lip-syncs Billy Idol singing the title song—"Rebel Yell (In the Midnight Hour)"—in celebration of her birthday, a performance that is more disturbing than charming.

Darren echoes the band members in the first story. He is a strange person; he has a collection of stuffed animals and invites the girls "to sit on the floor, along with the rest of the animals" (44). He has taken the birthday card out of Christina's backpack while she was asleep, showing the sort of indifference to private property that Lorraine's "home invaders" had exhibited in the first story. While the band members are fairly harmless, however, Darren is a threat to their innocence, as the Billy Idol song is generally interpreted as being about a one-night stand— hardly an appropriate subject for a song addressed to underage girls— with a title inspired by a brand of bourbon. To Christina, he is attractive precisely because he is dangerous; as the girls walk through his house's stone archway, "Christina feels as though it's night and she is home alone, listening for a knock at the door, feeling the danger of opening it, the danger compelling her forward" (43). Now, as he "sings" to her, she "wants more than Lorraine, more than a basement view, a tin of toffee, watching the world blow up on TV. She wants to know, most of all, what it is she wants" (45). She wants experience. The angel imagery of the first story recurs, but with a different tone: the person being addressed in the song is called "a little angel," an entirely human figure, and Darren is trying to seduce one or all of the girls. Christina begins to feel dizzy, and we suspect that the drinks he has given them are either alcoholic or drugged (45). She goes to the bathroom and he follows her in, making a pass at her. She is willing—whether influenced by her drink or not—and tells him she knows what he feels: "Like there's too many radios playing at the same time, all on different stations" (46). That is what she feels as an adolescent: too many voices, too many pressures, too many conflicting desires. The world of music into which he tries to draw her is a fantasy world, and when Pam turns on the bathroom light to save Christina from his advances, Christina "notices that his hair is thinning on top and she sees through it to the black roots at his pink scalp" (46). He is a predator, not a latter-day Orpheus.

Instead of leaving immediately, the girls revert to childhood, even getting into a food fight with her toffee, as Darren looks on in horror. As the girls bicycle home, Christina listens to Yo-Yo Ma again, her musical refuge in a way from the sexually charged song she has just fled. Now, it evokes a more violent image: "Yo-Yo Ma's music makes her think of a wolf, now. In one of those wilderness films, a wolf standing on an outcrop of rock, howling at the moon" (47). Once again, she associates it with Calvin, and the violence and finality of his death:

> And then the music is full and charged, like a suicide note that is romantic and terrible, but sad, too, because the person is gone and can't have the satisfaction of knowing that people have cried. Or know that their writing has been analyzed, words remembered forever. It's not fair, she thinks, that you have to die before people pay that kind of attention. She looks for Calvin in the streets. Long hair, black Johnny Walker T-shirt, looking like a hundred others at Grant Park High.
>
> (48)

The cover of the cassette shows the musician concentrating on his playing, "the music the only living thing for the moment," and then she connects his love for music to her mother's: "Like Lorraine, keening over Christina's bed most mornings" (48). She comes home to find Lorraine waiting for her with a lit birthday cake, and "she wants to grab Lorraine, to wind her arms about her mother's neck and cradle her head against her" (49). Of course, she will not admit her tender feelings and instead insults and argues with her (49). It is all an act, a performance of which they are both aware, much like Darren's fake singing of "Rebel Yell." At the end they plan to watch a movie together—but not before Christina writes a line in her journal largely intended to provoke her mother, who she knows will read it:

> She would like to write a poem, something for Calvin, call it Opus 85. But instead she writes, *Life is dull and boring and sometimes I think that if Lorraine doesn't get off my case, I'm going to take off. I have places to go*, she writes, because she suspects that Lorraine reads her journal.
>
> (50)

Lorraine is obviously not the only creative writer here.

The stories, then, are linked by character and by certain key motifs and themes. The mother and daughter provide the primary link, and each has her own say. However, the structure of the mini-cycle creates irony by portraying the daughter through the mother's point of view from a later time period, and then the daughter through a slightly distanced third-person viewpoint at an earlier period when we already know things about her from the first story. We know, for example, that there will be no serious rupture in their relationship because "I Used to Play Bass in a Band" depicts them as remaining close, if in a constant state of loving disagreement. Both are attracted to odd people, one because of their vulnerability and the other because of the danger they represent. The divorce is a fresh wound in the second story, but we enter the second story aware that the characters will heal in time. Among the shared motifs are suicides of young men whose despair is triggered by a lost loved one: a family member in one case—Jason never recovers from the loss of his mother—and a lost romantic love in the other. Throughout the mini-cycle, forms of housing symbolize the fondly remembered past or the less comfortable present, and Lorraine and Christina both seek familiar versions of "home" even though continuity is hard to find, and moving house is a common refrain. Lorraine does get the new house she promises her daughter in the second story, but by then Christina is living on her own, anyway. The most prominent motif, however, is artistic creativity. Both stories feature classical and rock musicians—real or would-be, whether present in the story or off-stage—who represent different types of and approaches to art. The classical musicians are intensely devoted to their art, while the rock musicians seem to be more aspiring than talented. Visual art also appears in both: van Gogh in "I Used to Play Bass in a Band" and the posters and Darren's all-blue decoration in "The Midnight Hour." Finally, both Lorraine and Christina write, although given that Lorraine is the only one who works as a writer, it makes sense that her story is the truly self-reflexive one. The structure of the mini-cycle highlights the characters' similarities and contrasts, all the while making us aware through the links of the constructedness of the mirror Birdsell has fashioned.

Robert Olen Butler has favoured the theme- or form-linked short story cycle as a genre presenting unique formal possibilities. Four of his story collections—*A Good Scent from a Strange Mountain* (1992), *Tabloid Dreams* (1996), *Had a Good Time: Stories from American Postcards* (2004), and *Severance* (more monologues than stories) (2006)—are cycles, and while varying greatly in approach, they exhibit some of the common features of theme- and form-based cycles. In each cycle, there is no single recurring protagonist; instead, in the theme-based cycles, the protagonists have similar experiences or, to use his term in describing the basic motivations of his characters, yearnings (e.g., Herzog 156), while in the form-based cycles, the stories have a similar structure. The stories in *A Good Scent from a Strange Mountain* are all first-person narratives told by Vietnamese immigrants to Louisiana, and throughout the cycle appear motifs like letters lost and found, snow as a symbol of death and/or North America, and manifestations of the supernatural (Nagel 224–44 *passim*). The characters in *Had a Good Time* are lonely and seek human connections they only occasionally achieve, while the stories in *Tabloid Dreams* are inspired by actual headlines in tabloid newspapers and feature fantastic elements normalized by the strange worlds Butler constructs out of these popular-culture and urban myths. Here, too, the main theme is loneliness, and the stories portray the characters' vain attempts at reaching out to others (Meanor 48). In such worlds, spacemen do come to Earth to woo poorly educated women, glass eyes do see, and John F. Kennedy was not assassinated after all (see Lohafer's article on the latter story). Yet while these cycles are constructed largely of stories about different characters, Butler has also employed mini-cycles as a further linking strategy. In two of his cycles, *A Good Scent from a Strange Mountain* and *Tabloid Dreams*, mini-cycles made up of two stories each perform special formal and thematic functions.

The related stories in *A Good Scent from a Strange Mountain* are "Mid-Autumn" and "In the Clearing." In a short story cycle featuring the theme of inter-generational relationships (see "Mr. Green," "Crickets," "Letters from My Father," and the title story in particular), these stories play a central role both structurally and otherwise. The cycle is made up of fifteen stories, and "Mid-Autumn" and "In the Clearing" are the eighth and ninth stories in the book; in terms of pages, they come slightly before the book's mid-point. Each is a monologue delivered by a parent to a child. In the first, a woman speaks to her unborn daughter, while in the second, a man addresses his son, from whom he was forcibly separated. Juxtaposed as they are, the stories form "companion piece[s]" (Nagel 234) expressing some of the volume's key themes. Nagel describes the extent to which the two stories are paralleled: "In each story an unnamed character expresses parental affection for a child, reveals a deep lament for a lost romantic love, and assumes a tone of resignation for opportunity irredeemably destroyed because of the war" (235).

As critics have noted, the cycle's major theme is the struggle for identity (see, e.g., Meanor 44–47; Nagel 225 and passim). Butler's Vietnamese immigrants strive to reconcile their past lives and their current existences, seeking to locate common ground between Vietnamese and American cultures (Cash passim). One way to accomplish that task is to seek out myths that may symbolize one or possibly both of the two cultures and perhaps connect them. The narrators depend on Vietnamese myths to articulate their pasts, presents, and futures, and express their hope that they can find a way to unite their Vietnamese and American identities into a coherent whole (Cash 37–38).

One of the features of Louisiana that makes it easier for these immigrants to settle into their new land is its landscape, which strikes them as similar to that of Vietnam. Certainly, Butler himself noticed the resemblance when he moved to Louisiana, as he has said in interviews; both are sensuous environments brimming with natural lushness, and Butler has said that that is one reason he feels at home in the state (Sartisky 168–69). The narrator of "Mid-Autumn" sees that similarity, too:

> Sometimes, like at this moment, I look beyond this yard, lifting my
> eyes above the ragged line of trees to the sky. It is a sky that looks

like the skies in Vietnam. Sometimes full of tiny blooms of clouds as still as flowers floating on a bowl in the center of a New Year's table.
(96)

In both stories, language becomes a key theme as the narrators strive for contact with their children. "Mid-Autumn" begins with the narrator telling her unborn daughter, "We are lucky, you and I, to be Vietnamese so that I can speak to you even before you are born" (95). The implication is that by being Vietnamese, they share not only a language but also the ability to perform this sort of communicative magic; above all, it is a Vietnamese custom to speak to one's foetus in this way. By contrast, "It is not a custom among the Americans, so perhaps you would not even understand English if I spoke it" (95). The cultural and the linguistic are therefore part of a continuum: neither can be teased out of the other. Her now-deceased mother spoke to her in this way, and she is now in the process of passing on a legacy of language, culture, ritual, and maternal love. As in the cycle as a whole, then, the story focuses on the problem of bringing the past into the present and, as a corollary and by extension, bringing Vietnam into America. The legacy is not all positive, however; she is certain that the words her mother addressed to her "were as a boy; she was hoping that I was a boy and not ever bringing the bad luck on themselves by acting as if I was anything else but a son" (96). It is this heritage of sexism that will provide the main theme and motivation for the narrator's own monologue.

The language the narrator uses to explain things to her daughter is coloured in a number of ways by her Vietnamese background. The way she communicates with her foetus is primarily through Vietnamese myth and legend. Indeed, even more than Vietnamese, myth becomes her true language, providing a way to connect with and teach her child. She begins early by describing the Rose Silk Thread God, who is the "genie" of marriage. Butler foreshadows her own fate as a bride by the way the narrator speaks of the traditional wedding ceremony: as something she heard about from her mother, not something she herself experienced (97). We know at this point, then, that there has been a cultural rupture of some sort represented by her merely second-hand knowledge of this god.

Much of the story concerns her unconsummated romance with Bao, whom she met at the Mid-Autumn Festival. She tells her daughter the Festival's origins, recounting the story of the emperor who yearned to go to the moon. A wizard made it possible for him to do so by climbing a rainbow, but as he had Earthly responsibilities, he could not remain in that land of enchantment (98–99). The emperor wished to return to the moon, but "the wizard came at his call and sadly explained that there was no return to the moon. Once you came down the rainbow, there was no way back" (99). During the Festival, the narrator and Bao stand together "looking up at the moon and trying to see the fairies there in the middle of the dark sea and we tried to hear them singing their poems" (101). She thus enters, or tries to enter, a similar world of enchantment—one that is, sadly, equally ephemeral.

The myth of the emperor's voyage symbolizes the narrator's own experiences: Bao joins the Vietnamese army and is killed in battle, and the narrator ends up marrying an American soldier. She misses out on the romance and also the ceremony of which she had dreamed. Emotionally and culturally, then, she has been cut off from what she has yearned for, and now has to settle for a life of fulfilling her quotidian duties. Like the emperor, she cannot stay in a land of wonder. It is noteworthy that she does not say she loves her husband, only that "he is a good man" (101). In other words, this is a marriage of necessity more than romance. Also, the myth symbolizes her physical voyage from Vietnam to America, from the land of myths to the land of houses "free from the mildew" (101).

She addresses her daughter primarily to educate her in her Vietnamese cultural past, but also to promise hope and a different life. For her daughter, she offers acceptance rather than disappointment over the fact the child is a girl and reassures her that she is loved. Also, she wants her daughter never to surrender her dreams, never to relinquish her mythical heritage or her yearnings: "I had my night on the moon and when I came back down the rainbow, the world I found was also good. It is sad that there is no return, but we can still light a lantern and look into the night sky and remember" (101).

Like "Mid-Autumn," "In the Clearing" is a monologue spoken by a parent in exile to a child who is not present in the conventional sense. The narrator echoes the previous story's ritual of speaking to unborn children as he says, "You were in your mother's womb when the North of our country took over the South" (103). Also, like the narrator of "Mid-Autumn," he is a reluctant immigrant who fled Vietnam only because of the Communist takeover: "I did not choose to run, not with you ready to enter this world. I did not choose to leave my homeland and become an American" (103). Once again, the Vietnamese relationship was a loving one, as he assures his son: "Your mother loved me then and I loved her and I would not have left except I had no choice" (103). His immigration, like that of the previous narrator, involved loss. The boy he left behind, we learn, now has a new father, just as the narrator of "Mid-Autumn" has had to find a new mate (103–04). His motivation, like hers, involves a wish to educate more than anything else: "I must tell you a few things about being a person who is somewhere between a boy and a man" (104). Ultimately, of course, what the narrator is doing is exploring his own identity and life, teaching his son who he was in Vietnam and is in the United States.

The images in "Mid-Autumn" are designed to evoke similarities between Vietnam and Louisiana, and focus on light, particularly moonlight; in this story, we also see common features of the landscapes, but the focus is on darkness. What the narrator says of his son clearly refers instead to himself: "As a boy you wish to be frightened. You like the night; you like the quickness inside you as you and your friends speak of mysterious things, ghosts and spirits, and you wish to go out into the dark and go as far down the forest path as you can without turning back" (104). The narrator, however, has had a different experience of darkness from that of an innocent, thrill-seeking child and warns his son not to seek it out because it contains real dangers (104). The narrator was a soldier during the war, and the dark jungle threatened death at every turn.

He tells his son about a patrol led by Lieutenant Binh; when one of the soldiers says that likely no one has ever been in the clearing they are resting in, the narrator responds, "Not since the dragon came south" (106). The officer misunderstands his reference to the Vietnamese creation myth, and their exchange later leads to the narrator's explanation of the myth to his absent son. Thus, once again we see Butler's narrator use myth as a primary way of expressing meaning; like the woman in "Mid-Autumn," the man in "In the Clearing" speaks in the language of myth and symbol as much as in Vietnamese. The narrator contrasts the day-time myths of Vietnam with the night-time ghost stories with which children frighten themselves and each other in the United States as well as back home. Indeed, he makes a point of comparing Vietnamese and American myths, referring to the story of George Washington and the cherry tree that he had been taught in school. But the Vietnamese and American approaches to myth are very different; in Vietnam, the myths are not distinguished so thoroughly from historical fact, while in his American school, where he is studying to gain his citizenship,

> the teacher immediately explained that this was just a made-up story. He made this very clear for even something like that. Just cutting down a tree and telling the truth about it. We had to keep that story separate from the stories that were actual true history.
>
> This makes me sad about this country that was chosen for me. It makes me sad for a whole world of adults.
>
> (107)

The platoon is ambushed, and most of the men are killed; that defeat is mirrored in the taking of Saigon, and the narrator's narrow escape (108). At this point, Butler establishes a further parallel between the two stories. Just as the emperor could not return to the moon, and the female narrator could not return to her romantic land of enchantment—her childhood, her romance, and Vietnam itself—so, too, does the narrator of this story realize that he cannot go home again. Binh takes him out of the country by motorboat, barely ahead of the Communist forces, and the narrator says, "when I realized I was leaving my country and my wife and my unborn son, I was only able to turn my face to him, for I knew there was no going back" (109).

On the final two pages of the story, the narrator recounts the myth of the gentle dragon and the princess. The tale features many of the themes of the story, and indeed the cycle, as a whole: loneliness, parenthood, and exile. The dragon and princess must separate—their family must be divided, just as the narrator's family and the narrator himself are permanently divided. The dragon and princess regain unity after death, on a higher plane, and the narrator hopes his own self and family will achieve reunification at some point and in some way. One force for reintegration is that very myth, one he tries to pass on to his son so that they can be reunited through story if in no other way:

> For a time in my life, the part of me that could believe in this story was dead. I often think, here in my new home, that it is dead still. But now, at least, I do not wish it to be dead and it does not make me feel foolish, so perhaps my belief is still part of me. I love you, my son, and all I wish for you is that you save your life. Tell this story that I have told you. Try to think of it as true.
>
> (110)

Note, too, that as in the previous story the narrator reassures his child that he is loved. Through love and acceptance comes the unbreakable bond between parent and child.

The cycle is about dualities: past and present, Vietnam and America, parent and child, men and women, peace and war, and so on. Perhaps this two-story mini-cycle is designed to embody in its bipartite form this balance and tension—and ultimate reconciliation—between such oppositions.

Butler employs a two-story mini-cycle somewhat differently in *Tabloid Dreams*. Rather than acting as a pivot around which the other stories develop, the mini-cycle brackets the others. Because they are separated from each other, they constitute an "exploded" mini-cycle—a form that we will look at in more detail in Chapter 9. The two texts come at the beginning and end of the book, and so we might consider them a framing mini-cycle for the collection as a whole. "*Titanic* Victim Speaks Through Waterbed" and "*Titanic* Survivors Found in Bermuda Triangle," by virtue of their prominent positions and links, express and reinforce the themes of the book as a whole.

As noted above, *Tabloid Dreams* portrays characters who are physically, emotionally, and spiritually distanced from each other, and their efforts to make connections. The narrator of the first story is the ghost of a victim of the sinking of the *Titanic* who haunts the water in which he drowned. That water has now become the contents of a waterbed, and he is ironically obliged to witness the sort of passions he denied himself in life. Butler makes full use of water's archetypal significance, as it symbolizes the flux of life and metamorphosis. Throughout the story, the narrator refers to his various manifestations since his death; he has been part of bodies of water and of people, he has risen in the air as water vapour (4, 11), and he has even been a cup of tea (12). But he is only superficially part of the living world; as he tells us in the opening paragraph, he is the medium through which fish swim, but does not partake of their lives (1–2). For Butler, life is a fundamentally sensual matter, and in interviews he rejects the abstract and intellectual approach to the world as a source of art (e.g., Sartisky 166–67; Herzog 159–60; Bonetti et al. 203). The narrator is an artist of sorts—he suddenly and surprisingly finds himself with an "impulse now to shape words" (2)—but he is a disembodied and therefore inferior one. His disdain for the physical becomes clear as he awaits his death: "I didn't mind so much, in point of fact, giving up a life in my body. The body was never a terribly interesting thing to me" (3). Only the pleasure he derives from smoking his cigar means much to him in a physical way. He even avoids alcohol on this final night of his life, as he wants "a clear head" (3). He goes on to declare his preference in the afterlife for a "propitiatory formality. A sensible accounting. Order" (4).

Much of what the narrator experiences is in the form of language, and often language he cannot understand. He hears indistinguishable voices on the ship, and again while in the waterbed, as if always missing the full meaning of others' attempts at communication (4–5). Later, after he dies and becomes water vapour, he seeks out others who have suffered the same fate in a passage that highlights his solitude and yearning for human contact, particularly through language:

> I wondered if there were others like me there. I listened for them. I tried to call to them, though I had no voice. Not even words. Not like these that now shape in me. If I'd had these words then, perhaps I could have called out to the others who had gone down with the Titanic, and they would have heard me. If, in fact, they were there. But as far as I knew—as far as I know now—I am a solitary traveler. (11)

He exists in and through language; indeed, his only reality consists of his self-narration. In a metafictional sense, then, the story creates as well as recreates his life and afterlife.

The narrator was a civil servant in India, and thus someone who was in a place but not of it. It appears that he has devoted much of his life, in fact, to avoiding engagement, preferring to remain aloof and alone with his cigar and drink (5–6). He describes himself as "an old bachelor" (6) and is hardly more in touch with his own people than those he helps to rule; during dances, he says, "I would think how the social rites of my own class sometimes felt as foreign to me as those of the people we were governing here" (6). Indeed, he sneers at "the pretenses the men and women made in order to touch, often someone else's spouse" (6). He is fundamentally an observer of, not a participant in, life, although when he encounters a woman on the deck of the sinking ship he admits, "There were certain things that I suppose were beyond my powers of observation" (7).

The woman is his introduction to the world of the sensual. They discuss somewhat dispassionately the fact that their ship is doomed, but as they speak, it is clear that his reactions are not as intellectual as he would like them to be. In fact, in an unintended double-entendre, he says at one point, while claiming to have maintained his dignity and self-control, "I felt a familiar stiffening in me, and I was glad of it" (8). Later, he reiterates the image of remaining stiff in her presence, but here it sounds more like *rigor mortis*: "I wanted only to be lying in a bed alone in a place I knew very well, a place where I could spend my days being as stiff as I needed to be to keep going." The implication of this passage is that he was just as dead while physically alive as he is now. He realizes with a shock what is happening to him as he stands at the railing with her:

> Is this an eddy through what once was my mind? A stirring of the water in which I'm held? I ripple and suddenly I see this clearly: my wish to comfort her came from an impulse stronger than duty would strictly require. I see this now, dissolved as I have been for countless years in the thing that frightened her that night.
>
> (9)

In this paragraph, we can see clearly how Butler uses the symbolic potential of water. The narrator may well be experiencing an actual "stirring" produced by the passionate activity above him on the waterbed. But that stirring is also internal, and the water represents the memory in which he has become absorbed. He swims both literally and figuratively in his own past, and as the story progresses, he sees once again how he has let so many opportunities for love and connection pass him by. Only after the fact can he see her as he recalls the light of the moon shining on her face (9). His vision thus improves markedly with the distance offered by time and the perspective of memory. But his reaction to her beauty then was to ignore, or perhaps it is truer to say to resist, it as he does again in memory: "I look away, just as I did then" (12). At his memory of her departure, he says, "Though I have no body, whatever I am feels suddenly quite profoundly empty. Ah empty. Ah quite quite empty" (13). At the thought, he cries out in pain.

At this point in his time on the *Titanic*, he returns to his room and dresses in evening clothes, clinging to his rituals and his meaningless dignity while fully aware he is doomed. He is also inuring himself to the disappointment he feels at his abortive encounter with the woman: "I straightened and stiffened with as much reserve and dignity as possible for a man in late middle age standing in his underwear, and I carefully dressed for this terrible event" (14). He returns to the deck, finds the woman once more, and helps her into the lifeboat, acting the part of the gentleman right to the end. He finally becomes aware of her beauty—now that it is too late—and then understands what she meant to him: "She stood there and she turned her face to me and I know now that she must have understood what it is to live in a body" (18). She represents all the physicality and sensuality he has avoided his whole life, embodying, in more ways than one, his frustrated yearnings. Meanwhile, the lovers on the waterbed have heard him cry out and peer inside at him; they, too, represent the sensuality he has spurned. The only thing that connects him to them is his voice and the story that he tells:

> I shape these words. I know that they heard me when I cried out. When I felt the emptiness, even of this spiritual body. I know now what it is that I've interrupted with my cry. These two above me were floating on the face of this sea and they were touching. They had known to raise their hands and touch each other.
>
> (19–20)

He now sees himself clearly, thanks to his memory and the story he has fashioned out of it: "I was already dead. I'd long been dead" (20).

The final story in *Tabloid Dreams* is narrated by the woman in the first story. As framing stories, the two tales thus reiterate the theme of separation and isolation in form as well as content, by being as far apart from each other as possible. The story permits us to see the events aboard the *Titanic* from her perspective, and as we learn, she is just as shy of human contact as he is. She is a temporal exile; apparently, her lifeboat was trapped in the Bermuda Triangle and emerged decades later, when everyone she has known is long dead. Like our other authors, Butler creates a number of parallels through imagery in his component stories. For example, one of the motifs is smoke: the male narrator recreates in miniature the ship's smokestacks with his cigars, and in the first paragraph of her story the female narrator thinks back to those same smokestacks, which take on symbolic meaning for her: "the smoke still slithered up from its stacks and for a moment the lights struck me as the lives still there on the boat and then the smoke struck me as the souls of those lives departing already, climbing to heaven from this death that was falling even at that moment upon the bodies" (185–86). Other parallels emerge as well. The male narrator seeks to maintain his dignity; similarly, while in the lifeboat, the female narrator tells her fellow women castaways, "Quiet! ... Keep your dignity!" (192). During the *Titanic*'s sinking, she hears the "sounds of people rushing, crying out" (196), recalling the male narrator's own crying out. Furthermore, as one might expect, the story is replete with water imagery. She says that she is afraid to bathe in a modern bathroom because of the rapid flow of the water (187). Water also means death to her, as seeing the water drain from the tub reminds her of the man she met on the ship. She sits on a vibrating bed whose motions recall the "stirring" of the waterbed in the first story. As we will see, the water imagery takes on special significance at the end of the story.

Like her male counterpart, the woman lives a life of the mind. She was a suffragette, and her narrative is larded with political opinions where one might expect a more emotional response. While she thinks of those who died, it is remarkable how distanced she feels from their suffering. They become an abstraction: "I was inclined, in the use of my mind, to think and speak often of the masses ... it has always been easy for me to think of humanity as just that, a monolithic thing, or at best a bipartite thing, men and women" (188). There is no evidence, however, that she has seen her own life in that bipartite way—as one involving both herself and another. For her, men are enemies, and she blames the sinking of the ship on their technological pride (186, 189). She constantly belittles displays of emotion, both her own and others'. In the scene in the lifeboat, as we have noted, she greets the other women's tears with scorn, and then contemns her outburst: "I understood that my anger at them was like their tears. I was frightened into a feeling that I wanted to repudiate as not truly my own" (192).

Her love of order, we learn later in the story, is inherited from her father, whose deathbed is described as "neat," with the covers in "a straight, orderly fold" on his chest (196). As he lies dying, instead of telling her he loves her, he says, "I'm proud of you" (197). She recalls that "he was always a man of the mind and the mind's energy surely crackled on beyond the body, it never needed the body ... I wondered if he'd had as little use for his body as I had for mine" (197).

She finds the modern world in which she has been thrown utterly disorienting. Much like the male narrator, she has entered a new and unfamiliar existence that presents her with endless surprises and challenges. Her main feeling, however, is one of solitude, saying, "I am alone" in an echo of the male narrator's sense of isolation (186). Being alone is nothing new to her:

> Not that I wasn't alone even on that night in April in 1912. It was a matter of pride to me, and would have been to any of my friends, all of them women who knew that we have a higher calling than the world had ever allowed for us, and who could travel alone as well as any man.
>
> (187)

Her isolation, along with the love of abstractions that produced it, comes painfully to mind as she remembers the scene in Venice:

> I was suddenly conscious of my solitariness there in that place, in that city, in that country, in the world. I had friends but we only had ideas between us and though the ideas were strong and righteous, I had not yet been naked in Venice except curled tight in a stone room with a tub of water and a sponge, wiping the scent of my body away, and quickly, never looking at myself, and then rushing back into my clothes. For all my ideas I was not comfortable in this woman's body.

And worse, it had its own intent: I felt a stirring in me at San Marco, a thing more like a need than a desire, a thing that I did not agree with but that would hear no arguments, no matter how clear and reasonable.

(190)

Throughout the remainder of the story, she continues to feel and attempt to deny her sensual yearnings. When she meets the man on deck, she tells us, "I felt a rustle of something in me before this man who was listening, a sweet feeling, even a legitimate one, I thought" (191). She is offended, however, when he asks her if she is travelling alone. She takes that as a slight rather than a solicitous gesture; her anti-male prejudices lead her to think he is questioning her ability to function independently. Her current crisis stems from the fact that it appears women have achieved liberation, and so her intellectual struggle has come to an end. To engage in that struggle, she has forsworn a life of passion, romance, and sensuality. She contemplates what she has given up and what she faces in the future. As she sees on television the skimpy modern clothes she is expected to wear, she wonders,

> What am I to do with my body now that the focus of my mind has been rendered obsolete? But this is not simply a problem of the new age. Indeed, if in my own time I'd been more comfortable in that fleshy self, I would perhaps have a function, or at least a prospect of pleasure, before me now.
>
> (194)

That leads her to regret the loss of the man on the ship; she wishes now that she had remained with him and had the kind of romantic encounter— however brief—that she had always avoided. But like him, she suffers from death-in-life. The closest thing she has had to a sexual experience came with a mine disaster that occurred when she was much younger, and she felt death enter her room:

> When I remember it now, it feels like what a man might feel like, stealing in on you in the night and touching you against your will, only you're sleeping and he's touching you very lightly so that he doesn't wake you.
>
> (194)

She feels the same sense of death on the *Titanic* and chooses emotional death over the physical kind that would inevitably come if she were to enjoy life, if only for a moment (195). She makes this choice despite the fact, as she now believes, "there was a connection between us" (195). She becomes acutely aware of his physicality, and for a moment does contemplate choosing to be with him: "I wanted to say, yes I will live, yes, I will receive this desire from you and perhaps in so doing I'll even apprehend at last what that actually means, to live, for this body of mine must surely have something more to do with it than I've so far discerned" (199). She desperately wants to reach out and to touch him: "I ached to put that hand on some part of his body ... there was a kiss yearning on my lips even then, though at the time I did not clearly recognize it for what it was" (199–200). But because they both try to maintain their dignity, their connection is fleeting, and when she sees its end she says, "something collapsed in me, as sudden and rock-heavy as the coal mine in Mingo County. It was too late for me. For this man, as well ... All these odd and sweet feelings I was having turned then into bitterness" (195–96). Like the man, she becomes a kind of walking corpse: "I was dead already, it seemed to me" (196). The irony of the situation is quite rich: in urging her to go into the lifeboat and live rather than stay with him, he has condemned her to a different but equally tragic kind of death.

The mini-cycle permits Butler to portray his characters from both within and without. The narrator of "*Titanic* Survivors Found in Bermuda Triangle" says that the man "seemed stupid at first" but then understood him to be "English and he was stiff," thereby echoing his own description of himself. He has clearly succeeded in conveying the impression he was striving for. She says that she found his eyes attractive, however, and so, like him, she sees the other as desirable but fails to act on that reaction. Interestingly, she says that he had "a woman's eyes"— the characters are obviously more alike than either imagined at the time (188). His double-entendres about being stiff find their counterpart in her image of the upended ship: "The great propellers at the rear were exposed, like a sexual part normally hidden from polite view but naked now in the throes of this powerful feeling" (188–89). She cannot see the man, but claims to know he is watching for her, to ensure she is safe; thus, both characters read the other in their own terms. As she straightens his tie before she goes to the lifeboat, she says of him, "his mind, which respects me and listens to me and considers me its equal, is so often filled with ideas that he neglects his body" (200). She is right about him, but just as correct about herself. At the end, she undresses, finally responding to her sensual yearnings: "At last I am standing naked, and I call to him, I cast the words of my mind out to the distant sea. Look at me, I say" (202), then she fills the bathtub and steps in. As if she knows the fate of her male counterpart, she seeks communion with him there:

> The water is cold. It takes my breath away. No matter. I sit and it rises up my thighs, my hips, my sides, and it is over my breasts, and it is beneath my chin, and it ripples there, like kisses. He is nearby. I slide quietly beneath the water. I will find him and we will touch.
>
> (203)

Both end their narratives immersed in water, yearning for and perhaps finding sensual union with the other.

These mini-cycles play vital roles in their respective story cycles. The two stories in *A Good Scent from a Strange Mountain* gain their formal strength by their juxtaposition; side by side, they reinforce each other, and due to their central position, they provide a fulcrum for the other stories in the volume. The mini-cycle in *Tabloid Dreams*, by framing the other stories, brings the book full circle in terms of character while emphasizing the theme of distance by their position at polar opposites of the text. The mini-cycles function through an ongoing tension between the independence of the component stories and their role in the pairings and the whole collections to which they belong. Like the components of Leacock's mini-cycle, the stories have a triple role: as distinct texts, as parts of mini-cycles, and as components of the short story cycles to which they belong.

References

Birdsell, Sandra. *The Two-Headed Calf.* McClelland & Stewart, 1997.

Butler, Robert Olen. *A Good Scent from a Strange Mountain.* Holt, 1992.

——. *Had a Good Time: Stories from American Postcards.* Grove, 2004.

——. Interview. *Conversations with American Novelists: The Best Interviews from* The Missouri Review *and* The American Audio Prose Library, edited by Kay Bonetti et al., U of Missouri P, 1997, pp. 201–16.

——. Interview. *Writing Vietnam, Writing Life: Caputo, Heinemann, O'Brien, Butler,* edited by Tobey C. Herzog, U of Iowa P, 2008, pp. 134–77.

——. "Robert Olen Butler: A Pulitzer Profile." Interview by Michael Sartisky, *The Future of Southern Letters,* edited by Jefferson Humphries and John Lowe, Oxford UP, 1996, pp. 155–69.

——. *Severence.* Chronicle, 2006.

——. *Tabloid Dreams.* Holt, 1996.

Cash, Erin E. Campbell. "Locating Community in Contemporary Southern Fiction: A Cultural Analysis of Robert Olen Butler's *A Good Scent from a Strange Mountain.*" *Songs of the New South: Writing Contemporary Louisiana,* edited by Suzanne Disheroon Green and Lisa Abney, Greenwood Press, 2001, pp. 37–45.

Lohafer, Susan. "Real-World Characters in Fictional Story Worlds: Robert Olen Butler's 'JFK Secretly Attends Jackie Auction.'" *The Art of Brevity: Excursions in Short Fiction Theory and Analysis,* edited by Per Winther et al., U of South Carolina P, 2004, pp. 32–43.

Meanor, Patrick. "Robert Olen Butler." *American Short Story Writers Since World War II: Fifth Series,* edited by Richard E. Lee and Patrick Meanor, *Dictionary of Literary Biography,* vol. 335, Thomson Gale, 2007, pp. 43–51.

Nagel, James. *The Contemporary American Short-Story Cycle: The Ethnic Resonance of Genre.* Louisiana State UP, 2001.

8 The Prototypical Mini-Cycle Plus
Clark Blaise's "Porter/Carrier Stories"

Most mini-cycles are made up of two or three stories, but Clark Blaise's mini-cycle, published in *Resident Alien* (1986), is a rare departure from that norm. The central fiction section of *Resident Alien*, entitled "The Porter/Carrier Stories," is made up of a fairly prototypical three-story mini-cycle, "South," "Identity," and "North," plus a novella, "Translation"—that is, a text in the genre that the mini-cycle seems designed to replace. Blaise does not switch the point of view from text to text, but the temporal and geographical settings and the plots are quite different as he explores his favourite theme: the crossing of borders.

Unlike Munro, Blaise did not have the opportunity to publish his stories together first in a periodical, and so the texts' publication history is both more conventional and more complex. "South" was first broadcast on the Canadian Broadcasting Corporation's "Anthology" series and published in the related anthology *Small Wonders* (1982) as well as the magazine *Canadian Forum* (May 1982). "Identity" was first published in *81: Best Canadian Stories*, a volume in an anthology series that mainly published reprints. An excerpt from "North" appeared in the literary journal *Writing* in the Fall 1983 issue. There is no record of any publication of "Translation" before its appearance in the collection; presumably, its length hindered its publication in a periodical.

The four texts portray Philip Porter's/Philippe Carrier's struggles as he seeks his identity and geographical and social place. Like many of the characters in Denise Roig's "After Quebec," Phil is the child of former Québecers now residing in the United States. As the son of a man who cannot settle in any one city or town for very long, Phil finds himself living on and crossing borders throughout his life. Two major incidents shape his destiny more than any other: a childhood accident that triggers the onset of epilepsy, and his father Reg's/Réjean's assault of his manager that requires the family to flee from Pittsburgh to Montréal, Reg's hometown. Phil endures not only constant moves but even (like Roig's characters) a radical change of name in crossing geographical, temporal, emotional, and other borders. Indeed, as Graham Huggan has argued, he is characterized more by his lack of secure, certain home and identity than by any specific national, cultural, or even linguistic selfhood (62).

The short stories in the trilogy are largely chronological, beginning with Phil's earliest experiences in the American South and proceeding through his movement northward to Canada. The titles explicitly refer to this transition and provide an interesting comment on it: "South," "Identity," and "North." It is worth noting that "Identity" and Phil's identity both lie between geographical locations; as Robert Lecker notes, like Phil himself, the story is a border entity, and so both text and character are equally liminal (191–92). In "Translation," the linguistic, cultural, temporal, and other dualities present in the trilogy come together, as Phil meets his Québécois translator and finds himself in constant motion between English and French, past and present, South and North, and so on (see Lecker 199–200).

The mini-cycle, then, reflects an overarching shift in geography, the primary aim of which is to portray Phil's mutable status. The stories are unified less by plot than by the various polarities that constitute his identity and place in the world. In his study of the book, Lecker goes into some detail about two of the primary dualities that define—if such a word can be used of the protagonist—Phil's life and self: past and present, and self and other, especially author and character. Blaise's growing self-reflexivity, Lecker argues, emerges as he blurs the boundary between himself as author and the persona he adopts in his fiction (162–65). Blaise melds autobiography and fiction, life and art, real and assumed self to suggest that the artist's truest identity is a dynamic one that encompasses both poles of such seeming binaries. Here, Phil must either reconcile or come to terms with the irreconcilability of his mythologized early childhood of security and certainty in an idealized family and the "divorce" (in many senses of the term) that permeates his later childhood and upbringing (Lecker 176).

Lecker's detailed analysis of the stories illuminates the four texts' treatment of Phil's progress from boy to man and from character (in his own story) to author, as Blaise's depiction of Phil's identity emphasizes its ever-changing nature. A study of the mini-cycle's form reveals how that shifting selfhood is represented by a number of motifs that recur throughout, with his name changes being only the most obvious example. The form as well as the thematic content reflects the fluid nature of self and the need to adopt various perspectives in order to view any identity— but especially an artist's—in its truest form. Thus, each story possesses its own internal structure while at the same time foreshadowing later stories and/or alluding to previous ones.

The references to North American, and specifically American, geography are among the clearest ways Blaise connects the short stories in the trilogy. The first story opens with a direct reference to its setting: "It was the South." Phil is about six years old, and the family is living in three rooms in their landlady's house but must move when Phil's father suffers a serious car accident. We learn early on, however, that Reg—as he is known in the United States—is not an American but a Canadian, and Phil's mother Hennie is also a Canadian whose relatives back home provide financial assistance (48). Canada is thus portrayed as a source of help and even salvation at the beginning of the mini-cycle. Bereft of resources, Phil's family is obliged to move, so Reg is both immobilized and forced to become mobile by his accident. As a salesman, however, Reg had always been peripatetic, and Phil recounts the many geographical shifts he had already been required to undergo even at this early age:

> I had started kindergarten outside of Atlanta and had put in a chunk of first grade in Gadsden, Alabama, and we had come to Leesburg, Florida, at the end of the first grade, before my father's accident, so that I was remembered by a few kids when second grade started.
>
> (50)

In their new home, the Porter family lives as a white family in the eastern and predominately Black part of town, and in the American South, much of one's social position depends on where one lives. As Phil says,

> It was a small town in those days, and a child revealed everything about himself from the direction he nosed his bicycle in from the stands outside of school. Each cardinal compass point indicated who and what you were, what your father did and what your prospects in life were going to be. I was an exception because our little laundry shed of a house was the last white-occupied structure on that side of town.
>
> (51)

His mother refuses to respect these racial barriers and crosses the social as well as geographical border separating black and white "by walking into Niggertown and running her hands over the heads of little girls and then standing in the yards calling up to women of her age, 'I'm your new neighbour. We live just on the other side of the streetlight there. I hope you'll come over for tea some afternoon'" (52). His best friend, Grady Stanridge, meanwhile, is securely ensconced in the white western part of town, and the second half of the story details a visit Phil pays to his friend's house. "South" therefore presents each of the "cardinal compass points" to which Phil refers, and as we will see, provides a foundation for the social and cultural implications of geography the entire trilogy depicts.

In "Identity," Phil is twelve years old, and the story recounts his life in Cincinnati and then Pittsburgh. Haunting the tale are his memories of the onset of his epilepsy; the past, in the form of his early days in other parts of the United States, keeps intruding as he struggles with the mystery of his condition's origins. He is certain that it began when he had a tricycle accident, yet we do not know where it might have happened, and in fact his mother's version of what really led to the condition calls into question whether the accident took place at all (62). Once again, geography is a significant theme, especially the degree to which Phil has no true home: "Let more bones break, more moves be made. Those early memories are from Cincinnati—a freak appearance in our lives, a town that did not claim us—from deep in America, a country, as it turned out, that did not claim me either" (63).

In Pittsburgh, Phil is portrayed on the roof of his apartment building trying to draw in distant television stations through a set of rabbit ears. He sees his greatest achievement as capturing signals from "Channel Nine in Steubenville, Ohio, or Seven in Wheeling, West Virginia ... there was rumoured to be a Channel Ten in Altoona and a Channel Three downriver in Huntington, West V[i]rginia" (64). It appears, then, that what makes Pittsburgh special to Phil is not so much its own existence as its ability to act as a doorway to the rest of the continent.[1] If Phil has a geographical identity, Lecker argues, it is North American rather than any specific or local one, and the signals symbolize his efforts at communicating beyond the self and the local (182).

At the end of "Identity," Phil comes home to find his mother frantically packing; that they are moving yet again does not surprise him:

> We'd moved many times before, and usually under bad conditions—to towns we didn't know and where we had no address. Those moves were chance things: pack up the car, flee a city and travel to a place where a job might be waiting. Then find an apartment after a few days in a squalid hotel, unpack, put the boy in school.
>
> (71)

Usually, she prepares for their moves very carefully, but clearly something has gone wrong. This is no ordinary move: Reg has assaulted his new manager, as we learn in the final story of the trilogy, and must move not merely out of town but out of country. The family heads north, and as they reach the border Hennie says to Phil, "In a minute we'll be going into Canada. Canada is where your father and I come from ... We're going to Montreal. We have relatives in Montreal" (74). Now, Canada is more than a site of aid; it has become a refuge. As a result, Phil is no longer an American, if he ever was one. Hennie continues,

> "Our name will change when we go over the border. Forget all you ever know about Porter. Our real name is Carry-A. Like this—see?" She showed me a plastic-coated green-framed card with an old picture of my father on it. I couldn't pronounce the name, but the letters bit into my brain. Réjean Carrier.
>
> (74–75)

Phil asks, "What's my name?" and his father simply tells him to "shut up"; his mother, however, says, "You can be anything you want to be"

(75). Phil's lack of certain identity now becomes a liberating as well as disorienting aspect of his life. Blaise could have explained Reg's flight from justice in "Identity," but chose instead to delay revealing the reason for the move in order to provoke in the reader the sense of dislocation that Phil feels. As Blaise establishes throughout the first two stories, Phil seldom knows the circumstances behind the family's frequent moves and so has become somewhat used to the constant, unexpected, and unexplained uprootings he endures.

In "North," the final story of the trilogy, Phil is living in Montréal. While he does not move in this story, geography continues to play an important role in his life. The city is divided into the English west and the French east, much as Leesburg was divided into a white west and a black east. Furthermore, his school has two separate entrances, one for the boys and one for the girls. As Lecker observes

> The initial distinction between boys and girls is gradually broadened to include a host of related polarities: male and female, father and mother, Catholic and Protestant, French and English, experience and innocence, age and youth. Carrier's movement "north" and over the border traces his attempt to bridge the gaps between all these polarities.
>
> (191)

Phil is required by history and his French Catholic school to obey these geographical strictures, but like his mother prefers to ignore them whenever possible. His new friend Mick tries to place him geographically; Mick asks, "Where you from—the States? Vermont?" and after replying, Phil notes that "Pittsburgh rang no bells for Mick Fortin. He only knew the cities that sent us tourists—Burlington, Plattsburgh, and half of Harlem, plus the cozy loop of the old NHL" (80). For Phil, Pittsburgh is now a memory, one he compares to the television signals he used to seek: "In memory, Pittsburgh came bursting through like a freak radio signal" (85).

Phil and his family live in the district of Hochelaga with Reg's brother Théophile, and Dollard, Théophile's son, is Phil's guide to the French-speaking and Catholic world to which Reg—now Réjean once more—has brought his family. Ironically, Dollard later gets a job at Steinberg's, a supermarket owned by English-speaking Jews, while we learn that "Two of Théophile's sons-in-law got big jobs in the States" (103), reversing the geographical migration of Réjean and the rest of the Carrier family. Phil once again tries to connect to distant cities and what is now a foreign country through a set of rabbit ears:

> We got a television set, the first anyone had seen, even though Canadian television was barely launched, rudimentary. That didn't stop me from buying the wires and rigging some rabbit-ears and tying

them to our chimney in an attempt to coax something, anything, from the air. Burlington, Plattsburgh—those towns that provided night-time English radio in my room—where were you when it really counted? Even KDKA in Pittsburgh came in, most nights.

(103)

Now Phil is looking backward, to a remembered home, seeking some certainty in an existence marked by perpetual change, and enacts his desire by trying to reverse both time and space. "North" presents the many pressures Phil faces to conform to other people's definitions of him, pressures coming from his immediate and extended families, from his present school, and one that, through his mother, beckons him. He reacts by refusing to conform and seeking his identity in a much broader and even international context. Hennie yearns to have her son become part of the English community, represented by McGill University (93). Milton Street, Pine Avenue, and Prince Arthur become the boundaries and markers of this more privileged world as Hennie takes Phil to visit an old professor friend. Phil rebels and wants nothing more than to return to his French school, resisting his mother's efforts to cross into the English area of the city, and thereby rise in class, through him.

Of course, the physical migrations Phil unwillingly experiences symbolize and trigger other changes as well. For example, with each move he must learn a new language, and so each story portrays Phil's linguistic as well as geographic transitions. Even in the United States, with its single national language, Phil must negotiate the many shifts in language he encounters in moving from state to state and South to North. In "South," Phil says that he likes the newspapers in foreign languages and typefaces that his mother uses as packing material (49). In the next paragraph, Phil says that the family hires "a coloured man" to move them into their new house in "Niggertown" (52, 54): Phil is being taught the racist language of "his" people, the town's whites. He is thoroughly embarrassed by the way his mother showers him with endearments no one else in the town would use: "She had the Canadian custom of smothering me with 'dears' and 'darlings' and even 'preciouses' in every conversation, and she even extended the custom to my little friends, as she called them. The one acceptable term of endearment—honey—she never used" (53).

The most radical linguistic change Phil undergoes is, of course, the switch from English to French. Suddenly, he metamorphoses from an English-speaking American to a francophone Québécois, and as "Identity" ends and "North" begins, we see him in full transition from one cultural identity to another. It is noteworthy that the motif of radio and television signals returns on the final page of "Identity" to mark this shift, as the family crosses into Canada: "My father found a radio station playing strange music in a foreign language" (75). The opening of "North" features the anglicization of the French words for "boys" and "girls"; he meets his newest friend, another English speaker in a French school, when Mick sees him baffled by the signs on the school: " 'Take the garkons,' he had advised, under his breath. *Garkons* was an early word in my private vocabulary. In the beginning, I had to trust strangers' pronunciations or worse, my own" (79).

Phil begins to learn French, but his mother has a much more difficult time: "In a week I knew some nouns and adjectives; no verbs, no sentences. French neutralized my mother's education; she was like a silent actress" (81). For her, the language represents all that is strange and even potentially dangerous:

> She was one of those western Canadians of profound good will and solid background, educated and sophisticated and acutely alert to conditions in every part of the world, who could not utter a syllable of French without a painful contortion of head, neck, eyes and lips. She was convinced that the French language was a deliberate debauchery of logic, and that people who persisted in speaking it did so to cloak the particulars of a nefarious design, behind which could be detected the gnarled, bejewelled claws of the Papacy.
>
> (82)

Hennie's continuing efforts to put Phil in an English school constitute a threat to his own efforts to assimilate: "English would obviously be easier, but not necessarily preferable. I wanted to belong, and no one I knew in Montreal spoke English, except my mother" (82). Théophile, a member of the St-Jean-Baptiste Society, will not hear of Phil's attending any but a French school, and that settles the question. Yet even though it is clearly impossible, Phil remembers that he studied and spoke to his classmates in English—clear signs of the unreliability of memory, a theme that takes on ever-increasing importance as the mini-cycle continues.

The French language makes its first appearance in the trilogy in "Identity," but only in association with sex. Phil's sexual awakening is a major theme in the mini-cycle, and it is sometimes associated with his linguistic transition. In "South," he is somewhat too young for such feelings, and yet the way he describes his father indicates that much of Reg's appeal for him lies in the father's virility. Reg is

> the manly force in my life, the dark, romantic, French, medieval, libidinous force in my life, the foreign element in my life, believing somehow that his eighteen siblings, his six wives, his boxing career, his violence and his drinking and his police record, his infidelities, in some way ennoble *me*, tell me I'm not just the timid academic son of my mother's rectitude.
>
> (56)

In the second story, Phil's friend is Peter Humphries, whose mother was divorced—*divorcée* was one of those words, probably the only one, that a 1952 Pittsburgh kid pronounced in a self-consciously French way, to imbue it with its full freight of accompanying *negligées* and *lingerie* and *brassières* and of other things that came off in the night and suggested a rich inner life.

(65)

Phil sees her as representing pure sensuality and associates her with a certain sort of language; his mother and his friend use different words for her: "My mother called her 'The Slut.'—Peter called her 'her' and 'she'" (68). Phil experiences lust for the first time, to some extent for his own mother, in an admitted case of "Oedipal longings" (70) but mostly for Peter's. Phil associates Mrs. Humphries with everything sensual and feminine, and the story's humour largely derives from his fumbling for knowledge:

Being with Peter, the only friend I had, was like standing at the tip of an enormous funnel; all the sexual knowledge available to pubescent, provincial Americans in 1952 was swirling past me, and not a precious drop was wasted, not with Peter and his mother nearby. I wasn't in their apartment that often ... but every time I entered it I was struck by the fumes of something lurid.

(66)

When Peter dresses up in his mother's clothes, thereby violating Phil's growing sense of the differences between male and female, the friends avoid each other for some time. The masquerade Peter engages in parallels and prefigures the change in identity the Porter family will enact when becoming Carriers at the end of the story.

Meanwhile, Phil finds his mother at her sexiest when she is scrambling to pack what she can as they are preparing to leave the United States. As in other areas of his life, Phil sees sexiness not as fitting a clear-cut set of defined features but as transcending any commonly accepted image:

Sexiness, if I am now to lift it from any immediate context or application to any particular woman, is (for me) an appearance that borders on slovenliness. Sex will never embrace me in tennis shorts, in a bikini, or in any fetishistic combination of high heels and low neckline. Sex is the look that says, "Help me out of these clothes," or shows that things she's wearing are a constriction, not an attraction.

(72)

He gleefully finds himself tutored by a girl named Thérèse Aulérie, for whom he develops an infatuation. She does not dress or wear make-up in the manner of the American teenage girls he knew, but Phil finds her attractive nevertheless (87). It should be noted that she represents the equally distant and mysterious realms of the French-Canadian side of Montréal as well as femininity:

> I came to think of my five hours a week with Thérèse as my parole from solitary. I came to understand my mother's use of the word "drab" to describe the interiors and the streets, the minds and souls and conversations of east-end Montreal. One big icy puddle of frozen gutter water, devoid of joy, colour, laughter, pleasure, intellect or art. School and home and church and the narrow east-end streets that connect them are the same colour even now in my memory, linked in a language that I didn't understand except through its rhythms.
>
> (91)

Note how Blaise combines in this paragraph a depiction of what Thérèse means to Phil, a description of her environment, and a reference to her language; for Phil, the personal, the geographical, and the linguistic are one. Thérèse, like Phil, has a name that crosses the linguistic border; just as Porter is an anglicized version of Carrier, Aulérie is a francized version of her "vrai *nom*," O'Leary (89). Thus, as Lecker notes, names continue to represent linguistic divisions and ironic contradictions: Mick Fortin, whose surname is French, is an anglophone, while Thérèse, whose real surname is English, is a francophone (192).

The linguistic and cultural divide between Phil and his French-Canadian compatriots shrinks as he learns from and teaches Thérèse; while she shares Catholic doctrine with him, he shares knowledge about the habits of American teenagers with her (90). In a sense, Phil becomes the ultimate translator, acting as a communication link (much like the television and radio signals) between English and French, the United States and Canada, boys and girls, and many other dualities. Throughout the story, Phil navigates carefully through a liminal space bordered by but not fully a part of these worlds. "North" ends with the French-named Phil and the English-named Thérèse sharing a thoroughly bilingual Sunday meal at Murray's Restaurant:

> I'd ordered and paid in English, and she'd been terribly impressed. She'd promised me she'd do it, but had gotten too embarrassed at the last moment. We were walking behind a group of old ladies in white gloves and wide-brimmed hats, the tea-drinking ladies of Westmount, and Thérèse had been frightened of them, afraid of what they might be saying about her. Just gossip, I said, mindless things, and I translated some of it, to reassure her. She shook her head and acted ashamed. "*Sh'peux pas!*" she declared, pounding the side of her head with her fists, "*Idiote!*", then giggled. "*Mais tu peus, non? You hunnerstan'* every word, *non?* Smart guy!" She took my hand

in both of hers and swung my arm like the clapper of the biggest bell
in th[e] world.

(105)

What she does not know is that he earned the money for such outings by
distributing flyers for a strip club, a business to which his friend Mick had
introduced him. His sexuality is now connected to a very cynical pursuit;
the raw lust he experienced at twelve has transformed into a more practical outlook at sixteen.

The trilogy also portrays the degree to which geographical and linguistic changes reflect and produce shifts, especially deterioration, in Phil's
and his family's social status. They are never rich but are at least reasonably independent at the start of the trilogy, but then arises a growing gap
between Hennie's social expectations and pretensions and the reality of
the family's decline in fortunes. "South" begins with an account of Reg's
accident; Phil says, "Until the accident we had been surviving in town"
(47). When Reg is sent home, he is confined to one of the BarcaLoungers
he had been selling; in a symbolic sense, then, he is trapped by the insecure job he holds. Because of his immobility and the exhaustion of financial help from others, the family has to sell off Hennie's most valuable
possessions and move. Phil's description of her luxury items reveals both
her alienation from her current social position and Phil's alienation from
her (see the list on p. 48). To him, "They meant nothing at all, to my
shame. A BarcaLounger now—that was a valuable thing" (48–49). Phil
identifies more with his father's taste and lifestyle. The family moves to
the Black neighbourhood, and it seems they have had to surrender even
a "proper" address:

> The new place was actually larger than the three rooms. It might
> have been called a house—it was detached but set back from the
> street, as a garage or a laundry house might have been. It gave us an
> address with an "A" at the end—something new in all our travels, "a
> sign" my mother said.
>
> (49)

To Hennie's distress, it even lacks indoor plumbing (50).

Hennie simply cannot fit in; she lacks friends and refuses to adapt to
Southern and poor—that is, working-class—ways (see esp. 51, 53). The
South has its own form of class consciousness, much of it based on race,
and Phil discovers that fact when he visits his friend's house. Grady's
home contrasts sharply with Phil's own: "His house was Florida Moorish,
with a tile roof, Mexican grillwork and rows of tall, narrow windows,
curved on top" (53). The Stanridges have an extensive garden, and Mrs.
Stanridge has her own set of "valuable" possessions to which she clings
as forcefully as Hennie did to her artworks, ceramics, and so on. When a

purportedly antique purple flowerpot appears to go missing (the colour perhaps signalling its true worth), Mrs. Stanridge blames her son and then her new cleaning lady. Phil sees the flowerpot on a shelf and points it out to her. Mrs. Stanridge says, "I promise I ain't never hiring a white woman to do coloured work again!" (56). The identity of the cleaning lady is not made explicit here, but Phil informs us in the next paragraph that Hennie has been reduced to cleaning "other people's houses" (56). One cannot help concluding that Hennie is Mrs. Stanridge's new cleaning lady, particularly when Mrs. Stanridge complains, "And her acting so superior. Like she was too good to clean a white lady's house" (55). If she is indeed referring to Hennie, the latter has clearly suffered a very humiliating social descent, as Lecker notes (178).

"South" is ostensibly about Phil's relationship with his father, whose employment and medical problems determine the family's economic and social fate. Yet the story deals more profoundly with Phil's inability to "see his mother" (57) in any meaningful way. Toward the end of the story, he tells us that as a boy he "deliberately mythologized" his father, and never understood his mother's higher-class background or the price she paid, the sacrifices she made, in and for her marriage. She ultimately does leave her husband, returning to Winnipeg to become a schoolteacher (56), and Phil finally acknowledges how much he has neglected her in his hero-worship of his undeserving but more colourful father:

> How easy it is for a boy and for a young man and even for a man now embarked on middle age to see his mother as nothing exceptional in the universe, nothing at all, an embarrassment in fact, against the extravagance of his father.
> Mother, why couldn't we love you enough?
>
> (56–57)

The family's decline in social position is made painfully evident in "Identity," although here Blaise's point is to demonstrate the unreliability of memory (see Lecker 179–80). In trying to recall the trigger of his epilepsy, for example, Phil first remembers his father sitting in a Queen Anne chair, then immediately dismisses the idea as impossible (61). By the time they reach Pittsburgh, the Porters can no longer afford a house; they are living in an apartment building, and both parents have to work to make ends meet (63). When they are forced by Reg's assault to flee the United States, they have to leave their furniture and take only what they can carry in the car. They cannot even stay in a hotel, but hide out in a motel parking lot looking for a licence plate to steal. In the course of her marriage, Hennie has gone from living in a house to renting an apartment to sleeping in a car (74).

Like "South," "Identity" presents us with Phil's ignorance of his parents' true selves, and of all they had subjected each other to and endured. The opening paragraph links the story to the earlier one: "Porter, Reg and Hennie. My parents for several years. Mysteries to me, to each other. Gone now, even in name" (61). In the end, Phil's parents' and his own identities become uncertain, as Phil learns that Porter is not their true surname and they must all become Carriers. The entire family's social place, in terms of class, ethnicity, heritage, and so on, undergoes a thorough revolution. As represented by the various legal documents that lie scattered around their old home in Pittsburgh (73), the only legacy his parents pass down to Phil is the lack of a clear set of personal or social boundaries.

In "North," Hennie's efforts to re-establish her former social position involve trying to direct Phil's education so that he will become what she used to be. She desperately wants him to attend McGill to avoid becoming like her husband's family. Now, Phil and his parents do not even have a home of their own. As for Phil's education, Hennie's view is that "English was the only language for an intelligent boy who didn't want to become a priest" (82). When his mother brings him to Eaton's, Phil learns later that she had been head of the store's furniture department, and Reg/ Réjean had been one of her salesmen. She then expresses her bitterness at what she has become: "I deserve it all, don't I? Sleeping on a floor in Hochelaga. No wonder they don't want to remember me—I must look a sight" (92). As a way of asserting her English and higher-class identity, she takes him for tea and scones at the cafeteria upstairs (92–93), and to visit her professor friend. Hennie, Ella, and Dolly (Ella's presumed lover) have concocted a way for him to attend an English school; as Ella tells him,

> "You can live with us, and we will send you. I know professors, I know musicians, writers, artists. We go out every night, or we have people here who are the leaders not just of this city, not just this country--"
> "— the *world*, darling. Ella is known all over the world."
> "That's not the point. The point is, we want to share this—what should I call it? Power? Connection? Good fortune?"
>
> (99–100)

Phil escapes, insisting that he be allowed to return to the French school where he has at least established some sense of belonging and identity. Referring to his father, but by extension himself as well, Phil says at one point, "The future would always be insecure" (104). He chooses that insecurity over both status and the prospect of being who his mother wants him to be (someone much like herself, or more exactly her former self). He would rather remain the social border-crosser he has become and find his own way through life.

Thus, each of the three short stories is structured with its own narrative arc, while the trilogy as a whole features a more extended arc that brings Phil from childhood innocence and a stronger sense of self to teenage experience and a refusal to be defined. Phil's sexual maturation understandably progresses from story to story as he grows up, and his romantic view of his parents is replaced by passions and then pragmatism. Meanwhile, motifs of national, cultural, linguistic, and other dualities inform the individual stories and the trilogy as a whole. Themes and images recur, yet each story treats them somewhat differently, communicating through its distinct nature the fragmentary, contradictory, fluid, and ultimately boundless identity Phil develops. Indeed, if he has any identity at all, it is a kind of transnational, North American one, and the trilogy could be described as portraying Phil's "North American education," to allude to the title of Blaise's first story collection.

It would be useful now to relate the trilogy to the novella that carries Phil's narrative to its conclusion. "Translation" brings together the motifs in the three short stories, offering a kind of closure as Phil finally determines what childhood event brought on his epilepsy: an incident involving his parents and a hot iron. Reg is now in a nursing home, and it is the scar on his body left by the iron that triggers Phil's memory; Phil is finally able to express his love for his father, and one can only hope that it is not too late for his father to get the message.

By the time "Translation" begins, Phil, in his forties, lives in the United States and has reassumed his childhood name of Porter. He is a successful author of fiction and has now published an autobiography, *Head Waters*, which has recently been translated by a small Montréal press as *Les Sources de mémoire*. Phil therefore has returned to his own headwaters in a sense, by moving back to the United States; the plot of the novella concerns Phil's meeting and relationship with his French-language translator, Madeleine Choquette, in Montréal, and he is thus re-enacting his childhood move to Montréal with his family. The novella revisits the themes and motifs of border-crossing. As Phil thinks back on his life, particularly since the period covered by "North," he pursues an affair with the older Madeleine—recalling his early Oedipal yearnings—and searches for his father. Even a cursory reading of "Translation" reveals the extent of the intertextual links between the novella and the earlier stories. Phil travels north once more, and his ongoing fascination with and experience of geography—places and their boundaries—are reflected in his perception of Montréal upon his return: "These were dangerous streets for Porter, the steep downtown slopes between MacGregor and Sherbrooke—Peel, Stanley, Drummond, Mountain—for it was in a tourist room between Burnside and St. Catherine on Peel that young Carrier had last lived with his mother" (136). He thus associates the city's geography with his movements through space, time, and social position. By using his American last name again, he repeats his father's name change and reverses the one he undergoes at the end of "Identity." The opening of the novella concerns the recurrence of Phil's epilepsy and his search for his condition's roots, echoing the first paragraphs of "Identity." Throughout "Translation," the narrative moves back and forth in time, from Phil's adulthood to childhood and back; that is, the largely, but not entirely, chronological sequence of the trilogy is countered, with the result that the stories' incidents are enriched by further detail.

Phil's relationships with his parents are the main concern of "Translation," as Lecker shows in some detail (see 204–08), and what happens is that Phil in a sense becomes his father while Madeleine becomes his mother. For example, the first line of section 7 is, "Porter dreaded the Canadian border. The simplest questions of an immigration officer were the imponderables of his life" (121), and this is exactly the sort of fear that Reg expresses at the end of "Identity" when he tells Phil to keep his mouth shut. As for Madeleine, in her role as older woman she reminds one not only of Mrs. Humphries but also of Hennie. Madeleine is even the same age, fifty-two (144), as Hennie was when she died. Moreover, in her role as an intermediary between languages as well as a romantic interest, Madeleine becomes another Thérèse. In addition, Phil learns more about who his father really was, even to the point of discovering he has a brother he never knew about (155). At the end of the novella, Phil tries to communicate across the vast distances that have separated them, in a manner reminiscent of his experiments with rabbit ears. "Translation" is thus both a recapitulation of and a site of possible closure for the elements that structure the trilogy.

Blaise has created a novella plus a trilogy that lies on the border between a set of independent stories and another novella. The three short stories possess their own internal structures, to a large extent (but not entirely) standing on their own as individual narratives, yet each enriches the other two, so that the whole trilogy exhibits a global unity created and reinforced by the stories' common features. Then Blaise provides a novella that mirrors and complements the trilogy while offering a slightly more coherent narrative that nevertheless presents a fragmentary, border-crossing vision through its varied spatial and temporal settings. Phil is shown throughout the middle, fiction section of *Resident Alien* as a figure of contradictory, conflicting, and diverse identities. The structural fragmentation of the complete mini-cycle, then, reproduces Phil's inner being and is therefore the most logical way for his life story and personality to be rendered dramatically for the reader.

Note

1 On the symbolism of geography and maps, see Huggan 56–57.

References

Blaise, Clark. *Resident Alien*. Penguin, 1986.

Huggan, Graham. "(Un)co-ordinated Movements: The Geography of Autobiography in David Malouf's 12 *Edmonstone Street* and Clark Blaise's *Resident Alien*." *Australian and New Zealand Studies in Canada*, no. 3, Spring 1990, pp. 56–65.

Lecker, Robert. *An Other I: The Fictions of Clark Blaise*. ECW Press, 1988.

9 The Exploded Mini-Cycle

An "exploded" mini-cycle is one whose component stories are not published together but are instead separated in the story collection. Our reading of the mini-cycle is inevitably affected by whether we read the stories sequentially or with a hiatus of one or more stories between them. If we are not aware that stories are linked, then returning to the same set of characters will come as a surprise after we have left them in an earlier story. As we saw in Chapter 1, the author will likely organize a story collection to create a certain effect, like this unexpected recurrence, but the reader will not necessarily read the stories in order and therefore may not experience the stories the way the author intended. The analysis to follow is based on what the authors seem to have intended by separating the component stories of their mini-cycles.

The stories in Steve Heller's *The Man Who Drank a Thousand Beers* (1984) are primarily linked by setting: all are set in Hawaii, but three are about the same group of characters and portray one significant event from different points of view. "The Rainbow Syndrome," "The Man Who Drank a Thousand Beers," and "The Rainbow Man" are about Joseph Kamahele's bet that he can drink one thousand bottles of beer in the space of ten days. Joseph, a large man, is something of a leader and even hero among the group of friends who convince him to attempt this questionable achievement. We watch his efforts from the perspectives of two friends and his son, Danny; Joseph's success would mean a great deal to the men who know him, but even more to Danny. "The Rainbow Syndrome" is the first story in the collection, "The Man Who Drank a Thousand Beers" is right in the middle of the book as the fifth of nine stories, and "The Rainbow Man" is the last story, their arrangement creating perfect structural symmetry in the book as a whole. That symmetry is reinforced by the similarity of the titles of the first and last stories and the fact that the middle one is the title story, acting as a prominent "hinge" of sorts for the collection.

The stories in the mini-cycle were first published in periodicals: "The Rainbow Syndrome" in *Cimarron Review* in 1977, "The Man Who Drank a Thousand Beers" in *Quarterly West* in 1981, and "The Rainbow

Man" in *The Texas Review* in 1980. There is no hint in the collection, apart from the titles of the first and last stories, that the three are linked; the table of contents offers no paratextual clues that they form a unit. Thus, the reader will finish the first one unaware that the characters will return, and perhaps leave it thinking he or she has gotten the only viewpoint on Joseph's efforts and their consequences that will be offered. The reader will therefore not expect to see the same characters and situation again in the title story, and from a different point of view. Returning to the characters and the circumstances of the bet this way may change how we respond in retrospect to "The Rainbow Syndrome"—an effect that will be strengthened when we come to the final story.

The first story is in third-person limited point of view with Burton Bettelheim—the name a likely allusion to the anthropologist—as the focalized character. Burton is an older man who adopts a somewhat superior attitude towards both tourists and the Hawaiian locals. His first action in the story is to step on to his balcony "proudly" (7). He very much does not want to be associated with others from the mainland, dressing in "plain khaki clothes, because although there may be thousands of men his age in Hawaii dressed in splashy colored tourist garb, Burton still knows what he looks like, by god" (7). From his heightened vantage point in a high-rise overlooking the beach, he looks down, literally and figuratively, on the goings-on beneath him. He can see only a "thin slice of the ocean" through a "crack in the wall of high-rises ahead" (7), images that symbolize his narrow vision, one that precludes sympathetic understanding of his friends.

That is not to say that his opinions are entirely wrong. We do not yet know why he thinks this, but he wonders "why, for Joseph Kamahele, the crazy three hundred pound Hawaiian who lives below him, everything has to be a test of manhood" (7). He is surely right to wonder, since the bet that we later learn about is a ridiculous, potentially fatal test of Joseph's strength and masculinity. When Joseph makes his claim, Burton responds, " 'That's a helluva lot of beer, Joe' ... thinking *you stupid fat-assed sonofabitch*" (9). Joseph foolishly wishes to prove that while he may be older he has not aged, that he is still the man he used to be, and for him "man" means someone able to hold his liquor. When the men are finalizing the rules of the bet, Burton asks what Joseph is risking, and Joseph's best friend, Henry Okuda, replies, "His pride, man" (12).

Were Burton a more sensitive individual, he might understand why Joseph wishes to engage in this macho display. Joseph's status is symbolized by where he lives among the high-rises and hotels that accommodate non-Natives: a "tiny wooden slat house, the cause of the gap, sandwiched between the two high-rises on the corner of Liliuokalani and Cleghorn Street" (8). As a Hawaiian he is in a subaltern position, and his "tiny" house—an anomaly among these tall buildings that disrupts the urban landscape Americans and others have tried to construct—is a reflection of that position, as well as his resistance to foreign domination.

He is not the only native Hawaiian in this situation, one marked by poor housing and lower social class: Burton is aware that "A distinctly separate community exists in the shadows of the big hotels. Slat houses of local people like Joseph Kamahele tucked between the concrete towers" (9). That stubborn native presence is also embodied in the plants and the fauna that they support:

> green growing things sprouting from every patch of soil splitting the pavement. From the ninth floor where he lives, Burton notices only the tops of trees, like the tall silver-ringed coco palm extending three-fourths of the way up to his balcony from the spot where the pavement way poured around it. A family of white doves nests serenely in its crown, suspended in quiet isolation in the gap between high-rises.
> Walking along Liliuokalani Avenue in the evening, he can see how the greenery holds its own against the encroaching cement.
>
> (9)

Joseph's reputed drinking prowess is another way for him to assert himself as a Native among colonizers and a man among men. The house is a shack overrun with cockroaches, and in an important image Burton "pictures the dimly lit living room inside the house, where roaches scurry away beneath the furniture and light seeps through the cracks between floorboards" (8). As later becomes evident, the cockroaches represent other furtive beings whom Burton disdains because they are beyond his mental grasp.

Joseph is not the only character facing his age and mortality. Burton has had a near-stroke or heart attack (9). Like Joseph, he also tries to deny the infirmities of age, and still "prides himself on his good eyes, though he has to admit it's tougher to see in the evenings now" (9). He is thus fooling himself about his perception, and his pride, a parallel to Joseph's, is what also prevents him from seeing his friends and himself clearly. He recognizes the danger that the bet poses to Joseph's health, but not the reason for Joseph's posturing, and certainly not his own self-blinding sense of superiority. Later, after Joseph's son pretends to run right at him on his skateboard, veering around him at the last moment, Burton considers complaining to Joseph about it, but realizes that Joseph will do nothing about it; "It doesn't seem that long ago that he didn't have to rely on another man's dispos[i]tion to deal with those who insulted him" (11). He has no choice but to admit defeat and his own powerlessness, something Joseph will also have to do later in the story. Burton cannot even drink any longer: "his system won't take it. It wasn't always like this. He had a hollow leg, people used to say" (13).

Danny is one of Joseph's three sons, all of whom Burton detests for their anti-social behaviour, referring to them as "the Three Terrors: Stephen, Kapono, and Danny, the oldest, who likes to throw Burton's laundry in the swimming pool" (8). When his neighbour Patterson asks him, "What would you do … if for just a moment you were their age again?" Burton replies, "Hide" (11). Later, as he looks down upon Joseph's house, he thinks:

> Kids seem somehow different now … He can't be sure he could communicate even if he *were* their age. It *would* be interesting, if for just a moment he could be … No. He resists. That's the first sign of senility, when you start fantasizing about youth.
>
> (13)

He hates children because he feels superior to them and their antics, yet he cannot help wishing he were young again himself.

Of course, there are few people (if any) he actually likes; he even thinks ill of Patterson: "He's too moon-faced, Burton thinks. Too romantic, like that fool sidewalk painter down on Kalakaua who calls himself the Rainbow Man—paints people as surfers, hula dancers, even sharks—anything they can dream up" (10–11). We will meet that painter later, as he is of course the title character of the mini-cycle's third story. Burton has no patience for dreamers of any kind. He resents Patterson's laughing at Danny's prank, then he himself laughs when Danny does the same thing to Henry later in the story (13).

The bet that forms the central focus of the narrative begins with a poker game involving Joseph, a wealthy Chinese man named Chun Lee, and Burton. Joseph has no respect for Chun Lee, who to his mind has sacrificed his humanity for the pursuit of money: "Money dry you up— make you skinny and bad-tempered. Before-time you used to drink pretty good. Now look at you … Now you got money and no time to enjoy it. Now you even too weak and skinny to drink!" (8). Joseph is unhappy about Chun Lee's distorted values and the loss of a former drinking buddy, someone able to join him in his alcoholic indulgence, even when Chun Lee explains that he has ulcers and is no longer allowed to drink. Joseph then says that in exchange for some of that money, he will demonstrate his undiminished capacities by drinking a thousand beers in ten days. The men lay out the rules and hide the beer bottles under the porch so that the social worker will not see them, something Burton objects to as too risky (11). When the bet begins, as Joseph downs his beers, Burton says, "I don't need this"; Joseph responds, "You need *something*, man … You too *sour* when you're sober" (12).

Now, Burton looks down from his apartment on Joseph's house, aware of what is transpiring as Joseph drinks himself nearly to death, and thinks back to his own struggles with substance abuse. He quit smoking ten years ago and will not start again: "You have to consider the consequences, he thinks—not like that crazy Hawaiian down there, who pretends all his problems will dissolve in bottles of Asahi and San Miguel. At least I don't have any moon-faced illusions about living in paradise"

(13). He cannot actually see Joseph drinking but feels self-conscious about observing Joseph's house. Perhaps he identifies with Joseph more than he is willing to admit, secretly hoping Joseph succeeds despite all his expressions of contempt for the man and the bet; Joseph's achievement would symbolize his own ability to fight aging: "Burton could almost imagine himself as the man who drank a thousand beers, sitting there triumphant, indomitable—" (14).

At the end of the story, Burton visits Joseph to check on his progress. Joseph has only drunk 314 beers in four days (14). A cockroach runs by, and Burton stomps on it but fails to kill it. It escapes through the floorboards instead, a sign of his impotence. "Nobody kill off ol' man cockroach! Not even Burton!" Joseph laughs, and "Burton feels his cheeks and neck redden. He stands stiffly. 'Hell with you'" (15). He leaves, furious at having revealed his weakness, especially before the man who, for him, represents virility and strength. He hears a noise beneath the house, and sees Danny hiding there, helping his father go through the cases of beer; like the cockroach, Danny has his refuge, a place where he can escape to and do what he wants to in violation of society's rules and preferences, and help his father, away from those who would stomp him out of existence. Both Danny and Burton want Joseph to succeed, for similar reasons—to protect Joseph's pride and help him maintain his status and reputation. In spite of all his own posturing as a voice of social propriety, Burton promises Danny he will not say anything. This time, he chooses not to tattle because of his own needs, not out of weakness.

As it turns out, Burton was right to worry; the social worker does catch Joseph. To prevent his sons from being taken away, Joseph sends them to Henry's house to hide out. Burton is glad he had nothing to do with the discovery (13–14). The final scene shows him as he "leans over the edge of the balcony as he looks out, putting things in order" (15); he is gathering and organizing his memories, but also trying to put the world in order from his God-like perspective. Joseph's other friends are disappointed in the forced cancellation of the bet; for his part,

> Joseph keeps right on drinking, though no one's keeping count anymore, pretending he's proving something to the world. Why kid yourself? Burton wonders as he looks out toward the ocean. It's like the roaches. You find your own crack by god. You don't have to be a goddamn dreamer to get along.
>
> (15)

However, Burton has already revealed himself to be another dreamer, another "sufferer" of the romantic "rainbow syndrome" referred to in the story's title. He has invested Joseph's effort with the same amount of hope as Joseph himself and the others, seeing it as a brave, admirable, and ultimately futile challenge to the effects of age and the social reality of powerlessness. Joseph's colonized status parallels his old friends' physical condition, and they wanted him to succeed for all their sakes. Burton goes downstairs and stands outside Joseph's house. When Danny comes by, they share a moment as Danny flashes him the thumb-and-pinkie skateboarder wave. Burton inhales the Hawaiian air deeply, "feeling the sharp rejuvenating thrill of pressure against his chest—maybe he will share a few with Joseph; the old hollow leg—until finally he exhales, releasing it slowly, reluctantly, as the boy behind him disappears into a crack in the shadows of concrete" (16). Through Danny, Burton has had a taste of youth again. Whether he can maintain that dream is another matter. The sensation in his chest echoes the one he felt when he had his near-heart attack (9); also, Danny is the "cockroach" in the story, the one who can live in society's cracks, and it is unlikely Burton can ever follow him there.

Three stories separate "The Rainbow Syndrome" from the collection's title story. Thus, not only does the mini-cycle comprise three texts, but so does each group of intervening stories. The stories are about non-natives living, working, and vacationing in Hawaii, contrasting their efforts to be part of Hawaiian society and life with Joseph's and his family's status as colonized locals. "The Man Who Drank a Thousand Beers" narrates the same events from Joseph's perspective, although again from outside: the story is also in third-person limited point of view. To a reader unfamiliar with "The Rainbow Syndrome," the description of Joseph in the first sentence as "the strongest man in Waikiki" (53) might be taken as an authoritative judgment by the narrator, but those aware of Joseph's self-image recognize this as his own view and that of the friends and other Natives who admire him. We know that Joseph is concerned about his pride, his reputation, his status among his peers. He, Chun Lee, and Burton are playing the poker game that leads to the fateful bet, and thinks, "He knew both were watching him, measuring him, as they played—but it was not *their* eyes Joseph felt" (53). Instead, "They were Danny's eyes he felt watching" (53); he can hear his sons outside, and it is Danny's presence, and opinion, he cares most about:

> Chun Lee and Burton only watched for weakness, waiting for him to make a mistake. Why should Danny watch like that? Danny had a special wave, extending only his thumb and pinkie, that he gave to show respect. Joseph had seen him give the wave to surfers and pool sharks and frisbee throwers. But not once since Alicia [his late wife] died had he given the special wave to Joseph. Why?
>
> (54)

Once the bet's rules are set, he detects "a small shadow in the living room window" (57), and, believing it to be Danny, shouts "Shakka, bra's!" as he drinks the first beer (57).

Joseph is a surfer who taught his oldest son (see 59–60) and wants Danny to emulate and admire his surfing skills. His reputation as a great surfer is important to him, and he basks in his friends' compliments, such as Easy Ed's "No wave too big for Joe Kamahele" (55). Easy Ed later adds concerning the drinking bet, "Nobody can beat Joe Kamahele!" (56). Joseph is their hero, perhaps even a superhero, and they count on him to represent and fight for them. When his drinking threatens to cost him his family, the community rallies around him, cheering for him to defeat Chun Lee and thereby all the people who have oppressed and dispossessed them. But Danny is the one whose admiration matters most to him.

Because of the shift in point of view, we gain insights into how Joseph sees the characters we met, and only knew, through Burton's viewpoint in "The Rainbow Syndrome." In that story, Joseph called Burton "sour," and here he thinks of him using the same adjective: "Joseph said nothing as he dealt the cards to his two opponents, sour old Burton and crafty Chun Lee" (53). Joseph thinks of Burton as "the bitter old Jew ... Burton hated Hawaii, and Joseph disliked Burton because he complained so much. But Burton was a lousy card player with plenty of money to lose. He was welcome in Joseph's house" for that reason (54). The dialogue during the poker game reported in the first story is repeated almost verbatim, with some notable exceptions, like Burton's querulous comments omitted in "The Rainbow Syndrome": he says, "My brother Morris—big man in real estate. *Hawaii*, he says. *Aloha Paradise. Condominiums*. So I move—and for what? A drinking bet. For this I left Florida?" While the others work out the bet's rules, Burton says, "Each year from Israel one thousand Jews move to Key West" (56) and later, "In Miami they have good Milwaukee beer" (57), again showing disdain for Hawaii and a preference for Florida—opinions not likely to win friends among Hawaiians.

As for Chun Lee, Joseph is aware not only of his wealth and influence but also how the community views him: "Most of Joseph's friends worked in Chun Lee's hotels, sold his orchid leis, and drove his taxi cabs. But they hated him for the hotels that blocked the ocean and the rich *haole* tourists who choked the beach" (54). He then makes a more egotistical comment on their friendship: "But Joseph knew why Chun Lee played poker in this tiny house—because Joseph Kamahele was the strongest man in Waikiki and had more respect than any hotel builder" (54). Joseph's self-image colours his view of how Chun Lee and others feel about him. It is the contrast between his own strength and reputation, and Chun Lee's physical weakness and the disrespect Joseph is certain he receives, that leads Joseph to call him "too weak and skinny even to drink" (54). While praising Joseph's surfing skills, Bigfoot says, "Chun Lee own the beach now ... But the ocean belong to Joe Kamahele" (55), and Joseph receives the comment with pleasure.

We learn more about Henry Okuda, since he is a close friend. Henry runs a souvenir stand, selling overpriced jewellery to tourists: "shark bait," in his words. Like Burton and Joseph, he also suffers from restricted vision; he has only one eye, due to a jellyfish sting attack, and uses his disability to intimidate customers: "Henry would block their way and make them look at him until they bought something. Henry aimed his bad eye at Chun Lee now, but the little Chinese stared back like a tomcat and said nothing" (56). Locals are less easy to manipulate, it seems. He sees in large part what he wishes to see: he is a supporter of Joseph-as-hero, and when Burton tells them the plan to hide the beer under the house is too risky, Henry declares, "Nobody scare Joe Kamahele out his own house … Right, Joe?" (56). Recounting a story about selling jewellery to a tourist, he says, "I tell her, I say, 'Lady, these shells here got stainless steel string—only big Joe Kamahele can break'" (58).

The bet begins, and at first the task is easy; more importantly, it elicits respect from Joseph's friends:

> He watched their faces as he drank and saw they were impressed, saw the strength he felt reflected in their eyes. He saw Henry Okuda's good eye wink and his green teeth flash as he cackled whenever Joseph downed another one. He saw Chun Lee's sharp eyes calculating the odds as the count changed. And Burton, rolling his eyes in disbelief and muttering something about thoroughbred racing at Hialeah.
>
> (57)

Of course, what really matters is Danny's reaction:

> Joseph could feel him watching, secretly, from the window. All three of his boys were supposed to be playing poker over at Hiromi's house. Joseph smiled. He knew Danny would sneak back and watch his father drink the beer. Watch to see if he could really do it. Joseph took a deep breath. He would show Danny this time. He wished he could show Alicia too.
>
> (57)

Remembering his late wife reminds him that Mrs. Nakamura, the "check lady" or social worker, has become Danny's new mother, and Joseph is seeking to regain his pride when it comes to her as well: "Joseph belched and spit on the floor. I show the check lady something too!" (58). As Joseph loses consciousness, Henry takes over his paternal duties, sending the sons to bed after telling them, "Your father do a great thing today … He show Chun Lee who be greatest man in Waikiki" (58). Joseph's preoccupation is clear: "Joseph thought he saw respect shining in the eyes of Stephen and Kapono as they listened to Henry's speech. Danny's eyes looked uncertain" (58). Danny has his own ambitions, and whereas his brothers are bragging about their father, he seeks to do better at school; however, when he shows Joseph his improved report card, Joseph considers it only relevant to the social worker (60).

The friends take turns watching Joseph as he drinks, partly to verify the count and partly to be there in case things go wrong. Burton and

Danny are thus not the only watchers in the mini-cycle; all take turns as observers, although the most important set of eyes are Joseph's internal ones, and the most important "sight" is the self-image he feels obliged to maintain in order to maintain the respect of his son and the others. He also feels a sense of responsibility to his brother, Tony, who has asked him to come see him perform at one of the hotel clubs. In spite of the risks to his health and the bet, he goes to see Tony's show; to his brother's embarrassment and anger, he drunkenly crawls up on to the stage (62–63), and Tony leads him away. It is evident that Joseph is not as strong or self-sufficient as he thinks. The stacks of cases under the house are shrinking, but after the mini-cycle's first story we know that it is not Joseph who is responsible for the diminishing supply of beer. The entire exercise loses its appeal: "Joseph knew he should feel good about the bet, but something was wrong. Since the night at the Moana, the best he could feel was numb. He tried to forget it, but could not. He had never been led away before. Removed by force, yes, but never led away" (63). Instead of feeding his pride and reputation, the drinking marathon has instead led to his humiliation.

Finally, he is caught by the social worker crawling under the house for more beer. She demands his financial records and his sons' report cards, leading to a physical confrontation. She threatens to take his sons—the source of all his pride—from him. Whatever positive things the bet might have meant are now lost. While his sons hide at Henry's, Joseph continues to drink himself into oblivion. Instead of strength, "he felt only numbness and the weight of the air that resisted him like water" (65): in other words, contrary to Bigfoot's brag, water controls him rather than vice versa, and he no longer owns the ocean. When the government moves to take his children from him, he is too far gone to concentrate on what he needs to do to keep them (65). Burton has a plane ticket to Florida and invites him to come along to escape the law and the friends who are abusing him, but Joseph refuses:

> He looked Burton in the eye. "Yeah, lot you know about it. You run away from here because you don't believe in nothing!"
>
> Burton blinked. For a moment he stared wide-eyed at Joseph—then yanked his hand from Joseph's shoulder as if it had suddenly turned hot.
>
> "You think you're strong," Burton said. "But you're weak." Then he was gone.
>
> (66)

It is likely the worst insult he could have directed at Joseph, someone who defines himself by his strength, but Joseph has allowed his pride to control him, and he is determined to win the bet no matter what the cost—even if it means losing the people he cares most about. If not for an intervention by a local organization, the ALOHA Foundation, he might well have had to surrender his sons, but their lawyer saves the family. Still: "What was the count now? He was losing; he could feel it. He was shaming himself in front of his boys and all of Waikiki. He felt his strength running out of him like the beer that passed so quickly through his body" (66–67).

Then comes his final humiliation: he hears the sound of running liquid beneath the house, just as Burton had heard something there in the previous story, and through the floorboard sees his son pouring out cans of beer (67). He is unsure that he really sees Danny's face there, and in a sense it does not matter if he does; the shame is internal as much as external, in his own eyes as much as Waikiki's, and he can "see" Danny's face looking into his own with anything but pride. A court hearing is held to determine what will happen to his sons. He barely knows what is going on, but we learn through other characters' actions and then words that he has won his case to keep them (68). Still, the bet is done, the beer confiscated, and Joseph must show he is a "real man" in a very different sense. Instead of being pleased, he is angry—the loss of his pride has been an unbearable defeat, no matter what a court says. All he cares about is finding the two most important people in his life: Danny and Chun Lee. Neither is around, but a tourist—embodying all the foreigners who have taken over his homeland and dispossessed him of wealth, pride, and a healthy community—tries to take his photograph: "His pink face was partly shaded by the wide brim of the hat, but Joseph could see the timid, embarrassed smile as the man tried frantically to work the focus on the camera. The crowd began to laugh and sneer" (69). His supporters wait for their champion to do something violent to the tourist, but Danny comes to take his hand. Danny is about to give his skateboarders' two-fingered wave, but Joseph stops him and leads him back through the surprised crowd (69):

> Joseph paid no attention as he plucked Stephen and Kapono out of the rebounding crush. He gathered the boys into his arms, lifting them above the amazed faces of their friends. As he broke through the edge of the crowd, he heard voices behind him begin to shout angry words at the tourists.
>
> "Ey, shark bait gone!" he heard Henry Okuda yell, but Joseph did not stop.
>
> (70)

Joseph has finally got his priorities straight, focusing on his sons—all of them, not just Danny—rather than the community he supposedly defends. He realizes that he must now earn love, not respect, and be a father, not a hero.

The final story, "The Rainbow Man," is a first-person narrative told by a man who is both a native of and a visitor to Oahu. Again, the title refers to the artist Burton refers to as a "moon-faced" romantic in "The Rainbow Syndrome," and the story's main theme is the idealization of real (i.e., fictionally real) people through the imagination. It is also a story about hero worship, and thereby brings together the themes of the other stories in the mini-cycle, expressing them through paradoxes and dualities, binaries in balance with each other.

Those paradoxes are evident in the first sentence, which characterizes the narrator as an outsider bringing his imaginative vision to Hawaii: "For a moment I am everywhere and nowhere—the brief miracle of displacement one experiences looking out at the Blue Pacific four thousand miles from home" (96). The word "home" is key here as an ambiguous designation. He says that he "distrusts" that feeling and works to get his geographical bearings, looking at Diamond Head on one side and the curving beach of Waikiki/Honolulu on the other. He states that he is "unmistakably alone" after describing the busy scene around him (96), meaning that he is emotionally solitary, an observer like Burton and other characters in the mini-cycle who seek detachment and engagement at once. He now sees "characters"—the first hint at the story's self-reflexivity—and the ones he notices are indeed characters with whom we are familiar: an old man with a metal detector who proves to be Henry seeking treasures to sell to the tourists, and a boy with a yellow surfboard who we know is, and whom Henry will later explicitly identify as, Danny (that he owns a yellow surfboard is revealed on p. 59).

The narrator is trying to become one with Hawaii, to see it as his home for reasons that become clear shortly, and in his effort he chooses one of these locals to identify with:

> Watching both of them—the old man intent, the boy uncertain—I know that, today at least, I am like the boy. For today is a day to be cautious, a day to question motives and review alternatives. My thirtieth birthday, a day when my mother and father are dead and most securely buried—and yet strangely they live again.
>
> (96)

He now reveals the explanation for these seeming contradictions, and for his connection to Hawaii: he was born in Hawaii to a Japanese-American mother and a South Dakota-born father, but grew up in Texas. The trip, then, is a homecoming, but only up to a point, since he remembers little of his time here. Hawaii has now killed both of his parents: his father because of the dreams it inspired of wealth and security after the war in which he had been in the Navy, and his mother, who has died quite recently, because of the lung disease she contracted while working with her father in the pineapple fields while she was a child (97). His visit is therefore a search for his roots (a voyage of a sort we will see again in the next mini-cycle) and insights into the lives and deaths of his parents. Hawaii is a crucible of identity for him, a place where his parents and he himself were forged and therefore a source of innumerable paradoxes. It is both home and exotic, who he is and has never been.

He remembers his father in two ways: Seaman William Taylor, a heroic fantasy figure he knows only through a photograph he once owned of his father in uniform (97); and "a fierce-looking giant" (98). Both are hero figures: "Seaman Taylor as a kind of distant playmate—a secret friend who traveled the world and yet shared my darkest moods and deepest thoughts in a way no real companion ever could," and he would recall the giant's "words and the tone of the voice many times when I needed the courage to face a bully, or the grace to accept defeat" (98). The narrator continues, "Through these memories—the giant and the secret friend—my father lived a double life" (98), and so, of course, does he. His imagination has turned a real man, his actual father, into a father figure, the product of both memory (if only as a photograph) and fantasy or wish-fulfilment. In other words, the narrator is an artist like the title character, creating images that render banal reality into something much grander and more appealing.

As he grows out of childhood and into adulthood, both versions of his father disappear. He loses the billfold in which he has kept the photograph of Seaman Taylor, and the giant "crept softly away later in my adolescence, when a firm hand and steady words were unwanted straps of dependence. By the time I entered college, Seaman Taylor and the giant were long dead" (98), only to be revived when his mother dies. He begins to yearn for his real/unreal father, feeling alone: "I have no other family, nor ... any real friends" (98) despite the efforts of his boss, Hollis Morman, to befriend him.

Henry comes over and asks if he can sit with the narrator, as if the narrator's thinking about companionship has summoned him, and the two begin to converse. They both watch Danny surf, and Henry tells the narrator who the boy is. Henry's hero worship of Joseph comes through again: "His father big Joe Kamahele—greatest man in Waikiki! ... Joe Kamahele strongest man, best surfer, greatest drinker in Waikiki" (99). The narrator finds the look that Henry gives him out of his good eye disconcertingly intense: "the *eye* startles me, aimed right between my own eyes like a gun barrel" while the damaged eye "is withered shut, as if its use were no longer required" (99): that is, Henry sees what he wishes to, in ways that he wants, and no other angle or truth is required. Henry is another Rainbow Man, "painting" Joseph in exaggeratedly bright colours: " 'Nobody has more respect than Joe Kamahele,' he goes on. 'Not even Chun Lee Chang who built the Sheraton and Ilikai'" (99). Heller reinforces the parallel between these two portraitists of heroes by having the narrator comment on Henry's Asian features, which of course the narrator shares. The narrator also tries to "read" Henry:

> It's something I can't control, this tendency to quickly see through the initial mystery of a face to the shallowest aspects of character just beneath it. Local color, I note sarcastically, regarding the contrast

between his pink flowered shirt and the black leather briefcase at his feet. A Fuller brush man in paradise.

(100)

He is right and wrong about Henry, who is certainly a salesman but far more than "local color"; what is most significant about the passage is its allusion to characterization. The narrator is bragging about—or lamenting—his ability to turn a real person into a character, and thus identifying himself as an author as well as a creator of images. Of course, merely by narrating this tale, he has assumed that role.

He continues to elicit details about Joseph from Henry, and when he learns about Joseph's plan to drink one thousand beers, he is astonished:

I almost laugh at the absurdity of it. "Really. Why, for Christsake?"
He shakes his head twice at my ignorance. "For respect only reason. He bet with Chun Lee Chang, richest man in Waikiki. No money stakes—only respect."

(100)

We now learn far more about the origins of the bet; Chun Lee had tried to create a monopoly on the beach, filling it with hotels, and Joseph had stopped him from taking every inch of it by destroying the survey sticks (101). Ever since then, he had become the community's hero. The narrator says, "I unmistakably recognize the man before me now. He is one of those men beyond logic and explanation—a grown-up believer in heroes, a man with moral vision as simple and singular as his one-eyed line of sight. Such men are easily deceived" (101). The narrator himself was a child believer in heroes and is certain that he has outgrown such romantic nonsense.

Now Danny comes up to them, and as he and Henry chat there is an underlying tension only the reader understands. Henry keeps asking Danny proudly about his father's progress, and Danny hesitates to say much about it (101–02). The narrator misinterprets Danny's discomfort: "Although the boy ignores me, I begin to feel a mute connection with him, wondering if, like me, he doubts the one-eye man's certain vision of his father" (102). It is true that Danny lacks Henry's faith, but not because he does not see Joseph as a hero—only because he is helping his father in secret. After Danny's departure, Henry declares, "Pretty soon now Danny proudest boy in Waikiki!" (102).

Reality and imagination collide the next morning. The narrator's two imaginary fathers return:

If I were nine again, I could share my uncertain mood with Seaman Taylor, or even the giant, whose firm voice would ring like a familiar bell across distant seas. But I am thirty, and they hide once again in my memory—though only two days ago I would not have been surprised to find the two of them in line with me at the airport ticket counter. Instead, I remembered again the tight-lipped expression on Mother's face whenever she spoke of Hawaii. On the plane I shook my head, reflecting how, in memory at least, she was accompanying me back to the exotic place of my birth—a trip she would have sternly resisted in life.

(103)

Real father and real mother clash with remembered and imaginary parents. He sees himself as a poor legacy of theirs, lacking their strength to overcome wars and dangerous work in pineapple fields (103). He feels a "lack of fulfillment" in his work, thinking he should be doing something greater (104).

At that moment, the story takes a strange turn. He hears squealing tires and sees below him that Henry has been struck by a taxi. A woman near the accident scene begins to cry, and the narrator recalls the last time he cried: at an act of love by a teacher toward a mentally disabled boy named Benny in his class (104). The accident scene is cleared, and that evening he sees Danny on the beach staring at the Sheraton Hotel:

I look up at the huge wall of lights and remember the Sheraton was one of the hotels built by Chun Lee, the man who bet Joe Kamahele could not drink a thousand beers in ten days. I look back at the boy and imagine the one-eyed puka shell seller spreading the news along the beach: Big Joe Kamahele is too sick to win his bet with the hotel builder. Big Joe Kamahele has lost, but he will finish and all Waikiki will be proud.

(105)

How does he know any of this, unless he has invented it himself? It may well be that from now on, the story is a product of his own imagination, that he is the Rainbow Man. He follows Danny to the International Market Place, where Henry has his stand, and is not at all surprised to see Henry there hawking his wares to the tourists. Danny stops in front of the Rainbow Man and sees what the artist produces: not realistic images, but the products of wishful thinking and the imagination, in this case a white woman surfing at Diamond Head: " 'I paint what you see in your mind's eye,' the painter says, and adds a final touch of blue to the ocean. 'Finished. Now it's yours.' " (105). When the narrator sees the painting and compares it to the woman who has ordered it, he notes the differences between the woman and her portrait:

the real woman is sunburned and peeling, while the figure in the painting is deeply tanned ... The real woman is chubby, almost fat, but the body of the woman on the surfboard is turned at an angle to obscure her shape. The real woman is forty or so; the age of the woman on the canvas is impossible to tell, but tousled hair and the bend of her body suggest youth.

(105–06)

The Rainbow Man has created a dream image, an idealized portrait that is more valued than reality. The painter says to the crowd, " 'On my canvas you can be whomever you wish. Close your eyes. Who sees a picture they would like me to paint?' Danny responds, and asks him to paint Joseph: 'big Joe Kamahele—strongest man in Waikiki!' " This is the Joseph he sees and wants to see. When the Rainbow Man says, "Your father must be a very big man" Danny replies, "Bigger than anyone ... Strong enough to beat Chun Lee Chang who build the Sheraton Hotel!" (106). Sure enough, the Rainbow Man depicts Joseph as "a giant hurling his great bulk against a gleaming wall of concrete and glass—the Sheraton Hotel": clearly an echo of the narrator's father-as-giant (106). The narrator wonders if the painting will be for the boy or for his father: "Which of them needs the illusion more? The father whose real life cannot measure up to the greatness his son has been taught to believe in? Or the boy who wants, against his better judgement, to believe?" (106). His contempt for hero-worship masks his own such thoughts about his father. He thinks he has grown beyond the need for such thinking, but his losses have made it clear that creating an imagined version of his father (and his mother) is a necessary comfort.

On his last day in Hawaii, he thinks, "Mother was right—these are islands of false hope and should be carefully avoided" (107). He has tried to keep his emotional distance, and thinks that Danny shares his observer's and cynical stance:

> there's no stopping the Hollis Mormans of the world. But the boy Danny is not like Hollis. Nor is he like the one-eyed puka shell seller, nor Benny the retard, nor Seaman Taylor who died in the Philippines. He is like *me*—doubting, hesitant, and—as he must inevitably learn— powerless. He may postpone the inevitable with a ten dollar painting, but, for both of us, the heroes must finally die. At least Seaman Taylor and the giant went quietly.
>
> (107)

However, he then sees Henry once again approaching his table at the same café where the story began and is still unsurprised to see him well. Danny is out surfing once again, so that the scene suggests that no time at all has passed (107). Henry repeats what he said during their first con- versation: that Danny is "like a son to me" (102, 107). Theirs is a rela- tionship of love, not merely shared respect for Joseph. He discloses that Danny gave him the picture of his father: an act of love. The narrator is stunned by what he now sees:

For a moment I do not hear his words as the scene around us dissolves into a blur. I try to gather my bearings, but see only the shell seller's good eye. A light radiates from there, and I see three figures: a tall sailor in white, whispering secret words whose meaning I've long forgotten; the huge, fierce face of a giant, his deep voice rumbling in reassuring tones; a young Japanese girl bent grimly over the dusty leaves of a pineapple plant, her small back arched strong against the sun.

(108)

He sees the reality of his imagined parents at last and comes to terms with them as both his real and his constructed forebears.

Although an observer throughout the story, and a creator at many points, the narrator has been as blind as Burton and far more blind than Henry. A tourist had offered Henry one hundred dollars for the painting, and now the narrator foolishly offers one thousand (108), in an obvious parallel to the thousand beers that represented Joseph's heroism. He wants this painted representation of both hero-worship and love, a replacement for the lost photograph and faded giant. Joseph has, in effect, become the narrator's father. Naturally, Henry refuses to sell it. Danny's gift to Henry reminds the narrator of the teacher's gift to Benny, and he begins to cry over this profound gesture of love, to the intense embarrassment of the people sitting around him.

Has the narrator invented the events following Henry's accident? Is he the author of the entire narrative? He brings a very different point of view to the events we have witnessed in the rest of the mini-cycle, a view from the outside that nevertheless seems to be aware of things depicted in the other stories. The various artists and storytellers in all three stories hint at the mini-cycle's metafictional nature. As a whole, the text demonstrates that no one perspective can provide a definitive picture of the characters or events; the shifting point of view, extending perhaps even to the (or an) author's own, subverts all narrative authority. Furthermore, the division of the mini-cycle into widely, albeit symmetrically, separated stories underlines its fractured vision, its refusal to offer coherence. Each story is like Burton's arrogance or Henry's disability: it gives us a single, limited angle on the characters, denying us the final word on any individual or incident while lending unity to the mini-cycle through shared characters, themes, and images.

The two linked stories in Nuala Ní Chonchúir's *Mother America and Other Stories* (2012), "Scullion" and "My Name Is William Clongallen," are separated by three unrelated stories and, in terms of setting, long distances and many decades. The collection as a whole is unified by the theme of emigration from Ireland and adjustment to life in the United States, and the mini-cycle depicts Mary Carter's departure from the old country and her son's return to it seeking his roots, thereby tracing a circular path.

Mary is the title character and narrator of "Scullion," a fourteen-year-old kitchen maid whom her so-far-unnamed employer has taken as his lover. It is important to note that we do not learn her last name here, either; the mini-cycle is about hidden identities, and as a servant, she is known by, and in terms of class and social convention in the household only entitled to, her first name. The fact that her surname is not revealed will have an effect on our reading of the second story, as we will see. Although it is an exploitative relationship, Mary does not consider herself a victim; instead, in her youthful naïveté she believes she holds an advantage over her master's wife because "Himself" prefers her and because of the secretive nature of the affair:

> Sometimes I want to say to her, "Your man has a better time in a short night with me than he has with you in a long week." But my mammy always says it is cannier to hold a secret under your tongue and not blurt it out from annoyance. I often feel a glow inside myself because the scutty bitch doesn't know a thing.
>
> (105)

She compares her own body favourably to her mistress's, describing the latter's as "slack and lumpy from having babies" (105)—an ironic line given how her own body and life are about to change.

Her desire for her master is both clear and unapologetic; this affair satisfies her at least as much as him: "He kisses me like a madman, slobbering his tongue all over my face and neck in a way that is so welcome to me" (108); afterward, "I feel the wetness seep under me and I like it" and she relishes the bruises from their love-making, "delighting in them as if they were jewels. I press on the sore spots during the day to remind myself of him; I poke their softness until the pain is hard to bear and I smile, holding my memories of his body and smell to myself" (108). Thus, it is anything but a one-sided affair as far as she is concerned. The problem is that she does not understand how little she and the affair mean to him.

Meanwhile, Mary despises her mistress, Ursula, out of jealousy perhaps and certainly because she does not like being ordered about in an arbitrary way. The early part of the story establishes her strong personality, a characterization that sets up her later decision to run away rather than submit to the will of her "betters." She refuses to accept the dictates of class, often challenging Ursula's treatment of her: Ursula complains to her sister, "Mary has a temper you see, Jane ... She is loose-tongued and prone to fits of anger" (106). Ursula's arrogant put-downs are not only directed at her, as Mary comments: "After a time, they lose the manners of their upbringing and start cackling and squawking like rooks" (106–07). Ní Chonchúir makes it clear that Mary has a mind of her own and the courage to fight for herself. She has powerful maternal instincts, more than is safe for her emotionally and in terms of her employment. She dotes on her employers' three daughters, and Cook, her friend, warns her, "Go easy Mary. The family are separate to us. All of them" (107). She is likely referring not only to the daughters but also to their employer, cautioning Mary to keep her distance from him.

The inevitable happens: when Ursula tells Jane that she is pregnant, Mary realizes that she is, too, and she reacts with something less than joy: "the shock settles over me like a cold cloak. I have been feeling peaked; my blood has not flowed. Something has been growing under my apron for months and I have chosen not to see it" (109). She informs her master, thinking he will be supportive, and begins to see the truth as he asks her what she plans to do with the baby:

> His face looks deformed in the flickering candle-light; it frightens me. I snuggle my head under his arm. "I will send the baby home to my mother," I say, though I know that no such thing will be possible.
> "Well then," he says, and pushes his hand between my legs.
> (109–10)

If she did not understand their relationship before, she must see it now.

The childbirths of the upper and lower classes take place in very different conditions: Ursula has a doctor and midwife while all Mary has to help her is Cook, and the rough nature of the room in which Mary bears her child is not revealed until the second story. Mistress and servant give birth at the same time, but Ursula's son is stillborn while Mary's is healthy (110). Cook, apparently knowing what is about to happen, tells her she should leave. Mary thinks, "But I have nowhere to go. My mammy is ashamed of me and has told me not to come home again" (111). Her master, who has long wanted a son, comes to take the child from her (111). Ursula did not know about Mary's pregnancy, and the family will hide the truth about the stillborn baby and pretend that the boy is hers. It is only when they take the baby away that we learn the man's name: "They name him William, after Himself" (112).

Mary now sees her true position. Her employers begin to raise the boy as their own, and she only gets to be with and nurse her son while the family is away in Dublin. It is while they are absent that Cook embarks upon her plan: she helps Mary run away with the baby (113–15). Cook offers money and a piece of advice: "Change his name, Mary" but Mary refuses to do so, likely because the boy was named after the master and she wants to keep the name as a memento of him. As it turns out, his name will change anyway. The story ends on a note of optimism—Mary succeeds in spiriting her son away. As for whether she makes it all the way to America, however, Ní Chonchúir leaves the ending open, and we do not learn her tragic fate until we reach the second story in the mini-cycle somewhat later.

The three intervening stories—assuming the reader reads them before turning to "My Name Is William Clongallen"—make the reader think that Mary's story is over and that we will never learn what happens to her.

We have no reason to believe she did not survive the journey. When we begin the second story, we also have no reason to believe that it has anything to do with "Scullion." In fact, Ní Chonchúir diverts us by opening the story with the narrator saying, "My name is Guillermo Dante"; we may not be aware that Guillermo is Spanish for William, and even so, that fact and the title will not immediately suggest that he is Mary's son.

The first hint that his identity is uncertain, and that the ambiguity of identity will be a major theme in the story, comes immediately after he declares his name: "the woman who I called Mama did not give birth to me ... It wasn't until my papa died that Mama told me who I was" (135). His physical features make him stand out: "in a family of dark-skinned boys, I alone was pale-eyed and fair" (135). His mother at first deceives him about his odd appearance, perhaps in a parallel to the way the master in the previous story tried to deceive his wife about the baby. In another parallel, his Mama overprotects him the way Mary dotes on children not her own, and Ní Chonchúir depicts their relationship in a way that also reveals the story's initial setting: "All of Brooklyn belonged to my brothers while I, it seemed, belonged only to Mama" (135).

Guillermo is twelve when his father dies and his mother tells him the truth about his origins. She divulges that his father had met "a poor young woman and her baby boy" (136) on a ship returning from Spain to New York via Ireland; he saw that she was ill, and after she died took charge of the infant. Guillermo's father named the woman as Mary Carter, but since we did not learn Mary's last name in "Scullion," the name still does not mean anything to us. Also, since Mary left Ireland under scandalous circumstances, there is every reason to believe this is not her real surname. Mama reveals, too, that Papa had erased any connection between the boy and his real mother: he changed his name to Guillermo and "brought nothing of Mary's; he did not even take the blanket you were wrapped in" (137). All he knew of Mary's background is that she "lived in a house called Clongallen with the Cookes" (137)—in other words, she has hidden the real name of her employers and pretended that Cook's "name" was theirs. Names and identities are thus closely connected in the story, just as they are in "Scullion."

Years later, Guillermo's wife Rosita convinces him that he needs to seek out his birth family. He is hesitant because he does not need to:

> "I'm from Brooklyn, Rosita, and Mama was all the mother I needed."
> "Guillermo, you are Irish by birth."
> "I am American," I said, ending the matter.
>
> (138)

Here, America is an identity, not a refuge as it was for his mother. In a further parallel, things change with the birth of a boy: "It wasn't until our eldest daughter had a baby boy, and I saw his helpless, beautiful form, that I felt the need to find out about my birthplace" (138). Guillermo sees himself in the boy—frail and "helpless"—and realizes he needs to know where he and his grandson really came from.

The story then recounts his trip to Ireland and his meeting with Cook. He does not fully grasp why his mother left, attributing her emigration to Ireland's dreary weather (138). He visits Clongallen House and asks for Mr. Cooke, but the only person living there is an old woman who tells him there is no such person and sends him away. He goes to the local pub and she tracks him down there; she is Cook, and invites him to come the next day for a talk (140). Throughout the experience, he feels disoriented, receiving strange looks and treatment from Cook, the barmaid, and even the landlord of his guesthouse. Like Heller's narrator, he is and is not home; he is Irish, American, and Spanish all at once.

Cook reveals his origins, but not her name; she identifies herself solely by her role, just as Mary did: "I was the cook for the family here. There's hardly a one of them left. What remains are beyond in England" (131). Ironically, then, William the elder had been determined to preserve the family line but failed, while Mary, his social "lesser," had managed to preserve both it and her own. In fact, Cook has the house itself now, presumably passed down to her by a family no longer interested in maintaining it. Cook's sharp tongue and tough manner are evident throughout the conversation; she is anything but a genteel hostess, throwing biscuits on a plate for him, and she describes Mary as "a bold girl and a good girl all in the one sack," explaining that "She broke her own mother's heart … By opening her legs to a man who'd never marry her" (141). She brings Guillermo upstairs to the attic room where he was born, which the reader can now see: "the floorboards were grey and runnels of water had made one wall green. I could hear rain thrashing down on the roof" (142). Here we get a more detailed picture at last of the circumstances of his birth, and the vast class difference that made Mary a disposable person for Lord Clongallen.

Cook has offered important information to Guillermo, and he responds in turn by telling her that Mary died on the voyage to America. For all her hard exterior, Cook reacts with shock and grief, letting out "a low groan" (142). She had been Mary's true mother, just as Mary had been Guillermo's; the bonds are real, whether genetic or emotional. She feels responsible for Mary's death and explains:

> "The master and his missus were going to keep Baby William—you—for their own; it wasn't right. You were Mary's child, first and forever."
> "Yes," I said.
> "I should have seen her right. The peteen …"
>
> (143)

She tells him that he looks like Mary, but he is unsure whether to believe her. It does not matter, since he has found the connection he has been seeking. He has no interest in meeting his half-sisters. Cook still refuses to give her own name but tells him his: "your name is Lord William Clongallen" (144). It is only on the final page of the second story that we see in full the name that had been kept from us throughout the first story, now applied not to the employer but to the son.

Guillermo shouts his name outside, accomplishing nothing more than frightening a pigeon. As he sits in his car, he realizes how empty his new-found knowledge is. Ireland is not his true home, and Mary is not his real mother except in biological terms:

> I longed to be home in Brooklyn. The journey before me looked endless. I rested my forehead on the steering wheel then sat up straight.
>
> "My name is Guillermo Dante," I said and started the engine and drove away.
>
> (144)

He has satisfied his need to learn his genetic roots, but what he has really learned is that national and biological origins are not the whole story.

The two stories in the mini-cycle, then, are about two different Lord William Clongallens, both of whom are linked to each other through Mary, and both of whom have false notions about relationships between parents and children. Lord William sought to pass off his illegitimate child with Mary as his legitimate son and heir with Ursula; Guillermo hunts for his biological parents and ultimately rejects them as, ultimately, irrelevant. The mini-cycle takes us on a cyclical journey, from Ireland to America, from real parents to genetically "real" ones, and above all from a real identity to an unreal—if historically true—identity, and back again. In a sense, the two stories draw both parallel lines and a circle, mirroring each other and bringing us back where we began. By separating the stories in her collection, Ní Chonchúir surprises us when she returns to these characters after leaving us to believe that she is done with them, and the emotional effect of our recognition is, to a lesser degree, like that of Guillermo, Mary, and Cook, who similarly confront surprising and sometimes shocking revelations. More specifically, like Guillermo, we learn who is who in unexpected ways; like him, we discover his identity gradually through the course of the second story, as the latter sheds further light on the situation and events of the first. We therefore recapitulate Guillermo's voyage of self-discovery through the process of reading his story.

Ní Chonchúir does much the same with the two linked stories in *Nude* (2009), separating them by a number of other unrelated stories, although all of the texts are linked by the theme of art and characters who are artists. The collection's first story, "Madonna Irlanda," portrays the early days of Magda Bolding's flowering as an artist in Paris after her loveless marriage ends in divorce (2). She entered the marriage as a virgin, a point that will become significant in the second story. Her mother had named her Magdalone—a "skewed-up versions of a Bible name" (1)—establishing an association with Biblical women that will be pursued in "Jackson and Jerusalem." Her name and actions throughout the mini-cycle reveal her to be an amalgam of the two important Marys in the New Testament. She moves to Paris to rejuvenate her creativity: "My will to paint had evaporated and I wanted the city to give me the jizz-up that eluded me in Dublin" (2). From the beginning, however, the story highlights Magda's disorientation in Paris at various levels: creative, emotional, and social. The opening line tells us that she is relying on her guidebook for information on how to behave with strangers to avoid misunderstandings but gets physically and socially lost anyway (1). That feeling parallels her condition during the marriage, in which she seems to have been equally lost. The story describes her gradual adjustment to life in the city and as an artist, as she finds her way in her new home thanks to her relationship with Micheal Farrell, another Irish expatriate.

Her relationship with Micheal is mainly one of artist and model. He invites her to be the model for his political painting, *Madonna Irlanda*. It will require her to pose nude, and she is extremely shy about that—a reaction that the second story will echo: "I've always hated undressing in front of people, even Victor" (8). To reassure her, Micheal says, "Bare flesh is just an ordinary part of the working day for me, Mags, so stop blushing, like a good girl" (9). Her fear is not just about physical exposure; she also has to learn to open herself to the city and to the world of art. Micheal shows her that one must choose between being an artist and a spouse: he tells her, "Art and marriage are a poor match ... They suck the guts out of each other" (5), as illustrated by his own relationship with the woman he refers to as "Her Maj" (5). Once they meet, he takes her to Les Deux Magots, the restaurant where many artistic couples, most of whom had had stormy relationships, had dined (4). At the atelier, she sees graffiti reading, "Rilke loves Clara"; later, Micheal informs her that their marriage had been a disaster, and that "Rilke offloaded Clara, and their daughter, and went his own way" (10). The conclusion is clear: she must decide between domestic happiness and art. She chooses the latter, and any potential love affair with Micheal is simply out of the question. When Victor writes asking her to come back to him, Micheal says, "Don't compromise yourself, Magda. You'll turn nasty if you do" (10). She must devote herself entirely to her art the way he has; at one point, as they look at *L'Odalisque*, the Boucher painting he will use as a source for his own, she says to him, "That's the kind of woman you understand, Micheal ... You couldn't care less about real women; three-dimensional ones" (8). For the true artist, it seems, that attitude is not a fault but a necessity.

Fully ten stories (and some years) later, Magda returns as a secondary character rather than as the protagonist. The narrator of "Jackson and Jerusalem" is a male model who comes to pose for Magda. Like Micheal, she wants to paint a variation of an existing image: "I love the idea of

Jesus as blasé teenager and divinity in one … this tableau I'm painting is of Jesus in the temple, talking to the priests. But, I want to represent Jesus naked, to show his power but, at the same time, his innocence" (68). Like Magda, Jackson is terrified at the idea of posing nude, and objects (67). He eventually agrees, however, and she later reassures him in terms that recall Micheal's: " 'Artists are like doctors, where the human body is concerned,' she said. 'Bare flesh is just part of the working day' " (69). The art is far more important than any conventional norms about nudity. Like Magda, Jackson must learn to put art first; when his father finds out what he is doing, Da attacks him verbally and physically, but Jackson fights back. From shame and fear, Jackson develops a sense of pride about his contribution to Magda's masterpiece. Instead of being merely a model, he becomes a collaborator, and when Magda sees the marks Da has left on Jackson's neck she hugs him in sympathy, but they choose "the best position for Jesus in the temple" together (72). The painting becomes famous, and Jackson gladly joins Magda for interviews, no longer self-conscious or embarrassed about being so completely exposed. At the end, he says,

> whether I knew Magda was mad famous or not, I still think I would have posed for her. She's a bit of a hippy—I knew that the minute I saw her—but she's the kind of auld bird who makes you feel like the most special person in the world when you're with her. That's one of the real gifts she has: making everyone feel important; as important as herself.
>
> (73)

By becoming both her model and her co-artist, he has become a participant, in fact an equal partner, in the production of great art, and that is worth the sacrifice of his privacy.

In both of these exploded mini-cycles, Ní Chonchúir employs a kind of misdirection in order to achieve the maximum effect of surprise when the reader finally realizes that the separated stories are linked. She interposes a number of stories that are unrelated except by theme—migration in one case, art in the other—so that the reader will assume that the characters have come and gone. Only later in each collection do the characters return, and with them the reader's recognition. The exploded mini-cycle thus strengthens the reader's sense of the simultaneous distinctness and unity of the component stories in ways that the story cycle, the volume made up entirely of linked stories, does not.

References

Heller, Steve. *The Man Who Drank a Thousand Beers*. Chariton Review Press, 1984.

Ni Choncuir, Nuala. *Mother America*. New Island, 2012.

——. *Nude*. Salt, 2009.

10 Marginal Cases

The texts we have been analyzing fit fairly well into my definition of a mini-cycle, but as one might expect there are others that are marginal or extra-generic cases. Like book-length fictional texts, these far smaller sets of texts cover a wide range, from single works made up distinct parts, much like novel chapters, all the way to related stand-alone stories that lack the unifying arc required for a mini-cycle. Publication history and paratextual elements are important clues as to what sort of text we are dealing with. Looking at a few examples will clarify the point and demonstrate how difficult it is sometimes to draw hard-and-fast boundaries between the "fuzzy sets" that are literary genres.

An early marginal case is in Sherwood Anderson's *Winesburg, Ohio*.[1] In story cycles and mini-cycles, titles matter; apart from other formal features, one way we distinguish between chapters in a novel and the component stories in a cycle or mini-cycle is that the latter are given their own titles, and they are often published in periodicals before being collected in a volume. "Godliness" is subtitled, "A Tale in Four Parts," and these are numbered using Roman numerals. Of those four parts, two are about Jesse Bentley, one is about Louise Bentley, and one focuses on David Hardy. In addition to the global title for the entire "tale," the "parts" that are not about Jesse Bentley are each given their own titles: "Surrender" for the story about Louise Bentley and "Terror" for the one about David Hardy. Is "Godliness" really one "tale" or four, or possibly even three? Critics are divided over what to call "Godliness"; in his study of the composition of *Winesburg, Ohio*, William L. Phillips treats the four parts as "individual tales" in his overall count of the number of stories in the book (10); Rosemary M. Laughlin refers to "Godliness" as "by far the longest and most structurally complicated tale" (97), thus seeing it as one story; John O'Neill also sees it as a unit, although, unlike Laughlin, he believes that in "language and form" the story "is simpler, less innovative than most of the other stories in *Winesburg, Ohio*" (67); Joseph Dewey writes of "the tales of Jesse Bentley" (251), that is, in the plural; and more recently, Jennifer J. Smith has said of it, "Anderson's three-story sequence, 'Godliness,' 'Surrender,' and 'Terror,' told in five parts, emblematizes the inclusion of longer, independent narratives within the cycle" (133).[2] She thus separates the two titled parts from the others, treating "Godliness" as referring solely to the first two parts despite what the text itself says. Judy Jo Small has a noteworthy, and perhaps unique, way of describing the text's form: "a miniature cycle of stories," one that "approximates the pattern of the larger cycle in which it is contained" (91).[3]

The text's compositional and publishing histories offer a few not very helpful clues as to Anderson's intention. Anderson wrote most of the stories in the book during a brief period from late 1915 to early 1916 and seems to have always wished them to appear together as a book (Phillips 13; on Jesse's origins, see Sykes). He published some of the stories in magazines, but the pieces "Godliness" comprises were not published before their appearance in the book. Jarvis Thurston has shown that "Godliness" had its origins in an abandoned novel to be entitled *Immaturity*, which Anderson worked on in 1917. When the project collapsed, he made a few alterations in some details, such as changing the main character's first name from Joseph to Jesse, and constructed "Godliness" out of these fragments while adding Louise's story so as to portray three generations of Jesse's family (Small 84–85). On the other hand, Small concludes, "The manuscript evidence does suggest at least that Anderson did not always intend to place all four parts together as a unit" (85).[4]

A cursory look at the three or four parts shows why an argument could be made that it is a mini-cycle. Again, among the markers of the genre is that the component stories feature shifts in point of view and/or major shifts in temporal setting, and both can certainly be found between the parts; on the other hand, there is a fair bit of change in point of view *within* each part as well. The common character is Jesse Bentley, a "grotesque" in Anderson's terms, as defined by the narrator in "The Book of the Grotesque," someone who has created a "truth" and insisted on living by it:

> It was the truths that made the people grotesques. The old man had quite an elaborate theory concerning the matter. It was his notion that the moment one of the people took one of the truths to himself, called it his truth, and tried to live his life by it, he became a grotesque and the truth he embraced became a falsehood.
>
> (24)

A grotesque is a person who has latched on to one "truth" as *the* truth, as a key to all wisdom and a guide for living, refusing to see the paradoxes and contradictions in life and human nature; the characters in the book suffer from "false ideas, false dreams, false hopes, and false goals" (D. Anderson, *Sherwood Anderson* 41), much like Chekhov's characters. As a result, the grotesque suffers incompleteness and frustration, and severe isolation and alienation, becoming unable to communicate or achieve community with others (Fussell 105; Hoffman 238; D. Anderson,

Sherwood Anderson 39–40; B. Lee 137). For Irving Howe, the book is "a fable of American estrangement" (101). Alienation is not inevitable; as David D. Anderson writes, "man could break down the barriers that separated him from his fellows through compassion and through sympathetic understanding" ("Sherwood Anderson" 250). But the grotesques in Winesburg lack that broad vision of humanity, that ability to sympathize, and so cannot break out of their shells. They have no one to talk to but George Willard, the budding author who eventually leaves the town, taking with him their only conduit to other people. George can make art out of the wide variety of "truths", the complex realities, to which he has been exposed by writing about the grotesques (Fussell 107–09).

Jesse is an ambitious farmer and religious fanatic who sees himself in somewhat traditionally Puritan terms as an agent of Providence, a man destined to found a nation in the Promised Land of America (Laughlin 99–100; D. Anderson, *Sherwood Anderson* 45). He identifies with, and even identifies himself as sharing the status of, Biblical patriarchs like Abraham and Jesse, father of King David. In Joseph Dewey's reading, "clearly Jesse wants to be possessed not so much by God as by significance" (254). When his wife gives birth to a daughter instead of Jesse's desired son and heir, then dies in childbirth, Jesse neglects Louise and invests all his hopes in Louise's son David. Scholars have discussed at some length the way that Jesse destroys himself by substituting ego and abstract belief for human communication, tenderness, and love (e.g., Dunne 71–73). In addition, Jesse shows us the harsh, Calvinist, and oppressive morality out of which the town's repressive, isolating, and alienating way of life emerged, providing historical background for the other narratives in the book (Small 87–88). John O'Neill argues that Jesse and his daughter embody the cycle's themes of loneliness and madness, and their stories are like biblical *exempla* of alienation (68). "Godliness" portrays the effects of Jesse's monomania on all three significant family members, showing how their minds and hearts have been starved of healthy affection and attention.

The first two parts recount the rise of Jesse from poor farmer to land baron. His father and four brothers live a brutish pioneer life that turns them into brutish men (64–65), while he is the smallest and most sensitive of old Tom's offspring, becoming a religious scholar and Presbyterian minister. When his brothers are killed in the Civil War, his father summons him home to take over the farm, and he runs it with the sort of religious fervour he otherwise devoted to his studies and Christian beliefs. Jesse's wife is too delicate for the hard life he imposes on her and himself, and so he is left alone to manage the farm. In his solitude and obsession with earning both material wealth and God's grace, he grows increasingly mad and gives his daughter none of the love she craves. He becomes a tyrant, an egomaniac convinced of his divinely sanctioned greatness, and a very lonely soul (67–70). On the other hand, Anderson laments the passing of such strong-willed, independent, and dynamic men in the modern age:

"Much of the old brutal ignorance that had in it also a kind of beautiful childlike innocence is gone forever" (71). Jesse's grotesquerie is partly a product of the industrial age (Dunne 71). *Immaturity*, in fact, was to have been a chronicle of America's changes as it moved from the pastoral to the industrial ages, leading to, as Anderson said, "the terrible immaturity and crudeness of all our lives" (qtd. in Small 85). Jesse becomes a religious fanatic because he has no other outlet for his active imagination; he is, in effect, a frustrated version of George Willard, the budding author (71–72). At the end of Part I, he has a quasi-religious vision of himself as a Biblical hero and his neighbours as Philistines who must be defeated in his rise to wealth and power.

Part II introduces us to his grandson, David Hardy, but then quickly shifts attention—albeit briefly—to his mother, Louise. Like her father, she, too, is a scholar and as frustrated in her intellectual pursuits as Jesse is in his imaginative ones. She ends up being a recluse, "a frightening social misfit" (Laughlin 97). She is unhappily married, becomes violent at times, and burns off nervous energy by driving her carriage wildly through Winesburg's streets (74–75). David is glad to escape his unhappy home by visiting his grandfather's farm, unaware that Jesse will see him as his proper spiritual and material heir in the absence of a son. David is also imaginative and is terrified by his own created demons when he runs away from home (76–77). The point of view remains largely that of David, who, when he is finally brought back home, sees a gentleness in his mother he had not seen before, as his near-loss forces her to appreciate him in ways she had not (78). When he eventually goes to live with his grandfather, he enters a world where he is largely happy, mainly because Jesse's sisters, like Jesse, treat him as the child they never had (79). For them, David's coming awakens "long-dormant dreams and desires to love and motherhood" (Laughlin 98). The focalization then moves between David's and Jesse's points of view; in this way, Anderson portrays both Jesse's ambitions for his grandson and David's fear of the old man. In the final scene of the part, David runs when his grandfather kneels to pray and seems to become someone entirely different. The scene sets up the text's climactic interaction between them: another bizarre religious ceremony that David misunderstands.

Part III, "Surrender," is the closest of the four to a discrete narrative. The focus shifts almost entirely to Louise, and we learn about how she became the person she grew up to be. She was a sensitive and intelligent person who received none of the love she yearned for from her father (D. Anderson, *Sherwood Anderson* 45), and became, the narrator tells us, "a neurotic, one of the race of oversensitive women that in later days industrialism was to bring in such great numbers into the world" (87). She goes to live with and work for the Hardy family, and there applies herself to her studies as per her own predilections and the wishes of Albert Hardy. She thereby provokes the resentment of Albert's two daughters (88–90), but also becomes attracted to their brother John, and eventually learns about sex when she is unintentionally an aural witness to Mary Hardy's encounter with her lover (92–93). Emboldened by what she has heard, she pursues John, they have sex, and she becomes certain that she is pregnant. It is on that basis that they marry, but then it turns out that she is not pregnant after all, and she ends up in an unhappy marriage living a life of bitterness and regret (96). Like many female characters in Anderson's work, she mistakenly believes sex will free and save her (O'Neill 69). Apart from the description of his emotional neglect of his daughter, Jesse plays no role in the "part," and so, in its relative autonomy, "Surrender" is very much like a component story in a mini-cycle.

"Terror" returns us to Jesse and David, and once again the point of view alternates between them. There is also the kind of temporal shift that we associate with mini-cycles: David is now fifteen, no longer the small child who benefited from the love and attention of his aunts and the life-affirming environment of the farm. Anderson begins the text by telling us the ending: "he, like his mother, had an adventure that changed the whole current of his life and sent him out of his quiet corner into the world ... He left Winesburg and no one there ever saw him again" (97). Anderson thus establishes thematic links to Louise's narrative in Part III and to what happens to George Willard at the end of the book. In addition, we are told that his father "spent much money in trying to locate his son, but that is no part of this story" (97). Calling "Terror" a "story" implies that it also has a degree of autonomy from the other parts of "Godliness" and reinforces the full "tales" status as a mini-cycle rather than a single short story.

Jesse has built up his farm into a great success, but at the cost of his sanity as he becomes convinced that he is a latter-day biblical patriarch and David is the scion who would beget the nation that would call Jesse its patriarch:

> Again he walked alone at night thinking of God and as he walked he again connected his own figure with the figures of old days. Under the stars he knelt on the wet grass and raised up his voice in prayer. Now he had decided that like the men whose stories filled the pages of the Bible, he would make a sacrifice to God.
>
> (99–100)

Meanwhile, like his biblical namesake, David has developed into a skilled hunter with his sling. Jesse takes David and a lamb into the woods, where he brandishes a knife intending to sacrifice the lamb. David thinks Jesse intends to kill him instead and defends himself with his sling. "Terror" alludes to a number of biblical stories, primarily Abraham's near-sacrifice of Isaac but also David's killing of Goliath when David fires a stone at Jesse's head and knocks him down (100–02). We are shown the incident from both sides, and therefore know both Jesse's real intentions and the reasons for David's fear, especially in light of what occurred at the end of Part II. Jesse thus brings about the destruction of his own dreams through his increasingly insane behaviour, which frightens his grandson to the point of fearing for his life (Laughlin 101). Jesse regains at least some of his sanity when he loses David; as he tells people, "It happened because I was too greedy for glory" (102). In regaining his sanity, he reacts to the loss the same way that Louise reacted to his near-loss in Part II. For his part, David "forsakes religion, forsakes family, to embrace hesitatingly and fearfully nothing less than the world itself" (Dewey 256), much like George does at the end. Thus, all three main characters, representing three generations of the family, are like the cycle's most important character in their own ways.

For Laughlin, the four parts of "Godliness"

> form a skillfully and intricately constructed tale. It is the only one in four parts in the collection, and we may hypothesize that as such it was an experiment with structure. The central climactic action in its mythic cloak occurs in the last part; the preceding sections present its causes and its prefiguration in past time; the impact of that ironic "sacrifice" is all the more powerful because the other parts (especially I and II) have shown the grotesque effects of Jesse's obsession on the lives of those related to him, particularly his daughter's.
>
> (102)

She is correct to argue that the four parts of "Godliness" compose a narrative whole, and as such are strongly linked. The text's narrative unity and its single title suggest that "Godliness" should be treated as one short story, yet the separate titles Anderson gave to the third and fourth parts and the substantial shifts in point of view in "Surrender" and temporal setting in "Terror" argue for the text's being a mini-cycle. Anderson's genre label—"a tale in four parts"—may be ultimately decisive, but the text is unmistakably on the border between the single short story and the mini-cycle.

Because it is a setting-based story cycle, characters in the book move in and out of each other's stories. "Paper Pills," "Mother," and "Death" bring Dr. Reefy and Elizabeth Willard together, interweaving their narratives as one might expect in this kind of cycle. Jennifer J. Smith considers the three stories "a divided trilogy, depicting the trajectory of Elizabeth Willard's life" (126). These stories would have to form a more unified whole distinct from the rest of book to be a mini-cycle in the same way the Pupkin/Pepperleigh stories in Leacock's cycle do. Nevertheless, they might well be treated as an exploded mini-cycle.

An even more challenging example is the pair of stories—if that is what they are—that open Alice Munro's *The Moons of Jupiter* (1982). The compositional and publication histories of the "Chaddeleys and Flemings" stories and paratextual elements make it very difficult to decide whether we are dealing with two stories that form a mini-cycle or one longer text that needs to be treated as a single story.

The text(s) began as one long short story or perhaps novella entitled, "Chaddeleys and Flemings"; it was intended to form part of a collection entitled "Rose and Janet" that was to include stories about two different but parallel narrators (on the history of the text and the collection, see Hoy, "Rose and Janet"). That collection formed the basis of *Who Do You Think You Are?*, which Munro later decided to limit to stories about Rose, removing the Janet stories entirely.[5] As for the story, Douglas Gibson advised Munro to break it up into two short stories. Following his advice, and revising the stories somewhat, she turned them into one called "Connection" and another she entitled, "The Stone in the Field." She published "Connection" in *Chatelaine* (November 1978) and "The Stone in the Field" in *Saturday Night* (April 1979). She then collected them in *The Moons of Jupiter* and reunited them under "Chaddeleys and Flemings," which she divided into "Chaddeleys and Flemings 1. Connection" and "Chaddeleys and Flemings 2. The Stone in the Field." Complicating the matter still further is that a third Janet story became the title story in the collection. Should "The Moons of Jupiter" be considered part of a two- or three-story (exploded) mini-cycle? It is printed separately from the other two, indeed as the final story in the book, and forms a coda for both the "Chaddeleys and Flemings" stories and the collection as a whole.

There are grounds for arguing both sides as to whether "Chaddeleys and Flemings" is one text or a linked pair, a two-story mini-cycle. The compositional history demonstrates that the stories were always intended to be a unit and thus to be read together. Munro did not reunite them as a single text in *The Moons of Jupiter* but retained their separate titles—up to a point. She restored their common title, and her using numbers suggests these are parts of a single text, like those in "Godliness." Scholars are divided, and even self-contradictory, over whether to consider it one text or two, however; Coral Ann Howells calls "Chaddeleys and Flemings" "a mirror story in two parts representing the double strain in Janet Fleming's inheritance" (*Alice Munro* 71) yet then calls "Connection" the "first story" (71). Ailsa Cox refers to "Chaddeleys and Flemings" as "[s]tories which piece together family history" (*Alice Munro* 42); later in the same study she calls it a "sequence" (76).

The "Chaddeleys and Flemings" stories would qualify as a standard two-story mini-cycle on some grounds. First, like so many two-story mini-cycles, the set appears at the beginning of the collection; second, the parts are linked by the narrator while offering mirroring narratives. Critics have analyzed "Chaddeleys and Flemings" in some detail and from various theoretical perspectives, and we do not need to devote much time to reviewing their work, but certain features should be considered to show how the stories function as both discrete and mirroring texts. Both parts or stories are about family connections: "Connection" portrays the visit of Janet's maternal cousins to her home, while "The Stone in the Field" is about Janet's and her father's visit to his sisters. The two sets of female relatives are opposites in a variety of ways, and the stories are linked not only through the common narrator but also through these comparisons and contrasts (see Blodgett 111, among others).

For example, the cousins work outside the home, and when they are listed on the first page of "Connection," their names are accompanied by their jobs, which are mostly—as one might expect given the times— extensions of traditional women's roles or reflective of conventional female interests: Iris is a nurse, Isabel owns a florist shop, and Flora (whose name links her to Isabel's business) is a teacher. Winifred is a "lady accountant": the only one with a non-traditional job and therefore subject to the label "lady" (1). Unlike the highly individualized cousins, the sisters are indistinguishable: "I could never get them straight. They looked too much alike" (25). The sisters are also in a way defined by their work, but of a purely domestic and traditional sort reflected in their spotless house. Janet says, "Work would be what filled their lives, not conversation; work would be what gave their days shape ... Work would not be done here as it was in our house, where the idea was to get it over with. It would be something that could, that must, go on forever" (26–27).

The cousins are fleshy and sensual beings, and Janet devotes much time to describing their bodies, highlighting their physicality: "Their bosoms were heavy and intimidating—a single-armored bundle—and their stomachs and behinds full and corseted as those of any married woman. In those days it seemed to be the thing for women's bodies to swell and ripen to a good size twenty, if they were getting anything out of life at all" (1).[6] Their sensuality is also reflected in their smoking (3) and drinking. By contrast, the sisters are "all lean and fine-boned, and might at one time have been fairly tall, but were stooped now, with hard work and deference ... Their faces were pale, eyebrows thick and furry, eyes deep-set and bright; blue-gray or green-gray or gray" (25). If the cousins exude vitality, the sisters come across as closer to death than life.

The cousins dress in outlandish or provocative clothes that also contribute to their air of the sensual, such as "corsets that did up the side with dozens of hooks and eyes, stockings that hissed and rasped when they crossed their legs, silk jersey dresses for the afternoon" (1), and "quilted satin dressing gowns" (2). They wear makeup and scent, asserting their femininity and desire to be seen (1–2). These sartorial and cosmetic displays border on and then become costumes: "They dressed up in old clothes, in old straw hats and my father's overalls, and took pictures of each other" (4), and put on a show as Iris "took the cloth off the dining-room table to drape herself in, and sent me out to collect hen feathers to put in her hair" (4). Janet's mother joins in, amazing Janet (4; on mothers as performers and "clowns" in Munro's fiction see Redekop, esp. 161–63). As Janet says, "Audience and performers, the cousins were for each other, every waking moment. And sometimes asleep" (4). The one performance Janet best remembers is their singing of "Row, Row, Row Your Boat"; the song comes back to her at the end of the story, holding a variety of meanings, including the fact that the four very noisy and exciting voices have now been reduced to only one through illness and death (18; see Howells, *Alice Munro* 73). Janet has inherited their performative nature; when she throws a plate at Richard for insulting Iris, "the pie flew out and caught him on the side of the face just as in the old movies or an *I Love Lucy* show" (18). The sisters favour no such overt displays; they wear plain clothing, eschewing the corsets and other additions that would emphasize their female forms, do not use cosmetics, either, and wear their hair more like that of girls than women (25). The aunt who shows Janet the fan system is also childlike in how she reacts to Janet's mother's summons: "the aunt and I looked at each other exactly as two children look at each other when an adult is calling" (22). Janet is disturbed by her aunt's lack of womanhood and the sexuality that goes with it (for a discussion of gender in the story, see Redekop 164–67). She reveals her genetic connection to them as she considers how little it would take for her to resemble them completely: "suppose I stopped doing anything to my hair, now, stopped wearing makeup and plucking my eyebrows, put on a shapeless print dress and apron and stood around hanging my head and hugging my elbows? Yes" (25).

The cousins are extroverted, loud and boisterous, constantly shouting and not shy about erupting in occasionally vulgar language. They are storytellers, filling the house with tales of dramatic events that may or may not be true, and Iris tells the same stories when she pays her visit to Janet, as if they are part of who she is (16). The cousins bring the marvellous into the family's unexciting life. As they are singing their round, Janet thinks,

> Life is transformed, by these voices, by these presences, by their high spirits and grand esteem, for themselves and each other. My parents, all of us, are on holiday. The mixture of voices and words is so complicated and varied it seems that such confusion, such jolly rivalry will go on forever, and then to my surprise—for I am surprised, even though I know the pattern of rounds—the song is thinning out
> (18)

The sisters are introverted, and one even "got up, and ran around the side of the house" at the approach of Janet's family car (25). As Janet's father tries to chat with them, it "was clear that only a great effort of will kept them all from running away and hiding, like Aunt Susan, who never did reappear while we were there" (27). Unlike the cousins, they speak only when spoken to, answering Janet's father's questions with short statements, their replies purely factual rather than expressions of feeling or opinion (27).

The cousins are aliens, even those who are still Canadian; they come from far away and exude an air of the foreign, worldly, and exotic, even in their language (3–4):

> In the larger world, things had happened to them. Accidents, proposals, encounters with lunatics and enemies. Iris could have been rich. A millionaire's widow, a crazy old woman with a wig like a haystack, had been wheeled into the hospital one day, clutching a carpetbag. And what was in the carpetbag but jewels, real jewels, emeralds and diamonds and pearls as big as pullet eggs ... Then she told how she had been proposed to by an actor, dying from a life of dissipation. She allowed him to swig from a Listerine bottle because she didn't see what difference it would make. He was a stage actor, so we wouldn't recognize the name even if she told us, which she wouldn't.

They are not only foreign but urban; all live in cities and find Dalgleish quaintly rural, and gush over Huron County's rusticity: "Breathe that air! Oh, you can't beat the country air. Is that the pump where you get your drinking water? Wouldn't that be lovely right now? A drink of well water!" (2). Dalgleish is, for them, an experience rather than a reality, a kind of tourist attraction: "They didn't think Dalgleish was real. They drove uptown and reported on the oddity of the shopkeepers; they imitated things they had overheard on the street" (4). The sisters are entirely local, long-time residents as they are of Huron County, and rural (24). They have apparently lived on the farm their whole lives, and when Janet's father wishes to tease them, he playfully accuses them of precisely the sort of behaviour the cousins have engaged in—or have claimed to, at least:

> He inquired whether they were doing much dancing these days. He shook his head as he pretended to recall their reputation for running around the country to dances, smoking, cutting up. He said they were a bad lot, they wouldn't get married because they'd rather flirt; why, he couldn't hold up his head for the shame of them.
>
> (27)

Their house is like the sisters: isolated, hidden, and difficult to reach, and thanks to their perpetual devotion to cleanliness as sterile as they are (26).

The Chaddeley cousins represent a life of movement and flux, and Janet's mother is also associated with them; in "The Stone in the Field," the family home is constantly changing because of her work as an antique dealer (19). Janet describes her childhood as a time when people were not interested in the old but wanted to convert it to the new, "covering old woodwork with white or pastel paint as fast as they were able, throwing out spool beds and putting in blond maple bedroom suites, covering patchwork quilts with chenille bedspreads" (20). The Fleming sisters represent the past and the static: they still drive "a horse and buggy, a horse and cutter in the wintertime, long after everyone else had ceased to do so" (22). They themselves are antiques, old-fashioned hold-overs from an earlier age (W. R. Martin, *Alice Munro* 134), and they have no interest in the new-fangled modern conveniences Janet's mother, "seeing life all in terms of change and possibility" (29), recommends. It is difficult to argue that modern, materialist values of the sort Janet's mother promotes *should* mean anything to these representatives of a simpler time.

Along with the contrasts, "Chaddeleys and Flemings" stresses certain important continuities pertaining to theme and character. The two sets of female relatives possess certain similarities as well as stark differences. Both the cousins and the sisters are "maiden ladies" or "old maids" (1), and both are tight-knit groups encouraging and aiding each other, if in pursuit of vastly different ambitions and lifestyles. Both sets of women are independent of men, even as they surrender the companionship and sexual satisfaction of romantic relationships, and are therefore socially unconventional (Rasporich 69; New 122). Like the cousins and their round, the sisters fade away over time, dying until there is only one left, Aunt Lizzie (31). They cannot resist the depredations of time no matter how much they want to freeze it.

More importantly, their speech and behaviour bring into sharp relief traits that they have inherited from their ancestors and that Janet, through her parents, has herself inherited. Munro's purpose is to show that Janet is a product of both the Chaddeleys and the Flemings, whether or not she realizes it or is willing to admit it (Martin, *Alice Munro* 133; Blodgett 109). Certain themes and their related family traits are reflected in Janet's and her families' beliefs, attitudes, and behaviour. For example, class is a significant theme here, as it is in much of Munro's fiction. Janet's family is poor, and that is why the cousins visit Janet's mother: "she was too poor to go to see them" (2). Despite her poverty, Janet's mother considers herself a member of an upper-class family that had suffered "a great comedown, a dim catastrophe" (8). She insists that those in her home use "genteel" language in her home (3), and to serve drinks to her cousin, Janet tells us, she "prettied up the glasses by dipping the rims in beaten egg whites, then in sugar" (5). She "polished the dessert forks, she ironed the table napkins" (12) when it came time to serve dessert. Like the cousins, she has little regard for Dalgleish, and fondly recalls her days in Fork Mills with its "stone houses, its handsome and restrained public buildings (quite different, she said, from Huron County's, where the idea had been to throw up some brick monstrosity and stick a tower on it)" and above all "the better quality of things for sale and the better class of people" (6). When Iris visits Janet in Vancouver, "her tone when she spoke of Dalgleish and my parents was condescending" (15). The cousins, including Janet's mother, rely for their sense of social status on an apparently upper-class family lineage, one that the four cousins predictably turn into a romantic and dramatic chronicle, although the truth proves to be far more ordinary and pedestrian (8).

Both stories are about connections—mainly family but other kinds as well—that require recognition and acceptance. In fact, the word "connection" itself recurs. Janet's mother appeals to her family heritage because it gives her a sense of social height, of the world outside Dalgleish that she misses, and an identity:

> the leading families of Fork Mills would themselves be humbled if they came into contact with certain families of England, to whom my mother was connected.
>
> Connection. That was what it was all about. The cousins were a show in themselves, but they also provided a connection. A connection with the real, and prodigal, and dangerous world. They knew how to get on in it, they had made it take notice. They could command a classroom, a maternity ward, the public; they knew how to deal with taxi drivers and train conductors.
>
> (6–7)

This is a world Janet's mother wishes she could be part of, where dessert forks, table napkins, and other signs of sophistication matter. For his part, Janet's husband sees only the Dalgleish in them, not the probably mythical gentility, and wants Janet "amputated from that past which seemed to him such shabby baggage" (13). In "The Stone in the Field," Janet remarks that she cannot believe the aunt who shyly drove her buggy in Dalgleish was a relative of hers: "the connection seemed impossible" (22). Later, she is ashamed when she neglects to keep in touch with the sisters: "It did make me guilty and bewildered to think that they were still there, still attached to me. But any message from home, in those days, could let me know I was a traitor" (31). Toward the end of his life, Janet's father becomes "very good-humored and loquacious under the influence of the pills they were giving him" (29), implying that he had been almost as taciturn as his sisters—that is, their silence is a family trait. We learn their father and grandfather had been the source of their devotion to hard work and resistance to change, their static way of thinking and living; the grandfather punished their father for using a wheelbarrow to bring feed to the horses: "he got beat. For laziness. That was the way they were, you know. Any change of any kind was a bad thing. Efficiency was just laziness, to them. That's the peasant thinking for you" (30). On the other hand, Janet's father gives them credit for surviving the difficulties of settling in Canada thanks to their hard work and pride: he tells Janet, "Pride was what they had when they had no more gumption" (30–31). Thus, pride, exhibited so frequently by Janet's mother, is also a characteristic of the Flemings.

Janet frequently exhibits the pride that she describes in, and has apparently inherited from, her relatives on both sides. She has married a man from a wealthy family for whom poverty "was like bad breath or running sores, an affliction for which the afflicted must bear one part of the blame" (12). Janet lists the cousins' jobs, but Richard's relatives "never referred to what they did at work as any kind of business. They never referred to what they did at work at all. Talking about what you did at work was slightly vulgar; talking about how you did was unforgivably so" (14). She wants Iris to make a good impression on Richard, or at least not embarrass herself and Janet—a desire ostensibly to prevent trouble with her husband. She does not send Richard to pick Iris up at her hotel: "I would not say I was afraid to ask him; I simply wanted to keep things from starting off on the wrong foot, by making him do what he hadn't offered to do" (13). She knows how Richard will react when he hears Iris's slang expressions (13–14). When Iris shows up in gaudy clothes and hairdo, Janet reacts with visible shock (15). Is her obvious "failure of welcome" only about Richard's reaction? What she expresses here is not only distress at how Richard will respond to Iris's appearance, but also pride in her own taste in furnishings. The fact is that, like her mother, Janet is something of a snob and is just as disturbed as her husband by Iris's vulgarity:

> had she always been like this, always brash and greedy and scared; decent, maybe even admirable, but still somebody you hope you will not have to sit too long beside, on a bus or at a party? I was dishonest when I said that I wished we had met elsewhere, that I wished I had appreciated her, when I implied that Richard's judgements were all that stood in the way. Perhaps I could have appreciated her more, but I couldn't have stayed with her long.
>
> (16–17)

Janet has now redefined herself, emotionally and socially, and Iris is a visitor not only from Dalgleish (if indirectly) but also from her earlier self. Again, like her mother, Janet has come to yearn for a better life, even if her dreams are inspired by the fantasies depicted in

> magazine advertisements showing ladies in chiffon dresses with capes and floating panels, resting their elbows on a ship's rail, or drinking tea beside a potted palm. I used to apprehend a life of elegance and sensibility, through them. They were a window I had on the world, and the cousins were another.
>
> (17)

What the cousins represented to her mother is precisely what they and the ads represent to Janet herself: a connection to wealth, high class, sophistication, worldliness. When Richard criticizes Iris, however, calling her "a pathetic old tart" and ridiculing her language (17), Janet throws a plate at him. As Lorraine M. York argues, she shows she belongs in the Chaddeley family by retaliating with a slapstick means of revenge (" 'Gulfs' and 'Connections' " 142). She is defending her family connection and perhaps reacting violently to his voicing of her own shameful thoughts. When Richard insults Iris, he is really attacking Janet; as W. H. New observes, "what Richard misses ... is not that Iris and the other cousins are *from* Dalgleish (they are not), but that the narrator is" (120).

Meanwhile, the Fleming sisters represent "the dour Scottish pioneer ethic of which Janet is also the inheritor" (Howells, *Alice Munro* 73). We seldom see her expressing much joy or pleasure in her marriage. She shares one aunt's capacity for storytelling—Janet creates stories out of her family and Mr. Black the way her aunt has with the clothespeg people. We have seen that physically she resembles the Flemings more than the Chaddeleys (25–26), and she says that "it was a face that wore better than theirs" (26)—a point confirmed when we learn that the sisters "lived a long time. They were a hardier clan, after all, than the Chaddeleys, none of whom reached seventy" (31). Her own longevity is embodied in her writing, which outlasts the models for her characters and freezes them in time the way the sisters froze their lives in the past.

Janet has also inherited a family tendency to struggle with the opposition between romance and reality; like many of Munro's characters, she is confronted with the paradox of the real and the marvellous (see Osmond, for example). Romantic myths about the Chaddeley family's history collapse in the face of facts about what work ancestors actually did (10), while Janet's mother's performance during the cousins' show astonishes her. Janet wants at least one of the sisters to have had a romantic encounter and builds up Mr. Black as a potential suitor, but the reality appears to be all too banal (32–34). She then constructs a story about Susan and Mr. Black while knowing all the while that it is just fiction (35): for Howells, "Her multiple interpretations serve as a meta-fictional comment on the way that an artist might use the raw materials of history" (*Alice Munro* 74). Through her imagination, she "would have made a horrible, plausible connection between that silence of his [i.e., Mr. Black], and the manner of his death" (35). On the other hand, her father surprises her by telling her about when he left home, because he broke an axe handle and his father "went after him with a pitchfork. His father was known for temper and hard work. The sisters screamed" (29). Janet asks, "Could they scream?" and he replies, "What? Oh yes. Then. Yes they could" (29). In her experience, this is not how Flemings can behave, but now she learns that at one time they were indeed able to express emotions. Did their oppressive father squeeze any spontaneity, passion, and expressiveness out of them? The point is that Janet and other characters are often said to be "amazed" or "surprised"—there are amazing, astonishing, and marvellous things in the very *real* people, objects, and places around them.[7] As is so often the case, Munro leaves much unsaid. Mysteries and secrets, like the real identity of Mr. Black, persist. The boulder under which Mr. Black was buried has disappeared, and the truth will never be known.[8] Even the cousins and sisters, with whom Janet is so closely connected, are not exactly who they seem to be. There are dimensions in the characters' lives that can never be found, depths and complications she will never fully grasp, as Janet eventually admits: "Now I no longer believe that people's secrets are defined and communicable, or their feelings full-blown and easy to recognize" (37). In Howells's words, "Janet comes to see herself in a new relation to her double inheritance" but "the solidity has vanished: some things are irretrievably lost, the dead do keep their secrets, and only traces of the past survive in the present" (*Alice Munro* 75).

Janet's connections go beyond family ties to her background as a whole, including the town where she grew up. Poppy Cullender, the antiques dealer for whom Janet's mother works, is much like the cousins in that he is considered unrespectable because of how he dresses and speaks—he wears "greasy black clothes" and speaks with a lisp (20)— and more importantly due to his sexuality. Like the cousins, he is a performer, his strange way of speaking a façade that he drops when speaking to Janet's mother (20). Poppy embarrasses Janet, and she uses a familiar word regarding him:

> If I had a friend with me, coming in from school, she would say, "Is that Poppy *Cullender*?" She would be amazed to hear him talking like an ordinary person and amazed to find him inside somebody's house. I disliked his connection with us so much that I wanted to say no.
>
> (20–21)

Whether she likes it or not, she benefits from that connection, as her mother earns at least a little money during the Depression from her work with Poppy.

The text's two-part structure permits Munro to show both the maternal and paternal legacies of Janet's identity, portraying each side of her family in a discrete narrative under its own title or subtitle. Janet's development as a person requires "acknowledging, accepting, and somehow resolving the oppositions and contradictions that meet in herself" (Martin, *Alice Munro* 133)—she herself is the connection between the families. Whether a single story in two parts or a mini-cycle under one global heading, "Chaddeleys and Flemings" makes full use of the division to portray both the gaps and the connections between people, and the need to apprehend the paradox that they are equally real, and inescapable, aspects of life (see York, "'Gulfs' and 'Connections'" 135–36).

Timothy Findley has presented his reader—albeit unintentionally— with another complicated case. *Stones* (1988) is a collection linked by the Toronto settings of its stories and a number of recurring motifs (Mackay 64; Schieder 22–23). The first two stories, "Bragg and Minna" and "A Gift of Mercy," are linked by character and appear together at the beginning of the volume, in line with the conventional handling of two-story mini-cycles. "Bragg and Minna" originally appeared in *Malahat Review*, while "A Gift of Mercy" was not published until it was paired with "Bragg and Minna" in the book. One could be forgiven, then, for believing that it was Findley's intention to compose a two-story mini-cycle. In truth, however, as he later revealed, his goal was to write a series or cycle. In his interview with Peter Buitenhuis in *Books in Canada* (December 1988), for example, he refers to the Bragg and Minna stories as "this series of stories" adding "and there will be more of them," then explains:

> coming back from Australia, I made a little note on a cigarette package that said whatever the first line of the story is. Yet it was almost a full year before I wrote that story. I walked around with those people for a very long time before I dared come to grips with them on paper. There they were, Bragg and Minna. Who the hell were they? ... I'm going on with the Bragg and Minna series.
>
> (20)

In a separate interview, with *Now* magazine, he says, "I've fallen upon two characters who don't appear to belong in a novel but in episodes that are more story-like in shape and size" (qtd. by Schieder 22). He wrote two more stories about them: "A Bag of Bones" and "Come As You Are," which he published together in *Dust to Dust* (1997). They had a similar publishing history as the first two, with the first initially appearing in a literary journal, *Exile*, while "Come As You Are" does not seem to have been published before its appearance in the book. Like "Bragg and Minna" and "A Gift of Mercy," "A Bag of Bones" and "Come As You Are" are set apart from the other stories in the collection. There are a total of nine stories in the book divided into three sets, and the two Bragg and Minna stories are printed sequentially and constitute the central set. The illustrations preceding the sets imply that each set should be treated as a unit of some kind. In the Table of Contents, the titles of the Bragg and Minna stories are set apart from the others by an extra space above and below the pair. In other words, Findley (one assumes that it was he) provides paratextual clues that the two stories are distinct from the others and linked to each other.

When Laurie Kruk asked Findley about the two stories in *Stones* in a 1993 interview, he said:

> Two then—and now, more. In *Dust [to Dust]*, there are two Bragg and Minna stories—and I'm sure there will ultimately be others. Perhaps a whole collection. They'll come out in story form first, but I also think that, at some point, if I have the energy to do this, their lives would make wonderful play
>
> (79)

What we have, then, is an incomplete story series or cycle rather than a complete mini-cycle.[9]

Further complicating how we read the stories is that we get the narrative of the Bragg and Minna relationship in jumbled chronological order, both within each story as present narrative alternates with flashback, and in the ordering of the stories in the two collections. In purely chronological terms, the first story, "Bragg and Minna," is the last or one of the last, and while "A Gift of Mercy" is set around the same time—after Minna's death—it portrays the relationship's beginnings. The other two are printed in the "right" order and are set during the relationship, portraying its breakdown over the issue of whether to have children. In her study of the stories, Laurie Kruk attempts to analyze them in their "proper" temporal order, dealing with the *Dust to Dust* stories first, but the stories are not so easily rearranged given their complex handling of time, and more importantly, such an approach obscures the effect Findley produces by ordering the stories the way he does. For example (assuming we read the stories in order), we enter "A Gift of Mercy" already knowing the characters' fates, and that knowledge lends a melancholy air to the story along with a sense that some of its tensions will be resolved in positive ways. Reading the stories in order of their arrangement in the two collections thus leads to a slightly different treatment of their mood, characterization, and themes—Findley's favourite themes of wars both military and domestic (as in his novel *The Wars* [1977]), Fascism (see Ingham), the meaning of masculinity, class, death, and so on, as well as the idea of monstrosity.

How, then, are we to read the texts? If they formed a completed mini-cycle, we could analyze them as such, but instead the four stories constitute a cycle or series fragment; they were never intended to form a coherent arc all on their own, although each pair has its own degree of unity. For example, Findley chose to begin his project with one story about the end of the Minna-Bragg relationship and one about its beginning, and to publish them in something like reverse order: a deliberate aesthetic choice. What effect does this choice have on our response, both emotional and critical, to this initial pair?

Consider the treatment of monstrosity in the stories. Monstrosity involves social attitudes toward what is "normal" and what is "monstrous," including homosexuality. As Kruk and Lorraine M. York have shown, Stuart Bragg has internalized society's views about homosexuals, feeling through many of the stories that as a gay man (actually, bisexual, as Findley himself points out in the *Books in Canada* interview [20]) he is not only seen as but *is* a monster. That is why he resists Minna's pleas to procreate with her. It is true that his family has a genetic legacy of genetic defects, and their child Stella is heir to them, but on a symbolic level the real problem is Bragg's self-hatred expressed through his term "genetic homosexuality" (14). What he needs to learn, and what he finally accepts, is who he really is; once he does that, he can embrace life fully as embodied in his disabled but vital daughter.

The first line of "Bragg and Minna" tells us that the latter has died. She has left behind a message: "*Bragg always said we shouldn't have the*

baby and everything was done a man can do to prevent it. Still, I wanted
her and she was born and now I realize I've given birth to all of Bragg's
worst fears" (3). Most immediately, she is referring to Stella and her
birth defects: twelve fingers and toes, and brain damage, although it is
interesting that she says, "Bragg's worst fears" and not their realization.
That is, she gave birth not only to Stella but also, even before Stella's birth,
the fears Bragg had that he could now pass on something he considered
monstrous. Domestic war is reflected in the conflict Minna writes about
over whether the couple should have a child. At this point, all the reader
knows is that they "shouldn't have the baby," not that he did not want
one, and we await the revelation of why. Minna is portrayed as compelled to have a child in spite of his objections, and her maternal, nurturing impulse will play an important role throughout the stories and the
couple's relationship.

The story is set during Bragg's flight home from Australia, where he
went with his male lover Col to fulfil Minna's request that her ashes
be scattered at Ku-Ring-Gai in the New South Wales national park
known for its aboriginal rock engravings. Stones are a recurring symbol
in Findley's work, associated with war (as in the story by that title),
memory, the past and the preservation of memory, and of course death.
Here, the site is a place for the disposition and memorializing of Minna
while at the same time learning from her and others. It is where stone
holds a message that transcends the individual, a kind of mythic call
that goes far beyond anything Minna can write. Because so much of the
story is in flashback, it portrays Minna as both an absent and present
figure—to put it another way, a *past* and present figure, or a *presence*.
For example, when Bragg comes up with a poetic line, "Everything had
gone awry," he immediately hears it in her voice (4). When a young
woman sits beside him on the plane, in the seat Col has temporarily
vacated, she reminds him of Minna, as if the latter has come back to life
(6–8). He tries not to think about her during the flight: "His mind flew
around the plane like a bird not knowing where to land. As always, it
wanted to avoid the subject of Minna but no matter where it perched,
she turned up—somehow—under its claws" (13). Despite her death,
Minna dominates both Bragg's mind and the story, highlighting her
significance for Bragg and what she means to him and to the stories as
a whole. She represents life-affirming power, and so even though she
herself is no more, her legacy of life and its perpetuation is what the
stories are truly about. Her view is reflected in what she says, or rather
yells, to him when pressing him to on the subject of having a child: "*If*
we don't fuck, we die" (6). Also, by this point in his life, Bragg has
largely accepted that he is gay and is not hesitant to admit to himself
his attraction to Stanley Nob, his Australian guide (5); the theme of
gender identity will become one of the most important in the rest of the
stories as Bragg struggles to reach this point. What he has not accepted
is homosexuality itself and his supposed "genetic homosexuality":

"This theory was that, since there had been genetic defects in other generations of his family—clubbed feet—cleft palates—mongoloid children—mental illness—maybe his genes were calling a halt. Maybe his genes were saying: *no more babies*" (14). The idea understandably infuriates Minna, and she compares his theory to the Master Race ideas of Hitler (14–15).[10] He tells her that he "was trying to save her from giving birth to monsters" and she replies, "MAYBE WHAT I WANT IS MONSTERS!" (15). What she appears to want is someone to take care of, and the more dependent the better; above all, she wants his baby, as it will be an embodiment of their love (16). Laurie Kruk argues that "Procreative sex is linked with life by Minna but with death by Bragg" (42). Stella's birth defects do not make her any less worthy of that love.

Because the story is designed to introduce the reader to the characters and the situation, the narrator does not limit himself to Bragg's consciousness but moves out of it to provide some background: "Colin Marsh and Stuart Bragg had met in Toronto before Bragg's marriage to Minna went on the rocks" (9). We then move into Col's focalization, the third-person narrator now presenting Col's thoughts and revealing that the "pinked triangle" (see Kruk passim) of Bragg, Minna, and Col has been a painful experience for all concerned. The story, we learn, will not be entirely in Bragg's point of view but strike a balance between the characters and their perspectives—and that includes the late Minna's. Death haunts all three—not just physical death but the death-in-life existence that they have endured largely due to Bragg's resistance to creating more "monsters" like himself.

Bragg goes to Australia, where Minna had fled with their daughter to put her up for adoption, in hopes of finding a sign of Minna's presence there. He leaves believing that he had failed to find one. In his search, he comes across evidence that she had passed through the park, and those signs are the first examples of motifs that will recur again and again throughout the stories, such as red and madness. Back in Bragg's point of view, we learn why his marriage ended: "The baby. That was the final bone of contention and the birth of the child had driven them apart" (13). This is how the reader learns that they have indeed had a child, and the child is physically the "monster" that Bragg feared. Minna finds Viv and Charlie Roeback, a childless couple, to look after Stella; the love they have to offer her is all they need to provide. Minna moves in with Stanley Nob, who takes care of her until the cancer caused by her smoking kills her. As Bragg and Col traverse Australia to visit the places Minna had been, they see the country's strange creatures, especially the platypus, which convince them it is a land of "monsters" if that is how narrow-minded people insist on seeing them (22).

The final scenes of the story involve finding the spot where Minna wished to have her ashes spread and the petroglyphs overlooking it. The pictured beasts include the weird "monsters" of Australia. One of the petroglyphs is of special importance: at first, the characters are puzzled by a figure that archaeologists have interpreted as a shaman (23–24), but only later do Bragg and Col realize the truth.

First, however, Bragg must come to terms with his homosexual side. The plane approaches San Francisco, and Bragg associates the city with homosexuality and AIDS:

> All his life, he'd been taught that he was an outcast—part of a scourge upon mankind. All the offshoots of this thinking had always seemed, to Bragg, to be so ridiculous and paranoid, he'd never paid attention. Now, there were people down in that city who were dying because of sex.
>
> (25)

He sees the insanity of being designated a monster and of people dying for no other reason than expressing their love for each other. At that moment, the "Janis Joplin girl" comes out of the washroom, having changed herself into a more conservative-looking woman like the Rosedale matrons Minna had fled. It is as if Minna has died once again. Now, Bragg understands why Minna wanted her ashes spread beneath the petroglyphs: "It was the joy and the liveliness—the sense of endless celebration that clung to all the figures in the rock. And the figures where the shaman stood—the very place where Minna's ashes fell ..." (25). That is when he realizes the strange figure is not a shaman at all but a child with "long, albino hair and one six-fingered hand stretched out" (26). It is an image of his daughter, someone who, like his own homosexuality, he must accept and accommodate: "The epiphany of the stone carvings leads Bragg to accept both the monster within and the monster without" (Kruk 43). He decides that he will retrieve his daughter and assimilate not only Stella but also his wife, even in how she used to carry Stella: "he knew right then, as he waited to debark the plane, that he would return to Ku-Ring-Gai with Stella on his shoulder. Or his hip" (26). The story ends with an affirmation of his masculine and feminine sides, his status as a bisexual man—that is, homosexual as well as heterosexual—a father, and someone who can love as widely and freely as Minna could.

The story provides a climax to Bragg's personal development, portraying him achieving wholeness and full self-acceptance. Findley then follows rather than precedes that climax with a narrative of Bragg's and Minna's meeting, that is, before he is in a position to have this epiphany. The opening of "A Gift of Mercy" informs us that we have moved back in time: "When Minna Joyce first laid eyes on Stuart Bragg ..." (29). Our knowledge of Bragg's hesitation to be everything he is and is capable of being, and equally our knowledge that he eventually triumphs over his inhibitions, self-doubt, and even self-hatred, colours our reading of "A Gift of Mercy." As Susan E. Billingham writes, "The subsequent stories are read through these elements, even when they are not stated explicitly, as Findley works backwards, filling in earlier segments of the narrative"

(206). We are aware of Minna's need to nurture, to be a mother or at the very least a caregiver, and so we understand her behaviour toward Libby Doyle, the "monstrous" bag-lady she takes in. We also understand Bragg's reaction to what Minna does on two levels: he is certainly justified in his suspicion regarding Libby, who does indeed steal from Minna, but his hostility to caring for others has deeper personal roots. He fears the monster inside himself—the homosexual self he does not want to inflict on another generation. In those younger days, he was obliged to hide who he was, and that is when he internalized society's view of him as a monster.

The café where they meet is "a rummy dive for drunks and crazies" and thus a place we know Minna would like working in, one where she can be with the Parkdale residents to whom she fled after leaving her Rosedale home. She is young and healthy enough to joke about death, above all the killing of her own mother (30). Findley has thus begun both stories in the first pair with references to dead mothers and paralleled whether they remain as "presences" in their loved ones' lives. Minna's hatred of Rosedale is later reflected in her unwillingness to move into the house on Collier, which is too close to Rosedale for her comfort (44). She is not the only one born into money, it should be pointed out; Bragg is also wealthy and therefore oblivious to money (48). Both characters highlight the theme of class in how they respond to being rich and poor.

Madness is one of the main themes of the story, given Minna's determination to take care of the local "crazies" who are patients at the Queen Street Mental Health Centre across from the café. She tells "one of her park-bench friends" that she has to "keep her eye on" the hospital because there is no way to know "what they'll do behind your back" (30), but her real motivation for observing the Centre is not fear but a desire to nurture the needy. References to madness continue through the opening paragraphs as she refers to herself in her mother's terms as "her cast-off, screwed-up daughter" and then her mother's new husband as a "masochist crazy enough to marry her" (30). The effect of these references is to dilute the meaning of madness and also to suggest that it exists in both Parkdale and Rosedale—that it crosses class and other boundaries—and, in fact, throughout his fiction Findley calls into question society's definitions of madness. During their marriage, they live across the street from a man who undresses and yells at streetcars, trying to get their attention (39), and then becomes violent when they actually stop during a traffic jam (40–41). Bragg spends much of the story trying as hard to escape the insane as Minna does to embrace them, and that is why he buys the house near Rosedale that Col will eventually also inhabit (44). When Minna brings Libby home, he both directly and indirectly calls her crazy (47), exhibiting his insensitivity along with his legitimate fear of what Libby might do. Minna claims she is doing research, and he asks, "What makes you think you have to do research, Minna? Tell me what it is you don't already know about these people ... What's there to know about these goddamned

people you don't already know? They're crazy, Minna. They're *crazy!*"
(47). He then tells her to go live with them, and when she asks why she
should, he replies, "Because you're one of them, that's why. You and the
goddamned Morrison café" (48). Minna's mother had had her committed
because she had acted out in public (53), but Minna is convinced that she
was only mad by society's definition, that is, being different and noisy
rather than silent. She sees herself as an unwanted child, her mother comparing her unfavourably to her "perfect" deceased sister Alma, and so
"Minna knew that in the depths of her mother's being she was offering up
the child she did not want to the same profession that had killed the child
she loved" (55). The importance of Minna's sense of herself as unwanted
will have implications for her writing.

Stuart Bragg comes into the Morrison during a blizzard, his hair "white
with snow" in an image reminiscent of the "albino hair" he will later see
on the child in the petroglyph (30). A further allusion to the previous story
and the petroglyphs comes when she thinks, "Bragg had the look of one
who bore a message—lost and uncertain as to whom the message must be
given" (31). As in "Bragg and Minna," he is preoccupied with the sending
and receiving of messages as revealed in his wish to use the café's phone to
make a call (32), and Minna's words are blown away by the wind when
she shouts at him outside during the blizzard, suggesting the difficulty of
their communication overall. As their marriage progresses, their ability to
talk to each other diminishes, and their growing silence becomes an issue
(see the references to Minna's silence on pp. 35, 43, and 45, for example).
Communication becomes the issue for Minna when Bragg throws Libby
Doyle out of their apartment: café owner Shirley Felton's policy of not
allowing phone calls is echoed, to Minna, in Bragg's attitude toward the
needy of Parkdale: *"no one is allowed to call for help"* (53).

Minna falls in love with him, and what attracts her is his apparent
neediness: "Strangers were her specialty and those who were pursued by
storms and demons made the best strangers of all" (31). Unlike the other
and more regular clients in the café, Bragg has a "look in his eyes of unrequited sanity" (31): that is, not unrequited love as one might expect but
a *lack* of madness, and he is someone who is "terrified of the light in a
world lit up with stark bare bulbs"—that is, he is vulnerable (31). She is
generous enough in her emotions (or crazy enough) to pursue him when
Shirley tells him he will not be allowed to use the café's phone and that he
must go across the street to the Centre to find a pay phone. Now Findley
switches the point of view to Bragg's, and by doing so returns to the
theme of madness, although it is now Minna who seems crazy: "her hair
was blowing across her face and he thought: she's mad as a hatter—*and
beautiful as anyone I've ever seen*" (33). We already know that they will
marry, and then form a triangle when Colin comes into their lives. The
story has already portrayed her as wilful, and now we see that quality
from the outside as Bragg sees that "it was so evident she wouldn't let
go until she'd had her way" (33). Readers of the first story know that

that will be the case when it comes to having children, too. They cling to each other as if in "deadly struggle" (34), a reference to the theme of war that will reappear in the account of the madman who fires his clothes as "missiles" at the streetcars on Queen Street (39), in the wartime songs that Libby Doyle sings (52), and Minna's self-description as "a deadly submarine" when she was finally released from the mental hospital (56).

Following the paragraphs portraying their meeting is one that brings us back to the narrative present of "Bragg and Minna": "By the time Minna died, the marriage had lasted just over twelve years" (34). Only now do we fully grasp that the story is really set in the same time period as "Bragg and Minna" and that it is a flashback, a recounting of memory, not a contemporaneous account. During this paragraph, we learn the meaning of the story's title: she moved to Australia to be *"just about as far apart as a person can get my dear ... A gift of mercy for us both"* (34). The paragraph opens with a reference to death and concludes with another on the theme with Minna's wondering whether one is supposed to celebrate the thirteenth anniversary with a game of Russian roulette (34).

We move back in time once more, in this case to a little more than halfway through their marriage. They are now living in the Collier Street home, which has too many bedrooms for Minna's taste because she fears they will no longer share one, and sure enough they take separate ones (44–45). We know that by this time Minna's desperation for Bragg's child has been met with stubborn resistance. Since she has already demonstrated her preference for "mad" company and mothering the "crazies" she meets—as a substitute for having any children—we are not completely surprised to learn that she has started taking in street people. Libby Doyle is her latest "project," and in many ways Libby suits her purpose very well. When Bragg sees her in Minna's bed she is, he thinks, "small enough to be a child" (37). She turns out not to be a child but an old woman, although when Minna found her, she was wearing "a pair of children's yellow rubber boots" (52).

She is not the only insane person who is described as childlike and whom Minna tries to mother. The crazy man across the street, we are told, wails "like a child" when his efforts to gain the attention of the streetcars fail (39). When he jumps out onto the street, she is so fixated on helping him that she puts her hand through her window just as he leaps from his, as if she can stop him.

David Ingham sees Minna as "probably the most sympathetic character in the stories" (49), but toward the end of "A Gift of Mercy," we learn that Minna is not altogether disinterested and generous in her desire to help the "crazies," as her desire to speak for the silent stems from her own experiences having been, or felt that she was, an unwanted child following the death of her sister Alma from untreated appendicitis (50–51). Alma had been her parents' favourite child, and Minna "is resented, imperfect, and alive, while a perfect sibling is dead" (Ingham 49). Her parents put her in the hospital after she had a nervous breakdown (or they thought she did) over their treatment of her. For her, "Queen Street West and, in fact, the whole of Parkdale offered a world of unwanted people—the only people Minna felt any affection for" because, it seems, she sees herself in them (51). She is speaking for herself as much as for them:

> The crazies touched and moved her beyond all others: the way they walked, the way they stood, the way they tried to speak. Just to be seen, Bragg. Just to be seen and heard and acknowledged. That's what they wanted. Witness. Not to be forgotten.
> "Where am I now?" they would say to her. "Can you tell me where I am?"
> Minna would listen and she would tell them: "here."
>
> (51)

Ingham remarks that "in giving words to the inchoate and inarticulate fury and pain of Queen Street, she reaffirms the worth of those lives others barely even acknowledge as human" (49–50). It is as if through the "crazies" she is asserting her own existence and need to her neglectful parents, who refused to see and listen to her. They are also "monsters" in the view of society, beings who are not quite human and therefore not deserving of love. Her compulsion to help them is therefore not entirely unselfish; it is, in fact, an unhealthy obsession or, as she herself puts it in her mind, an "addiction" (52). Gillian Mackay comments that Minna "champions the dispossessed and attacks the sinister repressiveness of the society in which she was raised. She manages to keep one step ahead of her demons by becoming a writer, in that way giving voice to the anguish she experiences within and around her" (64). When Bragg kicks Libby out of their apartment, Minna is frozen by the image of Libby hanging herself so that she would be "free at last of her storms and demons" (53)—that is, the things that haunt herself. She becomes a writer not so much out of a passion for literature as a desire to "plot the overthrow of silence" (56) that has beset herself and all the others labelled "insane."

Bragg's closeted gender identity proves to be a problem when he and Minna move into an apartment above a restaurant catering to the gay community: "The clientele that hung about their doorstep was a trial at times. The very young were very beautiful and Bragg would turn away and walk round the block, attempting to gain control of himself" (38). He is too inhibited to let himself be who he is and be attracted to them; later, while Minna is dealing with the "streetcar man," he is busily writing, struggling to come up with "a two-beat word for *inhibition*" (42). As Minna is recovering from the cuts to her hand when she punched through her window, he continues to search for the right word and unconsciously describes himself and their marriage:

Stricture.
Hindrance.
Restraint.

None of these was right.

It took him roughly half an hour to decide. The word he chose was *impasse.*

(43)

Minna writes lines in the margin of her notebook that could also have been his own: "*and what of me? I cannot articulate and have no desire to tell where I have been and where I am going. Surely this is dangerous. What am I hiding? When will it surface?*" (43)

The stories are about precisely this kind of concealment and confusion. His sense of his homosexuality as monstrous is reflected in his fear about what Minna would say if he continues to challenge her bringing Libby, whom she found standing in the rain, into their home: "He was absolutely furious because he felt the trap of reason closing around him. Surely, all of this would end with Minna saying *only a monster would have left her there ...*" (46).

Meanwhile, gay artists and culture surround him. When spring comes, it is accompanied by the sound of an Elton John song (40). To get back at Minna for bringing a stranger home and introducing a third person in their supposedly secure twosome, Bragg goes out at the end of the story and brings home Donald Murray for a homosexual one-night stand (56–57). It is the beginning of the end of their marriage:

There, she thought. It's done. We've come full circle from the day we met and now our lives will never be the same.

She was thinking of what Bragg had told her about that call he had wanted to place from The Moribund Café.

"I was going to phone a man I'd met and make him a gift of my virginity."

(57)

He had suppressed his gay side for her and now was letting it free, but at the cost of his closeness with Minna. It is only when he brings Col home that she learns to accept and accommodate his bisexuality—something she manages to do better than he can himself. It will be some time before he is able to redefine the "monster" inside. Rupert Schieder notes that it is Bragg's sexuality "that determines the progress and outcome of the narrative. He is, perhaps significantly, one of the few characters who achieve a positive resolution" (23).

The two stories thus form a unit of sorts, even if they are designed to be part of a larger cycle or series, because of their compositional history—as the first Bragg and Minna stories—and the way they were published. We will never know whether Findley was in the process of constructing a cycle, one that would have formed a larger unit out of the shorter components. The Bragg and Minna stories offer a tantalizing glimpse into the creative process, as we watch a linked set of short stories come close to, without reaching, their final aesthetic status. Perhaps we can call them a de facto or truncated cycle.

The marginal cases discussed illustrate the wide range of ways short stories can be linked, showing that there are blurry lines between the multi-part short story and the mini-cycle, and between the mini-cycle and the series that might well have become something else had the author lived to fulfil his or her purpose. Similar analyses can be and indeed have been made of other liminal forms, such as the fix-up novel and the weakly linked story collection.

Notes

1 On the themes of the book in general, see Burbank, D. Anderson, Howe, Rideout, and Stouck, among others.
2 Unless it is a typographical error, I do not know what she means by "five" parts.
3 This is the only instance I have found where another critic has talked about a short set of linked stories using a term similar to mine.
4 Critics have debated the place of "Godliness" in the book as a whole, some, like Howe, seeing it as not fitting well into the cycle, while others argue the text, in its themes and motifs, is well integrated into and is even essential to it (see, e.g., Howe 106; O'Neill 68).
5 As a result, *Who Do You Think You Are?* became a prototypical character-linked cycle.
6 For feminist readings of gender and the body in the story and Munro's work generally, see Rasporich, Irvine, and Kamboureli.
7 On this element in Munro's fiction, see Conron; the studies by W. R. Martin, esp. *Alice Munro* 1–4; Hoy, "Dull, Simple"; Dahlie, *Alice Munro* 226; Carscallen, etc.
8 The one clue Munro leaves us is that one of the sisters makes Janet a one-legged soldier out of a clothespeg, about whom she constructs a story (23), and it turns out Mr. Black was a one-legged man and perhaps a soldier (33). That is of course no coincidence, and the sister's intensity in presenting the toy soldier to her niece must mean something.
9 Findley has also written linked stories about brothers Neil and Bud Cable, including "About Effie" (1956) and "War" (1958).
10 Findley treats the theme of race in similar ways, since racial discrimination, like homophobia, also involves this sort of othering of those considered "monstrous"; see Lorraine M. York, "A White Hand Hovering over the Page" *passim*.

References

Anderson, David D. *Sherwood Anderson: An Introduction and Interpretation*. Holt, 1967.

——. "Sherwood Anderson after 20 Years." White, pp. 246–56.

Anderson, Sherwood. *Winesburg, Ohio.* Introduction by Malcolm Cowley, Penguin, 1976.

Billingham, Susan E. "Fraternizing with the Enemy: Constructions of Masculinity in the Short Fiction of Timothy Findley." *Yearbook of English Studies,* no. 31, 2001, pp. 205–17.

Blodgett, E. D. *Alice Munro.* Twayne, 1988.

Burbank, Rex. *Sherwood Anderson.* Twayne, 1964.

Carscallen, James. *The Other Country: Patterns in the Writing of Alice Munro.* ECW Press, 1993.

Conron, Brandon. "Munro's Wonderland." *Canadian Literature,* no. 78, Autumn 1978, pp. 109–23.

Cox, Ailsa. *Alice Munro.* Northcote House, 2004.

Crowley, John W, editor. *New Essays on* Winesburg, Ohio. Cambridge UP, 1990.

Dahlie, Hallvard. *Alice Munro.* ECW Press, 1985.

——. "The Fiction of Alice Munro." *Ploughshares,* vol. 4, no.3, Jan. 1978, pp. 56–71.

Dewey, Joseph. "No God in the Sky and No God in Myself: 'Godliness' and Anderson's *Winesburg.*" *Modern Fiction Studies,* vol. 35, no. 2, Summer 1989, pp. 251–59.

Dunne, Robert. *A New Book of the Grotesques: Contemporary Approaches to Sherwood Anderson's Early Fiction.* Kent State UP, 2005.

Findley, Timothy. *Dust to Dust.* HarperCollins, 1997.

——. "The Return of the Crazy People." Interview by Peter Buitenhuis, *Books in Canada,* Dec. 1988, pp. 17–20.

——. *Stones.* Penguin, 1989.

——. "Timothy Findley: 'I Want Edge.'" Interview by Laurie Kruk, *The Voice Is the Story: Conversations with Canadian Writers of Short Fiction,* Mosaic, 2003, pp. 77–99.

——. *The Wars.* Clarke, Irwin, 1977.

Fussell, Edwin. "*Winesburg, Ohio*: Art and Isolation." White, pp. 104–13.

Hoffman, Frederick J. "The Voices of Sherwood Anderson." White, pp. 232–44.

Howe, Irving. *Sherwood Anderson: A Biographical and Critical Study.* Stanford UP, 1966.

Howells, Coral Ann. *Alice Munro.* Manchester UP, 1998.

——, and Lynette Hunter, editors. *Narrative Strategies in Canadian Literature: Feminism and Postcolonialism.* Open UP, 1991.

Hoy, Helen. "Alice Munro: 'Unforgettable, Indigestible Messages.'" *Journal of Canadian Studies,* vol. 26, no. 1, Spring 1991, pp. 5–21.

——. "'Dull, Simple, Amazing and Unfathomable': Paradox and Double Vision in Alice Munro's Fiction." *Studies in Canadian Literature,* vol. 5, no. 1, 1 Jan. 1980, pp. 100–15.

——. "'Rose and Janet': Alice Munro's Metafiction." *Canadian Literature,* no. 121, Summer 1989, pp. 59–83.

Ingham, David. "Bashing the Fascists: The Moral Dimensions of Findley's Fiction." *Studies in Canadian Literature,* vol. 15, no. 2, 6 Jun 1990. pp. 33–54.

Irvine, Lorna. *Sub/Version.* ECW Press, 1986.

Kamboureli, Smaro. "The Body as Audience and Performance in the Writing of Alice Munro." *A Mazing Space: Writing Canadian Women Writing,* edited by Shirley Neuman and Kamboureli, Longspoon/NeWest, 1986, pp. 31–38.

Kruk, Laurie. "'Double-Voicing' Family in Findley's Short Fiction: Pinking the Triangle, Drawing the Circle." *Canadian Literature*, no. 212, Spring 2012, pp. 34–48, 203.

Laughlin, Rosemary M. "Godliness and the American Dream in Winesburg, Ohio." *Twentieth-Century Literature*, vol. 13, no. 2, July 1967, pp. 97–103.

Lee, Brian. *American Fiction 1865-1940*. Longman, 1987.

Mackay, Gillian. "The Naked City: Timothy Findley Goes Home to Toronto." Review of *Stones*, Maclean's, 14 Nov. 1988, pp. 64–65.

Martin, W. R. *Alice Munro: Paradox and Parallel*. U of Alberta P, 1987.

——. "The Strange and the Familiar in Alice Munro." *Studies in Canadian Literature*, vol. 7, no. 2, 1982, pp. 214–26.

Munro, Alice. *The Moons of Jupiter*. Toronto: Penguin, 1995.

New, W. H. "Re-reading *The Moons of Jupiter*." *The Cambridge Companion to Alice Munro*, edited by David Staines, Cambridge UP, 2016, pp. 116–35.

O'Neill, John. "Anderson Writ Large: 'Godliness' in *Winesburg, Ohio*." *Twentieth-Century Literature*, vol. 23, no. 1, Feb. 1977, pp. 67–83.

Osmond, Rosalie. "Arrangements, 'Disarrangements' and 'Earnest Deceptions.'" Howells and Hunter, pp. 82–92.

Phillips, William L. "How Sherwood Anderson Wrote *Winesburg, Ohio*." *American Literature*, vol. 23, no. 1, Mar. 1951, pp. 7–30.

Rasporich, Beverly J. *Dance of the Sexes: Art and Gender in the Fiction of Alice Munro*. U of Alberta P, 1990.

Redekop, Magdalene. *Mothers and Other Clowns: The Stories of Alice Munro*. Routledge, 1992.

Rideout, Walter B. "The Simplicity of 'Winesburg, Ohio.'" *Shenandoah*, vol. 13, no. 3, Spring 1962, pp. 20–31.

Schieder, Rupert. "The Overthrow of Silence." Review of *Stones*, by Timothy Findley, *Books in Canada*, Dec. 1988, pp. 22–23.

Small, Judy Jo. *A Reader's Guide to the Short Stories of Sherwood Anderson*. Hall, 1994.

Smith, Jennifer J. "Sherwood Anderson and the Contemporary Short-Story Cycle." *Sherwood Anderson's* Winesburg, Ohio, edited by Precious McKenzie, Brill Rodopi, 2016, pp. 121–43.

Stouck, David. "Anderson's Escapist Art." Crowley, pp. 27–51.

Sykes, Robert H. "The Identity of Anderson's Fanatical Farmer." *Studies in Short Fiction*, vol. 18, no. 1, Winter 1981, pp. 79–82.

White, Ray Lewis, editor. *The Achievement of Sherwood Anderson: Essays in Criticism*. U of North Carolina P, 1966.

York, Lorraine M. *Front Lines: The Fiction of Timothy Findley*. ECW Press, 1991.

——. "'Gulfs' and 'Connections': The Fiction of Alice Munro." *Essays on Canadian Writing*, no. 35, Winter 1987, pp. 135–46.

——. "'A White Hand Hovering over the Page': Timothy Findley and the Racialized/Ethnicized Other." *Essays on Canadian Writing*, no. 64, Summer 1998, pp. 201–20.

Conclusion

The mini-cycle is a form-based genre, one in which a number of authors have worked even when they were perhaps not aware of its history and prevalence. It is one of many forms made up of linked shorter fictional texts, ranging in coherence from the chapters of a novel to the weakly linked story collection. It offers authors, casual readers, and scholars both opportunities and challenges. Our discussion of writing and reading practices demonstrates the range of ways that creators and their audiences can approach texts like these, and the distinct possibility that what an author strives to achieve through a set of linked texts is not necessarily what a reader will experience even at the most basic level: reading the stories in the order in which the author arranged them.

The mini-cycle, like the story cycle and the story series, is inextricably connected to the material circumstances of its publication. Like all short stories, the components of a mini-cycle have depended to a large degree on periodicals, or their media equivalents, for initial publication; it is almost always the case, however, that the mini-cycle, like the story cycle, achieves its full realization only with book publication. Unless the stories are published together, they cannot form the linked and unified aesthetic whole the author intends. On the other hand, the exploded mini-cycle reveals that stories may retain their discrete identity not only by their status as short stories—rather than, say, novella chapters—but also by their being published separately from other component stories. The author of a collection containing an exploded mini-cycle strives to accomplish certain aesthetic tasks involving, for example, reader surprise and reconstruction of the exploded text. Where there are no paratextual clues to the linked nature of the components of a mini-cycle, the author obviously wishes the linking to be unanticipated and thereby create particular effects—assuming, again, that the reader reads all the components and does so in the "correct" order. Should the reader not be suitably obedient and fail to read the stories in the assigned order, the result will be a very different experience—cognitive, hermeneutic, and so on—from the one that the author presumably sought.

We have seen that paratexts matter greatly in a form that most often is read within another form. Titles, tables of contents, and other extratextual elements play an important role in signalling to the reader how to approach the component stories in a mini-cycle. Referring to the component stories as "parts" in a single "tale," for example, leads us to treat texts like "Godliness" as single units; titles that look no different from the titles of unlinked stories in the same collection, like "Chance," "Soon," and Silence," among other one-word story titles in *Runaway*, encourage us to treat the stories as entirely autonomous until the character names tell us differently. Both reader expectation flowing from such paratextual factors and the reader's actual experience are part of the final effect.

Finally, as we have seen, the bipartite or tripartite structure of the typical mini-cycle has a definite aesthetic function. There are reasons an author chooses to create a mini-cycle—a form that balances textual unity and diversity—rather than a single, longer narrative. Some of those reasons are practical, as the limitations of print periodical publication constrain authors when it comes to how long a text can be. The internet obviously eliminates that restriction, but most of the time authors still have to write within periodicals' length requirements. Aesthetic reasons for writing mini-cycles have been our main concern here. These analyses of individual mini-cycles have focused on how the division into component stories has contributed to the authors' efforts to move the narrative from one character's point of view to another's, or from one temporal and sometimes geographical setting to another. The mini-cycle provides an explicit, clearly visible formal means to make these shifts, as the author composes individual short stories with their own perspectives and contexts, while he or she simultaneously unites them in a broader narrative, character, or thematic arc. Like its book-length cousin, the story cycle, the mini-cycle makes full use of the form's possibility to strike a dynamic balance between individual and set, element and compound, the well-formed unit and the well-formed whole built from those units. Whatever the author's philosophical and aesthetic goals—to convey the fragmentary nature of experience, say, or explore the formal possibilities of fiction—the mini-cycle offers many wide-ranging structural opportunities for the writer of short fiction.

Index

For Product Safety Concerns and Information please contact our EU
representative GPSR@taylorandfrancis.com
Taylor & Francis Verlag GmbH, Kaufingerstraße 24, 80331 München, Germany